VAL

BIRTH OF THE STORM

BOOK 1 OF DEMON STORM

Birth of the Storm
Book One of Demon Storm

First edition. June 13th 2022
Copyright © 2022 Valerie Storm
Written by Valerie Storm
Cover design © 2022 Jessica Moon and Chad Moon
Cover art © 2022 @Ginkahederling
Map © 2022 @Dewiwrites
Formatting done by Mandy Russell

Published by Shadow Spark Publishing
www.shadowsparkpub.com

TABLE OF CONTENTS

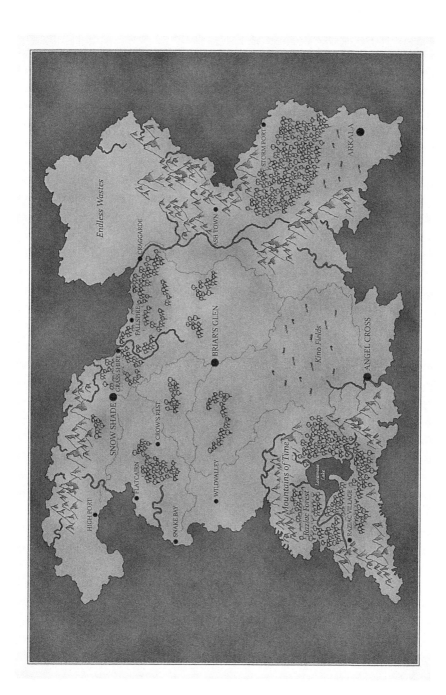

Endless Wastes

STORM PORT

ARKALA

ASH TOWN

CRAGGARDE

FALLSHIRE

BRIAR'S GLEN

Kino Fields

ANGEL CROSS

GRASS SHIRE

SNOW SHADE

CROW'S REST

FLATCAIRN

WILDVALLEY

Mountains of Time

Crossroads Lake

HIGH PORT

SNAKE BAY

Raziac Forest

RAZIAC VILLAGE

PROLOGUE

A woman and man sat on a couch in Zina's main room. The former was resplendent despite the plain, floor-length silk dress draped over her muscular form. A curtain of moonlight silver hair cascaded down her shoulders to her hips.

In contrast, the man was rugged, bare-chested, with hair darker than the blackest night. Zina had no clothes he could borrow; instead, he'd torn a table cloth and tied it around his waist. While they dressed to conceal their natural nudity, they did not attempt to hide their ears or tails, wolfish in appearance. The woman's tail was long enough that the furry tip poked out from the bottom of the dress.

CHAPTER ONE

Oh no, no, no no.

A slew of curses flew through Kari's mind as she raced around thick trees, ascending the mountain.

I knew I shouldn't have done it.

If only she hadn't gotten so close! How often had her mother told her? "Don't go too far from our home, Kari. Humans live down there, and they hate us. Humans hunt us. We don't belong in the same space, let alone the same world."

Today, though, she'd done it anyway. She'd gone down the mountain so she could see a little piece of their village. And she'd used the power. Oh, how she could howl in frustration! Usually her ability wasn't so obvious, but in the excitement, it had sparked free of her control and given her away.

What would her mother say? Her father?

A breathless whimper escaped her throat at the thought.

Father always said it was dangerous to do!

Kari's chest heaved, her paws pounded the ground, and her tongue dangled from the side of her panting mouth. She pumped her legs, willing herself to move faster as she ducked around dense bushes that snagged her fur. Fear of being caught by humans after so long paired with dread of what her mother and father would do. Home was close now.

Maybe her mother would understand this time. Kari had wandered down the mountain on rare occasions and usually Mother was angry, but it seemed that she was beginning to understand Kari's curiosity.

Then again, Kari had never gone *that* far down before.

She was still a young demon, and the thought of staying on this mountainside while the whole world was out there, waiting for her to explore it, tugged at her mind. How could her parents expect her to remain oblivious to it? They'd had their fun on the land of Taris before settling and breeding. When would it be her turn?

Later, her mother would say. When was later?

The musky, wolf-ish scent of her parents was in the air now, and with the smell came the natural silence of the peak. The prey of the mountain didn't dare trespass up here. Kari slowed to a jogging pace, shaking out the chill that had settled on her fur.

She was the only child of her parents, and they were the only wolves on the mountain, if not in the whole world. She envied the human children in the village who had siblings and friends to talk with and play alongside. For as long as Kari could remember, she had longed to see them closely—much closer than the occasional glimpse across the distance she'd managed when exploring the woods. *Just* see them, for it had been drilled into her mind for ten long years now: humans are dangerous.

That truth didn't change the fact that she was bored and lonely, though. Her mother would understand that, wouldn't she?

The northernmost cave at the mountain's peak loomed before her. The late morning sun peered over the tops of trees to spread golden light over snow-laden ground. Kari's claws *tapped* as she left behind the wet, cold, snow-strewn earth for the stone floor of the cave.

Perhaps called by the sound of her claws or her heavy breath, her mother emerged. Much larger than she, and with silver fur instead of tawny, Kari's mother looked down at her with yellow eyes. She looked pleasantly calm before reading the look on Kari's face. Her pupils were probably dilated with fear, and she was still panting from both the run and the terror of being seen, as well as what that might mean now.

Damnit damnit damnit.

Kari, what happened? Her mother's voice reverberated in her mind. She usually had a light, amused lilt to her voice that lulled Kari into calmness. Now, she sounded hard and angry. Kari's ears dipped back, and her tail drooped.

How to tell her? Even though they shared a mental link for communication in their wolf forms, her mother could only hear the thoughts Kari wished her to hear. Kari could lie about the entire incident—the humans hadn't seen her as a wolf, anyway. She'd been in her humanoid form; she was at least smart enough for that. She had even been sure her ears and tail weren't visible. The humans would have virtually no idea that Kari had been anything other than a strange human child.

Kari. Her mother spoke again, glaring.

She had to tell her something, now, before her father came back from hunting. Her mother could be intimidating, but his anger was legendary.

Kari bent down on her front paws and whimpered.

They saw me, Mother. I…I was playing with the sparks, and—

Who? Who saw you?

By the way the silver wolf bared a tiny glimpse of her teeth, Kari imagined she knew who.

You mean to tell me you went down there? Her mother's mind-words didn't shout, yet they were icy and clipped, disbelieving. *You went down the mountain? You got close to the humans?*

Abandoning all pretenses, Kari crouched and rolled over to expose her belly.

I'm sorry, Mother! I...I was curious. I just wanted to see them!

Her mother's eyes flashed with anger and a low growl built in her throat.

To Kari's surprise, she did not react further except to turn away and head back into the cave. Kari moved onto her belly and watched her.

Had she understood? Maybe this little mistake of hers wouldn't be so bad after all.

They will come, her mother thought, the sound dimmer to Kari now that she was farther away. *And when they do, they will not like to find us. We will have to kill them.*

But why would they follow me, Mother? Kari asked, getting up and scampering after her. The cave entrance opened into a wide, short tunnel that expanded into a large cavern more than big enough for the tiny wolf pack. *I didn't show myself. Not my real self.*

Her mother snorted angrily. She had sat in the center of the cavern, no doubt to wait for Father.

Why did you not heed me, Kari? she asked. *Did you truly think that a small girl alone in the snow would not draw some sort of attention? They will come to find you because that is what humans do.* She snorted again, resigned now. *They will imagine you are lost and need help.*

Kari avoided her gaze and let out another whimper.

It wasn't that she was particularly averse to fighting or killing humans if she must, she reasoned with herself—it had been a vital part of her upbringing. Sometimes you have to kill the humans to survive. If you hesitate, they would kill you. Her parents had told her plenty of stories about the time before she was born.

That was all she knew, though—stories. She'd never even gone hunting on her own. At roughly ten summers counted, she was still too young for that.

How many times had Kari, playful and full of energy, wished for a bloody battle? She might not be as big as her mother—certainly not her father—but she had a skill even they didn't have.

4

With the moment upon her now, though, Kari didn't feel ready at all. She couldn't have summoned a spark of electricity to her fangs if she wanted to.

I doubt they will pursue your trail this day. Humans plan. They will gather a party first, prepare themselves, her mother finished, oblivious now to the panic that was restricting Kari's breathing. She rolled her great shoulders and let out an angry huff of a breath before turning her eyes on Kari. *Come here.*

Her eyes glowered, shining like the moon at its peak. Her tone, though, remained tensely soft. Kari, her head low and her tail tucked in, approached and plopped down across from her.

They sat there, mother and daughter, Kari with her head lowered in deference. Surely Mother would scold her now. She'd been foolish to believe it wouldn't come.

Kari held back a whimper, waiting for the flash of teeth, the snarl...

There's a lot you don't know, her mother said instead. *Some things we could never tell you. It...never felt like the right time.*

Frowning, Kari lifted her head. *Like what, Mother?*

Her mother's lips pulled back from her teeth. *Do you remember the story I told you about our creator?*

Kari blinked, laying her head on her paws. *Yes. He created us, but no demon ever saw him. Most don't even know about him. You said he probably didn't really exist.*

The silver wolf nodded. *Some have said he was a very powerful being, with strength and abilities the likes none of us could ever imagine.*

Kari's head shot up, her ears stiffening. *Are you talking about my electricity?*

Her mother frowned this time. *Not exactly. Before we came to this mountain, your father and I heard tales of this creator. If he ever did exist, it was likely he was killed. Why else would our lord forsake us to the humans?* She shook her head and let out a huff of air. *Kari...there are many who would hurt you in the same way.*

5

Kari stiffened. *Why, Mother?*

Her mother looked away from her, to the cave entrance. *Your father and I have tried to keep you safe, but...*

Her thoughts trailed off, leaving Kari's mind woefully empty. She inched closer until their paws were almost touching. She pressed her nose to her mother's paw. *Well, we can leave, can't we? We can hide someplace else.*

Her mother surprised her by rubbing her head against Kari's. A soft lick traced her jaw with a tingle. Kari stared with wide eyes. Mother was rarely so affectionate.

Yes. After this, I think we will leave. I will talk to your father.

Kari could hardly stop herself from leaping for joy. They would leave! She would see something besides these pine trees and stone cave!

She nudged her mother happily, earning another soft lick.

If we are separated, I want you to find Zina. She's in the south, in a grand forest, one full of mysteries. She will be able to explain and keep you safe.

Safe from what? What do you mean?

The sound of padded feet and something dragging over stone made her mother perk up. She stood, leaving Kari and their conversation. Kari knew better than to try and call her back.

Her father appeared from the quickly darkening forests, a hulking black mass with glowing eyes, and her mother met him at the cave entrance. Kari could not break into their mental conversations unless invited, but it was not hard to discern her father's feelings toward the news. He dragged the large buck he had caught and laid it in their sleeping cavern before turning on her. His teeth were bared, his shoulders raised.

How could you be so foolish? Kari flinched as his voice roared in her mind. *Did I not tell you to keep that power of yours inside?*

Kari bent before him, whimpering. *I'm sorry, Father.*

He huffed, teeth bared, and turned away. *Eat,* he commanded.

Dinner was a solemn affair. Her mother and father ate with the usual ripping of meat, though there was a heavy silence in the air. Kari glanced between them before hesitantly clamping her jaws on her share. She focused and soon felt a tingling sensation in her jaws. It laced through her bones, down her teeth, and into the meat held tightly there.

Electricity—it arced along the meat, cooking it until it was softer than stringy, and her mouth watered in anticipation of eating. Her father cast an imposing look in her direction and snarled; the sparks ceased instantly. Lowering her head in obedience, Kari began to eat.

Kari… Her mother's mind touched hers, cautiously thoughtful. Kari's ears pricked, waiting for her to continue. Her father turned his massive head in her direction.

Tomorrow the humans will come. Of that, we are sure. You will stay in the cave while we handle them—

Kari lifted her head from her meat. A sputter of sparks left her teeth before dying away, earning her another growl from her father. Her ears flattened.

I could help, Mother! I should learn how to fight. Let me—

Yellow eyes narrowed warningly. *No.*

Kari quailed, lowering her head. *Who is Zina, Mother?* she asked instead. *Is she a demon you know?*

Father looked to Mother, and this time Kari heard him.

Will you tell her all? His thoughts came harsh and indignant. What did he not want Kari to know?

She is a friend, her mother said, ignoring him. Kari could sense the hesitancy behind the word *friend*. *She is strange, yet I know she will help you. That is—*

The crunch of snow combined with the crispy swishing of moving bushes cut her sentence short. Her ears perked and a low growl settled in her throat. Kari's father climbed to his feet, his hackles raised. He faced the entrance to their cave.

What is it? Kari asked, jumping up too. Her mother snapped at her and she leapt away, her ears bent back.

Stay, her father grunted before darting outside.

Mother, Kari began again; the larger wolf growled. *Is it the humans? I want to help. Please!*

Quiet.

Kari obeyed as well as she could. Her claws tapped against the stone of their cave and her tail twitched, swishing nervously.

Her mother lithely climbed to her feet. *They've come.*

Kari stared at her, not comprehending. *Who?*

Then the sound of voices, human speech, was on the cold night air. Kari stiffened, her fur standing on end.

The humans. The humans were here. They had followed her, as her mother had said. And now…

Her legs trembled, but she forced them to still. Sparks of lightning came to her teeth, but they fizzled out too soon.

Kari had wanted to fight them, but now that they were here, she was…

Mother, what do we—

A ferocious, snarling growl broke the night apart. Kari knew her father's anger better than anyone, yet she had never heard him so furious.

Your father will handle what he can, her mother said. *We will wait.*

Kari silently laughed at herself—of course her father would deal with them. By dawn's light, the snow outside of their cave would be stained with blood. Any humans who had come up here would meet a quick end or be forced to flee.

Her mother moved, each step slow and cautious, her tail and head low. Kari followed, not nearly as elegant, until they stood within the shadows of the entrance.

Will we help now, Mother? Kari pulled back her lips and felt a tingling sensation begin in her jaw. Fresh sparks darted along the tips of her teeth as her insides thrummed with energy.

Her father had never approved of her electricity because it was akin to human magic. However, it would give her an edge over the humans. She knew it.

No, her mother snarled after a moment.

The electricity fizzled out again as Kari frowned. *But...*

The snarling, roaring grunts of her father were louder now, sometimes followed by sharp human yelps of pain.

This is no different from other prey, her mother responded with a flick of her ear.

Kari understood. It wasn't unusual for the two of them to go in separately; a single wolf made the prey wary, waiting for the rest of the pack to show up. It made them watch their backs or look for exits, instead of fighting as well as they might.

Another human's scream of pain meant it was working, though Kari remained nervous. They were only humans, not entirely worthy of honorable deaths. They wouldn't even be eaten. So why was her father taking so long? Why was her mother hesitating?

Kari tried to look around her mother's thick, silver-furred body and failed. She huffed.

How many are there, Mother?

The ruckus outside—boots stamping in the snow and humans shouting as they tried to coordinate with each other—meant her father was fighting more than the anticipated two humans.

Go back inside, Kari.

Kari clacked her teeth. The electricity would not come again. *No, I want to help!*

Her mother glared at her, yellow eyes glowing in the dimness of the cave. Kari's ears bent back.

Another yelp reverberated through the air—this one didn't belong to a human. Kari's heart thudded heavily in her chest.

Stay here! her mother commanded before she bounded out of the cave.

Kari's paws tensed, her claws scratching tiny marks into the stone. She waited a single breath, then edged closer to the entrance, careful to stay hidden so she could survey the scene. Already her insides were tingling with more electric power, and she knew she could help her parents.

Maybe once her father saw how useful her electricity was in a fight, he would appreciate it more. She knew she could sear flesh; she'd done it countless times on the meals Father brought home. That would be enough to distract the humans, to give him the edge he needed to finish this.

Then her power wouldn't simply be a strange oddity, something that true demons should not have, if her mother's tales of demonic origins were to be believed. Her electricity could be an extra strength.

If she could prove that, maybe Father would help her to hone it.

As her gaze took in the sight of snow dotted with specks of blood, she faltered. She'd seen animal blood before; her mother's shiny snout was still flecked with it from their dinner. Something about the sight of this blood was different and filled her gut with squirming worry. Steam wafted as it melted through the snow, sinking deeper, shining as it did so. Starkly bright and crimson against such crisp, clean whiteness. It was a common sight for one who hunted, yet Kari struggled to tear her gaze away.

Near the edge of the clearing laid a still human body, facedown. Four more of them, three male and one female, were crowded away from her father, their weapons raised to keep him at bay. The massive black wolf, his teeth bared with his snarl, lunged at them. He danced in and out of range, never making the same move twice; unfazed by the bloody gash on his side.

Kari gritted her teeth, eager to join her parents despite her trembling.

Her mother leapt into the tense standoff, a flash of silver that darted in to clamp her jaws on one of the male's legs. He dropped his long dagger with a loud howl. The woman jabbed with her spear, but Kari's mother had already retreated.

10

Kari relaxed again as the skirmish unfolded, feeling foolish for letting even a pinch of fear get ahold of her—these humans were no match for her parents.

She knew that killing so many humans—who'd probably told other villagers why they were venturing up the mountain—meant they'd have to leave the cave quickly when the fight ended. Kari allowed herself to imagine where they might go after this. Maybe her parents would be willing to find somewhere she could make friends, instead of hiding away as they did. There must be other demon children like her in the world. Despite assurances that her ability to call electricity was impossible, she thought there had to be others that could do it.

And maybe Kari could learn why her parents preferred seclusion, when, based on stories she'd heard about her parent's youth, it wasn't the usual demon way.

Another human fell under her father's attack, clutching his arm to his chest and his weapon discarded. Kari was thrilled. One dead, one disarmed, and one weakened by the bite on his leg. Though the one with the wounded leg had recovered his two-handed hammer, he wavered, all confidence in the fight gone. With the woman and single man left, the fight was all but over.

The woman's spear found the shoulder of the large black wolf. Kari's father yelped, and before he could counter, the man's hammer came up to smash his head. There was a horrible crunching sound, and then he rolled away from the fray, motionless.

Time was frozen. Kari could see the rise of his body that meant he was still breathing, but he did not get up.

Father? Father!

Nothing. No low growl or even a whimper to signal that he heard her. Fear strangled Kari's heart. As the man raised his weapon in both hands to strike again, something bubbling and hot invaded her mind. It frothed in her chest, forming lava-like bile. It was fury, burning and intense. It devoured her fear and hardened her resolve.

Baring her teeth, Kari tensed her legs, about to jump in herself until a deep, angry *No!* engulfed her thoughts. Kari's head swung around to see the silver blur that was her mother tackle the woman with the spear to the ground.

The human fell under the weight of Kari's mother, her spear flying away from her hand. Kari stood frozen as her mother held the woman's arms down with massive paws, a snarl lighting up a once loving face.

Stay there, her mother commanded again. *We will handle this.*

Kari's whimper was inaudible. Her thoughts raced too quickly for her to respond.

How could they handle this? Her father had still not gotten up.

Her mother's eyes glowed and her teeth snapped out, preparing to rip the woman's face off.

The man was there again with his hammer. He swung it upwards, catching Kari's mother in the side. She flew off the woman and rolled away, her body crumpled and broken. Kari's blood froze, as cold as the icy air. She willed her mother to get up again.

Mother? Father?

She could feel her mother's mind-presence throbbing quietly, brushing the edges of Kari's consciousness, yet she did not respond. On the other side of the bodies, the man helped the woman to her feet. She smiled at him and brushed herself off. The other two humans who were not yet dead were offering weak cheers at their success. The one with the wounded leg had fallen to the ground, and his weaponless companion was tying white wads of something around the bleeding wound.

Shift, Kari.

Kari's attention flew back to her mother. Her breathing was shallow, evidenced by the feeble rise and fall of her chest, as she commanded again: *Shift. Now.*

Kari didn't understand. She turned back to her father, forcing herself to look beyond the reddened snow surrounding him. He would get up soon. It was one hit. He'd taken worse swipes from a bear.

KARI.

Her mother's voice screamed in her mind, before it cut off suddenly, a syllable half-formed. Kari let out a whimpering sob and retreated into the shadows of the cave. She shifted into her humanoid form and came out on all fours as a tiny, cowering, and very naked girl. The cold air chilled her skin, making the tiny hairs all over her body stand straight up. A cutting breeze curled its way around her shoulders, but she didn't so much as shiver; her demon blood kept her comfortable. Her wolfish tail was small, barely more than a stub that flicked uneasily; her minuscule ears, too tiny still to see and only a couple of shades darker than her blonde hair, bent backward.

I did it, Mother! Mother?

Kari's mind was full of buzzing silence, devoid of any thoughts except her own.

From the ground, she lifted her head. Her mother's eyes remained yellow in death, though blank and lifeless. Kari's hands shook and her throat burned as something wet invaded her eyes.

"Dear, are you okay?" The woman was at Kari's side, her voice soft. Flinching, Kari pulled away and glared, baring her teeth. The woman looked taken aback but kept her voice soft.

"Poor thing," she continued. Her eyes trailed down Kari from head to toe, eyes widening at the sight of her bare body. "You must be freezing! What are you doing out here all alone? What's your name?"

As she pulled off her overcoat, the men approached. The one with the bitten arm supported the limping one.

"What is it, Anne?" the man with the hammer spoke, stopping beside the woman. He froze when he saw Kari, who was flinching away from the woman's coat. She raised her gaze to his face.

He was an older man, his face lined with wrinkles, and his short, russet hair laced with gray. He *looked* weak, Kari thought blankly. How could he have beaten her father? She glared at the hammer in his hand.

It is because of their cowardly use of weapons, either to outrange or outbrute demons. They have no real strength of their own.

Distracted, she allowed the woman—Anne—to place her coat over her thin shoulders. Warmth enveloped her, and so did a repulsive human smell.

13

"It's true, there really was a girl out here?" the man with the hammer muttered to himself. To the woman, he said, "She's in shock. Come on. We can take her home and see if she recovers from whatever's happened to her out here."

"We'd best hurry. We have to drag Billy's body down with us, too," the limping man said.

"Yar, I'd hate to leave him here," murmured the one supporting him.

You killed them. You killed them. YOU KILLED THEM.

Kari's angry thoughts were tangible, choking her, but she swallowed them back. She wouldn't have a chance of surviving a fight with all of them. Her mother had wanted her to change forms—why? Her fingers twitched and she tried to keep her eyes and thoughts away from her parents. Their blood would paint the snow. Kari clenched her trembling fingers into fists.

"Will you come with us?" the woman asked, reaching for Kari's hand. Her eyes were soft bark, her face framed by waves of similar colored hair.

How could you do this? Kari wanted to scream. *How could you kill my mother?*

They thought she was human, one of them—that was the only reason Kari was still alive. Her wolfish ears were so tiny, hidden away in her locks of golden hair, so these idiotic humans did not yet suspect that she was anything other than one of them. Even her tail was too small yet to draw attention.

That was why; her mother had wanted Kari to blend in with them. Her mind screamed, wild and scrambled with panic; how safe could she be with the humans that had killed her parents?

Kari's anger was quickly fading into a deadened feeling, her stomach empty and fluttering with unease.

Mother and Father are... she couldn't complete the thought. Her body trembled, and every breath took energy she didn't have. She wanted to slump into the snow and freeze to death.

"Perhaps we'd better leave her, Anne," the man with the hammer mumbled, gently caressing the woman's shoulder. "She's mad. And I'm surprised she's not bitten by the frost. No matter how long she's been out here, she should be dead."

The woman clicked her tongue angrily. "How dare you! Abandon a child out here to this horrid weather? No! Why else would we have come all the way up here? Why would Billy have given his life if not to save this child?"

The man with the hurt arm grinned. "At least we got some good furs for it."

Kari stiffened beside the woman.

No. No, no, no…

"Ah, don't say that," the man with the hammer said. "Billy was a good man."

Anne shot them a glare before turning back to Kari. She reached forward and gently laid her fingers on the back of Kari's hand. Her skin crawled from the touch and her focus slowly returned.

"Your nails are so long," the woman murmured.

Yes. Long and strong enough to rend flesh, at least. Kari could slice her throat with them.

Yet her mother ordered her to shift so that they would not kill her. Kari must remain alive, if only for the sake of her mother's last command. She jerked her hand away from the woman.

"My name…Kari," she croaked.

The man with the limp made a noise of dissent. Anne ignored him. "Kari is your name? You poor thing. Are you alone?"

Kari gritted her teeth.

"Come on, Anne. It's getting late."

"Come, Kari. My name's Anne. We'll get you home and fed and warmed up. How does that sound?"

Kari allowed the woman to tighten the coat around her body but bared her teeth again when the woman bent to pick her up. Looking concerned yet determined, the woman instead gestured for her to follow.

The men were hefting large, furred bodies onto a wooden sled. Kari squeezed her eyes shut. She forced her head to the east, instead, where she knew her father's hunting trail was.

He'd emerged from there only hours ago. She wondered how he'd caught the buck; had it been difficult? She snorted to herself. Of course not. He was a master hunter.

Her frail smile fell.

Was.

Kari's humanoid feet crunched in the snow, the sludgy frost seeping between her toes. The woman looked back at her intermittently, her face soft with compassion. Kari's jaw tightened so much it ached.

I will kill them, Mother, she whispered in her mind, though the soundless void was enough to make her breath hitch. *I will kill them for you and Father.*

CHAPTER TWO

The humans huffed and talked little as they walked, and Kari tuned them out easily. Anne stayed close by Kari as the men hurried on to their village. Kari kept her eyes down, focusing the entirety of her attention on every twig and rock they passed by.

These people were obviously from the village at the bottom, the only human civilization around for miles. Kari couldn't help but notice the irony of the situation. She'd always wanted this. She'd always wanted to see the human's way of life, to possibly even make friends within the village so near her home. Of course, she hadn't thought the cost would be so great.

The sky was aglow with golden, morning light when the humans and Kari finally left behind the thickest of trees and entered the village proper, where all the men except the one with the hammer left Kari and Anne behind.

As the trees were traded for buildings, Kari was overcome by the smells: the scent of baking bread and meat, smoke and fire, wood, leather, and sweat, and on top of it all was the overpowering stench of humans. They crowded thin streets between buildings, too numerous to count.

New sounds rang through the air that made her flinch the deeper they descended, passing building after building; the clang and cling of metal hitting metal, shouting voices, doors slamming shut and creaking open. Tiny human children ran by them, their screams piercing, their scents sweeter, yet still sickening.

Kari narrowed her eyes at the flailing-limbed children as they disappeared into town, and saw so many humans her gut clenched. Dozens upon dozens…no, hundreds.

How could she ever survive this place?

She glanced around the grubby-looking humans, following Anne with numb steps, and noted a head of bright yellow hair.

There was a young girl, like her, but this one wasn't screaming like the others. She stood beside a stocky, dirty man, who shared angry gestures with another. The latter spat and glared, poking the former in the chest and pointing to the young girl. She cringed, her lower lip quivering.

Kari watched them, intent enough to forget the insufferable ringing and talking, or the smells. Her jaw unclenched and her brow loosened.

That girl looks exactly how I feel.

"I'm meeting the boys at the skinner, Anne. I'll be back."

Kari spun as the man with the hammer spoke. Her stomach tightened at his words, but she forced herself to think of her mother's last wish.

I must survive now.

Anne waved in response and lead Kari inside the house they'd turned toward; a dingy place with a peaked roof, two musty windows, and a single faded door. The sounds and smells dampened as they entered the house. Without the distractions, Kari found it was harder to breathe. Her chest was full of thick viscous pain drowning her heart and sticking in her lungs. A sob welled in her throat; she swallowed it with difficulty.

Anne removed her warm layers and hung them on a metal hook beside the door before turning to her.

"It's a real shame about Billy," she mused. "He has a family and all."

Kari heard her words through a dull echo.

I had a family, too.

She bit her lip and pushed the thought away, instead focusing every bit of her attention on this new place.

She'd never seen the inside of a human home. They stood in an open space, as wide and spacious as her cave had been. Instead of stone walls and floor, though, there came a brighter room with lots of wooden tops. To the left was a doorway, similar to the cave tunnel she'd walked through a thousand times.

Anne carefully pointed out everything for her.

"We eat there, at the table," she explained softly, pointing at a large bit of carefully carved and flattened wood that could be seen through the doorway. She saw more as she looked, and Anne pointed to these things one at a time.

"We make a fire there, in that pit. Joseph keeps the salted meats in that box against the wall. There's some bread and fruits in the chest next to it..."

She rambled on until Kari felt herself drooping again. She longed to lie down and never get up, to leave behind this world and find her parents in the next one.

"Are you tired, dear?" Anne asked. "I'll show you to your room. You can lay down a bit until we have something to eat. You can warm up, too, poor thing...maybe we have some clothes you can wear..."

Kari shuffled alongside Anne toward the leftmost entrance, and down a short hallway. At the end were two doors facing each other.

Anne gestured to the door on the right. "Joseph and I sleep in here. We won't be far if you need us. You can stay right across."

Kari couldn't scrounge up an answer. Anne opened the left door, revealing a small space with a wide wooden dresser, and a four-legged frame of wood on which lay a long, bumpy-looking pad.

Anne led the way over to the frame and laid a hand on the misshapen cushion. "You can sleep here." Her eyebrows scrunched together, and a frown pinched her lips. "Joseph and I have no children, but we always keep a bed ready anyhow…for guests, maybe. It's freshly made, stuffed with straw, you know…should be comfortable."

She spared a smile, possibly hoping Kari would return it with some sort of reaction. Kari refused to meet her eye.

"I'll leave you to it. There's blankets in the drawers here," Anne moved to the stand beside the bed and pulled out the top drawer. "And clothes you might wear in here." She bent to pull open the bottommost drawer and revealing various styles and colors of human shirts and pants. "You can keep the coat, too, if you'd like."

When Kari still didn't respond, Anne gave her one last smile before slipping out of the room, closing the door with a gentle *snap*.

She threw off the coat that smelled so heavily of Anne before dropping to her knees beside the drawer stuffed with fresh clothes. She had to wear something if she was to try and fit in at all.

She thrust her hands into the neatly folded things, grateful that these items smelled less abrasive, and tossed them out until the entire floor was covered with a mismatch of colors and shapes. Kari picked out the least obnoxious shirt and matching pants and dressed. She hesitated as she pulled the pants up over her tiny tail. Warm and wet tears sprang to her eyes.

She must give up everything she knew. She must play the part of a small human child and honor her mother's final instruction.

Her tail, though small, still bent at an annoying angle when stuffed into the pants. Dressed and looking as human as she could manage, Kari shuffled to the bed and ran overlong nails over it. She had often wondered how humans slept, certain there was no chance they would sleep on the hard ground. Now she knew.

She frowned at her hands. Unlike humans, her long nails were sharp and strong enough to shred bark and flesh. Of course, now they would simply be another thing to separate her from them.

She angrily chewed them off, spitting the broken pieces onto the floor and sweeping them underneath the bed. Sitting on the bed, she investigated her hands. Her fingernails were nothing more than jagged stubs, leaving her even more helpless.

Alone and still, her energy quickly waned. She had dressed like a human, so she would sleep like one. She would eat and breathe, maybe even speak and act like them. She would learn how humans lived, as she always wished.

Her weakness overtook her. Kari slumped forward, head in her hands, and began to sob.

Kari hadn't even realized she'd fallen asleep when a soft knock made her jerk up with a gasp. Anne's ever-cheery voice came from behind the door, quickly reminding her where she was and why.

"Kari? I have some food on the table if you have an appetite."

Her stomach offered a low rumble and she dug her claws into the straw mattress. Would Anne force her out of the room if she didn't respond and follow? Drag her to their 'table,' where strange human food would be forced upon her?

Her stomach tightened into sickening knots. She'd never eat with her parents again. Her father had promised to take her hunting in the summer, and now he never would.

Her misery threatened to swallow her up. Her vision swam. She blinked furiously, holding back another thick sob that had built in her throat.

"Kari?" Anne's voice came again.

She was lost. She'd obeyed her mother's last wish and lived because of it, but without her parents, she had nothing except her memories and the things her parents had taught her. In hindsight, that wasn't much. She knew which part of a deer was the best meat, what kind of trees birds preferred to nest in, and how to shred the skin of prey with her teeth and claws.

Was she to give that all up for these humans?

Anne's footsteps retreated, leaving Kari alone once more. Once she was sure the woman wasn't coming back, she crawled into a ball and closed her eyes.

The door creaked open, and a thin sliver of amber candlelight pierced the inky darkness that had enveloped Kari's room. She flinched as the light fell on her and saw Anne entering. The woman's eyes widened in surprise before relaxing. She offered an apologetic grin.

"Sorry—I didn't mean to wake you. I thought I'd leave this for you."

She crossed the room and laid a wooden plate on the bed. There were slices of fruit, a hunk of brown bread, and a few strips of cooked venison on it.

"We'll be up awhile yet if you'd like to join us," Anne said before leaving the room again.

Kari blinked away the crustiness of tears from her lashes and moved to the edge of the bed. As she'd hoped, her parents had been there in her dreams, welcoming her home. Now that she was awake, that only made her feel empty.

She reached for the plate and pulled it onto her lap. The meat smelled good, but she had rarely eaten bread or fruit in her life. Sometimes, when bright red kikno berries fell from bushes in the winter, her mother would offer them to her. Meat always tasted better, though, especially when she was in wolf form.

Was she to leave it *all* behind? Forever?

No, Kari thought angrily to herself. *Just until I can avenge Mother and Father.*

She shoveled the food into her mouth without even tasting it. When she was done, she dropped the plate onto the floor amidst the mess of clothes she'd left.

If nothing else, she must live to do that. Even if it meant staying with the humans Anne and Joseph until she was strong enough.

She would eat their food and sleep in their bed for as long as it took.

I will do it, Mother. I will kill them.

Anne didn't bother her again until the next morning. This time, determined to *try* to do what her mother wished of her, Kari steeled herself and followed the woman out to the main room for breakfast. The acrid scent of burning wood filled her nostrils as soon as she left the hallway; a crackling fire wafted lazy smoke from the fire pit in the cooking space. Kari wrinkled her nose, but made herself approach the table.

Joseph was already there waiting for them, a plate of food in front of him. His left arm was wrapped tightly in white cloth and held to his chest in a sling. The image of her father snapping his arm flashed through her mind, and she grinned.

He glanced up as the two of them entered. "Mornin'."

Kari's smile slipped from her face in an instant as she met eyes with him briefly in answer. Unlike Anne, his gaze was cold and hard, more predator than prey. She took a seat at the far end of the table.

"So…" Joseph began once Anne had laid some food in front of Kari. She'd expected more bread and venison, but instead, the plate had thin strips of salty-smelling meat alongside some gelatinous white-and-yellow stuff. Kari wrinkled her nose at it.

"I was thinking, if you're going to stay here, you might get some learning done," Joseph continued once Anne had taken her place beside him.

Instead of looking at him, she stared down at the white-and-yellow thing beside her meat. It looked familiar, but it was different somehow…

Joseph cleared his throat and finally Kari peered up at him.

"Something wrong with the eggs, Kari?" Anne asked.

Eggs. She'd had eggs before. They were a delicacy, only gotten if they were lucky enough for the birds to drop them from their nests. Her parents didn't believe in stealing the young, so it was only once they fell to the ground that she could eat them. These were different, though. Cooked, Kari guessed. She picked up a strip of meat and bit it.

"Have you ever had any sort of learning?" Joseph asked.

"No," Kari replied, her voice raspy from lack of use and her crying the night before. She ate the rest of the meat and reached with her fingers to begin eating her egg. Anne gently pushed a pronged piece of metal to her. Kari picked it up, incredulous.

"For the eggs," she whispered with a smile.

"We'll go introduce you today. Alright?"

Kari shoveled the eggs into her mouth before looking up at Joseph again. He was insistent. He wasn't soft or kind like Anne, and he looked at Kari with furrowed brows, his lips twisted at the corners. He was as uneasy with her presence as she was with his.

Was "learning" required to fit in with humans? By the look in Joseph's eyes and the persistence with which he'd pursued it, Kari imagined so. What sort of learning did he mean? Did humans teach their young to hunt and forage? She gave a weak, noncommittal shrug.

"Good," Joseph said with obvious relief. "We'll go after my morning work. Alright, Anne?"

"Sure. I need to do some housework anyway."

After breakfast, Kari watched Anne wash the dishes and the counters, her thoughts far away in the forests. Only when Anne sat down with bundles of thread ("for knitting," she explained), did Joseph finally poke his head in the front door.

"Kari! Come along now!"

"Oh! One second," Anne called as Kari stood. She laid her thread aside and lifted a pair of long and lumpy leather shoes.

"I found these slippers in some of my old things," she said, holding them out for Kari. "They'll help keep your feet dry, at least, until Joseph can get you something proper to wear."

Her feet? Kari looked down at hers, bare, and to Anne's, which were encased in simple slippers, the edges lined with tufts of rabbit fur.

Her mother had once told her about the shoes that humans wore to protect their feet.

She took the leather shoes and pulled them on. They were loose, and when she stepped, it felt wrong. Normally, she felt each miniscule groove of the ground; every rock, patch of grass, or swirl of dirt was noted when she stepped. With these infernal *shoes*, that was all gone. Her feet were blind in a way she could have never imagined, and she had to be mindful of them as she followed Joseph outside.

"I'll have dinner ready for when you return!" Anne said as the door shut.

Anne and Joseph's house was near the edge of town, away from the hustle and bustle of morning, but that was the only thing that made it stand out from the uniform structures. From what Kari could see, every house was built nearly identical except for the openness of door-ways or shapes of the roofs. She walked down a faded cobble-stone path lined with buildings, following Joseph as they entered the thick of the village.

He briefly explained things as they walked, rightly assuming she didn't know most of these "commonplace" things. She learned this town at the base of the mountains was called Snow Shade, because of the way snow fell upon the village in winter. He pointed out the "shops": butcher, bakery, an inn, and half a dozen other places.

The building for learning, which Joseph called a "school," was a wide, one-story structure lined with windows and a set of tall double doors right in the center. Human children of various ages milled in and out, some of them looking Kari up and down with expressions of mild shock, interest, or suspicion. She stared back at them, equally puzzled by their appearance, from their combed hair down to the various shoes they wore. Her own leather slippers were downright shabby in comparison.

Joseph led her down a hallway, past two open rooms to a door at the end. This he opened for them, closing it once he had entered behind her.

A woman stood in the small room, rearranging numerous books on layers of worn shelves. She turned at the sound of the door opening.

"Mr. Holt. To what do I owe the visit?"

Joseph laid a hand on Kari's shoulder. His grip was hesitantly gentle, yet she still stiffened at his touch.

"Anne and I found this girl outside town. Seems to have no family, and says she's never been to school."

The woman turned her brown eyes to Kari. Her face had contorted into a look Kari had seen often enough on Anne to note it right away—pity, though mingled with surprise and interest. Her hair was a lighter color than her eyes and tied back away from her face and neck. The smile she offered was kind, although it did nothing to ease the nerves twisting up Kari's insides.

"We can situate her with the beginner group until she catches up," she said, crossing the room to a small wooden table. "Most of them are smaller than she is, but we'll be able to see what she knows if we start there." She shuffled through the papers on top of it, finally withdrawing a sheet with many lines and poising an inked quill over one of them.

"What's your name?" she asked kindly.

When she didn't reply, Joseph said gruffly, "Kari."

"Is there a last name?" the woman asked after scribbling this down. "A family name?"

"She can take mine…"

Kari's stomach tightened. "Kasente."

You are Kasente, *her mother said. A strong wolf. Never forget that.*

"Kari Kasente?" the woman asked, looking at Joseph. He jerked his head in confirmation and she wrote it down. "Welcome to our school, Kari. We meet here for class five days a week, from morning until late afternoon. We don't expect certain clothes, per se, but…"

She gestured at Kari's feet. Despite Anne's assurances of dryness, the bottoms of the leather slippers were soaked. Kari glanced behind her to see a trail of tiny footprints made of wet mud.

"We'll see the cobbler," Joseph said.

She nodded her approval and held out her hand. "I'm Mrs. Landry."

Kari stared at her hand. Slowly, her gaze rose to Mrs. Landry's face.

Mrs. Landry smiled and dropped it. "We'll see you tomorrow, bright and early. I will get you acquainted with the class you'll be with until we can get you caught up."

Joseph thanked Mrs. Landry and led Kari back out to the village. The light orange of afternoon was sinking over the buildings as he led her around the corner to a shop filled with leather and silk shoes. He talked to the wizened man behind the counter for a time before finally returning to her, a pair of leather slip-ons in one hand.

"You're not cold, are you?" he asked as if knowing the answer already.

She shook her head. He muttered "Strange," before handing her the shoes. She traded the slippers for them and found that they fit well enough. Satisfied, Joseph led her out again, leaving Anne's old shoes with the cobbler.

The three of them ate dinner together that night. Kari quickly shoveled her food as she had that morning, wanting to be hiding in her room. Anything was better than sitting at the same table with her parent's murderers.

CHAPTER THREE

School began the next day. Though Anne was cheerful as they walked along the road, Kari's instincts screamed for her to flee. Anne and Joseph had been accepting of her behavior so far, assuming she was half-mad from living in the wild, but she had no idea how human children would react to her.

A day of school consisted of two breaks and three sections of class time. She had been assigned to the room of Eli Belle, a friendly man who tried his best to put her at ease. He introduced her to the class in a jolly manner.

"Everybody, this is Carrie Kasente. She will be joining our class for a little while. Now, I know she's a little older than you—"

"It's not Carrie," she murmured. "Kari. Car-ee."

Eli looked abashed, but quickly recovered with a smile. "Right. Kari. Choose a seat, and we'll get started."

They began class as they usually would, he said: a lesson on reading, in which Kari found she was very far behind, even being with younger children. She'd never needed to read, and found she understood nothing of the language she had spoken her entire life.

After their first lesson and subsequent break ended, the second part of class focused on numbers. With this Kari had much more luck; she could count five apples, give away three, and be left with two. Eli was pleased, and despite the consistent trembling in her stomach, she felt a semblance of pleasure in the work she did.

Nonetheless, no amount of Eli's continuous approval of her could dissolve her knowledge that she did not belong with these children. They stared at her and whispered behind their grubby little hands, thinking she could not hear them, but her wolf-like hearing picked most of it up.

"*Care-y* is so scary."

"She sits funny."

"Her hair is so ugly and plain."

"She's *weird.*"

Kari gritted her teeth, determined to ignore them at all costs. Her life, and the honor of her parents, depended on it.

As Eli finished their lesson in math and sent them off for lunch, she felt their stares turn into scowls. Their whispered words became louder, wondering at her oddness, the way she walked and spoke.

She clenched her fists and kept her eyes down as she followed her group outside to a large space behind the school. She found a bare spot of dirt and sat down against the building to look at the lunch Anne had given her: tied inside a bundle of cloth were an apple, a small hunk of bread, and some more dried venison.

I can do this, she thought viciously to herself. *I can do this.*

She laid it all on her lap, prepared to eat when a small, shoed foot came out of nowhere to kick her in the leg. Her food tumbled from her lap; the apple bounced across the hard dirt-clouded ground; the bread rolled and hit the building behind her; the meat hit the ground soundlessly.

Kari froze as she stared at her ruined lunch. Giggling filled the air, and she was soon surrounded by the thin limbs of children's legs, each with a different style of clothing and shoes.

"You're so weird," one of them, a boy, said. She slowly raised her head to glare at him, a snide child with an upturned nose and sharp, cruel, hawk-like black eyes.

"Where'd you come from? 'Cause it's obvious you ain't from here."

The dozen kids surrounding them giggled. Some of the girls broke into a small song, their high voices grating on her ears: "Kari, Kari, she'll be sorry."

The boy with hawkish eyes sneered as he spoke over them. "My mama said there'd be a new orphan in town, some kid who lost her parents."

Kari was on her feet in an instant, fists clenched. She could hit him now, probably hard enough to break his neck. She hesitated, knowing that doing so would draw attention to her and what she was.

The boy looked taken aback, then laughed when she didn't do anything. The other children echoed the grating sound.

"I mean, did you even *have* real parents? My parents would never let me run around soundin' so dumb...I mean, did you guys hear the way she said—"

Kari's fist flew before she could stop herself, slamming into the boy's chest. Though she held back her strength enough to send him stumbling backward rather than cracking his ribs, he gasped in surprise and stared at her with wide eyes.

"Don't talk about them," she hissed through her teeth.

It took no time at all for the boy to collect himself. "Get her!"

Kari was overcome by a rush of bodies, all of them jumping on her at once, swinging legs and fists at anything they could reach.

She huddled in on herself, covering her head and stomach as best as she could while she winced. She could not fight all of them at once. Even if she had decided to rip them apart, there were too many.

Gods, she hated them. She hated them to her core. The memory of her mother using her last moments to protect her rang free, riddling her thoughts with guilt and sadness.

It wasn't until the end of the lunch break that a loud voice broke apart the onslaught of their attacks.

"Hey!" the adult yelled. "Stop that! Back to your classroom!"

The children broke out of their assault with the ease of practice, leaving Kari as a curled-up ball of bruised and bloodied skin. Only when she was sure the last footsteps had retreated did she relax, unfurling herself and crawling onto her hands and knees.

"Kari, are you alright?" Eli was there, bending to help her up.

She knocked his hand aside with a low growl. His soft expression muddled with confusion, but he said nothing as she climbed to her feet and limped her way back inside.

Her ribs hurt so badly she felt sick and certainly no longer hungry for lunch. The pain was constant and intense, enough to make her vision blur. She alternated between resting her head in her hand and on her desk without a single complaint from Eli.

It wasn't until the last lesson of the day that she felt most of the worries drawn from her mind. Even the sneering classmates, their hatred evident in their beady, malicious eyes, could not distract her from history. For this was the time of day when they studied the world they lived on, focusing on their home continent of Taris. Eli revealed an enormous map of it: dotted with mountain ranges, trees, one large river and several small ones, and villages. She took it all in, absorbing the sight.

"First, we'll go over the leaders of the many towns across our continent."

Finally, something useful, she thought eagerly, her pain forgotten.

"All of you, of course, should know our own Lord Isaac Toler, grandson of Louis Toler, legendary warrior in the last Great War." Eli tapped the northernmost town labeled Snow Shade. He proceeded to the right, touching each town in sequence. "Then there is Lord Hill of Grass Shire and Lord Shaw of Fallspire, both significant for our trade here in Snow Shade. Lord Victus of Craggarde..."

The words quickly turned to a droning buzz. Allies of Snow Shade were unlikely to be a friend of hers, a demon. Lord Kira at

Crow's Rest was another ancestor of a renowned warrior, while Lord Grall of Ash Town and Lady Viitala of Storm Port had nothing important to their names. Kari noted High Port, Flatcairn, Wild Valley, and Snake Bay in the east. Then, finally, her vision trailed south. Unlike in the north, the villages here were sparse and distanced. Between two mountain ranges was a vast, unlabeled field.

Eli's stick landed on a thickly detailed forest in the south-west corner of the map. "Lord Izulu of Raziac Village, quite young but with much mettle, I've heard. The family Izulu is known well—"

Kari stared at the village, ignoring what Eli said next, and remembered her mother's words.

If we are separated, I want you to find Zina. She's in the south, in a grand forest.

Was this the forest her mother meant? Kari furrowed her brow. It was so far. She glanced around Eli's map, noting other, smaller clumps of trees. Did she mean the one in the east corner, north of Arkala? Or the scattered trees around Grass Shire and Fallspire?

"There is Snake Bay," Eli explained. "Unlike other villages, run independently and under the control of a specified leader, Snake Bay runs according to the will of the people…"

Kari slumped in her chair. *Mother will never find me, so why do I care about finding this forest and this Zina?* Tears stung in her eyes, making her blink furiously. *That doesn't matter now. I need to avenge them before I think of anything else.*

After a brief lesson on Snow Shade's history—with a particular focus on the Toler family's colonization of Snow Shade—Eli's class was dismissed, and the children broke away to return home. Kari headed outside with them, slammed into walls by the bumping shoulders of various children. Soon Anne in her simple brown dress and smiling face was there, waiting for her so they could walk home together.

"How was your day? Was the meal to your liking? I can pack something else tomorrow…"

The thought of the lunch strewn over the dirt was enough to make Kari's anger boil again Her hand trailed to her ribs, where she was sure there would be bruising at least for a day or two. She was shocked to feel they didn't hurt at all.

Kari paused, putting pressure on her abdomen. She felt the bones beneath the simple shirt and trailed her clawed fingers down each one…with no pain.

"Kari, dear? Are you alright?"

Anne had stopped to cast a concerning glance over her. Kari slowly dropped her arm to her side again.

"I'm fine."

That night the three of them ate dinner together again. Joseph asked about Kari's day but when she ignored him, he turned his attention back to Anne. They talked pleasantly together as Kari retreated to her room.

She closed the door behind her and removed her clothes so she could study herself more closely. The flesh of her stomach was unblemished, her sides the same. Even her legs were unmarked, leaving no trace behind of the beating she had received that day.

Kari remembered dimly a time when she had foolishly tried to climb a tree as a pup. She'd made it up well enough, her ability to leap and dig her claws into hard bark more than any fleeing squirrel could anticipate. She'd found out that wolves were not meant to climb vertical slopes; her claws had scrambled, and she had fallen. The ensuing pain of a ruined limb was enough to make her scared of trees for years afterward.

Her mother had watched over her for days until the leg healed and explained that demons heal much, *much* faster than humans, but it always takes time. There is no instant recovery, not without magic. Kari's leg had taken many days for her to be right again, still much faster than a human, but not instantaneous by any means.

The pain she'd felt after being attacked had not been unbearable. It was enough to warrant something that would take her demon blood some time to fix—internal bleeding, a cracked rib? Something. Even a few bruises would have been expected.

Instead, she was looking at bare flesh. Not a scratch or even a spot of slightly discolored skin...nothing at all. She pursed her lips.

How?

CHAPTER FOUR

Kari quickly settled into a routine with the humans. Wake up, breakfast, writing, mockery, math, hiding from the other children to contain her rage, history, home, dinner, bed. She hated every minute of it; growing more dejected as the hours passed, as the children eyed her cruelly, and Eli skipped over her in class.

The physical attacks of her peers were never as bad as they had been that first day, but Kari was always victim to some type of vehemence; hateful words whispered as they walked by her in the hallway, or swift kicks as they rushed past her to go home. Any marks left behind would be gone soon after she had been hit, and their words stung less and less with every day, yet she still felt broken.

School went on for five days straight, giving her two free days every week. These would be her solace, her recuperation. She could do this until she grew enough to be stronger than them.

On the seventh day of every week, she learned that Anne and Joseph attended "church" with the other villagers.

Her mother had briefly talked to her once about human religions. She knew that they worshipped many high beings, but could only name one for healthy crops—the goddess Mina—and one for safety in battle—the god Akima.

Mother said demons had no need for gods and goddesses—their creator was a god in his or her own right, even though he or she was unknown by most of the demon race. When Kari had questioned this, her mother had no answer.

Kari learned that the people of Snow Shade did indeed pray to Mina, as well as a few others who she had no hope of remembering. She sat through that first time in utter silence, her fists clenched against her legs, and refused to go again.

What did the goddess of crops care for her, a lonely wolf demon? She would never need to worry about the wheat coming in or the fertility of soil like a common human farmer.

So the pattern of her new life continued day by day, week by week. While the humans focused on their monotonous lives, Kari fixed her energy on learning the histories of Taris, and a little of their written word—anything that could aid her when she was strong enough to avenge her parents.

The slow, steady weeks turned into months. Snow fell heavily, coating the village as Joseph had said it would. Kari was forced to wear a thick jerkin and snow hat to keep up the pretense of being human. She hated the hat, as it required her to focus harder to hear, but at least it would do well to hide her ears when they started to grow.

She adapted to school, gathering as much information about the humans as she could. She brushed off their mathematics after she'd learned the basics, and her writing was better after many weeks of practice. History she studied carefully, sure that this would aid her in the future. Eli moved from known villages onto the past, touching lightly on demonic history in conflict with the humans.

To this, Kari listened rapturously, though her mother had explained most of it already. The way the human told it, hellspawn spewed from the earth in the form of demonic creatures. These demons feasted on humans until they found a way to fight back with holy magic, the white light that burned away demon souls.

Not all of them kill humans, even though they could, Kari thought.

The hawk-eyed boy continued to plague her at every moment. Since that first day, he had gotten a few more shots in at her, producing bruises or drawing blood. She never backed down from him, learning early in her life on the mountains that to show weakness was to die. Yet every time they managed to overcome her with their numbers, her rage boiled, and she wondered what she'd do about it.

Two months after her arrival, she was alone during their midday period. Every day, she considered ways to stop their abuse, and every day she came up with nothing that wouldn't give her away.

Kari sat, back rigid, and watched as the boy and his friends appeared on the school grounds. Another day would pass like the dozens of others, and she would only grit her teeth and swallow back her anger.

Instead of making for her, though, they went to the edge of the field their school claimed. A small girl clutching a leather bag was wandering by, her light hair messy and her stitched leather clothes made by unpracticed hands. She was familiar, Kari thought, though she couldn't think from where.

The girl stopped when they called out to her, their voices sharp and cruel, the way they spoke to Kari. She grimaced.

They had found someone else to torment.

The girl shook her head and tried to leave, but the hawk-eyed boy and his entourage of friends surrounded her. She recoiled as they began to poke and prod at her. Kari twitched her head and flexed her ears as they spoke.

"Yer that weird forest girl," one of them said in a scathing voice.

Kari's brow furrowed. *Forest girl?*

37

"Yeah, I seen her pa in town. He's a dirty old man!"

They shoved the girl; she clutched her bag tighter and shut her eyes.

"I bet she don't even speak. She grunts, like an animal!"

They all laughed, shoving her between them. She fell hard, still holding her bag. Kari scrambled to her feet and moved toward them.

One of them nudged the hawk-eyed boy and whispered, "Lian, *she's* comin'."

He turned to watch her advance, a wicked grin on his face. "The freak's come to help the weirdo," Lian said. "Grab her!"

The children swarmed Kari instead, forgetting the girl with the bag. Kari planted her feet and swung her fists, beating them back before they could wrap their tiny, cold fingers around her arms. Beyond the scrabble, the girl watched them with wide, sky-colored eyes.

Go, Kari wanted to yell, but her focus sharpened on the bullies. She spat in their faces and kicked, growling and roaring. When they overcame her, pushing her to the ground, she saw the girl with the bag had disappeared.

Even as a breath of relief filled her, someone's fist connected with her lip, drawing blood. Kari's vision darkened. When it cleared, she saw young Lian looming over her. Kari glared hatefully at him, despising his cowardliness. His minions waited with bated breath.

"I'll smash your face," he promised. "Then even your adopted parents won't like you anymore."

As he raised his foot to do so, he paused. His eyebrows knit together, and his thin face was overcome with confusion. He leaned down to her, so close she could smell his breath, heavy with sweets.

"What is it?" the other children murmured, their voices laden with worry and surprise.

"What's wrong, Lian?"

"Hurt her!"

"You...how'd you do that?" Lian whispered.

Kari's look of confusion must have been apparent, because Lian grabbed her face with his icy fingers, squishing her cheeks, and popping her lip outward.

"You were bleeding!" he yelled.

The feel of his hold invoked something within her, a hot desire unlike anything else she had ever realized. It was burning, fiery, the need to hurt.

Don't touch me, she thought viciously, and her hand snaked out from beneath the bodies of four children, easily upending them onto the icy ground. She wrapped her fingers around Lian's upper arm.

His face contorted with anger before the electricity that shot up Kari's arm pierced his flesh.

He screamed and flailed away from her, his body seizing. Frozen with shock, his minions merely watched as he flopped around. Foam flecked his lips and his eyes popped open. Kari spared him a glance before taking advantage of their distraction. She shoved them all away and raced back to the school.

Lian didn't die, though part of her wished he had. Human healers were summoned to examine him, and somehow, they saved his life. There was relief in that, and the question of what exactly had happened naturally followed.

His minions had been quick to point their stubby fingers at Kari; the outcast, the weirdo, the one with no friends. Even so, there was no proof, no way for them to know she could electrocute someone. Anne was called upon all the same, and Kari left school early.

She was sure the humans would figure her out, and when Anne sat her at the eating table, Kari expected to be thrown down and killed on the spot.

She clasped her hands, wondering how many adults she could take down before they could stop her.

Anne sat down beside her, her own hands flat and entirely weaponless on the table. "Would you like to tell me what happened?"

"You know what happened," Kari croaked in response.

"I know what *they* say," Anne replied with a tilt of her head to indicate the school. "I want to know what *your* story is."

Kari couldn't stop her eyes from narrowing suspiciously. What sort of tactic was this? What did it matter what she thought? The humans would be here any moment to kill her for attacking that boy and almost killing him, for trying to burn his insides into ash…

Hurting him felt so good, she thought, but that wasn't right. Her mother and father had taught her differently than that.

And her father…*this* was why he hated her electricity. It was dangerous, he'd say, volatile.

"Kari, dear?" Anne murmured. "Please talk to me. I can't imagine you hurt that boy. How could you have? But there will be an investigation into it, and the more I know, the better." She hesitated before adding, "The more I know, the better I can protect you."

"What's an 'investigation'?" Kari blurted without thinking, quickly tightening her lips in annoyance with herself.

Anne's smile was kind. "Some people, the Council of Snow Shade, will want to look into what happened because it was so bizarre. That poor boy suddenly collapsing the way he did…and if they cannot reach a verdict, the lord will be involved."

"The lord?" Kari wondered, and a memory clicked in her head: a brief lesson when Eli told them that most villages across Taris are headed by 'lords,' humans of a higher power who rule over the others in their town. She hadn't liked the sound of it then, and she certainly didn't like the sound of it now. How could one human be in charge of so many others? Did they have special powers that offered them control? What else could make one human so special that he was above all the others?

"That's right, dear. Our Lord Isaac has always been fair and kind. I doubt he would even be bothered with this since no one was *seriously* hurt."

Anne's emphasis on the word almost made her smile grimly. What she was saying was that Lian had not been killed, but it was a near miss, and Kari knew it.

She couldn't tell Anne what actually happened. Any knowledge about her ability would cause *more* curiosity about her. They'd want to know how and where she learned such a skill at such a young age. A human child could not have such powers. Her father once said it took years of training for humans to learn even basic magic.

If they thought Kari had magic, they'd start to wonder how she learned it. They'd question who her parents really were. The less they knew about her, the better.

How could she draw the attention away from herself? There were so many fingers pointed at her now, all from those disgusting little children.

I wish I'd hurt them, too.

"Kari?"

Anne was waiting for an answer, something to placate her curiosity about the incident.

There will be an investigation.

"Nothing happened," Kari finally answered. "He just fell over."

Anne searched her face, then visibly relaxed. "Alright, dear. You'll be kept out of school for a day or two, and during that time, some of the Council may come to see you. You won't miss much learning, though, don't worry about that. Eli sent a letter that you're going to be leaving his class and moving up after all of this is over. Isn't that great?"

Anne's words were drowned out as Kari's mind buzzed with anxiety. They'd come to see her? Of course they would. She knew someone must, for she was the one directly involved with Lian's incident.

What would they do? Her ears flicked uneasily beneath her hat. How did they plan to determine if she was guilty or not? And if they found her guilty, what would happen? Kari's palms were wet, her pulse beginning to quicken. They couldn't know that she used electricity to hurt him, could they? Without Lian awake, it would be hard for them to know any facts, right?

Still, she worried. Even after Anne softly patted her hand and got up to make dinner, Kari remained at the table, her nails digging into the wood. Two months. She'd made it two months, all to have it blown on a rush of uncontrollable anger because Lian had touched her face. Kari's mind was a rush of horrific imaginations of what would happen in the coming days.

What would she do now? Wait for some humans to come question her?

Anne served dinner and Joseph arrived home. The two of them talked quietly in the kitchen, snippets of their conversations registering through Kari's dazed state.

"Heard about the boy—"

"He's alive, but Kari is—"

"The Council informed the lord—"

"To our *house*?" Anne's sharp words drew Kari's full attention.

"No, she'll go to him," Joseph responded. "It seemed to me the Council already decided…"

Kari suddenly pushed away from the table and, her stomach twisting, darted down the hallway toward her room. She slipped in and closed the door behind her, sliding against it to the floor.

She would be questioned about what happened, and not by a simple group of humans as Anne had thought. She would be taken before the lord of Snow Shade.

Again, she found herself wondering about 'lords.' How did this one keep track of all the people in this town? How did he manage them? He must have some sort of magic of his own, some special ability. Would that ability be enough to tell him that Kari hurt Lian and used a type of magic to do so? That she was a demon?

Kari dug shallow gouges into the wooden floor in her worry before she finally crawled to the bed and sat upon it.

Her entire life depended on her ability to live with the humans here. If one of them learned what she could do or what she truly was, it was all over. Her mother and father would have died for nothing.

Disgust and fear riddled her insides. What could she do now?

Soft footsteps sounded from the hallway. With lightning-like speed, Kari crawled under the blankets on her bed and feigned sleep, managing to slow her breath enough as the door opened.

"Kari? Are you okay?" Anne's voice whispered in the dimness of her room. When she didn't answer, Anne stepped forward as quietly. She laid something on the floor and retreated. Once the door snapped shut, Kari peeked out from beneath her blanket to see a wooden plate with that night's dinner.

Did Anne and Joseph know that her death would come any day? Did they have any inkling that she might not be what they thought, that she *had* hurt Lian on purpose, and with an ability no one of her age—or species—should possess? Or did they really, truly expect nothing to come of an "investigation"?

She slipped off the bed and gathered the plate, picking at its contents without thinking about it.

What should she do? Should she wait, see the council or the lord as was expected of her? That's what a human child would do, Kari reasoned with herself. A human child could not be at fault, because they couldn't have electric powers.

Yet a human child wouldn't have been in the situation with Lian in the first place. Even if he had bullied another human, their face wouldn't have healed before his eyes, upsetting him further. And a human certainly wouldn't have reacted in their rage by electrocuting him.

She laid the plate aside, half-eaten, and stared across the room.

What now, Mother? What do I do?

The evening sun was slowly sinking past her bedroom window, allowing darkness to descend upon the world. Through the frosted panes she could see some of the village, and beyond them were the tops of trees.

The sight of them stirred something inside her. She belonged there, not here. She belonged out in the world, not hiding in this dingy room with an unknown fate awaiting her. She could meet the lord of Snow Shade and gamble that he would choose to kill her for her transgressions…Or she could run.

She should have done this long ago. Rather than going with the humans, she should have run, not stayed to play house with the human scum who killed her parents. She need not even abandon her mission for revenge. She could come back for them any time.

With shaking yet silent footsteps, Kari crossed her room to the window. She was small enough to slide behind the dresser and strong enough to slide the window open, despite the frost holding it shut. It creaked noisily, making her flinch. After waiting several heartbeats and hearing no approaching footsteps, Kari heaved herself up to the sill. She hesitated only a moment, then slipped out into the night.

CHAPTER FIVE

Snow Shade was silent as Kari plodded around the front of the house. Everyone had disappeared into the safety and comfort of their homes for the night, preferring to avoid the freezing temperatures. She tugged her jerkin around herself and darted away from Anne and Joseph's house, heading for the tree line.

She knew she would be happier on the mountain. She could be herself and learn to hunt.

She slipped in and out of the shadows of buildings. Some of their windows glowed in the darkness, so she avoided them as well as she could. She didn't need anyone recognizing her and wondering where she'd gone.

The northernmost exit of Snow Shade had no guard towers; the trees and bushes were a good enough barrier from unwanted visitors. She broke through those bushes, the same ones she had been spotted within only months ago. The mountain was ahead of her, its pathways obscured by many trees.

She broke into a run, her breath fogging in the air. Soon the trees loomed above her, impenetrable dark creeping between the trunks. She slowed to a jog, and then a walk, before finally stopping.

The scent of the forest was upon her, a heady, earthy smell that made her want to leap forward, but she hesitated. Her fingers twitched at her sides.

She wanted to be gone; away from these people who, at the very least, would deem her too dangerous to live among them. She wanted to be up on the mountain peaks again, hunting squirrels and whatever other easy prey she would stumble across.

Kari didn't know if she could handle it. She couldn't bear to see her home again. She closed her eyes and could imagine it clearly, but it was wrong, sprayed with blood and smelling of death. Her parents lay side by side, their eyes blank and lifeless.

A branch snapped somewhere to her right. Kari twisted around, her teeth bared.

"Who's there?" she hissed, trying to keep the tremble from her voice.

A head of blonde hair poked out of a small huddle of bushes. It was a girl, not much older than her, with cheeks rosy from the cold and eyes wide and blue, like the sky.

The girl Lian had been bullying, the one she had effectively saved.

"What're you doing?" Her voice was light, interested.

"None of your business."

"I think I know you," the girl continued despite Kari's tone. "You stopped the others from..." She trailed off.

"They bully me," Kari muttered. "I was going to make it end anyway, with or without you."

The girl watched her. A ray of moonlight peaked through the trees, glinting off her golden crown of hair.

"Are you afraid of the forest?" she asked, stepping out from the bushes to stand not ten feet away. A softly sweet scent brushed the air, the smell of flowers. As Kari had noted before, her clothes were obviously handmade by someone with little skill. "There's nothing to be scared of," she continued. Her hands were gloved with the same shoddy type of leather work. "My papa and I live up there. He doesn't like me to come down here, but sometimes—"

"Up where?" Kari interrupted loudly.

The girl blinked. "The mountain, of course."

"How…how could you live up there?"

"Well…the same as those people, I suppose…? Only we do our own hunting."

Kari stared at her. She couldn't emphasize her question without giving herself away, could she? How could this girl live on this mountain without her having known?

The girl shrugged her thin shoulders and threw out her hand in an offer of a handshake that Kari had seen the humans do in Snow Shade many times. Even though they were still several feet away, she said happily, "Anyways, I'm Kiki. What's your name?"

Kari said nothing and made no movements. She was speechless. Who was this girl, out here in the middle of the night, spouting stories about living on this mountain? *Her* mountain?

Kiki dropped her hand to her side. "Papa said that's how it's done. I haven't gotten to try it before."

"Who…what…why the hell are you here?"

The blush on Kiki's face deepened. "Sometimes I come here… to watch others. Papa doesn't like to come down here much at all, only for trading. I like to see them, though, even if they're a little mean."

When Kari only stared at her, Kiki smiled.

"Do you want to come play with me? There's some flowers—"

"It's late," Kari snapped. "Shouldn't you be at home?"

Kiki quirked a brow at her. "Shouldn't *you?*"

"This place isn't my home—"

"You wanted to see the forest, right?" Kiki interrupted, her voice high with excitement. "Let me show you! Please? I don't have anyone to show, but they're so pretty, even in winter…"

"I don't have time for flowers," Kari scoffed.

"Then what're you doin'?"

"I told you, it's none of your damn—"

"Because you looked troubled. Papa always said village folk have nothing to be troubled about, but that's silly. Anyone can be upset about *something*."

"I'm not 'village folk,'" Kari sputtered angrily. "I was running away!"

Kiki's eyes sparkled with interest, but not the same way as the other children Kari had come to know the last two months. "What're you running away from? Sometimes I want to, you know. I love my papa, but I hate living in the forests. It's so lonesome," she whined.

Her words struck Kari to the core, tangling up her insides with the sadness that still lingered and the vengeful rage that accompanied it. She staggered.

She couldn't go back up the mountain. She couldn't look upon her old home and the place where her parents had laid dying. The agony would be too much.

What do I do?

A hand touched her arm. Kari twitched, pulling away from Kiki's grip. Her touch was gentle and retracted easily.

"Sorry, was I rambling? Papa says I do that a lot."

Kari stared at her face, pale in the places where the cold didn't flush the skin. Her eyes were bright, her smile cheerful.

How did this child live on the mountain? And where had she been when Kari had raced down to see the villagers, desperate for evidence of living life somewhere, anywhere, else?

Kiki's smile faded at the look on Kari's face. "I think, whatever's caused you trouble, you shouldn't run from it. Papa always said that never helped anyone."

"What could your father know about me?" Kari rasped, unable to summon even a spark of anger. The idea of climbing the mountain slope seemed impossible, a lifetime away.

"Nothin', I guess, but he's pretty smart all the same. You know, he raised me all by himself since my mama died. Refused to ask for help, especially if it meant going to towns like this one. Even with the demons on the mountain, my papa was strong. He's never run away from anything." Kiki glanced back to the trees. When she turned back to Kari, it was with an apologetic smile. "I gotta go home now. Papa told me not to go far, he'll be mad if he found out I came all the way down here again."

Kari opened her mouth to speak, her questions numerous. Why did her father choose to live away from society? Who was she?

"The forests aren't scary, so come and play sometime. I'm around most nights," the girl continued as she retreated to the darkness of the bushes and trees. "When Papa isn't havin' me hunt with him. But the hunting is rare right now, so…"

"Try more east," Kari blurted out before biting her lip. Kiki looked back at her curiously and Kari, resolved, found her voice. "Try more east of the slope. The deer prefer it there. There's…there's no wolves."

The girl's smile widened. "Okay, I'll let my papa know! Thanks…" she hesitated halfway through the bushes; her body nearly enveloped in the black of the night.

"Kari," the young wolf demon muttered. "My name is Kari."

Kiki smiled one last time before disappearing into the bushes with a quiet rustle.

Staring at the place where Kiki had first shown herself, Kari remained motionless. She was uncertain again, a demon who lost her parents, forced into the role of a human child and adopted by the ones who took their lives.

I think, whatever's caused you trouble, you shouldn't run from it.

As much as she hated to admit it, Kiki was right. Kari's father would have disapproved of her trying to run away from a problem.

She had to face it head-on and deal with the consequences…ones she wrought when she shocked that stupid boy.

If she had heeded her father's wishes never to use her powers, maybe it wouldn't have happened.

You are Kasente. *A strong wolf.*

Kari clenched her fists and slowly turned away from the forests that would lead to her mountain peak cave. Just as she had run back home to tell her mother of the mistake she'd made when being sighted by the humans, she must now return to Anne and Joseph's house and await the appearance of their lord. If he would decide her fate, then so be it. She would fight for her life, though. As a demon would, as her parents did.

The sun was breaking the horizon when she slipped back through her still-open window. Her room filled with a thin layer of frost in the night, but she didn't care. She shut the window. Warmed by her determination, climbed beneath her dampened and chilled sheets.

CHAPTER SIX

Kari woke groggily to a light knocking on the door; shivering, she sat up as Anne entered her bedroom.

"By the gods, it's cold in here!" the woman gasped. "What happened? And why is everything damp?"

Kari rubbed her eyes as she swung her legs off her bed. "I opened the window last night. Some frost got in."

And, she thought, *the smell of the trees is so much better than your stinking fires.*

Anne rubbed her arms, her brow furrowed. "Well…I will try to clean it up later. Come to breakfast."

Joseph was already at the table, digging into his eggs. Anne served Kari, then herself before sitting at her husband's side. As Kari fought the eggs with her fork, Anne spoke.

"I heard something in town yesterday."

Kari perked up. Joseph grunted for her to continue.

"Sally said her husband spoke to one of those scouts. You heard we lost one?"

"Yeah."

"Well, one came back. Said they were attacked by something strange."

"I heard them talking. A mutant, they said. Fools." Joseph scraped the last of his eggs into his mouth. "There isn't anything out there but nasty, old demons. They'll make any excuses for not doing their job."

"Sally said there've been other stories of these monsters…odd things. Not demon, but not human either."

Kari glanced between them.

Joseph pushed from the table. "Real men don't have time for fairytales, Anne. I've got work to do."

"All the same," Anne pressed, "do you think Lord Isaac will hire some help? Hunters, maybe?"

Joseph scoffed. "Gods know this town can't afford that, Anne. Those damn Masters of Glimmer View are too expensive for little towns like ours."

Anne lowered her head. "I suppose all I can do is pray for our safety. Yours, specifically. When you go out hunting—"

Joseph shook his head. "Our gods don't care about a lone man like me. And don't bring that nonsense about angels into it, neither. They don't exist." He looked to Kari. "Good luck, girl."

Anne pursed her lips, but before she could say anything more, Joseph left. The door slammed shut behind him.

Kari stared after him. Mutants, not demons? And angels? Her mind whirred from the conversation, as well as Joseph's final words. *Good luck.* For what?

Anne straightened with a small, gasping sigh. "Kari, I'm sorry. I meant to tell you last night before you went to bed. Joseph heard that our Lord Isaac will see you today, after a meeting with the Council. I will escort you as soon as you're ready."

Kari's fluttering insides turned into an uneasy knot. Her vision swam, and her body threatened to topple over.

Anne gathered their dishes and retreated to the kitchen. "Choose something nice to wear, dear. We want to make a good impression for the lord."

Kari wandered back to her room, her vision blurring and her stomach trembling. She began to sort through the clothes on the floor. It took several minutes before she finally extracted a nice enough dress, the color of faded bark, and changed into it. She pulled the leather coat over it and put her hat back on before returning to the main room where Anne was waiting.

"Ready, Kari?"

It was still early in the day, the sun barely shining its warmth over the streets as the two of them walked through town. Shop owners waved to Anne as they took the usual path toward school. She brushed off their gossiping questions with false laughter and guided Kari around the seamstress's shop.

They stopped in front of a two story building made of elegant black and white stone. A set of glossy steps led the way to double doors, lined on either side by shining windows. Kari stared up at its majesty, the gold-lined gables, and peaked roof, as Anne led her up the stairs. A pair of leather-armored guards held vigil on either side of the entrance.

"Name and business?"

"Kari to see the Council," Anne answered, prompting the guards to nod and open the doors. Anne smiled at Kari. "Come on, dear."

Kari stepped into a high-ceilinged room with shining floors and too many halls branching in every direction. In the center of the room was a high wooden stand with four men behind it. Anne led Kari to them.

"Name?"

"Kari Kasente," Anne said.

"Noted. You may leave. We will escort the child home when the questioning has been completed."

Anne hesitated, looking concerned. Kari, too, was taken aback, although for a different reason—their words implied that she was not heading straight to a death sentence.

"I will see you for lunch, perhaps," Anne said with a small smile before turning and leaving her with the Council members.

"Kari Kasente," one of the men boomed once the front door had closed again. The speaker was the oldest looking of the four, with wizened, scowling eyes and puckered lips. "Do you know why you are here?"

Trembling, she raised her head to meet the speaker's eye. "The hurt boy—Lian."

"Correct. His current state is…questionable. Only you could give some insight, being the one who was involved in the confrontation. Now…"

A balding man with dark, stern eyes leaned closer. "How did you know Lian?"

Kari blanked at the question. Didn't they already know? "We go to school together."

"How are your interactions?"

He and his friends attack me constantly.

Kari shuffled her feet. "We don't get along well."

The man nodded and bent his head to write on a paper in front of him. The man next to him continued the interrogation.

One by one, the councilmen of Snow Shade drilled Kari with questions, sometimes repeating the same one several times. What happened that day? Why had she been found in the mountains by herself? What happened to Lian? How was her home life? What was her friendship with Lian like? What…

By the time they had asked her for the fourth time how she knew Lian, Kari's mind was mush. She answered the same thing, every time, every answer clear. At first, she thought perhaps the men were senile, asking her repeated questions because they'd forgotten. Eventually, she caught on: they were trying to catch her in a lie, however insignificant it might be.

The realization irritated her.

"How is your life at home, Kasente?" the man on the right asked.

Kari couldn't hold back her clipped reply. "I've answered this enough."

"Do you refuse a response, child?"

Before Kari could release the scathing reply at her lips, a door slammed shut, the sound echoing across the massive room. The Councilmen fell silent at once; a cold air passed over all of them.

Down one of the many hallways came a new figure, lined on either side by elegant women. As the three of them came closer, Kari took note of the middle-aged man in the center: tall and handsome; his cheek bones well-defined and his jaw smooth; hair dark and green eyes framed by delicately styled eyebrows. His clothes were sophisticated, of much richer thread than Kari had yet seen; he walked with the air of one who worried for nothing.

For all his prettiness, Kari could only think one thing: arrogant. His self-importance was evident in every step, the look in his eyes bleeding overconfidence. This man was no doubt the lord of Snow Shade, and Kari found herself disappointed.

"Gentlemen."

"Lord Isaac," the Councilmen echoed.

"Is this our young lady? I have waited many hours now to see her."

Had it been that long? Kari thought blankly of the breakfast she had not finished, and her stomach rumbled weakly.

"Our apologies, Lord," one of the Councilmen said. "We—"

"That is enough," Lord Isaac interrupted. "Come, child. We don't want to waste any more time, do we?"

Before Kari could process what was transpiring—his appearance, his words, and the irritated faces of the council men—the lord's women surrounded Kari and ushered her after him. She stumbled, grabbing her hat to keep it from falling as they quickened their pace. They followed Lord Isaac back down the hallway.

He walked as few others in Snow Shade did, with his back straight and his head held high. The long sleeves of his tunic rustled with every movement, and his loose-fitting breeches were lined on the sides with glittering gold buttons. Even his handsome leather boots made a statement with a gentle, constant, *tap, tap* at every step.

Kari followed him and his women to a door near the end of the hallway. Here they entered a new room, much smaller than she imagined, but no less elegantly furnished. A shining maple bookcase, table, and chairs filled the space. Lord Isaac crossed to the largest seat available, a throne-like chair facing the door, and sat. The women steered Kari to a chair directly opposite of him and then disappeared from her vision. She heard their gentle footsteps as they tip-tapped around the room, busying themselves.

Lord Isaac smiled kindly at her, yet his eyes twinkled with something belying the compassion he was attempting to portray. Kari stared at him, refusing to return his smile.

"So," he began, "how pleasant it is to finally meet you, child. I am Isaac, Lord of Snow Shade."

He spoke carefully and clearly, showing his teeth whenever he opened his mouth. Kari clenched her fists in her lap.

She'd been taught mild pleasantries by her parents and picked up on more human ways of polite greetings while she'd lived in Snow Shade. Yet even thinking about uttering one of those to this man was difficult. How could a human demand respect from her? He was not *her* lord.

"I will not bore you with more pointless questions. I believe we both have the same desire to finish this business and get on with our lives?"

Kari bit her lip and nodded.

He grinned pleasantly. "Then I ask for merely a pinch more of your patience," he said and snapped his fingers. The sound was sharp and sudden, but Kari's flinch was ignored. One of his women appeared at his side with some sheets of paper. She passed these to him and moved out of sight again.

"The official analysis is that poor Lian's body received some type of trauma. A shock that caused his heart to sputter for a moment made him collapse. My healers cannot determine *what* the shock was, or how he sustained the burn on his arm."

Kari barely stopped herself from chewing her lip. There'd been a burn inflicted, too?

"I do not expect one as young as you to have answers for me. There is only the word of your peers, them being children themselves. So, until young Lian awakens and can give some insight, I am having this matter dropped from the record."

For a heavy moment, Kari stared at Lord Isaac. She was quick to snap her mouth shut as it hung open in disbelief.

"W-what?" she muttered before she could stop herself.

She'd expected all sorts of things; blame, threats, warnings, promises of finding the truth, that she hurt him and would pay the price...not this leniency.

Lord Isaac's laugh was cheerful and clear, embodying the same confidence he carried when he walked. "Dear girl, don't look so shocked. Did you think you were here for punishment?"

Yes, Kari thought, biting her tongue. "Can...can I go home then?"

"Oh, certainly you may. But first, I must beg your assistance in another matter I have been dealing with as of late."

Kari's eyebrow rose of its own volition. Her fear long since forgotten, she could only stare at this curious man, this man who was like no one else in the village. Rather than demand her assistance, he merely smiled at her. Waiting patiently for some type of confirmation that, yes, she would help him.

What could she help him with? She was a mere child, as he'd just stated, and from his own words regarding her peers who'd witnessed the incident with Lian, she knew he granted them the amount of responsibility one might give a cow.

"I don't know how I could aid you...but I will do what I can," she answered reluctantly, unsure what she was agreeing to.

Lord Isaac looked pleased. "Wonderful. I only need to know one thing, dear girl, and then you may be on your way. You're new to Snow Shade. By now, everyone has heard your tale, coming down from the northern peaks, found living on your own. No one can possibly discern your past, but…"

Kari almost rolled her eyes. *Here we go. More useless curiosity, wondering about something that is none of their business.*

Humans.

"I suppose you have heard the villagers gossiping about mutant demons nearby?"

Kari recalled Anne's worries from that morning, and Joseph's dismissal of them. "I heard they were…not demons, exactly."

"Quite. I had one captured, and I…well, have you ever seen a demon up close?"

She bit back derisive laughter. "No."

He nodded at the expected answer. "As you should not, as young as you are! This thing—and the others like it—are nothing like demons that have been recorded in the last hundred years. They are not animal-blooded, for instance."

Kari's hands fiddled in her lap. Was this lord lying to her? "Not animal-blooded?"

"Correct. These *things* come here, and unlike true demons, they do not desire to hurt my people. Rather, they seem to be searching for something."

Kari bit back her fury at his blatant ignorance. "What?"

Lord Isaac watched her, searching for something within her face. She kept her expression impassive, lightly curious.

"They seek a demon. For reasons I cannot fathom, these purple-skinned beasts are rampaging my land in hopes of finding this one demon." He sighed, waving a hand. "Yet that is all outside my village. You see, there has been talk in Snow Shade. It is quiet talk, for sure, yet it reaches the ears of my confidants." He steepled his hands and leaned closer. "Can you keep a secret, Kari?"

Her mouth drying, she nodded.

He grinned, pleased. "Word is that there are demons *within* my village. They sneak in and out of reach, yet no matter where I look, I cannot find them. My people have been able to learn one thing only: a name. At first, I wondered if this named person was connected to the purple-skinned mutants, but no interrogation could draw out any truths. It is unfair to ask you, perhaps, but I am out of options. If anyone has a seed of knowledge, why not the strange girl from the mountains?

"Tell me, child, have you heard the name 'Rathik'?"

Kari sat very still, absorbing all he'd said. Demons were in Snow Shade? Where, how? What did this Rathik person, or the not-demon creatures apparently skulking about, have to do with them?

Lord Isaac's expression slipped into an annoyed scowl, one a spoiled boy might make when told "no" by his mother.

"At most," Lord Isaac continued in a sigh, "I can discern that Rathik is the ringleader for the demons infiltrating Snow Shade. Perhaps these creatures are his pets, gathering demons and hording them within my village. I desire to interrogate him, but I don't know where he resides or how he sneaks them in. It maddens me."

"No...Sir. I don't know anyone by that name."

The lord briefly searched her face. Satisfied by what he saw, he smiled again. "Very well. Thank you for your agreeing to come see me today," he said as he stood from the table. Kari copied his fluid motion. "Mila and Mika will see you out, and one of my guards will escort you home again."

"That's not necessary. I can make my way."

His smile widening knowingly, Lord Isaac's eyes twinkled. "Yes, I suppose you are quite tired of adults watching your every move, aren't you, child? I was young once. Off you go."

Unable to believe her luck, Kari stepped away from the table and turned to exit the room. His two women stood beside the door, holding it open for her. She spared them a glance before slipping by. Then she was quietly making her way back down the hallway, the exit within her sights.

She was alive. Alive and without having to hurt anyone. She had not even been threatened by the humans' precious lord, though Kari hadn't liked one bit of him. His false kindness was not missed by her, neither was his inattention toward Lian's wellbeing. The lord did not care if Lian was hurt. He merely cared about potential spies within the town of Snow Shade.

What a useless ruler for them to have! Kari could have pitied the humans, if not for being distracted by her relief to be free of his presence.

She strode through the main room and past the tall stand with its council members who ignored her. She hoped to never see these old men again, but there was much time still. So much time until she would be ready to complete what she considered now to be her main goal.

Kari was greeted by an evening sky when she finally stepped outside again. She stared down the lined path that led into the main part of Snow Shade, thinking of her day and the woman who was no doubt at home anxiously awaiting her.

I will see you for lunch, perhaps.

Kari was tired in body and mind. Even so, she could not muster the will to return to the place she reluctantly called home. What else would she do?

Her eyes trailed to the trees in the distance. With an odd tingling in her gut, she recalled the night before, and the human girl who had risen from the forest's depths to greet her.

With slow steps, Kari headed north through town.

CHAPTER SEVEN

The humans of Snow Shade milled back and forth, not sparing the barest attention for the small girl who slipped by their shops and down alleyways that would lead her to the forest.

Part of Kari questioned loudly what she was doing. What did she gain going to see the human girl from the mountain? She was the oddest human Kari had ever known, and Kari didn't even know how to find her again unless she was in the exact same spot.

Was it any better to go back to the murderer and his wife, who would pester her and demand to know how things went with the lord?

Kari kept her pace up, darting around corners and down side paths until the first of the trees loomed above her. For a long moment, she stood under their shadows, her weight on her toes as if she might leap forward at any minute. Yet she stayed where she was.

The girl had been nosey and talkative, and she'd said she was lonely.

Like me.

Kari's fingers twitched. Had she become one of those demons so easily? Fearing, even despising, humans? Even her parents never *hated* humans; they merely thought of humans as an annoying or dangerous neighbor who must be kept at a distance.

We do not kill them for sport, Kari. Not as our brethren might. There is no point. We must share this world.

Kari squeezed her eyes shut.

I want revenge. That's all. The rest of them can live.

Demons were not inherently evil. She knew that. Some might want to fight and kill, but her parents hadn't.

Kari's ears flicked as she opened her eyes. Her legs tensed, and she dove into the trees.

The earthy smell welcomed her like an old friend, banishing all the human smells she detested. Her leather boots were crunching over twig-and-leaf strewn snow, and she paused to take it all in, to savor it.

A vision of snow painted red, of empty yellow eyes, made her eyes snap shut. She froze and placed a hand on a nearby tree. Her nails dug into the tough bark.

Why did it have to happen...?

Kari shook her head and looked around her. The day's light was fading, but her wolfish vision allowed her to see the thick trees, the scruffy bushes. It was getting late; she couldn't stay away too long, or Anne would be agitated when she finally returned.

This is foolish, Kari thought. Who knew if that girl would show herself tonight?

Quiet footsteps crunched over snow and fallen branches. Kari spun to the direction the sound originated. Before she could form an idea of who—or what—made it, a tiny face appeared out of the huddle of bushes, barely distinguishable in the growing darkness.

"Is that you, Kari?" Kiki whispered.

"If it wasn't, what would you do?"

Kiki's face withdrew. Hardly a second later she was climbing over the shrubs, stumbling and grunting, until she was standing in the same clear space as Kari.

"Well, I suppose I'd run..." she said once she'd brushed off her clothes.

Kari couldn't help but recall the memory of being spotted by a handful of children and their parents when she had been caught spying.

"I didn't expect to see you so soon," Kiki said with a wide smile.

Kari fidgeted, tried to think of something sarcastic to say, and failed. "I...didn't want to go home yet."

Kiki's eyes danced with understanding, but she didn't comment on it. "Well, it's getting dark, but do you want to see the flowers? They're not far from here."

Kari chewed her bottom lip. "Flowers? It's the dead of winter."

"You don't listen well," Kiki said with a roll of her eyes. "These ones are different. They're pretty, no matter what the season."

Kari hesitated, feeling foolish to be in the woods, seemingly making friends with a human girl. She should've...what? Gone to that house with those people? Those people who removed her only family from the world?

Whatever she should've done, she shouldn't have come here.

Before she could protest, Kiki's leather-clad hand was grabbing hers without permission, tugging her toward the bushes. "Please," she pleaded. "Please come see them. I promise, promise, *promise*, you won't regret it."

Her eyes were far too wide, her face too innocent. Kari could not know her, could not dream of ever seeing this girl as more than a human, an enemy.

Kiki tugged again, and before Kari could consider another thought, her feet were sluggishly moving. Her boots crunched over the snow again as she forced her way through icy leaves and branches, ducking into the deeper parts of the forest after Kiki.

They were still close to Snow Shade, but the mountain was brimming with life Kari had always taken for granted. Night birds sang quiet, haunting songs, and bugs that could stand the cold buzzed among the frosted greenery.

Kiki let go of Kari's hand and led the way, walking a well-memorized path through the trees. The smells were a fresher type of scent than the regular earthy smells of the mountain—Kari realized she'd never ventured into this part of the woods. It wasn't very far, as Kiki had said; not more than a quarter of an hour later, the two of them came to a wall of bushes so tall and thick with winter berries it was impossible to see beyond them. Kiki glanced over her shoulder.

"Just through here," she whispered and ducked into the hedging. Kari hesitated and followed her.

They stepped into a wide, circular clearing edged entirely by those same thick bushes. To Kari's amazement, there were flowers. Hundreds and hundreds of them, floating daintily on thin green stalks. Their long, curved petals glowed in the light of the rising moon.

"They're pretty, right?" Kiki stepped carefully to avoid squishing any of them. Kari stayed on the outskirt, reluctant to enter this place of strangely tranquil beauty.

"What are they?" she whispered, kneeling to touch a single petal.

"Papa said they're called morthiem lilies. It takes all year for them to bloom, but in winter, they're so pretty."

"This is bizarre," Kari murmured. She had, until now, seen winter as a dead season, the end of most life and the worst time for hunting. Yet here these little flowers were, thriving in the dead cold of the night, pleasantly happy while the human crops withered.

"I come here all the time, whenever Papa doesn't need me," Kiki was saying. She managed to find a clear spot in the center of the area and sat down, even though the ground must be freezing. "I love it here."

Kari couldn't help but silently agree. The clearing was beautifully aglow with the moon's rays; the flowers gave off a gentle, soothing smell, and there was no sound except the natural life of the night. It was a haven, a place outside the rest of the world. Despite Kari's constant tension, she felt a semblance of peace.

This felt like a place she could stay, at least for a little while. It was Kiki's hideaway, but could it be hers? When things were too much, could she come here?

"I...need to get back."

Kiki stood, brushing herself off. "Yeah, I think I should too."

Kari waited for Kiki to join her before heading back through the bushes.

"Hey," Kiki said as Kari turned to leave, "you're in the village, right? So, you get their learning?"

Kari pursed her lips. "Yeah."

Kiki's excited intake of breath would have been missed by someone with weaker ears.

Kari glanced over her shoulder at the girl. "Why?"

"Well...Papa said I couldn't go. He hardly wants me talkin' to those people at all. It's silly."

Was it? Kari wondered. After what she had seen Lian and the others do, would Kiki be any safer than Kari was around them? Even as a human, she was outcast from them. Maybe her father knew that.

She and Kari dug their way back through the hedges that shielded the clearing. Once they were on the other side, Kiki grabbed her hand again.

"Will you...will you teach me sometime? I know simple stuff that Papa teaches me. I can read a little. But I...I want to leave this place someday! I want to see other places. I want to go to other towns, and mountains, and forests!"

Kari gently shook her off, annoyed that the girl's touch didn't unnerve her the same way Anne's might. "I don't know...There isn't much to know."

Of course, that wasn't true. Already Kari had learned a lot of arithmetic, types of things her parents would have never bothered to teach her. And the land...she had already memorized parts of Taris, especially the forests. In case she ever decided to find Zina.

Kiki's eyes were determined, her lips tight.

Kari sighed. "I can tell you some things. Maybe we can...meet here again. At the lilies. Sometimes we have practices we have to do at home, so I can show you that."

Kiki's smile showed all her teeth. "Okay! I told Papa what you said about the eastern hunting, so he's takin' me that way tomorrow. What about the next day? Do you think you could come to the lilies then?"

Kari shrugged. What else did she have to do after a day of school? Go back to that house, eat dinner with Anne and Joseph? "Yeah."

"Great! I'll see you." Kiki waved as she turned away, back to wherever home was for her. "Goodbye, Kari!"

"Bye," Kari muttered as the girl disappeared. She turned away, back to the path that would lead her to Snow Shade.

CHAPTER EIGHT

Kari could run much faster than a human, and soon she was at the door to Anne and Joseph's home, her breath only slightly heavy. She adjusted her hat to make sure it was still covering her ears and entered.

Anne appeared from the kitchen as the door creaked open. Kari hadn't even realized how elated she felt until the sight of Anne drove that all away again.

The woman didn't notice or care for the abject look on Kari's face as she crossed the room in quick strides, dropped to her knees, and grabbed Kari's arms in a tight grasp. Kari flinched away, but the woman wouldn't let go.

"Where have you been?" she asked in a choked voice.

"Your-the lord kept me late—"

"I went there looking for you when you never came home. They said you'd left already. That was nearly three hours ago!"

Kari gritted her teeth. This was the life of a human child, as she'd learned watching other human parents scold their children. She had known Anne would worry.

"I walked around town a while," Kari finally managed. "The weather was so nice."

Anne searched her face with not-quite-angry eyes. She sighed and released her. "Sorry. I just…I worry. There's been talk about dangerous people in the village lately, and I…as a mother, I…"

Anne's words trailed off. Her face flushed. Kari stiffened.

"Not that I'm your *mother*, but…" Anne sighed again. "I'm sorry, Kari. Do you want some dinner? You must be hungry. You barely had breakfast. I can—"

"No, I'm fine," Kari replied in a clipped voice.

Anne had the grace to look embarrassed by the verbal blunder and allowed her to slip past. Kari made her way down the hall, briefly catching the sound of Joseph's snores as she opened the door to her room.

The old man doesn't care about me and what I do, so why should Anne? Kari thought scathingly.

Anne had cleaned her room and organized the clothes Kari had strewn about, piling them neatly beside the bed rather than putting them away in the drawers again. She fought the urge to destroy the neat little piles and instead sat down on the bed, her body numb.

Gods above and below, I do not belong here, she thought as she dug her nails into the thick blanket that now layered her bed. *She is not my mother and she could never hope to be. And one day, I will…*

Her angry thoughts trailed off, making room instead for thoughts of the forests, Kiki, and the enchanting morthiem lilies. There was beauty and things to appreciate in the world; she would just have to wait a little while to see it. And once she had avenged her family, she would see much, much more.

The next day passed in a blur. Anne decided to pretend the night before had never happened, and Joseph did not question the heavy silence between them. Officially cleared by the lord, Kari returned to school, where she met her new teacher and classmates.

Within the first hour of the new class, Kari realized how much she should have appreciated Eli and what she had deemed as useless niceties. Her new instructor, who insisted he be called Mr. Hodges, was a sneering older man with not a scrap of patience for Kari's stumbling over words. He called her out and openly mocked her, forcing her to try and try again until the class had broken out into fits of giggles. Then he berated her for wasting his time.

By the end of the day, Kari was exhausted. Her classmates had not attempted to physically abuse her as Lian and those of his age did, but with Mr. Hodges' constant complaints, she hadn't been able to retain much from the geography and math lessons.

She returned home to a quiet dinner with Anne and Joseph, where they finally asked her about the meeting with Lord Isaac. Kari declined to mention the man's curiosity about a 'Rathik' who was wandering about town, only repeating what the lord had said about her guiltiness being dropped.

"That's wonderful!" Anne cheered at the news. "I knew they would, dear. They had no reason to blame you."

In her room that night, Kari lay awake, dreading the coming days if they would be any type of repeat. How did one survive like this, even as a human? It was harder than it should be, even if she was learning useful things. When she finally came of age, she doubted she'd even be fit enough to destroy anyone.

I can teach myself, the thought jolted through her mind. *I can go to the forests after school and practice. Anything would be better than nothing.*

It was an idea, at least. The only problem was finding a time and place where she could train in solitude, for Kiki was around and Kari couldn't handle another slip-up.

Kiki.

Kari was to meet her tomorrow evening, but she had only started receiving learning appropriate to her age. She wouldn't have much to give the girl of the mountain. What would be the point of attempting to teach her so early on, or at all? To make friends? Did Kiki want that?

Did Kari?

The next day went on much the same. Kari stuttered and misread the words Mr. Hodges wrote so much that he finally took pity and left her alone the rest of the day. She ate the lunch Anne packed her and studied all the arithmetic and geography that Mr. Hodges went over. As the end of the day neared, she found her attention waning.

"As you return home tonight, I want all of you to find something to describe to me in great detail. Any old thing will do—an old hat, your mother's dress, whatever suits your fancy. But I want *details*," Mr. Hodges told them. "And tomorrow we will begin to study how local fauna and flora have evolved and changed over the centuries. Pick a flower and bring it in, or choose a wild animal you may have seen. If that's not too difficult."

Kari milled out with her classmates and met Anne outside. Her stomach twisted into loose knots. How would she convince Anne to let her go see Kiki without telling her anything? The uncertain anxiety was quickly smothered by a wave of indignant annoyance. She did not need to tell Anne anything, she simply needed to go.

For dinner, Anne laid out strips of venison, and the three of them ate. Kari devoured what Anne served her, thinking of sneaking out her bedroom window again. That would be the best way to avoid unwanted questions from the humans.

"How's school?" Joseph's gruff voice came from across the table. It took Kari a moment to realize he was talking to her, something he rarely bothered to do. "You've been put in with the other kids your age, right?"

"Yeah," Kari answered uncertainly.

"Bit hard?"

"A little."

"Fitting in? Making friends?"

"Joseph," Anne hissed.

Kari glanced between them, slow understanding dawning on her. Was he suspicious now, because she did not play the right role as a human child and get along gleefully with her peers? Did he, perhaps, speak with her new teacher who no doubt had plenty of crude words to describe her?

She could never forget that it was Joseph who landed the killing blows to her father *and* mother. He had orphaned her, and while he had agreed to take her in as his own, the sin was still there. What right did he have to question her and how she would live? He didn't even know who, or what, she was.

"Why should I try to make friends?" Kari replied airily.

Joseph scowled. Anne looked concerned. Kari shoved away from the table.

"Thank you for dinner," she said before returning to the hallway, catching a mere snippet of Joseph's annoyed words as she left the main room behind.

"Bizarre girl, Anne, I'm telling you—"

Kari's smile was faint, but it was still present, for she knew that if she did nothing else violent, Anne would protect her at all costs. Anne, who wanted so badly to be a *mother*, who wanted to love Kari and be loved in return.

Her love would protect Kari for as long as she required it.

It took nearly a quarter of an hour for Kari to shove handfuls of shirts and pants underneath the sheets and punch them into a shape that might vaguely resemble her. By the time she was done, it looked like a mess, but it would have to do. If not, though, Kari was sure Anne would accept any story if she came back safe.

Without another thought, Kari was crossing to the window and shoving it open. Cold air blasted her face as she climbed up and hoisted herself out. This time, she was careful to close it before turning toward the mountain.

Rarely had she put much effort into something like this. Even the things her mother or father had asked of her were done with utmost laziness; anything it took to get the job done as fast as possible. Now here Kari was, sneaking out and attempting to cover her tracks, all so she could go meet Kiki.

A human girl. A human girl who was becoming her *friend*.

Kari scoffed as she made her way around the house and through the village all the same.

For the third time, Kari found herself under the trees again, smelling the earthy scent and running her fingers over the frosted bark and bushes. She couldn't deny how good it felt to be outside the village. This world outside of the humans completed her.

One day, she would get the courage to climb the mountain again, to see the place where she had lost everything.

Kari soon left behind the main path for the depths of the foliage, stumbling until she finally came to the massive hedges Kiki had shown her. She slipped between them and entered the clearing filled with flowers.

The morthiem lilies were like a dream, a sight she would never have believed; knee-high at their tallest points, their petals fluttered in the light breeze and spread that soothingly sweet scent around the area. In the center of them all sat Kiki, her blonde hair tied back and her gaze turned upward.

She turned at the sound of Kari's footsteps and smiled. "I didn't think you'd come!"

Kari frowned down at her. "I said I would."

"Yeah, but people don't always do what they say. Sit down with me!"

Kari carefully nudged some lilies aside, finding them surprisingly yielding.

The two girls sat together under the faint light of the moon as it began its ascent. "How was the hunting?"

Kiki lit up. "Oh, it was wonderful. Papa was so happy. He let me have this—"

She dug in a side pocket of her worn pants and withdrew a shard of bone as big as her hand. One side was pointed, but the other was jagged, hacked off with little skill by a dull blade.

The sight of it made Kari's stomach squirm. Deer were good meat, sure, but hadn't she always preferred their antlers whenever Father managed to bring some back? Hadn't he promised she would get her own one day when she took down her first kill?

"Do you want it?" Kiki asked, holding it out.

Kari's eyebrows drew together. "It's a present from your father. Why would you give it to me?"

"I'll see more of them," Kiki said with a small roll of her shoulders. "And you came today for me."

Kari shook her head. "No, I couldn't take your father's gift. It's precious."

Kiki leaned forward, grabbed Kari's hand, and forced the piece of the antler into it. "Keep it," she said sternly. "It's my gift to *you*, for coming here to be with me."

Kari sighed, but rubbed a thumb over the smooth bone, savoring its feel.

"Well, it's payment for nothing. I've only just joined others my age and I'm behind still. I haven't learned much."

"That's okay! I'm happy with anything, anything at all!"

Kari stared at her for a moment, torn between exasperation and disbelief. "Are you always so cheery?"

Kiki giggled. "Mostly. Sometimes Papa gets upset, but…"

"No, it's…it's good," Kari said. "It's good to be happy."

"Are you not? Is it because of your family?"

Kari clenched her fists, her claws digging into the antler bone. "They're not my family," she ground out. She let out a deep breath and forced herself to relax. "You can help me with the work Mr. Hodges gave us."

Kiki rolled with the change of conversation smoothly, easily forgetting or ignoring Kari's sudden anger. "Okay! What is it?"

Kari looked around her. "I have to…describe something. Anything. And come to him with something we can study…fauna or flora, he said, I think."

Kiki pursed her lips. "The morthiem lilies would work, but…"

"What?"

"Well…I like this place. I wouldn't like anyone coming here."

Kari laughed scornfully. "Don't worry. If I told him about these flowers, I'd never tell him where they were."

The thought of sharing this sacred place with anyone was ludicrous. Those humans in Snow Shade would ruin it, defile it with their greed and disrespect. They'd already ruined enough for her. And Kiki, too, if her father's feelings towards them were any indication.

Kiki visibly relaxed. "Okay, then. What kind of words would be used to describe them…?"

"Pretty," Kari said quietly.

Kiki giggled. "Luminous."

Kari glanced at her. "What does that mean?"

"Glowing," the girl replied, reaching out to touch a single glittering petal.

"Yeah. That. I think Mr. Hodges would be shocked if I used a word like that."

"He sounds mean."

Kari gave a jerky shrug. "All humans are. Or…most of them."

Kiki said nothing, pressing her arm gently against Kari. Kari stiffened, but didn't move away. Instead, she noted an oddly comforting warmth in the pit of her stomach.

"What about their color? They're kind of purple, don't you think?"

"I was thinking blue," Kari replied with a tilt of her head.

The two of them talked until the moon had risen far into the sky. Then they went their separate ways, promising to meet again the next day. Kari walked back to Anne and Joseph's house with a small yet definite spring in her step. For the first time, she looked forward to the next day.

CHAPTER NINE

Kari's life began again. She still went to school, wavered with the work given to her, and despised the house in which she lived, but she felt differently over the following months. As the snow melted and color bled back into the world, she saw Kiki more. The human girl from the mountains quickly became what Kari had always imagined a best friend would be, someone to rely on and with whom she could share things.

She listened to Kari's general complaints about Snow Shade, and in exchange, Kari listened as Kiki whined about being tired of the mountain and hunting.

"Why do you always laugh?" Kiki demanded one day as they sat in the field of morthiem lilies. With the dregs of winter cold gone, the flowers changed drastically. Under the gentle warmth of springtime, they became stubby, colorless little things.

"Sorry," Kari said with a chuckle. "It's funny to hear someone talk about this place the way you do."

She tried to teach Kiki more of what Mr. Hodges tried to impress on his students. With Kari's help, Kiki was able to understand basic grammar and complicated math. Together they drew simple maps of what Kari could remember of Taris, and they made imaginary plans of going to the places depicted one day.

As Kari drew the thicker forests she recalled from maps in class, she wondered if her mother's friend Zina would actually be waiting for her, somewhere.

At home, Joseph remained surly and doubtful of her. Anne continued to be doting and gave Kari more space as she started to "cheer up" and "make herself at home." Kari allowed Anne to think this was possibly her doing, that her love had been powerful enough to make the wild girl from the mountain peaks suitable for village life.

When the sweet-smelling air made way for the warmer gusts of summer, Lian finally woke from his sleep. The news made Kari panic until it was revealed he didn't remember the details of what happened. He did not point any fingers at Kari, except to state that she was strange, an outsider. She gladly forgot all about the pathetic human boy who attempted to defeat her and failed.

Snow Shade reveled as the heat grew, bringing sweet blue and red berries, as well as more deer from the mountain. Travelers pawning their wares swarmed the village for a few weeks, leaving Kari to skirt the edges of town until they'd left. School slowly got easier. Kari's peers laughed at her less, happy enough to ignore her. Mr. Hodges offered her rare and grudging praise for her work. Things were looking up for the orphaned wolf demon girl; she settled into the life of a human child, only occasionally worrying about the future vengeance she must one day face.

Now that future was muddled because Kari was forced to wonder about Kiki. Once she was old enough, would Kiki really want to leave this place and her father behind? And how could Kari possibly kill Anne and Joseph without the girl knowing?

These thoughts became the new troubling force within her. She was certain of what she must do—her honor as a wolf and a demon relied on it—and she was worried how it would affect this new person in her life.

The winds cooled, and the vibrant greens of the forest began to dull. Kari made her way to them, thinking of the many months that had passed since Anne and Joseph had taken her from the mountain.

The breeze was sharp and crisp, blowing stray leaves from their branches. Kari fastened a hand over the hat on her head, one she was forced to wear all the time as her ears had begun to show above her hair. It was such a disastrous and simple thing that if the hat should fall, Kari would be exposed. The façade would be broken, all her hard work would have been for naught, and she would have to escape before the humans tried to kill her.

Thankfully, though, other children had a similar habit of wearing caps all year around, a sort of fashion trend Kari didn't understand but grabbed onto gladly. Of *course,* she loved the stupid thing, of *course,* it was because Joseph had picked it out especially for her, and of *course,* she never wanted to take it off because she was a silly child.

Whatever it took to preserve herself.

Thick orange and brown leaves littered the forest floor, crunching noisily under her feet. Brambles and twigs were crushed as she headed for the hedges hidden within.

Kari's tail, too, had grown sharply over the passing of summer, and it was even more of an annoyance than the damned hat. It was uncomfortable having to hide her tail within her pants, where it remained bent for hours. Only the nighttime saved her when she was able to hide it underneath blankets.

How can I handle years more of this? she asked herself so often it was an echoing, ringing thought, but the simple answer was that she would do it because she must. There was no other option for her. Either she risked an impossible life on her own in the wild, or she masqueraded with the humans until she could take her revenge and be old enough to take care of herself properly.

The hedges around the morthiem lilies withered with the warmth of summer, their branches and leaves drying up. Now that the cold was approaching again, though, they were changing from gray-brown to dull green. They crackled less than usual as Kari pushed through and stepped into the private clearing where she was to meet Kiki.

The morthiem lilies had begun to revive again in what Mr. Hodges had said would probably be an endless cycle of rebirth, a thing uncommon in most of the world. They'd retreated into stagnant, motionless buds; now they were flowering, pushing out pure white petals, their tips furled. Kari made her way to the center, gently brushing her fingers against them as she moved past.

It was rare that she showed up first. Usually, Kiki was here waiting on a day like this; when her father did not need her, and she could be what she deemed a "normal kid."

Kari grinned at the thought. Though Kiki had no idea, she was always the only normal one. Kari had to pretend to be like her and the others that she lived with. She had to pretend to be a human child.

The wind howled, making its eerie noises as it rustled leaves and branches. Before Kari could register what was happening, the wind was swooping over her, ruffling her hair, and throwing her hat several feet away.

"Damn it," Kari growled as she got to her feet.

A small, nearly insignificant gasp made her freeze. Her wolf ears cocked of their own volition towards the sound, and she slowly turned to see who or what had spotted her. Part of her already knew, though, and dreaded seeing the expression of horror that would be on her face.

Kiki stood at the far edge of the clearing, the measly and now very useless hat lying between them. Her eyes were wider than usual, her hands covering her mouth. Kari's heart shuddered.

Oh gods, what do I do?

"Please...don't scream," Kari rasped, finding her voice crackly with panic.

My only friend and now I have no one again what do I do

Would she have to kill Kiki now?

79

The thought was brief, coming and going within milliseconds, and it made Kari's blood cold.

No. I wouldn't do that. Never.

"Kiki," she managed when the girl said nothing. "I…"

"You…you're a demon?" she interrupted in a whisper, slowly lowering her hands to clasp them in front of her chest.

Kari swallowed. "Yes."

"But…how? How do you live in the village? How…"

"Please," Kari pleaded, desperate now to keep her, and realizing too late that it had been foolish to dream of being close to this human girl. "I'll explain. I don't want to hurt you. I never have."

Kiki hesitated. Kari dug her claws into the palms of her hands. She'd have to run now, wouldn't she? She could no longer stay here. Kiki would tell them all.

"I thought…I thought Snow Shade hated demons," Kiki whispered. She hadn't moved yet, hadn't tried to flee.

"They do. When it comes up at school, they all talk about it. How despicable and dangerous demons are."

"Why are you here, then?"

Kari's lips tightened. She had never dreamed of telling anyone, but now she had to, didn't she? She had to tell Kiki everything in order to keep her friendship. She had to make Kiki understand.

"They…the two I live with, the humans, they killed my mother and father," she hissed. "I lived on this mountain too. I lived at the peak."

Kiki gasped again, but this time it was in understanding. "The wolves?"

"Yes. I never knew you were here. I don't think my parents did either. When…when they died, the humans took me down with them. They decided to keep me. And I couldn't leave. I…"

Kari hesitated now, her chest tight. She could not tell a human that she wanted to kill another human. No matter the reason, it was

80

evil of her, only adding to the fact that she was a demon and should be killed.

Kiki came to the conclusion on her own. "You wanted to get back at them, so you stayed."

Kari gritted her teeth. "I'm sorry I didn't tell you, Kiki. When I met you, I wanted so badly to have something else, something besides revenge. But I have to avenge my family."

When Kiki didn't say anything, Kari's stomach and head buzzed.

Run or talk? Run, run.

"Please understand, Kiki," she managed, her body straining with the effort it took to keep her feet firmly planted. "I would never hurt you. *Never.* And after I do this, I will leave Snow Shade forever. I'll never come back, and I'll never hurt anyone again if I don't have to."

"You're going to leave?" Kiki's words were quiet, hurt rather than fearful, but Kari heard them clearly. "When?"

"I…I don't know. I need to get stronger. I can't fight them like this. Not now."

"How do demons get stronger?"

Kari stared at Kiki. "I don't know," she said repeated. "Time? Training? I never asked."

"Papa always said if I were to come across one, it'd be too late, and that's why I shouldn't go very far. He said they run fast and are much stronger than us."

"Maybe one-on-one," Kari said humorlessly. "But a whole village would be difficult."

A tense silence fell between them with Kari fidgeting and Kiki watching her. After a moment, Kari looked away, the ears that had betrayed her flicking uneasily.

"Should I go? I won't tell anyone about your flowers. I won't come back."

Kiki slowly frowned. "Why should you leave?"

Kari's brow furrowed as she turned back to Kiki. "What? Is that a serious question?"

"Well…yeah. I don't care if you're a demon, Kari. They always sounded scary, sure, but *you* are not scary."

Kari grimaced, but she couldn't fault Kiki for thinking that.

Kiki crossed the clearing with slow, hesitant steps. Kari stayed where she was, her legs tense and her hands shaking. Kiki picked up the hat as she went, and when the human girl was finally at Kari's side, she smiled shyly.

"Can I…can I touch your ears? Do you have a tail?" She handed Kari the hat.

Kiki's voice was more light-hearted again, the fear gone from her expression and tone. Kari's shoulders slumped in relief. "Yes, but it hurts all the time to keep it hidden."

She tilted her head so that Kiki could run a single finger over one of her ears. The girl giggled.

"They are so soft! It must be hard to live this way. Is making them pay really worth all of this?"

"Yes. I will never see Mother and Father again. The least I can do is take the lives of the ones who took them away from me."

Kiki pursed her lips thoughtfully. "I understand, I think…if someone took my papa…" She paused and shook her head. "I can't imagine it."

"I never could have imagined I'd be here, either," Kari muttered. "Mother and Father…they seemed invincible to me. But the group of humans was too much for them. That's why I have to be careful and make sure I'm ready before I make my move."

Kari could hardly believe she was here, having this conversation with a human. Yet Kiki didn't look at her with fear or hate. Instead, there was an expression that Kari had never seen on a human's face, except perhaps Anne. Anne's was different, though, more pitying. Kiki didn't pity Kari. She was sad *with* her—she understood Kari's pain.

"Have you practiced at all?" Kiki asked. "Fighting, I mean."

"Well…no. I don't have anywhere to practice. I've thought about coming here, but…"

"But you didn't want me to see you, huh?"

Kari smiled sheepishly. "Yeah. I didn't want to run you off if you saw me."

"What can you do? Can you break a rock? With your fist?"

Kari stared at her. "What do you think demons are? No, I can't do anything like that."

"Well, what then? You must have *some* type of ability, right? A special strength or skill? How else would demons be so fearsome?"

"I think we're fearsome because humans don't know us well," Kari said thoughtfully. "Like...like a bear, or a big animal. We're stronger, sure, and we have sharp claws and teeth, but there isn't much else."

"And faster, too. I bet you'd beat me in a race."

"Definitely."

Kiki glared. "You don't have to sound so smug. You can't even break a rock!"

"Well, I'm sure a really strong demon could! Just not me!"

"*Well*, you won't ever be able to if you don't even plan to try."

"Now that you know my secret, I'm not worried about coming here and practicing," Kari said with a weak laugh.

Kiki's face lit up. "Yeah! Can I watch when you do? Maybe we can do that together when you come to show me the things you learn."

"I wouldn't want you to get hurt," Kari began, but Kiki interrupted her.

"How would I get hurt? I'll stand out of the way!"

An image of Kari's father popped into her mind, his eyes boring into hers and his mind speak roaring through her head.

Lightning is dangerous. Lightning makes fire, and fire destroys our home.

She hadn't even tried to summon a spark since she hurt Lian. It *was* dangerous, and she didn't want to have to think about trying to explain away a house fire.

"What are you thinking about?" Kiki asked. "You look worried all of a sudden."

83

Kari rubbed her arms. "You might still get hurt if you were with me. You asked if I had a special strength." She hesitated. How much was *too* much to tell Kiki? She didn't seem too well-versed in the history of demons, but wouldn't the idea that Kari could potentially destroy things with sparks from her fingertips be terrifying? "I do," she finally continued. "Most demons have a lot of strength and speed, and that's all, I think. But I can…"

"What?" Kiki asked when Kari paused again. "What is it?"

Kari inhaled, then exhaled slowly. "Step away from me."

Once the girl was several feet away, Kari held out her hand, palm up, and called to the static that lived inside of her.

An exhilarating charge ran through her body until she managed to center it in the palm of her hand. There, half a dozen tiny sparks appeared to dance between her fingertips and her wrist. The sight of them was thrilling, and breathtaking, and felt…*right*.

Kiki gasped. "Oh, wow!"

Kari clenched her fist and the sparks were discharged, settling into the lines of her skin until they were nothing again. She relaxed, not even realizing she had been holding her breath.

"I can summon lightning. I've never really tried to do that before. Father didn't like it."

"That's so cool! But…demons can't usually—"

Kari grinned weakly. "I'm the only one, according to my mother and father. But it's dangerous. I…accidentally hurt that boy with it."

"Which boy?"

"Lian," Kari said. "The one who bothered you that day, with his friends."

Kiki's mouth fell open. "Oh."

"He was a stupid boy. I didn't want to, but I could have really hurt him."

Kiki frowned. "Well, he's okay, right?"

"Yeah," Kari replied hesitantly.

"He wasn't very nice, and cruel people *should* get what they deserve. And I think if you don't want it to happen again, you should learn to control it."

Kari stared at her—Kiki was right. Kari would have never imagined that she would be conversing with a human this way. Kiki had barely flinched when Kari had mentioned avenging her mother and father. Did she truly understand? Did it not scare her that one day Kari might kill a human?

"I'm not surprised you didn't tell me," Kiki said. "I understand. People are mean, like you've said before…and sometimes we have to hide ourselves to *be* ourselves. You know?"

Kari nodded. That was why Kiki and her father hid away on this mountain rather than live in Snow Shade. They were outsiders from the humans, too.

"I want to keep being friends," Kiki continued. "I don't…I don't know about you hurting the people you live with, but I think I understand. I want to help you learn to control your powers. And…" her face reddened.

"What?"

"Maybe you could teach me how to do it, too."

Kari smiled weakly. "Humans can learn magic like this, so it's not impossible."

Kiki's face glowed with hope.

CHAPTER TEN

As frost colored the leaves and wilted the grass, Kari realized a year had already passed since she'd lost everything. Every icy breath that lifted strands of her hair recalled that day, that walk down the mountain. The hollowness in her chest wasn't quite gone, and in quiet moments, Kari could forget everything but her pain.

The anniversary meant something else entirely to the humans who had brought this ruin on her, as she learned when she sat down for breakfast with Anne and Joseph one morning. Anne turned to her with a more protuberant smile than normal.

"Kari…I've been meaning to ask, and since we're coming up to a year now…" Her gaze flicked to Joseph, who did not reflect her joy. "Well…I'll just ask. Do you know when you were born? We can celebrate!"

Kari felt her expression hardening, stone-like. Demons did not celebrate days of birth. Unlike humans, who died needlessly from old age, demons could live to be more than centuries old. Kari's own mother had been such an age, though no one would know by looking. With so much time to pass, why be concerned with age?

For Kari, her years on this world were a baseless number, a signifier as to when she would be allowed to hunt with her father. For Anne, it was more. And as with everything else, she would be forced to endure it.

"I don't know."

Anne either didn't notice her apathy or didn't care. She placed her hands on the table and stood. "Then I declare this day to be it! We will celebrate every year on this twenty-ninth day of the cold months!"

A younger, pre-Kiki Kari might have lost her temper at Anne's joviality. Yet Kiki had talked about birthdays once or twice, and Kari had known it would come for her, too. It was a human thing to do. She released her breath and her fury along with it.

"What do you think, Joseph? I could make some pies. Do we have any berries left?"

"Maybe," Joseph grunted. "I'll look."

Kari had no intention of spending an entire day with these two reveling in the loss of her previous life. Fortunately, the timing was advantageous: cold weather meant the coming of Snow Shade's Midwinter Festival. This was the time for the traders in town to sell their wares at the highest prices of the year.

Kiki had talked about it for the last several weeks, and they agreed to meet. While Kari found the idea of walking around so many humans abhorrent, it was the perfect excuse for her to be out of the house.

As Anne looked to her again, Kari stood from the table. "I'll be out."

She couldn't deny a flicker of joy at Anne's crestfallen face. "Oh…okay. I'll have something ready when you come back!"

With a grin that was slow to fade, Kari slipped out the front door.

The ground was mushy and dark. The children could be seen out in their finest winter things, their faces pink as they chased each other down the streets. Anyone who could trade did so, lugging crates or bags full of salted meats, bread, leather, or even shining, valuable stones. A few traders from outside of town appeared as well, offering exotic items like spices or fancy cloth.

"Pa only recently started letting me do this," Kiki said as they walked the town. "He used to just bring me along sometimes." She pursed her lips at the thought. Kari grinned. "But this year, I'm making my own trades," she continued proudly, patting the sack at her waist. In it was all manner of plant-life that could be used for wounds, illness, poisons, and even seasoning food.

Kari was skeptical, but as they stopped again and again, she watched Kiki trade handfuls of leaves for bread and cheese, and sometimes for coin.

"You could pick up any stray oak leaf and these fools would pay for it," Kari murmured as they left behind a recent deal.

Kiki smiled. Kari glanced at her.

"*Do* you sell oak leaves?"

"No!" Kiki laughed. "These are real plants that do real things! My mama told me about most of them before she died. Of course, there's still plenty for me to learn, too."

Kari resolved to swipe a book on plant life for Kiki as soon as she could find one.

It was a fascinating skill to have, and one Kari could understand. If these plants helped humans to heal their wounds the way some unknown magic helped Kari...

"Anne asked about my day of birth this morning."

Kiki's smile fell. "What did you tell her?"

They paused so Kiki could make a quick trade with an older man: two apples for a handful of bright, purple, thorny leaves. When the man moved on, Kiki handed her an apple.

"I said I didn't know," Kari replied, rolling the fruit between her fingers. "And she proclaimed that it would be today, so they could *celebrate*."

She barely resisted throwing the apple at a building as they passed.

"It's my favorite time of year," Kiki mused, her voice quiet. "It's fitting for my best friend."

Kari glanced at Kiki to see her grinning. Snorting, she took a bite of her apple to hide her own smile.

When the festival ended, Kari and Kiki relaxed in the forest, where they counted Kiki's earned coins and ate bread.

"If I can keep trading like this, we can make lots of money!" Kiki said, her glee contagious.

"It would be easy to make a living like this."

They chattered, making childish plans for their small pile of silver coins. When the sky was drowning in hues of violet, they parted ways.

"Happy birthday, Kari!" Kiki giggled, disappearing into the trees.

Grinning, Kari grudgingly returned home, where Anne was happy enough to not be perturbed by her late arrival. When Kari sat at the table, she served pastries sweetened with berries.

"Do you like them?" Anne asked, hands clasped under her chin, and received no answer.

"Makin' friends, huh?" Joseph asked as Kari picked at the little tart. "Saw you with that girl out there." Kari's only response was to nod. Joseph watched her. "She's the weird one, ain't she?"

"Joseph," Anne chided.

Biting back a snarl, Kari shrugged. "I don't care if she's weird. I like her."

She leveled her gaze with the old man, hoping her eyes told him everything she could not say aloud.

I hate you. One day, you won't be here to taunt me and remind me of what I lost.

If Joseph saw any of Kari's hatred, he ignored it. "It's good, Anne," he mumbled around a bite of pastry.

In the following years, whenever Kari could escape Anne and Joseph's company, she spent her leisure time with Kiki. They wandered the forest around Snow Shade, spying on young wood-gatherers, who Kiki insisted on seeing as often as possible.

"That one, there," she pointed to a boy with long hair the color of chestnuts, "I fancy him. I've heard the others call him Asher." Kari saw little about him attractive, except perhaps his muscled arms that would at least make him useful. "What about you?" Kiki asked as she attempted to smooth her flyaway hair.

"Not for me," Kari replied, containing a smirk.

Kiki pursed her lips. "You wait. I bet you'll find a nice boy some-day, one who will accept you right down to your attitude!"

"Yeah, right," Kari laughed.

They went to yearly festivals; aside from the Midwinter Festi-val, Snow Shade held a gathering in spring that Kari had missed the previous year. When the trees were bright and lively, and the winds were warm and sweet, traders came from all over Taris. There was less interest in Kiki's plants than usual, which left Kari and Kiki to peruse outsider's wares. In Kari's case, this meant spying on the sellers more than their merchandise; it was her only chance to see what awaited her outside of Snow Shade.

Taris was full of strange humans, she realized in those days of the Spring Festivals. Though many sold necessities or rare gems and furs, others peddled anti-demon charms. If Kari hadn't been afraid of ousting herself, she would have proclaimed they did not work when a toothless woman held up a rusty old necklace for them to see.

Others were less eccentric. There were any-weather clothes and ability-enhancing potions that Kari shook her head at, for neither she nor Kiki had enough money, even if they did work. One man shouted his figurines of a winged woman with a cold gaze and cropped hair were modeled after, and blessed by, a real angel.

"Kinera, the Seraph of Nalmi! Look, I swear it!"

"Wow, she's beautiful," Kiki breathed. Kari pulled her away before the man could notice them.

When there were no festivities, the girls spent their time in the forest. Thanks to Kari's time in a human school, she could make a defined map of Taris with dirt, rocks, and twigs. Kiki squatted next to her until she finished, then pointed out various towns.

"Ooh, Crow's Rest sounds nice. Or High Port. We could see the ocean!"

Kari finished placing tufts of short, fuzzy leaves to represent the largest southern forest, a place called Raziac, and wondered if that was where her mother wished her to go.

She pulled herself out of the thought; whoever Zina was, Kari no longer considered her a priority. For months now, it had been all about her vengeance and leaving with Kiki.

"Mr. Hodges said Briar's Glen is the biggest place. And Snake Bay is good for travel because it's on the coast." Kari grinned, looking up. "But *demons* are welcome there, too."

Kiki giggled. "I'd love to see other types of demons!" She poked the pile of twisty twigs that represented Snake Bay. "But crossing the sea must cost so much. And it'd be scary, too, getting on a big ship," she finished in a hush.

Kari bumped her shoulder. "We don't have to do that. We can earn money first, then figure something out."

When they'd decided that Briar's Glen would be the best for their plans, they focused on training. While Kari's hand-to-hand combat and control of her lightning strengthened every day, Kiki's desire to learn magic did too. Kari knew humans could learn magic—reinforced by history lessons that detailed the use of fire magic in decades-old wars—but neither of them knew where to begin. When Kari asked Mr. Hodges for advice, he scoffed.

"A thoughtless girl like you, who can hardly pull two words together, learn *magic?*"

She'd left before he could berate her any further. They would find another way; they had plenty of time.

CHAPTER ELEVEN

Months became years, and with each passing season, Kari grew stronger. They accomplished little in the way of Kiki's dream for magic, but the girl had waved it off.

"Later," she said. "Once we leave here, I'm sure there will be tons of opportunities for me!"

Kari relented and fixated on honing what little fighting skills she had.

On her fifteenth "birthday," Kari awoke with a sense of fatigue that was underlaid by exhilaration. She had gone through countless human days, and while she tired of the charade, this year would be the one for which she'd waited. She felt it in her bones, the tightness in her muscles, the certain clench of her gut.

Anne pushed away her plate, all traces of the celebratory red berry pie she served gone, and smiled brightly at Kari.

"Another birthday! I can't believe it's been so long since we found you."

"Aye, and you're nearly at the time in your life," Joseph said in his slow, even tones. "An adult, like."

Kari glanced at him. It was common for young adults of Snow Shade to aid their parents in whatever it was that they did. As their adoptive child, she would be expected to help Joseph with his hunting. She laughed privately and scornfully at the idea. She never would help the man who'd proudly killed her father.

She managed a thin smile.

"We couldn't spend much for the occasion, I'm afraid. But Joseph made something up all the same! Show her, honey."

Kari reluctantly turned her gaze to the man of the house, the man who for the last few years had looked at her with barely concealed distrust. She was sure he knew, or had an inkling, that she was not what she appeared to be.

Joseph's smile wrinkled his eyes, but Kari could see slyness in his gaze, some cunning thought hidden behind his jovial appearance.

She tensed as she waited for him to act and found herself surprised as Joseph pulled something from his pocket, something flappy and dark brown, made of nicely-stitched cloth and leather.

It was a hat.

"Yours is a bit worn out. Thought you'd want a new one."

Joseph had given Kari her first one, the same one she had worn for a couple of years until her ears had outgrown its use. She'd then gotten a new one from Kiki, whose father liked to make clothes from the animals he hunted. Of course, Kari did not have to hide herself with Kiki anymore; given what they did hidden in the forests, the measly leather-and-fur hat had quickly become scuffed up and generally unsuitable for public wear.

"Thanks," Kari said, reaching across the table for it. He kept the cap out of her reach, though.

"Take yours off and Anne can toss it," he said in a careless tone. "It's junk anyway."

"Joseph, don't be rude," Anne scolded.

Kari's insides flared at his insult toward the thing that Kiki had given her, all the while keenly aware of what Joseph was trying to do.

How to handle such a situation? Her claws twitched. Would this, perhaps, be the moment when it would all be over, when it would all finally end, and she could leave this place?

Her gut squirmed.

No…no. Not yet.

Kari forced the muscles in her face to relax. She shrugged. "I still like it."

"Where'd you get it from again? I forget what you told us."

She hadn't told them at all. She'd flat-out refused an answer on the thing or anything at all concerning what she did in her free time.

Kari turned to Anne. "I'll be late today."

"Again, dear? It is your birthday, I suppose…"

Kari nodded and stood from the table. Anne got up too and gathered their plates while Joseph eyed Kari with his beady, frustrated eyes. She rounded the table and snatched the hat from his hands before he could blink. The motion was quick, lightning-fast, and Joseph merely glanced down at his empty hand. His lips tightened and his eyes widened. Kari smiled.

"Thank you for the gift," she said as she turned to leave the house.

Kari tucked Joseph's gift in a pocket of her pants as she left Snow Shade for the mountain forests. She'd grown a lot in five years, becoming thicker and leaner with muscle. She was, as Anne so rightly put it, nearly an adult—a grown woman with extra parts. Her ears were so much more noticeable than they had been on that fateful day, and her tail had become longer and bushier.

95

As soon as she was deep enough in the safety of the trees, she loosened her pants to relieve the pressure on her tail and removed the hat from her head.

Confident strides carried her off the main path, over hard earth and into the lusher parts of the forest. She slid easily around thick trees and wormed her way into the clearing where Kiki was waiting for her.

Kiki had grown into a young woman, too. Her hair was longer, still a pale yellow. Her child's fat was gone, leaving her face angular and her cheekbones defined. Her clothes remained ragged, but her dazzling sky-blue eyes continued to sparkle with joy. As Kari entered their secret place, she thought fondly how the two of them could appear to be sisters.

"Hi, Kari!" Kiki called over her shoulder. She fiddled with something in her hands. As Kari approached, she could see the small unfurling buds of morthiem lilies being twisted into a circular shape by Kiki's long, deft fingers.

"Hey," Kari answered as she sat down.

"Papa gave me the whole day today," Kiki said happily, and Kari was relieved. The day before, they had been uncertain if Kiki's father would need her in the afternoon—if he did, Kari would be forced to go "home" or stay out here by herself, and neither option appealed to her.

"Good. I have some things I want to try later. But first, this…" She removed the hat from her pocket and dropped it between them. "Look at my birthday gift from Joseph."

Kiki glanced at it. "That was nice of him. Why aren't you wearing it?"

"He used it as an attempt to get me to show myself. For all I care, it can burn."

"One day he'll learn, won't he? It has to be hard to keep it hidden the way you do…"

"One day he'll be dead, and it won't matter."

Kiki didn't say anything for a moment, still fiddling with the lilies in her hands, twisting the stems together to make braided shapes.

"You are still resolved to do it?"

Kari raised her hand to eye level, well away from the flowers. Lightning flared to life in the form of two tiny sparks that darted between her thumb and pointer finger. They danced easily at her command, but still required most of her attention to keep them there. Even after five years, this small control was difficult.

"Yeah," she answered. "I am." Kari knew her friend was troubled by the thought of taking another mortal's life. She chose her words carefully, reminding Kiki that it wasn't for blood that she would kill, but vengeance. "I couldn't live with myself if I turned away now."

Kiki had been Kari's de facto trainer, helping Kari to hone her skills so that she would be strong enough to finish this task she had set herself. The reason for that training no longer mattered to the girl; it was just another thing they did together. As far as Kiki was concerned, within the following year, she and Kari would leave this place forever with no deaths left behind. The training was her way of repaying Kari for sharing what she'd learned in school.

"I…I know," Kiki replied quietly.

Somehow, she had convinced herself that demons were not evil at the core. Kiki believed that demons only became tainted once they chose to do malevolent, hellish things—like murder.

Kari countered by reminding her of the supposed history of demons: *they spawned from the earth and spread death and destruction, born of wicked intent and nothing else.* If she was even a little hesitant to avenge her parents, it only meant she was not quite demon enough.

"I promise you it won't change me," Kari interrupted. "Not one bit. I'll always be me, and once it's done, we'll leave and start all over."

"Yeah, okay."

They fell silent. Kari flicked her fingers, extinguishing the sparks, and yawned. They would train again today; Kari wanted to practice more with moving her electricity into other objects. She'd worked for nearly a year controlling it within her grasp, and it had taken the years after that to learn to make larger, more significant sparks. Now, though, she wanted to be able to send it places, to charge a weapon with the volts or burn a tree to a crisp.

She imagined it'd be easier now that she could summon it at will; now, it was a matter of keeping it where she wanted it.

Kiki let out a happy sigh. "Finally," she said, turning to Kari. "Here!"

She held out the lilies she had been fiddling with. They were fashioned into a circlet, the nearly budded flowers poking out intermittently around the ring. Kari couldn't help but grin.

"What is that?"

"A new hat—a wreath, actually, I guess. But it would definitely distract from your ears."

Kari placed it on her head and laughed. "Yeah, right."

"Happy birthday, my dearest friend. Now, shall we get to your training?"

They rose together. "I know the library in Snow Shade has books about magic. I bet there's some to help with learning. I'll try to grab it sometime."

Kiki led the way out of the clearing with a smirk over her shoulder. "If we leave to other places, you won't be able to steal all the time, you know. People work hard for their things, so we have to, too."

Kari shrugged. "I can always threaten them for things instead."

Kiki rolled her eyes and Kari laughed.

It was late, and a light sprinkle of snow had begun to fall when the two of them finally decided to leave for the night. Kiki disappeared into the woods while Kari turned back to Snow Shade. Her clothes and hands were muddy, but she proudly carried a small ball of brown muck that she had scooped from the chilled ground. It crackled quietly with the power of her lightning.

Snow Shade was quiet. It was much later than Kari had anticipated, and she quickened her pace, taking more shortcuts than usual.

Would Joseph mention to Anne how Kari had taken the hat from him? Thinking back on it, it had been a foolish thing to show off to him like that. Kiki was right. It was only a matter of time until he found a way to reveal her.

A gasping, grunting sound caught her ears as she turned a corner and faced a dark side road between the bakery and the skinner. Kari froze, her eyes catching the silhouette of a large shape leaning against the baker's shop. The longer she stood there, the more her eyes adjusted, recognizing a large, muscular body and elongated face.

"Get away," a voice hissed at her.

Kari tightened her grip on the ball of mud in her hand. There was an unfamiliar, bitter smell in the air—not a human scent at all. "Who are you?"

The male laughed darkly. It was a hissing sound, not unlike a snake. "You are more foolissssh than other humansss." There was a rustle as he stood and stepped out of the shadows.

He was six feet tall compared to Kari's meager five, towering over her with a scaly snout and yellow eyes; every inch of his revealed skin was covered in tiny green scales. Kari's mouth dried and the electricity in her mud ball sparkled loudly. She dug her claws into it, trying to regain control.

A demon—a real, menacing one—was in Snow Shade.

Kari stepped back from him, but the man advanced, a thick lizard's tail unraveling behind him to slide along the frosted earth.

"Rathik sssaid we would be sssafe here, but we are conssstantly finding resisssstance," he hissed. "Patience, he asssked. But I can wait no longer. I need to kill sssome of them, that will teach them to put usss down like thisss." The demon reached at Kari with long claws. "I'll sssstart with you, you little whelp!"

Kari leapt away and threw the ball into his face. It exploded into a muddy mess, splattering his eyes with muck and electricity. He stumbled back a step and screeched in pain, his long fingers going to his face. Kari's ears bent at the sound—what if the humans heard?

"W-what are you doing here?" Kari managed through her clenched teeth. She tensed her claws, prepared to fight him, but he was so much bigger than her. The lightning that came to her fingers was weak and sporadic in her fear.

The lizard demon glared at her, his jagged black teeth bared. "You…you are not human, are you?"

Kari hesitated a heartbeat before answering. "No."

His eyes narrowed. "Ssso the humanss have demon petsss now, do they? Or are you a mere halfling?"

It was Kari's turn to bare her teeth. "I am not born of them!"

"Then you are a traitor to our caussse, brat," he hissed, lunging at her again. Kari was too slow this time and his fingers wrapped around her upper arm, easily pulling her toward him. Her hands went to any part of him she could reach—his chest, his arms, his face. Her claws hardly made a scratch on his scales.

"I don't know what you're talking about!"

"Good, then I will have killed you before you tell your mastersss."

He thrust her against the nearest building. The air was forced from her lungs, and before she could react, his large hand swiped at her. Long, jagged claws slashed her across the face and sent her rolling away from him.

Kari lay on the cold, hard ground. The pain was blinding, her blood warm as it dribbled from her face and pooled under her cheek.

The lizard demon's footsteps were loud to her, the sound sending echoing vibrations through her body.

He stood over her, his laughter more of a hiss. "You are sssso weak. It isss good of me to end your misssery." He knelt, grabbed Kari around the arm, and lifted her easily. She twisted in his grip and growled. Lightning sparked at her command, but it glanced off his scales, too.

His other hand wrapped around her throat, easily ignoring the punches and kicks she threw at him. He squeezed until she struggled to breathe. She choked and gasped, her feeble claws going to his hands, tugging at his fingers. Her vision blurred, the world swimming all around her.

This is how I'm going to die? I will never see Kiki again. I won't…

Her choking gasps were becoming mere gurgles, her struggling fight weakening.

No. No! I have things I need to do!

As the lizard demon tightened his grip, something snapped. It was as if a flash of fiery light burned the inside of her mind. It dispelled all the pain and panic with waves of fire, sharpening her focus onto one thing.

She had to survive.

Thunder rumbled through the sky, long and loud, and the lizard looked up.

Crack!

The lightning that struck was ferociously loud and blinding, a vibrating scream that shattered the sky, blasting the lizard away from her. She fell back, landing shakily on her feet as he slammed into the wall opposite, his flesh charred and smoking.

Her ears rang with the sound of the thunder blast, and she had no doubt that any nearby humans would certainly have heard it too; the thought of humans coming upon them was brief and easily ignored. Instead, Kari's mind was a blur. She felt her body moving; she tensed her legs and leapt, landing on the lizard before he could even begin to stand. Her claws, charged with thick ropes of electric energy, shredded into his vulnerable chest and belly.

She was destroying him. She was so powerful, so strong, and it was such an intoxicating feeling, nothing else could compare.

The lizard shrieked in pain and raised his hands to defend himself, reaching up to scratch Kari's eyes out. She growled, and his arms were slammed into the ground, immobilized by her very thought. A needle-thin spear of pain flashed through her mind, but Kari only winced, the discomfort quickly forgotten.

"You should not have threatened me," she whispered.

She laid a hand on his chest, felt his thundering heartbeat, and unleashed all the electricity she could summon from her body. It flowed in endless currents, flickering from her in erratic sparks, and sank into the lizard demon's heart.

No other scream escaped his throat. The pure energy only allowed his eyes to pop and his mouth to fall open. He was dead, leaking thin rivers of blood from yellow eyes.

Kari slowly stood and stepped away from him. Rain had begun to fall in icy droplets lit by intermittent flashes of lightning. The rain washed away the feeling of fiery anger. Kari tossed her head back, allowing the shower to patter her entire face.

Her body was drained, but she felt relief in the exhaustion. She'd done it. She'd defended herself and taken this demon's life with her own hands, hands that now trembled. Was this what it would be like, to kill Anne and Joseph?

It would be different, wouldn't it, to kill humans? There wouldn't be nearly so much fight in them.

Frowning, Kari searched for something else within herself: remorse, fear, or something more demonic. Pleasure in taking a life, as Kiki feared. There was nothing, only the breathless recognition that she had survived a real fight, and with minimal damage to herself.

A hand slowly went to the cheek he had slashed, only for fingers to touch cool, unblemished flesh. Spots of dried blood remained near her chin, and even that was being taken by the rain.

She'd healed again, like when Lian used to bully her. This was faster, though, taking no more than minutes.

She looked down at the lizard demon, thin curls of smoke drifting from his chest. He had been so much faster than her, and stronger. Her training had done very little to save her from his attack. So why was she still standing? What had given her the sudden burst of power to overcome such a battle-seasoned demon?

Thunder roared above her. The sound filled her with brief exhilaration and her lips tightened. Had she been the one to make the storm? She raised a hand to touch her head. And stopping the demon from moving with her thought—did she do that, too?

Kari shook her head, forcing her mind to focus on the situation now. More questions, more things she would have to learn later.

Shouts shattered the silence. Kari froze, her ears pinned, and darted around the back of the building as hurried footsteps of a dozen humans approached, pausing at the opposite end of the alleyway.

She cursed herself. What would they do with they saw the demon's body? She should have been more careful, quieter. She recalled the clamor the lightning—her lightning—made when it came down.

Her back pressed against the wall, she edged to the corner to listen, her heart pounding so hard it took her breath.

"It's...it's a demon," a man gasped.

"But it's dead!" a woman responded shrilly.

"Yeah, and how?"

"One of those misshapen beasts?"

"Lord Isaac said they couldn't get in!"

The humans argued amongst themselves. Kari, breath held, slipped into the shadows of the trees before they decided to search the area. She darted in and out of bushes, making her way steadily toward the house. As she rounded a final building, something moved at the corner of her vision. Her head snapped to it, only to be greeted by the sight of the dark road: empty, desolate, and now flooding a little with rainwater. Kari frowned and continued.

As she walked, she looked down at her hands. The lightning had come to her so easily, and it had been so powerful. It had coursed through her veins, charging her entire being with its power. In that moment, she could have destroyed anything. She recalled a blistering heat in her gut, a surge of such raw fury that she had been blinded to all else.

Kari touched her middle, where the heat had burned inside of her, insisting she survive. It had left as soon as the danger passed, leaving behind a tingling, itching feeling she'd never felt before—a vibrating hunger.

Had that heat inside of her been responsible for the lightning? What was it? A demon's fury, perhaps, lending her extra strength in times of need?

Another thing her parents had not explained.

When Kari finally returned to the house, a frantic Anne greeted her, fussing over her drenched clothes and haggard appearance. Kari grunted until the woman left her alone, and then retreated to her room. She peeled off her clothes and curling up under the dry warmth of her blankets.

Her dreams were vivid and wild, filled with crackling thunderstorms over an endless field. She stood outside of herself, seeing another Kari in the center of the storm, her long hair blown about, and her muscles tensed. While the sky darkened, filling the air with booms of thunder, Kari tried to look upon her dream self. Before she could, she awoke.

CHAPTER TWELVE

Though mutterings of the demon followed Kari on the walk to school and during her class the next day, she could only think of her lightning bolt and the heat in her belly that had accompanied it. Hunger, a ravenous desire to thrash and hurt.

Now, on a new day, that feeling was absent. No matter how many times she thought of the demon, her fear, or the way it had felt to draw blood, she felt nothing.

Letting out a huff of air, Kari drew circles on her desk. What did it mean? Her mother had never described a feeling like that, not ever.

"We have a guest today," Ms. Lier said, her smile strained. "She is a…ehem…magic user from Glimmer View."

Kari raised her eyes, head propped up by her hand. Glimmer View? Her eyes darted to the map against the far wall, even though she knew it would not be labeled there. What was Glimmer View?

Ms. Lier beckoned at the doorway. "Please come in, Miss… Kiean?"

A tall, finely-built woman swept into the room, her dress color-ful and lurid. Sunlight draped over ivory leggings, with loose sleeves that swayed around her arms when she moved.

"That is correct," she said as she passed Ms. Lier, sparing not even a glance for her. She swept back long, golden hair, revealing a pair of dark purple earrings, and looked around the class.

Kari straightened at the sight of her eyes, colored just as her dress, though without the warmth of a sun's rays.

"My name is Tzara Kiean. And I will teach you, today, about the basics of magic."

Thus began a lecture so stiff with facts and statistics that the children around Kari began to slump, their minds treading other in-terests. Even Kari found Miss Kiean's knowledge unserviceable—she already knew that it took quite a long time to learn magic, and only humans could do so.

That was what made her own lightning so disturbing.

The classroom was quiet, with few looking ahead when Miss Kiean finally paused. Kari looked up at her again to find her grazing each face with those coldly yellow eyes. Miss Kiean explained those away as part of magic, too—it changed your physical body, such as hair or eye color.

"All of this to say that the world is dangerous, children. Though my village trains people like me to protect you all, the lives of demons cannot be easily cut short by magic alone. Why, on my way here, I stumbled across an ungainly creature of immense strength. Were I not trained so diligently, I would not be here today."

Kari's fingers, limp upon her desk, twitched. This woman had met and killed a demon? Or one of those bizarre mutants she kept hearing about, perhaps?

"For that reason, I will be taking names after your day has ended. I cannot personally train you, but I can refer this village to others from Glimmer View if the need is great. Thank you."

Miss Kiean bowed her head, then turned and left the room be-fore Ms. Lier stood from the desk she'd slumped into.

"Yes…well…" She cast a strained smile. "Back to work."

Kari was the first to leave the classroom as soon as school was over. She swung her head around every corner and into every open doorway, searching for that woman's bizarre dress. It was such an unusual sight in a place like Snow Shade, where the usual was leather and cloth colored in nothing but browns and greens.

Around a final corner and beyond the entrance, Kari spotted her. She faced away, hands behind her back. Even her boots were yellow and certainly not leather. How impractical.

She slowed to a stop, allowing a sea of children to pass between them. Not one paused to speak to the newcomer, the magic-user.

"Miss...Miss Kiean?"

The woman turned, brows raised, and found Kari. She smiled.

"Yes?"

This woman had spoken of killing demons—of course, as all humans did—but she had also spoken of learning magic. From a *real* master.

Though Kari stood tall, Miss Kiean loomed over her. "I have a friend who is interested in...learning magic."

Miss Kiean's smile widened. "Oh, excellent. Where is your friend?"

"Well...she lives in the forest. With her father."

"Ah." Miss Kiean glanced over her shoulder as if she would spot Kiki peeking at them from behind a building. "Well...at this rate, it would be difficult for me to convince the leaders of Glimmer View to send anyone down here. They certainly would not for one child."

Kari's insides deflated. "Alright."

As she began to walk again, Miss Kiean touched her shoulder. She flinched, and the woman quickly dropped her hand.

"Does your friend know about the different elements and their properties?"

Kari's brow furrowed. Did Kiki know those things? "No...I don't think so."

Miss Kiean sighed. "Many do not. I suspect the information is here, somewhere...my mother insisted every village have such knowledge accessible." Her mouth pinched at the corners. "Whatever your friend chooses, be sure she stays away from fire. I have seen it wilt the minds of people."

Kari blinked at her, unsure what to say to that. Miss Kiean laughed at her expression.

"Anything else?"

Kari opened her mouth, paused, then asked, "What about demons?"

Miss Kiean's smile slipped so quickly that Kari's insides chilled. "Demon magic, you mean?"

Though instinct told her she needed to run *now*, Kari nodded. Miss Kiean knelt so they were eye-level.

"If you ever see a demon using something akin to magic, you will run to the nearest letter carrier and alert the leaders of Glimmer View. Do you understand?"

Kari's throat bobbed. "Yes."

Miss Kiean's grin returned. She straightened. "Tell your friend I do apologize. However, there are surely books here in Snow Shade. That is a good start as any until she can find a master."

"Right," Kari muttered. "Thank you."

She walked away, peeking over her shoulder as she did. Miss Kiean looked away, and Kari broke into a jog.

Panic swirled her thoughts, even though she knew it was unfounded. Miss Kiean's reaction to her question about demon magic was unexpectedly direct and only cemented what Kari already surmised: she would be hated and feared far more than other demons for her power.

The lightning bolt she called down seemed more menacing than thrilling, now.

Her feet carried her away from school, down a path she didn't normally tread. The trees loomed beyond buildings. She needed to see Kiki, but Kari paused in front of a door that said *Books.*

Heart shuddering, Kari entered without a second thought.

Small. Two side rooms branching from the entrance, with scarcely filled shelves against the walls. There was no way such a shop would have anything useful; even so, Kari approached the bespectacled man who held vigil across from the door.

She twisted her fingers together. "Do you have anything that could tell me about…demon powers? Magic?"

He snorted and gestured to a shelf against the wall. Kari followed his direction and perused the titles there, narrowing her eyes at the many long, difficult words she could not understand.

She began to pull books at random. They were thick, small, old and tattered, or glossy and leather-bound. Sitting and flipping through them, though, relayed the same idea that Kari had already deduced from conversations with her parents as well as human schooling.

Magic takes many years to learn, and decades to master, but anyone with the time and dedication can learn it.

Only one branch of magic can be learned by any one person at any one time, and each has a subskill. Lightning Masters can move at a speed faster than sight; Water Masters learn the basics of healing; Fire Masters acquire the skill to change their physical form; Light Masters, though their lifespans are lowered considerably, can practice minor spells of other elements…

Was this what Miss Kiean meant about elemental properties? Kari reread the line about Water Masters several times before putting that book away. Kiki would love to learn magic for healing.

Demons have never been recorded to possess the magic of elements and are not any more susceptible to magic than any other being.

Kari shook her head. Why had Miss Kiean reacted the way she did, as if she knew of a demon with powers like hers?

"Holy" magic, that of a divine core and more reliant on one's spirit than actual knowledge from tomes, is particularly dangerous to demons and is the surest way to kill them.

109

Kari snorted, replacing the book. Perhaps that was why her parents had chosen the mountain by this particular village; there was no real temple here, and thus no men of great purity to endanger them.

Ultimately, Kari relented. Despite what Miss Kiean had said—confirming demon magic *did* exist—there was no book on such a thing. According to the knowledge in Snow Shade, demons had nothing other than superior strength and speed, no matter their breed, age, or lineage. Not even halflings were capable of magic. And there was certainly no mention of a tingling, burning, or hungry sensation.

Biting her tongue, she shoved the books back haphazardly, wherever they fit. She picked up the last one, about to squeeze it between two much larger books when the title caught her eye.

"Magic for Beginners," she read quietly. Her pulse jumped. She glanced to see if the bespectacled man was watching her, but he was gone from the front of the shop.

Shoving the book underneath her shirt, Kari ducked outside. Though the humans around paid little attention to her as usual, she felt as if she were being watched. At least Miss Kiean was nowhere within sight.

Holding the book close to her body, Kari twisted around, eager to get back to Kiki.

She bumped into someone with such force that she stumbled and fell. The book slipped out of her grasp to clatter onto the dirt.

A man above her cursed. "Sorry, miss."

Kari tried not to flinch as he grabbed her around the elbow and hauled her to her feet with easy strength. Would he know she was stealing? What would he do?

Her eyes darted to his face, taking in the helmet of a town guard, and her breath froze in her throat. Surely he would report her, or worse. She'd heard from classmates that people who stole lost their fingers or hands, depending on the price of the item. Her chest constricted, her fingers twitching until she noticed the man's skin.

His helmet concealed his face, except for the tanned, brown flesh around his eyes and mouth. Her own eyes widened at unnaturally colored patches marring that skin. Blues and greens…shiny, like the scales of a lizard or snake.

He grabbed the book and handed it to her, his lips lifting in a half-smile. "Careful with that."

Kari could only stare as he hurried to a nearby house and slipped inside. Before the door shut, she caught a whiff of something bitter. Though it nagged at her senses, she wrinkled her nose and retreated to the forest.

Kiki was waiting for her in their clearing. When Kari charged in, her eyes widened.

"You're late! Are you running from something?"

Would the guard pursue her? Somehow, Kari doubted it. He'd seemed as if he had more important things to worry about.

She shook her head. "No, I…I had a long day. First." She tossed Kiki the book. Kiki scrambled to her feet in time to catch it with a gasp. "Now you can start."

Kiki lowered her gaze to the cover. Mouthing the title, she flashed a wide smile.

"Thank you! But…" Her smile faded. "Did you steal it?"

Kari waved a hand, plopping down beside her. Kiki frowned as she joined her, cradling the book with ridiculous care.

"What happened?"

Kari let out a breath and told Kiki about the demon attack. How she had been scared witless until that feeling overcame her. How lightning fell from the sky at her command.

Kiki's hands went to her mouth, the book forgotten in her lap. "Oh, Kari. You could've…died…or…" Her eyes widened. "You summoned real lightning? From the sky?"

"It's what I've been training for, isn't it? That is the sort of power I could have in the future. Only…" She frowned, touching her chest.

"You can't recall that feeling again?"

"No. I *feel* it, way deep inside. It's a tingle in my gut, you know, when you're very excited? It wasn't there before. It's…itchy. Like if I could just…" She dropped her hand with a sigh. "I wish my parents had explained anything about why I'm like this. Even that woman had something to say about my powers."

"What woman?" Kiki asked.

Kari's head snapped up. "Oh! We had a woman come to school today. A real magic-user. When I said I had a friend who wanted to learn, she suggested books." She pointed at the book in Kiki's lap. "Since they can't bring anyone down here."

Kiki looked down at the book, tracing the spine with a finger. "What did she say to you, though?"

Even now, hours later, Kari could recall the gravity of Miss Kiean's expression when she'd mentioned demon magic.

"She told me if I ever saw a demon do something like that, I should tell the magic users. I assume so they could…"

Her words faded into silence, leaving an edgy space between them.

Kiki cleared her throat. "Well, I won't tell on you."

Kari cracked a grin. "Thanks."

"And forget that woman. She doesn't know you like I do. This power of yours isn't something to fear. It's great! Although you should practice it more if you don't want to hurt someone else." Smiling wide, Kiki inched closer so their legs were touching and cracked the book open on their laps. "Read with me! Maybe it will have something useful about control."

They bowed their heads over the pages, legs and shoulders touching. Kari's heart warmed, grateful for this one human, her best friend.

CHAPTER THIRTEEN

When Miss Kiean was nowhere to be seen in town the next day, Kari felt a weight leave her shoulders. She had always known her electricity was something to keep well hidden, but Miss Kiean's grave reaction had only added to her constant tension.

With one less worry, Kari listened to stray conversations about the dead demon found in Snow Shade. Over the next few days, the chatter quieted, and Kari breathed easier. Even so, she spent countless hours wondering: why had a demon been in Snow Shade? Who was Rathik? And was there truly any connection to the mysterious creatures she kept hearing about?

While the pressure on Kari lessened, though, Joseph's nerves rose. His eyes followed her every movement, and he asked more questions. Kari stayed out of sight and dodged what inquiries she could, knowing she'd have to act soon. She packed away food, sneaking whatever she could from Anne's kitchen when the humans were asleep or out of sight. She also found a water skin and decided to pack spare clothes, as she knew shifting would destroy her clothes.

She and Kiki would leave Snow Shade and travel to Briar's Glen. Kari was sure they could do odd jobs to earn money. If nothing else, they could survive in the world as Kiki and her father did now, at least until they could find a home. Kari was satisfied enough to know they would leave and do this together.

As for her personal goals, Kari had no solid plan of action. How to complete the task she had set upon herself? When would be the best time? For if enough ruckus was made and anyone else came running, Kari would have to make a quick getaway. She needed an escape plan.

Although Kiki was uncomfortable with it, she helped Kari to strategize: an attack in the early morning or night, when visitors were unlikely, would be best. Kari would do best to escape straight into the forest rather than Snow Shade's southern gate, as that would be where the town's meager guard would go first. Once things settled, the two of them could leave.

Kari finished gathering her things, shoving as much food and clothes as she could into a traveling pack. Kiki's father, who was well aware of Kiki's desire to live a more normal life, would be giving the human girl her own traveling pack. Once Kari's bag was ready, she snuck it into the clearing of morthiem lilies and hid it there.

Of course, there was still that matter of when—when exactly would be the right time?

It was a chilly morning before the last day of school when Kari woke and headed down the hall, her mind swirling with plans and ideas. She would wake earlier to catch Joseph off guard, then finish Anne while she slept. Or maybe she could follow Joseph out and get him where no one was around—either way, Kari was certain she had to do them separately.

These thoughts were interrupted as she stepped into the main room and saw Joseph at the table. Wrapped in a thick leather coat, he leaned casually in his chair. Kari paused at the sight of him, all her plans turning to a messy mush in her mind.

"Morning."

"Morning," Kari replied in a cracked voice.

"Anne's sleeping still," Joseph said, leaning forward to wrap his hands around the steaming cup in front of him.

Kari didn't get his point, or why he was here. "I figured you'd be gone already."

"Mmm…the other hunters been going early. What? Did you think I was going with them?"

"I don't really care what you do or when."

Joseph sipped his drink. "I think you might, girl. My actions concern you, after all."

"What?" Kari felt fear tingling in her stomach and forced it down.

"I'll only ask you once, girl, so tell me true. You owe us that." Kari waited while he took another sip, her breaths hard. "What are you?" Joseph finally asked. "You're no girl, I know that. What did we bring into this house?"

She felt her brow furrowing into a glare before she could stop it. The question caught her off guard, even though part of her knew Joseph had probably been wondering this for a long time. Though her claws tensed, and her muscles tightened, she forced herself to relax.

"What do you care, old man? Your wife is happy, is she not? She always wanted a child. Thanks to me, not you, she's had one. Would you take that from her?"

Joseph's face flushed with angry color. "If you're a demon—"

A door creaked open, and they froze. Anne's soft footsteps were approaching, the gentle padding of a serene woman, wholly unaware of the tense conversation going on in her home. Joseph's eyes widened as he looked at Kari, all the anger gone from his face. He looked pleading, or scared, and Kari was taken aback by the drastic change in expression.

"Joseph? Kari?" Anne's sleepy voice came. "What're you doing?"

If Kari had any inkling that she would do it now, it was gone. In one smooth motion, Joseph stood from the table and turned to leave the house, taking her chance of revenge with him.

"I'll be home fer dinner, Anne," he said over his shoulder as he left.

"He's acting odd," Anne murmured. "Are you hungry, dear?"

Kari watched the door close. What if Joseph said something to someone? Before the fear could settle, she shook herself free of the worry. If he was going to tell anyone, he would've already. His words were proof he suspected her and was trying to catch her in some sort of act. She tried to rack her brain, thinking of when he might have followed her or seen her some place. The forests were impossible; if Kari did not catch his obvious human scent out there, at least Kiki would have seen someone.

"Kari, dear?"

"Yeah," Kari mumbled. "Yeah, I'm hungry."

The day passed in a cloud of apprehensive slowness. Kari could hardly spare attention for the lessons, and Ms. Lier grew steadily more frustrated before finally snapping at her. It was useless; Kari's thoughts were elsewhere.

She had no choice now. She had to act tonight or leave immediately, before Joseph could reveal her existence.

Even knowing this fact, Kari dawdled. She couldn't decide the right timing nor the way to do it; instead, she made excuses, dragging her feet on the way home. What if the humans overwhelmed her? What if the guards came before she could slip away? Perhaps she wasn't quite ready to take a life.

Her stomach bubbled with unease at what she was to do, and when she finally came within sight of the place she only technically called home, it was nearing nightfall. The sun teetered on the edge of the horizon, threatening to sink the world in darkness.

Now would be a good time. Villagers bustled around Snow Shade, making plenty of noise as they made their way home for the night. Still, her steps dithered. Would she flee from this, as she had fled up the mountain five years ago?

Grinding her teeth, Kari forced herself to grab the door handle and push it open, steeling herself.

This moment felt good, she told herself. She was ready.

She froze as her sharp ears caught the sharply tense voices coming through the door before it was fully open.

"I'm telling you, Anne, she's not human!"

Kari's breath caught in her throat; she strained to listen.

"Oh, don't say that, Joseph—"

"She's always been weird, and she goes to the forests at night—"

"The mountain was her home for all we know—"

"And what about the boy, Lian? He didn't just collapse, Anne! And he wasn't quite right after what happened—"

The conversation ended abruptly as Kari finally pushed the door open and stepped inside. Anne and Joseph sat at the dining table, but when Kari entered, they both stood.

"You're finally home, dear," Anne said with a strained smile.

Kari looked at Joseph instead. The hatred in his eyes helped to harden her resolve.

"I want you to understand my intentions before I go through with this. I'm not a murderer."

Anne frowned; Joseph glared.

"Honey, what do you—"

"You killed my parents," she spoke over Anne to Joseph. "On the mountains all those years ago, you killed them. And I could never forgive you for that."

"Mountain? Where we found you? Sweetheart, you were alone…"

117

"The wolves!" Kari snapped at Anne so fiercely that the woman stumbled back and fell into her chair. "Can't you see?" She ripped her hat off, tossing it aside. Her ears, tawny against her blonde hair, flicked. Anne gasped. "I'm not one of you. I'm a wolf demon."

Kari moved toward Joseph, who finally summoned some form of courage. He hefted his hammer, hidden underneath the table, and swung it at her. Had he been planning to kill Kari himself while she slept if Anne had been more cooperative?

She ducked under his swing and thrust a fist up into his jaw. Joseph fell back with a grunt, dropping his hammer to the floor with a heavy *thunk*.

Kari leaned down to grab the front of Joseph's scruffy shirt before he could attack again, lifting him with no effort.

"You won't slay me the way you did my parents."

"We should've killed you," Joseph growled, his hands going to hers. "We should've—"

With her other hand, Kari gripped his head and twisted it. His angry words fell away in a puff of air as his neck broke, flopping to one side. Kari lowered him until he was kneeling at her feet.

With one motion, the man who had killed her parents was dead. There was no elation at the thought, no blessed joy; only the cold burn of vapid satisfaction that was quick to recede. Kari dropped him unceremoniously to the floor. His body laid flat, unmoving; this wasn't the justice she had hoped for.

Anne's gasp was loud and sharp enough to hurt Kari's ears. She turned to find her sitting in the same chair, her eyes wide and welling with tears. Her trembling hands covered her mouth.

"You were kind," Kari muttered. "But don't misunderstand. That was never going to save you. You speared my father, after all. You remember?"

Anne shook with her cries and didn't answer. Kari stepped closer, stopping when she was within arm's length. Still, the woman didn't move, frozen at the sight of her husband's still body.

Is this right, to take her life too?

118

Kari's teeth clacked as she ground them.

"If you had known I was a demon, would you have kept me still?"

Anne finally looked at her with watery eyes. "It would never be a-allowed," she muttered through her sobs. "They would've killed you. Killed me!"

"In other words, no," Kari said. "You don't deserve it. My parents were left to bleed out in the snow, and I know you scavenged their bodies for all they were worth." The words were a bitter taste in her mouth. "I'll make it fast, like him."

Kari gripped her shoulder with one hand and raised the other, her claws poised to run the woman through.

She hesitated.

Did Anne deserve this? Her blind love had been a shield that Kari had gladly used, and Anne's repayment would be to die?

Even if she is worth sparing, I can't leave her here, Kari argued with herself. *It would be too dangerous.*

Something tugged at her gut, a hot sharpness. It was that tingling burn.

She is still human. She still helped to kill your parents.

They would have wanted this.

The voice spoke harsh words, but they were ones she'd thought. Kari's arm trembled.

Do it. Be done with it all, and we can leave.

Her arm moved without conscious thought: it thrust forward, her claws spearing straight into Anne's chest. Bones *snapped* and *crunched,* and Kari's hand was doused in warmth. The woman coughed, grabbing her; Kari ripped free again, taking the heart that had tried so hard to love a child it had never truly known.

Anne slid to the ground in a heap. Kari dropped the heart and stared down at her.

Her revenge was finally complete, but Kari felt nothing. Even the tingling burn was gone.

After using the water basin in the kitchen to clean her hands, Kari strode back through the main room, eager to leave this place for the last time.

She had done it. She had avenged her parents, and while she felt a heavy weight had left her shoulders, Kari didn't feel better. She felt righteous, not unlike the snake demon's death, yet the aching emptiness where her parents had been was not filled.

Kari quickened her pace. She longed to talk to Kiki. Kiki would support her, even after what she'd done. Perhaps she would even berate Kari's dissatisfaction with the way she felt.

Well, Kari, didn't I tell you it wouldn't be worth it?

It wouldn't matter. They would leave this awful place, and Kari could forget everything that had happened here. She could look forward to a new life, one that was hers. A life she could be proud of, one worthy of her parents' sacrifice.

Kari reached the forest edge quickly and dove into the depths, making her way toward the clearing.

Her breaths were coming in heavy gasps as she pushed her way through the hedges protecting the area. With Snow Shade permanently behind her, Kari felt scraps of excitement.

Kiki was sitting in the middle of the field when Kari thrust through the bushes. As Kari hastened to approach her, a metallic scent disturbed the tranquil sweetness of the lilies. She froze in her tracks, recognizing that smell easily—it was the same sharp scent she'd just left at Anne's house.

"Kiki…?" Kari whispered. The girl didn't respond, and cold dread filled Kari's stomach. "Kiki, speak to me!" She forced herself to move, not caring if she smashed the pretty blooming flowers that surrounded them. The smell of blood was strong, filling her nose. Kari covered her face with a hand and dropped down behind Kiki, reaching out a shaky hand. "Please, Kiki…"

Her fingers touched Kiki's shoulder and the girl fell back into her arms. Her eyes were dull, her skin pale, cold, and bloodless. Rivers of red poured from a cut throat, the wound deep enough to reveal bone.

Kari's vision blurred. "Kiki," she garbled, gently shaking her by the shoulders. "Kiki, Kiki!"

Kiki could say nothing. She could merely stare at the sky, her azure eyes glassy and empty of the naïve, lively girl who Kari had loved.

Chapter Fourteen

Kari's howling sobs carried through the night. She clutched Kiki to her, praying and hoping that somehow, someway, she would be okay, that this would all have been a bad dream.

I'm sorry, I'm sorry, Kari silently begged, sure this was some sort of punishment for having killed Joseph and Anne. *Please, I'm so sorry!*

A pale pink dawn rose into the sky. Kari, her eyes puffy and her throat raw, was frozen. She lay with her head on Kiki's, unable to believe this had happened. *Why? Why take her from me, too?*

Kari slowly raised her head. She traced Kiki's jawline and froze, her hand hovering over the wound on her throat. The severed skin was completely even, not jagged around the edges like from a knife wound.

Dull rage burned inside of her. Who had done this?

She lifted her head to the sky and breathed in deep, trying to catch an unfamiliar scent, any hint that another person had been here. Only the metallic tang of blood filled her nose, making her sick.

The pain in her heart was agonizing, made worse by the fact that Kari had no idea who to blame for this, except herself. If she had been here earlier, this wouldn't have happened. She could have protected Kiki.

A choking sob left her throat; she couldn't stay here anymore.

It took the rest of the morning for Kari to lay Kiki's body in the flowers, her eyes closed, and her hands crossed over her chest. The budding lilies sparkled in the morning light, the flowers that Kiki had loved more than much else.

Kari's eyes blurred with tears. Her body numb and weak, she plucked some lilies and tried to thread them together the way Kiki once had for her. Twisting, tying, curling the stems around each other. She would do whatever she could to make sure Kiki looked as peaceful as possible. When her father came looking and found her, Kari knew Kiki would not want him to remember her any other way.

The stems unwound in her fingers. No matter how she grabbed and moved them, they fell loose in her lap. After the third failure, Kari's shaking hands ripped up handfuls of lilies and instead arranged them around Kiki's head and chest. There was no elegance and little beauty, but when she finally stood up, the wound in Kiki's neck was concealed by hundreds of curling petals.

If she weren't so still, she could have been sleeping.

"I'm sorry, Kiki," Kari whispered, her voice cracked by tears.

She wanted to stay here by her side but knew she couldn't; Kiki would have been irate to know she hadn't followed through with their plans. Kari had no choice but to try and live the life for both of them. Heavy, every breath a chore, Kari steeled herself and left the forest with her bag slung over one shoulder.

Skirting the edges of Snow Shade was easy, and no one spotted Kari as she melted out of crackly woodland. Soon she faced an entire world, the freedom she'd hoped for, yet it was bitter and sickening.

What was she to do now? She and Kiki had made plans, but Kari wasn't sure if she could follow through with them. They would have gone south, making any possible trades with other villages for food and supplies, and made their way to Briar's Glen.

Going there now made Kari feel hollow. Yet what else was there for her to do? Travel aimlessly, hoping she found something to fill the gaping hole in her heart?

If we are separated, find Zina.

A hoarse chuckle bubbled free. Kari shook her head and began to walk.

What could the mysterious friend of her mother do for Kari now? Everything was lost.

She made her way south, the only direction that felt right. Perhaps she was obeying her mother's final wish to one day find Zina, or maybe she found herself drawn to the towns in the south rather than any other. Her lessons in school told her how small Grass Shire and Fallspire were; less human populace would make a demon stick out even more than usual.

So, she followed the old trade roads south. She shed her clothes and stuffed them into her bag to save them from shredding as she shifted forms. The cracking transformation of her bones only served as a reminder of Kiki; Kiki, who had accepted who she was and now would never leave the vicinity of that wretched town.

She tossed her head and ran. The short walls of a town whose name was slow to come to her—Crow's Rest—passed on her right. She quickened her pace, swallowing hard around the lump in her throat.

She had to escape it all.

When night fell, Kari slept hidden beneath bushes. Her fur kept her warm, yet she was alert, waking to every sound. When she did sleep at last, her dreams were edged with unease: she stood in the plains, the sky thundering and dark above her. Other times she saw Kiki in the field of morthiem lilies. On these days, she woke with swollen eyes and a dry throat.

It was a bright, sunny morning, her fourth since fleeing Snow Shade. Kari stretched, then shrank back into her humanoid form before pulling her pack closer. Her claws sifted through her clothes before scraping the bottom of the bag. Frowning, she upended it. There were the few pairs of shirts and pants she'd packed, followed soon by a few fist-sized hunks of stale bread, goat cheese, and a water skin.

Kari gathered the food. It would do for breakfast, but what would she do for her next meal? The plains were quiet so early in the morning. Kari's stomach tightened—she had never caught any food on her own.

As midday approached and Kari felt her stomach start to grumble, desperation twisted within her. She lifted a hand and called lightning to her fingertips. It answered as tiny, wild sparks that danced and glittered. With a frown, she looked at the grass that surrounded her, covering the entire world in a sea of green, and clenched her claws to stifle the electric energy.

She could not rely on her weak lightning prowess for getting food. One wrong move and the entire area would be a burned, blackened mess.

Instead, Kari shifted forms. She had to learn eventually. Her heightened senses allowed her to easily sniff out the living things that hid in the tall grass all around her. The only problem was being fast enough to catch them.

The first tiny beast—a rabbit, she knew by scent and instinct—escaped her paws. Snarling, strap of her bag in her mouth, she pounced again and again. A squeaking mouse wiggled free and darted away. Birds were out of the question, though she wasn't above trying; they squawked, their wings scuffing Kari's ears as she ran after them.

She learned to walk quietly, to sneak up on the tiny creatures hiding in the grass. She could smell them even if she couldn't see them. The sound of their scurrying movements and hard breaths weighed on her ears. She stayed low, each step meticulous. When she bounced for the tenth time, she dropped her bag and snapped out with her teeth.

The squirrel she'd caught screamed, though it was cut short when her electricity flared. She ate, then retrieved her bag and continued, confidence making it easier. A rabbit was next, then another squirrel. They were in abundance in the fields, and she ate until her belly was, at last, full.

Kari quickly adapted to the life of hunting prey, listening, and calmly waiting for the right moment to strike. As her days of traveling turned into weeks, there was no mistaking the heaviness that weighed her down.

She was exhausted, desolate, and alone.

The realization saddened her as she continued southward, dimly registering the sight of buildings on the not-too-distant slope of a hill. Things would have been very different if Kiki had been with her. With Kiki, Kari had been able to be herself. The girl had been the perfect solution to her desire to see the humans and have friends; Kari had been able to share things with her, and Kiki never looked down on her for anything.

Kari found herself brooding over this so deeply that she did not even notice the approaching humans until one of them screamed. Her massive head swung around to see a group of them, along with a wooden caravan pulled by a horse. There was at least a dozen, mostly men with a handful of women, and all dressed in simple brown tunics of traders. They froze as one, watching her with wide, staring eyes.

The woman who screamed was in the front. Her hands flew to her mouth, but not before a whimper escaped. Kari watched them, ears bending back.

She should have expected travelers and stayed away from the main road. *Stupid, idiot,* she chided herself and took a deliberate step back from the humans and their caravan.

A man touched the woman's shoulder, gently shushing her.

"Just a wolf, Ma. See? It's leavin', no problem. Quiet down now."

Kari was thankful that she was not in her humanoid form. The group of travelers visibly relaxed as she crept away from them, their tension dispelled with a chorus of released breaths. When she had disappeared behind a large rock, the caravan moved on, wooden wheels cracking noisily against the hard earth. Kari shifted forms, dressing as she waited tensely for the sound of the humans chattering to fade.

When she peeked out from her hiding place, it was to see the traders making for a massive town she hadn't noticed in her brooding. It was much, much bigger than Snow Shade, with tall and sturdy outer walls that blocked the view of the town from outside. Guard towers capped it in various places, and Kari could see the dark specks of more guards walking the tops of the wall.

The entrance was a smaller iron gate, and the trading caravan made for it. A few posted guards pulled open the gate with the piercing sound of screeching metal, and as the people followed the caravan, one in the back turned to glance around the area.

She was dressed differently than the traders, donning a simple gray tunic and pants. She hefted a massive bag on her back, but it seemed not to weigh on her. Kari watched her, brow furrowed, and froze when the woman's eyes locked with hers.

Kari's insides squirmed with fear, urging her to flee before the woman screamed at the sight of a demon so nearby. Perhaps she would even guess Kari had been the wolf they'd seen.

The woman did not scream. She smiled and turned back to the town, disappearing behind the gates as they closed again.

Kari stared, her mouth dry. She swallowed hard.

Was that woman not scared of her? Were demons…welcome here? Should she approach?

Kiki would have insisted they at least check it out, and Kari knew even human acceptance would be welcome. Hell, she could even deal with occasional nervous glances if it meant she could enter this place in peace.

With one last breath to steel herself, Kari descended the hill.

The town's sign met her nearly halfway down, signaling with wide, curly green letters that this was the town of Briar's Glen. Kari recalled from her teachings that it was the biggest town on Taris and the best for trading. It was also the place she and Kiki had considered going to first for supplies or money.

And like most places, they probably turned away demon kind with the utmost prejudice. Without a human companion, she had no chance.

Kari paused, ready to turn and flee, when she noted the sight beyond the iron gates: a wide marketplace filled with people. People pulling carts, waving their wares around, shouting, and all amongst that, children running back and forth.

Humans everywhere, and the sight of so many filled her with cold certainty.

Humans would not trust her.

As she turned, ready to jog out of the shallow basin Briar's Glen made home in, a voice shouted from above.

"Hey! Who approaches? Announce your name and business!"

She froze and turned back to the gate. Shielding her eyes from the sun, she looked up to see a man in gleaming silver and leather armor atop the wall, facing her.

Kari opened her mouth to speak, but only a squeak came out. She cleared her throat and yelled back, "My name is Kari. I'm passing through!"

As she spoke, she caught a hint of movement near the bottom of the gate. A group of four or five humans was posted there, and she had hardly noticed them for all the attention she had paid the town. They all turned to her, postures, and expressions, lax.

"'Ey!" one of them called. "'Tis a demon! Bin awhile since we saw one of them, huh?"

The guards straightened, hands going to their swords. Kari's pulse quickened.

"Demon filth!" another spat. "'Ow dare you come 'round 'ere?"

Kari found her voice. "I was just passing by. I'll leave."

"Ha!" one of them guffawed. "So you can come back with all your little demon friends? I don't think so!"

"Yeh! 'Ow's 'bout we jus' kill you 'ere?"

They drew their weapons and advanced. Kari's heart thumped as she watched them, each pounding beat urging her to flee.

She turned, her legs tensed to run when a whistle in the air made her head turn. Something clipped her cheek and she stumbled back, hand going to the cut. Her gaze lowered to an arrow, embedded in the earth beside her.

"Don't move!" the guard at the top of the gate shouted.

As her teeth clenched, lightning crackled to life at her hands. The advancing guards froze.

"That…that's not possible!" one of them yelled.

"'Ey!" another shouted, nudging him. "Tha' powers the one tha' woman talked about, innit?"

"Right," the first guard said, shaking himself. "Get her!"

What woman? Kari wanted to demand, but she could only focus on the power in her hands. Gritting her teeth, she flung out her hands, unleashing the electricity. It arced off the nearest guard's metal plate with little more than a *zzzt*. He flinched, but the electricity had already dissipated.

They stood still, stunned by her show of power. Then their surprise turned into amusement as they laughed loudly.

"No big deal, eh? We capture this rare demon and get rewarded!"

Kari's face warmed with shame. Why could she not call the power of the storm like she did against the lizard demon?

"'Ey, hurry up!" the guard from the gate yelled. "The Magistrate will be around for the checks soon!"

One of the guards lunged at Kari, the blade of his sword menacingly sharp. Instinct carried her backward. She swung her arm out, underneath the blade's arc, and her claws swiped at his leather-clad forearm.

Kari lost her footing and fell to the ground as he let out a hiss of surprised pain. She looked up at him. The leather that had covered him so carefully was shredded in four fine lines by her claws, and beneath the ragged brown mesh, bright red blood could be seen. It dripped, staining the ground.

"Bitch!"

Kari glanced at her claws. It was nothing like when she killed Anne, but the blood was there as proof. She had hurt this human, much easier than she had anticipated.

She was not helpless. She could kill these humans, and if she wanted to survive, it was exactly what she had to do.

She jumped to her feet and leapt at him. The guard fell back with a grunt as she slashed wildly at his face and chest, tearing open flesh and leather easily. His screams fell on deaf ears and his blood painted the earth.

The swish of heavy metal made Kari duck, her hair ruffled by the swing of the sword. She jumped off the current guard and bowled into the next closest one, tearing into his arms and stomach. He dropped his weapon with a panicked cry and tried to shove her off.

Kari slashed and growled, leaving the human a pitiful bloody mess before turning to the next in the group. She felt that tingling, boiling rage filling her gut, and jumped at the others with a renewed sense of vigor.

Fresh sparks flew from her claws as they tore into flesh. Blood and screams splattered the air around her, and Kari recognized an enlightening sense of pleasure. She had not felt this when she'd avenged her parents.

Their deaths are not required, her mother had said once. *Humans are our enemies, but we are not lowly creatures like them. We do not kill for sport. We are wolves, proud and honorable.*

Nonetheless, her mother's wisdom did not change the fact that she was enjoying this. It smothered every other feeling and thought, made the sadness go away.

Kari's bloodlust was blinding. She barely moved out of the way as one of the men, a young boy with a pale face, jabbed his sword at her side. Kari twisted out of the way, and instead of piercing her, the blade scraped along her ribs. With an angry hiss, Kari snapped her hand out, wrapping her bloodied claws around his face. The lightning in her palm flared free, and the young guard was blasted back. He hit the ground and lay still.

She turned to the rest of them, ready to continue fighting, but they retreated. The first one she attacked was dragged away; his chest so torn apart it was a wonder he was still alive.

Kari watched them go, her teeth bared and chest heaving. The anger in their eyes was gone now, swallowed by fear, and the sight of it brought sense back to her. The tingling, burning fury in her gut was fading. She looked down at her hands, trembling and bloody.

She leapt back at another whistle of air. As the arrow hit the earth, she threw a glare at the guard atop the gate. His aim was poor, but if she didn't leave, he might actually get a hit on her.

More guards would come. Briar's Glen was much bigger than Snow Shade; Kari had no doubt they could summon a small army.

The guard nocked another arrow. "Call the deacon!" he shouted over his shoulder.

Kari knew the word *deacon* from school. A reputable holy man, capable of exorcising demon souls. Before the guard could properly aim, or this holy man could show himself, Kari turned and fled the valley.

The bloodlust faded as soon as she left the town behind, and Kari did not pursue it again. As her heart calmed, so did her thoughts; she did not want to kill humans unless it was necessary. Anne and Joseph had been an exception, the only one. Even though the guards had attacked her first, she shouldn't have done as much damage as she did.

Maybe Kiki was right about murder darkening her soul.

131

Days passed slowly. Kari continued to hunt what she could in the plains, but it wasn't enough. When a rattling caravan lumbered up the path behind her, the thought of stealing food came hard and fast.

How easy it could be: she could scare them by growling and using her lightning, then steal their food and be on her way. No harm done. The caravan came closer as she stepped off the path, watching it approach. The shapes of humans appeared, walking alongside it.

Even if some of them had weapons, Kari was sure she could get something before they hurt her. She doubted any of them were trained to fight demons.

Her fingers itched and her feet shifted, ready to move. Instead of leaping down the path toward the caravan, though, she backed away and hid in nearby bushes. The caravan passed by, the humans chattering amiably. She sighed, resigned.

That night, Kari dreamt of bloodied fingers and howling screams, and was glad she had refrained, even as she woke shivering and hungrier than she had ever known.

Exhaustion crept into her bones. Her pace slowed. She walked more and slept less, determined to avoid more nightmares as long as she could. Her feet dragged with each step, but still she walked, determined to find a place that could be home.

She had been roaming aimlessly, farther into the wilderness, when she noted the dance of orange light in the distance. Kari paused, considering who or what she would encounter if she neared the light ahead—a human, probably, maybe even a few of them.

Her stomach was tight with hunger, and she was so very tired of the pangs in her gut disrupting her sleep. Maybe the humans would have food. She could threaten them and take some of it—just a little, enough to satiate her.

Her pace quickening, she made her way to the flickering light.

CHAPTER FIFTEEN

Kari had expected to see *some* humans on her way south. They had to travel, even at night. Still, she thought it absurd that they would alert others to their location with such a bright beacon. Though she hadn't seen any herself, surely other demons roamed these plains? What if one saw the fire and decided to attack the humans gathered there?

Kari crept closer, each step careful and quiet as she approached the camp. She thought to get a sense of how many humans she would be dealing with when the smell of cooking meat reached her nose. Her thoughts of caution were dashed away, and Kari lifted her head to breathe it in—venison, maybe. Her stomach rumbled angrily.

It'll be mine, she promised herself. She allowed herself to get closer before slipping behind a meager bush. It was frail and crackly, but adequate cover in the darkness. She peered at the campfire again and noted the silhouette of a single human.

It was too easy, but she hadn't come all this way to question her luck. Even if there were no other humans around right now, they could be back any minute.

Kari leapt up and plunged into the light of the camp, only to flinch at the girl's gasp that pierced her ears.

The sight of a woman alone was so outlandish that Kari faltered. That could only mean her male companions couldn't be far—Kari had to hurry.

Ignoring the woman's wide eyes and gaping mouth, she faced the fire. Roasting above the flames dripped a small slab of meat, ready for Kari to take. She reached for it, eager, only to hiss when the campfire licked her wrist. She snatched her hand back with a frustrated growl.

"Are you hungry?"

Incredulous, Kari snapped her head up as the woman climbed to her feet.

"D-don't move," Kari warned, raising her hands, trying to hide their trembling. "I don't want to hurt you, but I will if I have to."

The woman reached out to grab the spike holding the meat. She lifted it away from the fire, the meat dripping still more juice onto the hissing flames.

"Here," she said. Kari looked at her. Her eyes, dark as the night sky yet warmer, didn't even dart to look at Kari's ears. Her thin face was framed by long brown hair that fell in waves around her shoulders.

She was familiar. Kari's gaze trailed over her ashen, loose-fitting blouse and earth-colored trousers, down to the leather bag by her side. It was even bigger up close.

The same woman from Briar's Glen—Kari recognized the bag. She hunched, seeming small and delicate without the hefty weight of it on her shoulders. Now she was here, kindly offering to share her food.

"You can take it," she continued. "I have plenty in my pack." The woman smiled as Kari took the meat, and as Kari turned to run with her prize, she spoke once more. "You can share my fire if you'd like. I find the darkness a little daunting." Slowly, she sat again, leaving Kari to stare.

The smell of the meat wafted to Kari's nose, but she was too befuddled to eat now. Share her fire with her? What did this woman think she was?

Still, the heat and light were soothing. She shuffled her feet.

"Your companions won't like me, even if you pretend to," Kari ground out. "And if you think I'm dumb enough to get caught by humans again, you're wrong. I'm stronger than other demons."

The woman chuckled, a sound that reminded Kari of music.

"Companions? I'm alone."

Kari's brow furrowed. "Don't lie. I saw you with them, back at the town."

The woman shrugged. "I left them a day or so ago. I prefer my solitary presence to those of my kind." She smiled. "Will you sit with me? The meat will get cold."

She turned around to rifle through her pack, effectively putting her back to Kari.

While the woman busied herself, Kari sat and devoured the meat. It was greasy, delicious, and still quite hot. Even as it burned her mouth, she continued eating until there was nothing left.

Dropping the wooden spike it had been on, she sat back with a contented sigh. She could sleep comfortably, not that she would nearby.

"My name is Vivianne." The soft voice made Kari jump. The human was smiling at her again. Gods, her eyes were like Kiki's. "My friends called me Viv when I was younger," the woman continued, laying a folded piece of paper aside and reaching into her pack again. "Are you from this side of Taris?"

Kari stared at her for a long time before realizing this woman truly wanted an answer. She cleared her throat and muttered, "No. I'm from the…far north."

Vivianne extracted a thin book and turned to Kari again. Her eyes lit up. "Oh, really? You know, I've toured Taris a couple of times and never made it to the top of the mountains. You know the tallest ones? Those are a bit too dangerous for me, I think."

Kari pursed her lips.

"I've thought about making a home somewhere here, but the hills are a bit much for me. I prefer flatlands, with lots of water…"

"Even if you didn't want the merchants' company, how can you be alone like this? Out in the open?" Kari asked.

"Where I'm from, we teach women basic defense. It's not seen much here on Taris, I know. I certainly couldn't kill a demon." She tilted her head at Kari. "Not that we have many at home. I could at least get myself some time to think of an alternative or get somewhere safe."

Kari's disbelief must have been evident; Vivianne laughed again.

"Where are you from, then, if not Taris?"

"Kestos. It's across the sea."

"I know where it's at," Kari retorted and fell silent.

Vivianne continued to smile at her as Kari looked around, noticing the paper that had fluttered open in the night breeze. On the parts Kari could see, she noticed drawn lines and tiny pictures: forests and houses. Her eyes widened.

The human nudged it to her. "It's a map of Taris. I bought it at Snake Bay, the coast town up the road. Last time I toured the continent, I got a little lost, so I thought this might be helpful."

Kari picked up the map and opened it. It was nothing like the maps she and Kiki had drawn and made plans with, nor even the ones she studied at school in Snow Shade. This one was gloriously detailed, clearly showing where the grasslands ended and began, where the little patches of forest were. Kari trailed the path all the way from her northern mountain home, wondering where she sat on the map now. There was Briar's Glen, and some other villages she had skipped by on her way south.

Vivianne's hand appeared to point at a place near the bottom of the map. A tiny town was detailed there, labeled "Angel Cross."

"I'm heading there before I officially begin. I'll circle the continent, ending back at Angel Cross again before I take my leave and return to Kestos."

Kari looked over the map. It had taken her nearly a month to walk from the northern mountains to where she was now.

"A trip like that would take three months," she said. "Or more."

"Maybe," Vivianne said with a shrug. Kari let her take the map back, tucking it under her large bag. "Anyway, I should get some sleep. I wake up early. It's better to walk in the morning." She hesitated. "Would you like to stay here? The light of the fire keeps away the demons who stalk at night."

Kari quirked an eyebrow. "I'm a demon."

"Well, you're a different sort. If you were to hurt me, you would've already, right?"

Kari twitched, hesitant to stand and leave. Being in the fire's light and warmth was a comfort she'd missed. She jerked her head in a brief nod. "Just for tonight."

Vivianne smiled brightly. "Good! I have a spare blanket, and bundles of cloth for a pillow…"

"I don't need any."

Vivianne nodded and set up her bed on the opposite side of the fire. She laid down, leaving Kari to stare into the flames. Soon her breathing became slow and steady, turning into soft snores.

Kari scoffed. What a naïve human, so trusting. The same way Kari had fooled the people of Snow Shade, she could have easily fooled this woman into thinking she was safe, too. The difference was that she had no reason to hurt her.

Kari shook the thoughts away, deciding instead to ponder the map. What an excellent resource that would have been when she had first started her journey! She wished furiously that she had taken one from Joseph.

Or…I could take hers.

The idea rose with a flash to Kari's mind. Of course—it was so simple. She could take Vivianne's map and be on her merry way.

Kari looked at the folded parchment, tucked nicely under the bulging leather bag. Yes. She could take it and leave…

Her chest tightened at the thought of stealing from this woman who had been nice to her. She'd given Kari her meal—possibly one she'd caught herself—and trusted Kari not to hurt her.

And there was the fire…it felt silly, except she couldn't help feeling safer with the crackling flames nearby—even the smoky smell was calming. She understood why Vivianne would feel safer with a lit fire nearby.

Kari lay beside the fire with a yawn. She'd sleep first, and when dawn came, she would take the map and leave.

The early morning birdsong woke Kari after the sun had risen. She sleepily opened her eyes and stretched, feeling well-rested rather than edgy and irritable. Part of her wondered if it was because of the fire; she berated herself for being childish. Campfires did not make enemies and fears go away. One's own strength did that.

Still, Kari thought reluctantly, *maybe I could learn to make my own, using my lightning. Then the nights wouldn't be so…*

With a jolt, she remembered the map.

It was only a few feet away from her, still tucked under Vivianne's bag, and beside it was the sleeping Vivianne. She was unmoving, her breathing calm. Holding her breath, Kari crawled over to the bag and reached for the map. She could take it and be out of here before Vivianne even woke…

With an almighty yawn, Vivianne stretched. Kari froze, watching her. The woman crawled into a sitting position, rubbing her eyes before flattening her hair with her hands.

"Morning!" she said cheerfully at the sight of Kari. "I'm a little surprised you're still here. Would you like some breakfast?"

Kari was speechless. Vivianne was so like Kiki, the way she looked at a demon with nothing more than polite friendliness.

As she got up to leave, her stomach betrayed her with a quiet rumble.

Vivianne chuckled and pulled her bag closer. She picked up the map and tucked it in her pocket before beginning to dig around in the bag. Within moments, she had extracted a hunk of dark bread and tore it into halves.

"So…what's your name?" Vivianne asked as she handed half to Kari.

"Kari," she replied before devouring the bread.

"That's a pretty name."

Kari didn't reply and the two of them ate in silence.

"I hope you won't think me too forward," Vivianne said as she buckled her bag and climbed to her feet. "I don't want to offend you. But you seem to be…wandering. I wonder, would you like to come with me to Angel Cross?"

The rejection that came to her lips faded before she could give it voice. Kari could not forget her grief and her loneliness, although she did realize how nice it had been having someone with whom she could sit and eat.

At the same time, she didn't know this woman, nor did she know what Angel Cross was. All the time in school, learning about Taris, Kari couldn't recall anything about it. What would Kari be going to if she went with Vivianne?

Vivianne's expression softened, perhaps reading the uncertainty on her face.

"I hear there's an actual fire mage in the area, but that certainly wouldn't mean my safety—"

Kari perked up. "Fire mage?" A magic user nearby? First Miss Kiean, now this one. What were the chances that she'd meet two in her lifetime?

Vivianne nodded. "She was said to be hunting a specific demon, so I don't expect I could rely on her in a pinch. Chances are she won't even go south. So come with me, Kari, at least for my sake. The journey from here gets a little more treacherous, and I could do with some protection. Walking will take me at least a good week and a half, maybe two. You don't even have to go all the way with me. The road forks a ways down, so we could go separate ways if you wish. What do you say?"

Kari looked at the remnants of the fire, reminded of the warmth and comfort it gave her. She thought about the meal they had shared—more certainly assured if the size of Vivianne's pack was any indication—and the calmness with which they had been able to converse.

She was going south anyway, and it wasn't as though she had other plans.

"Alright," Kari mumbled.

Vivianne smiled and slung her bag over her shoulder with ease, even though it must have weighed a few dozen pounds. "Great! Let's get going."

Kari had become accustomed to traveling in silence, one with her thoughts, but that changed with Vivianne. Even more than Kiki, this human enjoyed talking, and Kari wondered how someone so carefree and innocent could have survived "touring Taris."

Vivianne told Kari about her hometown in Kestos—how wide and reaching the flat lands were, how she loved the river north of her home. There weren't many forests, but Vivianne preferred it that way. She loathed the last leg of Taris, she said, because of the great forest in the southwest.

"What about you, Kari?" Vivianne said midafternoon on their third day together. "You're from the northern mountains? What brought you out here?"

Kari could have told a stranger anything of substance about Vivianne at this point—her favorite food (bear meat), where she lived (a village called Lightglen), or her family name (Coreum)—but Kari couldn't think how to respond to Vivianne's questions about *her* life. Kiki hadn't liked the idea of Kari avenging her parents, and she'd had a better understanding of the situation. How would Vivianne react knowing Kari had spilled human blood?

Instead, Kari shrugged. "Exploring, I guess. You haven't yet told me exactly *why* you travel."

Vivianne didn't look terribly pleased about the change in subject, but she came to a stop and pulled her bag off her shoulder.

"I'm a scribe," she said, opening her pack so Kari could peer inside. Kari had expected clothes, or food, or even weapons. She did not expect Vivianne's large, bulging, over-stuffed bag to be filled with bundles of quills and pens and old tomes of varying sizes.

"I gather stories and histories, then I write them in my books." Vivianne reached in to extract a thick volume inlaid with a beautiful leather cover. "I mostly do it for fun, but there are some in Kestos who pay well for the histories from Taris. Not many from Taris care for what I have, except those in Angel Cross. That's why I'm heading there first."

Kari looked up from Vivianne's bag. Her face was positively alight with excitement, but Kari was confused.

"You walk around the *entire* continent—a few months' worth of time, at the absolute least—so that you can write things down? Things that happen to ordinary people, at ordinary times, at any day?"

Vivianne's smile didn't falter. She replaced the tome and pulled out another, smaller one. She flipped it open and turned a few pages until she came to whatever she was looking for.

Vivianne cleared her throat and read:

"The scaled things we called demons took us to their home city of Nagaris. It was a place unlike anything I had ever seen having grown up, primitively you might say, in the Jungle of Nagura.

…Their leader, who I had recently learned was named Vasthra, took us to their Lady. She sentenced my tribe to death in their colosseum."

Vivianne looked up at Kari, her eyes glittering. "Does that sound like an everyday happening? This is one of my favorites…I was so fortunate I could meet her and that she was willing to tell me her story."

Kari screwed up her face. "Scaled things? Nagaris?"

Vivianne nodded. "Nagaris was a demon city on Kestos. It no longer stands. Some hundred years ago, it was burned to the ground by the very person who told me this tale. And this is only one of the many histories I have recorded. Sometimes people have need of the past…why things happened, when, who was involved. I'm happy to be able to provide that. And who knows, maybe one day you'll be reading one of my collections!"

Kari doubted that but didn't say so. Vivianne put her things away and slung her bag back over her shoulder.

As they started walking again, Kari felt a nagging question at the tip of her tongue. She chewed her lip but felt silly wanting to ask.

"Have…have you met other demons like me?"

Vivianne looked over at her, and upon seeing the look on Kari's face, her brow furrowed.

"Wolf demons, you mean? No, Kari, you're the first I've ever seen."

Kari pursed her lips. If other demons had an ability like hers to call lightning, she would have expected them to at least share her animal blood.

"Not just wolf. But…"

She hesitated, then held out her hand. Vivianne watched while her face scrunched in concentration. When the sparks appeared, Vivianne gasped, clamping a hand over her mouth.

"By the five gods!"

Kari's lightning fizzled out. She curled her fingers, scoffing at herself.

Vivianne slowly lowered her hand. Despite what Kari had done, something that should be impossible, she appeared rather calm.

"No, Kari. Not even that. How do you…?"

"I don't know." Cold disappointment was forming in her chest. If this woman didn't know, this *scribe* of the world, who else could possibly provide answers?

Vivianne looked thoughtful. "Well, just because I haven't seen that before doesn't mean it doesn't exist. Hundreds of years ago, when demons first manifested, they were so different from the demons we see now. They evolved, and there's always a chance for…mutations."

She said the word with caution. Kari rolled her eyes.

"It's fine," she muttered. "I've been alone a long time. This makes no difference."

Vivianne's smile was small, but certain. "You don't have to be forever. On Kestos, there's a group of people *and* demons…I think they called themselves the Council of Balance. I met them once or twice. They're a little eccentric, but they're learned in things many others aren't. It's possible, maybe, they could explain that."

She pointed at Kari's previously electrified hand.

Kari shrugged noncommittally, and Vivianne, sensing her disbelief, changed the subject. While she described the long boat ride from Kestos to Taris, Kari's mind wandered to the Council of Balance. Maybe she could meet them one day. Maybe they would have the answers her parents didn't.

As the days dragged on, Vivianne's cheeriness melted the despair that had become so familiar to Kari. Vivianne was lively and bright, her dreams wide and endless. She had her family in Kestos, but since her youth, she'd longed to see everything she could of the world. Her desires had taken her to lessons in writing, at which she excelled. From there, she gathered the necessary materials to begin the life of a recorder. She set out on an adventure that would be filled with thrills, tribulations, and exhaustion. Most of all, though, Vivianne was grateful.

"I love being able to meet all these people! So many of them have stories to tell that no one cares to hear. Not only are they helping me, and others too, but they are getting to talk about their experiences. And everyone loves the chance to talk about themselves!"

She was so reminiscent of Kiki, who had longed so desperately to travel the world. If Kiki had a chance to live, would she have become a scribe like Vivianne?

Kari found herself becoming quite comfortable as their days together turned to weeks. She could no longer lie to herself or rely on her pride. She was becoming happy with this human, this companion to travel alongside.

Maybe, she thought, *this is my saving grace. This is where I start my life over.*

Chapter Sixteen

Though the days were peaceful, and the nights were completed by the warmth of the fire and full bellies, Kari's dreams took a sharp turn the further south they walked. She began to wake in a cold sweat, her eyes burning with visions of being lost in endless darkness while Kiki gargled her name around a mouthful of blood.

Kari tried to hide the unease the dreams caused her, but Vivianne noticed her reluctance to sleep more than a few hours at a time. After a few nights of this, she breached the subject.

"Would you like me to tell you a story?"

Kari blinked. "What?"

"A story," Vivianne repeated. "It might help you to sleep."

Kari stared blankly, trying to catch a sense of the joke. Vivianne's unwavering gaze and straight mouth betrayed nothing funny about what she was suggesting.

"Children need stories for sleeping. I'm not a child anymore."

Vivianne's lips twitched. "Maybe, but even adults have night terrors. Something traumatic in the past can upset your whole life if left alone."

Kari didn't reply.

Vivianne sat back on her hands. The light of the fire reflected in her eyes. "Humor me. Let me think for a minute…"

Kari lay back on the hard earth with a roll of her eyes. Even so, she remained quiet, waiting for Vivianne to begin her tale.

When the silence had comfortably cloaked them, Kari was startled as Vivianne exclaimed, "Ah!" and turned to her. "The tale of the first demons. Have you heard about demonic origins?"

Kari nodded and explained what she knew. The teachers of Snow Shade had some to say about that—how the demons had spawned from Hell to spread chaos and death, but there weren't many specifications. How and why did they suddenly come, where was Hell?

Vivianne smiled. "Fortunately for you, I have the stories," she said as she cleared her throat. "The first demons appeared hundreds of years ago from a place recorded as *Yutemi*, not Hell. Back then, demons were remarkably different from the sort we see today, like you. They were big, barely humanoid, with hard, sometimes leathery skin. They came in a variety of types: some with wings, some with three arms, some with five eyes. There are a few different tellings of it, but the thing most agreed on is how they came to be on Earth. And the most common is this.

"Humans were thriving as a race, overcoming war and famine all around. Still, there were some who lived in sin. They killed other humans, ripped apart families and lives. Some of the more devout will tell you these are the ones who started what has been deemed The Fracturing." Vivianne leaned forward to continue, the thrill evident in her quivering pupils. "One day the sun was blotted out. There was no light to be had, not even by candle or campfire. Then, out of the darkness came a burning, blistering red glow. The earth had broken apart, swallowing homes and people by the thousands. The radiance that came from the fissure was a hellish light. It drew some to it, mostly those who followed sin.

145

"The first of the hellspawn crawled from the dark depths that day, but they were…formless. Blobs of evil with barely definable shapes. When the wicked humans approached, the demons latched onto them. Some will say the demons sucked out their innards like a spider, others that they ate them whole."

Kari's face twisted in disgust. She could never imagine actually *eating* a human.

Vivianne laughed at the look. "It's gross, no? But that is how it is said the first demons became humanoid. Hundreds crawled out of the ground that day, devouring sinful humans. The ones who could not find a tasty morsel had to contend themselves with animals…and that's how we have demons like you!"

Despite Kari's earlier reluctance about the story, she found herself curious. "Where did the fissure open?"

Vivianne pursed her lips. "That's the part of the story I don't like. It isn't consistent. Most will say it opened in the village hidden on the south western corner of Taris…but there is no mark on the land to prove it. A fissure like that would take eons to heal."

Kari turned her head to look south. In the distance, she had been able to see the tops of mountains during the day, the range that kept that corner of Taris excluded from the rest of the world.

"Still, others say The Fracturing is what split Taris and Kestos apart. You can't rely too heavily on legends as old as these, but they are fun to tell."

Kari looked back at Vivianne. "It was nice to listen. Thank you, Viv."

Vivianne smiled widely. "Glad I could be of service. It is my life's work, after all."

Kari stifled a yawn and gave her a grin in return. "Goodnight."

As Vivianne told her more stories, she found calmness in her dreams again. Vivianne read from her small notebook, telling Kari the tales of those who had lived a hundred years ago or more—the story of a man who traded his mortal soul to save his lover, or the rarely-told legend of a woman who could glow as bright as the sun and banish darkness with a wave of her hand. All such extravagant stories that Kari had to wonder how much truth they really held.

The two walked, and though Vivianne did most of the talking, Kari felt herself forgetting her grief and warming to this human. What histories did she know that could relate to Kari? What would Kari see if she traveled with Vivianne? Would she find others like her, more orphaned young who had their family taken from them?

Might she, perhaps, find something to explain the lightning that coursed through her veins?

By Kari's estimation, they'd been traveling together for a couple of weeks. They made camp against a thicket of leafy bushes. After the fire was lit and some squirrels were cooking, Kari leaned back on her hands. She felt like a kid, waiting eagerly for Vivianne to tell another story.

Vivianne brushed off her hands and sat back on her haunches. She smiled. "What should I tell you tonight?"

Kari chewed her lip, thinking. By now, she'd heard so many Kestosian and Tarisian legends: the mystery of Nagura Jungle, now a sweeping, barren land; rumors that a prophet once walked the lands before disappearing a few centuries ago; and supposed sightings of angels, easily dismissed as bird-blooded demons.

Thinking of angels made Kari think of Nalmi, where it was said good souls went after death. The sobering thought of death drew her gaze to their fire.

"What happens when you die?"

Vivianne, masterful storyteller that she was, barely hesitated to reply. "No one is certain. Some say reincarnation, others that worthy souls are offered a place in Nalmi. Angelhood."

Kari tilted her head. "What does it take to get into Nalmi, any-way? Besides not being a demon."

Vivianne's grin was humorless. "Honor, faith. Those who be-lieve in actual angels see death as a homecoming."

Kari crossed her legs and propped her elbows on her knees. "Killing isn't allowed. Right?"

Vivianne pursed her lips, turning a few squirrels so they could brown evenly. "I think there's some allowance for self-defense."

"But real, willful taking of a life...you go to Yutemi, right?"

Vivianne sat back. "That's what they say. You must be very wicked to go to Yutemi...they say that's where evil souls quarrel for dominance."

Kari propped her chin in her hands. "Do demons go to Yutemi?"

Vivianne straightened as if she'd been caned. "Not necessarily. There may be another place for demons after death that—"

She cut off as Kari sat up. There'd been movement behind Viv-ianne. Something big enough to be seen from a distance. She squinted.

"What is it?" Vivianne turned around, staring into the distance. The sun crested the horizon, barely coloring the land in warm light.

"I...saw something..."

Vivianne pulled her bag closer. "A demon?"

Kari pushed herself to her feet. Ahead of her, miles of rolling hills laid out. Except for the random breeze ruffling blades of grass, all was still.

She was about to turn, surveying elsewhere, when movement caught her eye. Something climbed a hill, racing toward them.

It was massive, with bulging shoulders, and running on all fours. Its movement was lumbering, beast-like, but its intent was clear: it headed right for them.

Kari stared, thin arcs of electricity popping to life along her knuckles.

"Kari, what is it?" Vivianne asked, sharply enough to bring her back to focus. She stood now, too.

"Demon." It had to be; no human could move so fast.

Vivianne swung her bag around and began rummaging through it. "It's coming fast."

The thing was closer now; Kari could see flesh so dark it appeared purple. Its arms were thick with muscle, yet distinctly humanoid. A slathering, elongated mouth—very non-humanoid—hung open.

What is that?

She recalled Joseph and Anne's conversation, weeks ago now, about a mutation. Neither demon nor human, but blood thirsty.

Kari shook the thought away and jumped forward. "I'll handle it!"

Whatever it was, she would stop it. She called more power to her sparks and felt a rush of pleasure as electricity burst to life over her fingers. She clawed the air and unleashed the energy.

Yellow volts shot forth in a volley, crackling and sizzling as they flew. Kari followed them, determined. She knew she could do it: she had torn the flesh of those guards at Briar's Glen. If she had to, she could kill this—

The purple-skinned monster skidded to a stop, long-fingered fists and bare feet scraping up clods of dirt. Kari's lightning struck an arm and seeped into its skin, stretched thinly over swollen muscles.

The creature shuddered as the electricity bled through its body. It tossed its head back, every inch of its skin rippling. Kari staggered to a slow, staring. Nearly imperceptible vibrations worked its way up that thick, bulging arm and into the broad chest. The creature closed its eyes, the only sign of discomfort in the clench of its jaw.

Then, the creature slowly lowered its head. It straightened, tossing its shoulders back. A smile formed, a disgusting grin that showed rows of jagged, black teeth oozing even darker saliva. Kari froze, the cold hand of fear gripping her spine. She could only stare, every muscle in her body seizing.

Kari shook her hands, but no more sparks would come. She swallowed hard and managed a glare despite the shiver trailing her back.

Her instinct told her the truth: she couldn't fight this thing. It was too big, too strong. It'd *absorbed* her lightning…as if she'd done nothing more than splash it with water.

Her mouth dried. If she didn't…if it got past her…

"KARI, DUCK!"

Kari flinched, cricking her neck as she twisted her head to look at Vivianne. She had something in her hand, a thin burlap sack that smelled *horrid*. Moldy death would have been more pleasant.

Vivianne pulled her arm back and launched it. The bag sailed, and Kari stumbled over her feet as she scrambled to get out of the way. The beast watched with polite disinterest, its smile just as wide, as Vivianne's bag hit the ground.

It burst, exploding in a yellow cloud followed by a scent so awful, it paralyzed. Though it was several feet away, the smell clogged Kari's nose. She gagged, then cried, tears pouring from her eyes. Putrid gas replaced the air in her lungs. Her nose, throat, lungs…everything burned.

Someone grabbed her wrist and hauled her away. Somehow, her legs worked. They carried her after Vivianne, who was unaffected by the smell.

"Cover your nose!"

Kari slapped a hand over her nose and mouth, but it was too late. Her throat was aflame, as if she'd swallowed a days-dead squirrel recently lit on fire. She gagged.

"I know!" Vivianne shouted. "I know, Kari! Just run! Please!"

Kari swallowed back a mouthful of acrid bile. She closed her eyes and followed Vivianne, her legs moving without direction. She nearly tripped, but Vivianne caught her and heaved her back into running.

Vivianne's gasps were heavy on her ears. Their feet pounded grassy plains. Ahead of them, Kari saw nothing but blurs of green through her seeping eyes. She followed Vivianne blindly, doing everything she could not to retch.

150

"It's following!" Vivianne panted. Alarm hitched jaggedly in Kari's chest. The hand clutching her arm was slick and cold. Vivianne was terrified, yet she'd been so brave. "I don't know what it is, but it's not a demon!"

What will we do? Kari wanted to ask, but her throat was clasped in flames. She couldn't think for the agony each breath took.

Vivianne slowed, throwing Kari forward a few feet. Kari's eyes snapped open as Vivianne grunted and spun, throwing another foul-smelling bag. It landed at the feet of the beast, again running like a misshapen animal. As Vivianne's bag burst, the beast staggered to a slow, snarling monstrously—the smell did not paralyze and nauseate like it did for Kari, but at least enraged. As the creature smashed the bag under a foot, Vivianne grabbed Kari's wrist and continued to sprint.

Kari wished desperately for the power inside of her to flare, to do something.

Lightning struck that lizard demon when I needed it! Come on! Help me now!

The sky didn't so much as grumble in response. Kari's heart sank.

"We're almost there," Vivianne gasped.

Kari opened her mouth to ask where, only to break into a fit of coughs instead. Vivianne tugged her wrist sharply.

"Don't stop!"

Suddenly, it was as if they ran into a barrier of aroma eager to suffocate. Kari's nostrils were assailed. *I can't do this. I can't breathe.* Her mind fogged with fuzzy panic. *I'll never breathe again.*

She couldn't move forward, but Vivianne towed her on. Her feet slid along dirt—they'd left behind the grass—and kicked up something long, twine-like. Fear strangled as it caught on Kari's ankles, tangling her feet.

With a grunt, she and Vivianne toppled to the ground. Kari kicked at the vines trapping her feet, the only sound able to escape her swollen throat a pitiful whine.

"Hold on, Kari!" Vivianne's fingers shook as they gripped Kari's ankle and undid the vines.

Somewhere behind them, the creak of hinges signaled a door being thrown open.

"Gods!" yelled a man.

"Help me!" came Vivianne's scream.

Meaty hands grabbed Kari under the arms. She was hauled away from the vines and dragged over dirt. Rocks dug into her back, the pain almost welcome—it distracted from the horrible smell and the terror crushing her chest.

A roar shattered the air. Kari cringed and kicked her feet. She had to escape. She had to run!

"Get inside!" the man ordered.

Feet pounded beside Kari. She was dragged over a bump—the threshold—and the door slammed shut. The man released her, and Kari slumped to the floor. She heard Vivianne wheezing beside her.

"We…we're…we're safe…" she said between breaths.

Her eyes were too swollen and watery to see much more than blurry colors: the smatter of brown impeded by the clash of dark mopped over an oval of off-white.

"Well," the man breathed, "that was exciting. Welcome to the Weary Traveler, girls."

CHAPTER SEVENTEEN

It took several minutes for Vivianne to catch her breath, during which other sounds came to Kari's ears. She heard the vague chatter of numerous people, whispering under their breath. Chairs scraped as their occupants moved, though no footsteps approached. The *clunk* of glasses on wood signaled drinking.

Though her throat throbbed, she refrained from coughing. Her breaths came shallow and unsteady.

Beside her, Vivianne shifted.

"I'll help ya move her, miss. There's a chair against the wall."

"She's a demon," Vivianne whispered. Kari's heart hammered so hard, she was sure everyone in the room would hear it.

"Customer's a customer," the man grunted. "'Sides, I expect that thing out there was more dangerous than you two."

Kari stiffened as the man hefted her to her feet. Vivianne—appearing as a blur of soft browns and tans—grabbed her hand.

"We're okay." She said it like a prayer. Kari closed her eyes.

She was plopped into a wooden chair. It was stiff and hard against her back, but at least she wasn't on the floor anymore.

"I'll get some water," the man mumbled, walking away with a creaking of wood.

Kari tried to swallow; it felt like her throat worked around a dozen knives.

"Just wait," Vivianne murmured. "I'm so sorry, Kari. I didn't know what else to do. Violet ivy repels demons, so I thought it must work." She bowed her head, resting it on Kari's shoulder. "I'm sorry. It must have been horrible."

With eyes burning and throat full of blazing daggers, Kari could have screamed. *Horrible* did not begin to describe it.

She leaned her head against Vivianne's, only to straighten as footsteps approached.

"Here you go."

A wooden cup was pushed into her hand. Kari eagerly tossed back a mouthful. Water, crisp and cold, doused her tongue and throat. Swallowing brought the flavor of sour mold and decay to the tip of her tongue, but her throat was soothed. Sighing, she splashed the rest of the water onto her face and rubbed her eyes.

"Gods," she groaned. Her voice rasped as the walls of her throat scraped together. She winced.

"Don't talk for a bit," the man suggested. "That stuff's potent. 'Swhy I put it out there."

Vivianne took the cup from Kari and handed it back to the man. "Thank you, Mister…"

"Adolphys Dunbar. I own this tavern." He stood. "I'll get more water. And food, too."

"Thank you."

Kari blinked the water out of her eyes. Her vision returned, revealing a low-ceilinged, hazy room full of tables and chairs…and humans. A dozen or so.

The chair dug into Kari's back. "Viv…"

"I know. We're safe here. Trust me."

She tried to steady herself, but her breaths came out as hard puffs. She gripped the edges of her chair, her claws digging into the wood as Adolphys returned. He was a tall, lean man with a mop of dark brown hair, the bangs sweeping his brows. He studied her with a similar level of wariness.

"There's a table, if you two'd like to sit for a bit."

"Please," Vivianne breathed. "I have money."

Adolphys nodded, beckoning with a hand as he turned away. Kari glanced at Vivianne, then stood and followed him. They walked around the edge of the tables, the eyes of every patron glued to them. At the opposite end of the room, Adolphys stopped at a small, empty table sat with two steaming bowls of soup, two cups, and a flagon of water.

"No one'll bother you, 'slong as you don't bother them."

"We won't," Vivianne promised. She fished in her bag, finally withdrawing a small pile of silver coins. "Can we stay a night?"

Kari clenched her teeth. "What about that thing?"

Adolphys shook his head. "The ivy will keep it out, guaranteed."

Kari wasn't convinced, but Vivianne handed him the money. With a tilt of his head, Adolphys meandered away, leaving them in peace.

Vivianne took a seat, so Kari did too. She sat stiffly, fists on the table, and blinked too frequently.

"How long until the blurriness goes away?"

Vivianne's face scrunched as she frowned. "Shouldn't be very long."

Sighing, Kari looked down at the bowl in front of her. It was mostly white, with chunks of yellow, green, and brown floating in it. She tried to breathe in the aroma, but could only smell the scent of death and anguish.

"It's some type of vegetable and meat," Vivianne said helpfully. "Rabbit, I'd guess."

Kari nodded and ate a spoonful. It was thick, creamy, and hot, but tasteless. "Where are we?"

"The Weary Traveler is a tavern a ways east, off the main path. It doesn't get many patrons lately." Vivianne looked down at her soup, swirling her spoon in it. She dropped her head into a hand. "Gods, if it had been closed…"

If the tavern had been closed…they would be dead. That creature, whatever it was, meant business. And for whatever reason, it was intent on them.

Kari pushed away the thoughts of that beast—bulging, salivating monster that it was—and swallowed a mouthful of soup. Each spoonful soothed her throbbing throat. "Thank the gods it wasn't. You saved us."

Vivianne leaned over her bowl. "You, too! When you attacked, that was so brave, Kari."

"Not brave enough. My power…" She flexed her fingers. "That thing brushed it off like it was nothing," she whispered.

Vivianne grabbed her hand. "Let's agree that we both did what we could. I mean, I suffocated you."

Kari exhaled through her nose. Vivianne grinned and resumed eating her soup.

"What is that stuff? I've never heard of anything like that. My parents only warned me about the blessed power."

Vivianne looked up. "Violet ivy. It's a plant founded on Kestos hundreds of years ago. I don't think it ever grows on Taris. The people here have to buy what they can." She took a drink of water.

"Your…foul, yellow powder was the same as those vines outside?"

"Yes." Vivianne scraped the last of the chunks of meat out of her bowl. "But mine is more concentrated. I don't know how Adolphys got violet ivy to grow out here, but that's what keeps this place standing."

Kari tapped her spoon against the bottom of her bowl. "Will it keep that thing out? And what about when we have to leave?"

"It wouldn't come near the ivy. As soon as we crossed, that beast backed away." Vivianne pushed her bowl to the edge of the table. "I plan to ask around tonight and before we leave, see if anyone knows about what that was and what it's doing here. With luck, someone will know a safe route to Angel Cross."

Kari lifted her bowl and drained it before stacking it on Vivianne's. "You really think it wasn't a demon of some kind?"

Vivianne tapped a finger on the table. "I...I don't know. It didn't react to my ivy bombs like a demon, but it hates the pure ivy..." She sat back and crossed her arms. "You remember you were asking me about Yutemi?"

Kari nodded.

"In the legends about demons, the ones that say demon souls came straight from Yutemi, there are ancient reports written by the first holy men of the time." She unraveled and clasped her hands on the table in front of her. "The first demons, it's said, weren't human *or* demon. They were something in between. Part of me wonders... maybe...if that was one of those. A proto-demon."

A chill doused the air between them. "Is that possible? For one to live for so long?"

Vivianne's shoulders slumped. "If you'd asked me that yesterday, I would have said no. Now, I'm not so sure." She drained her water. "It isn't as if one could just come from nowhere. It had to be born or made."

Kari swirled her own water. A proto-demon. Maybe that was why it was so much stronger than her; if it was a first-generation demon, it surely had strength she couldn't fathom.

Vivianne tapped her hand, drawing her eye. She smiled. "Let's go to bed. We'll think more clearly after a nice rest."

Kari nodded. They stood and rounded the tables again. The door to the rooms was in the corner opposite.

Keeping her head low, Kari followed Vivianne. The room had quieted some since they arrived, but she still felt plenty of eyes on her. Even so, no one leapt out at her or shouted curses. She and Vivianne made it to the other end of the room without issue. They faced a hallway lined with doors.

Vivianne paused at the threshold and faced Kari. "I don't suppose you'd know anyone here, would you?"

Kari blinked. "No. I lived in Snow Shade my entire life. And… none of those people would come this far south. Why?"

Vivianne's eyes darted to the side. "There's a woman. She's in the center of the room, seated by herself. Her hair is so bright red, its hard to miss her. She's watched us since we sat down."

Kari followed Vivianne's glance. She hadn't bothered to look at the humans in the tavern, but now she saw them: gruff, bearded, thick-shouldered men took up most of the room. The few women were bony and long-faced with straw-colored hair.

Except for one, a woman in a brown cloak. She leaned back in her chair, perfectly balancing on its back legs. Her hair was a bright shade of red, like the core of a fire. And her eyes…

Kari's stomach dropped. The woman's eyes, an odd golden color, were locked on her. When their gazes met, the woman's lips curled. Despite the heated glow in her eyes, Kari felt cold.

"Let's…let's go," she grunted.

Vivianne ducked down the hallway. Tearing her gaze from the scarlet-headed and yellow-eyed woman, Kari followed.

CHAPTER EIGHTEEN

The only unlocked door was at the end of the hall. Vivianne pushed the door open, revealing a small, square room with a single bed, a short table topped with a stubby candle, and a rickety rocking chair.

Vivianne dropped her bag beside the door and propped her fists on her hips. "The bed isn't quite big enough for both of us. I'm used to sleeping on the ground—"

"I don't need the bed, either," Kari argued. "If it wasn't for you, we wouldn't even be here."

Vivianne shook her head. "Agree to disagree." She crossed the room and lit the candle. It flared, reminding Kari of the red-haired woman in the main room.

Who was she? Kari had never seen anyone like her before, but the way she watched them—and smiled—was reminiscent of hunter spotting prey. Her eyes, strangely yellow, reminded Kari of that woman, Miss Kiean, who came to Snow Shade to lecture them on magic. Her own magic had made her eyes an unnatural color. Did that mean the woman in the bar was a magic user, too?

Kari closed her eyes. And what about the purple-skinned monster? What if it waited for them outside, right now? What if it watched them through the windows?

She moved to the window against the back wall and folded her arms over her chest. The panes reflected her own face amid a sea of obsidian glass.

"Are you okay?"

Kneeling beside her bag, Vivianne watched her.

Reluctant to turn her back on the window, Kari slid to the side and pressed her back against the wall beside it. "On edge," she admitted quietly.

Vivianne's eyes softened. She stood, a large tome in hand, and sat on the bed. "Join me."

Kari dropped down beside her, hands braced on her knees. Vivianne cracked her book open with a sly smile.

"I'm going to tell you the story of Tabias and Vitro, two friends who defied all odds."

A burst of reluctant laughter expelled from Kari's lips. "How did they do that?"

"They were a human and a demon who, despite their many differences and the disapproval of their families, remained good friends."

Kari rolled her eyes. "I see where this is going."

"Hush, and listen." Vivianne cleared her throat and held up her book. She began to read, describing in great detail the story of a young boy who set traps every day, hoping to catch a juicy rabbit to feed his family. One day, he found something much larger struggling in his hanging net: a demon with mottled skin and wings too small to function.

"The demon was very irate at having been caught," Vivianne explained. "And thrashed wildly, cursing so loudly Tabias was fearful that other humans would hear him. 'Quiet down!' he told the demon, who responded by cursing."

160

Kari sniggered. She'd leaned her head against Vivianne's shoulder, her eyes closed. Though anxiety laced her bones and made her edgy, exhaustion had begun to drape over her like a blanket.

The page crackled as Vivianne turned it.

"After some time, Tabias cut the demon free. He was speechless, and stunned, when Tabias offered his name. 'I'm Vitro,' the demon grumbled. He was not pleased to have been caught by a human trap, but secretly found Tabias quite nice. The thought warmed him—"

"Is this story even true?" Kari mumbled. Vivianne's words had begun to blur into images in Kari's mind; she imagined a short human boy, standing over a grumpy-faced demon sitting on the ground.

"Of course it is!"

Kari smiled, and Vivianne continued her story. Tabias and Vitro visited again, but one day, Tabias was accosted by a starving bear. Kari's heartbeat quickened at this point in the story, wondering what would happen next, before her uneasy mind softened into dreams.

The sun's rays flashed between tree branches outside the window that Kari hadn't been able to see the night before. She groaned, throwing an arm over her face. Then she shot up.

When had she fallen asleep?

She scanned the room for Vivianne, already annoyed that she failed to insist they sleep in relative discomfort together.

The young, traveling story-teller was in the rocking chair, legs drawn up and arms draped over her large bag. The position must have been horrendously uncomfortable, but her face was peaceful, her snores quiet and calm.

Kari shook her head and threw her legs over the edge of the bed. The floor creaked as she stood. "Morning, Viv."

Vivianne shifted, rubbing her face in her bag. She sat up and rubbed her eyes with her fingers. "Did you sleep well?"

"Better than you, I bet."

Vivianne smiled as she climbed out of the chair. She stretched, arching her back. "You needed that more than me, my friend."

Kari shook her head. "Let's get some food and information. I want to know if that thing is going to be waiting for us."

Vivianne sobered. "Me, too. Let's go."

She grabbed her bag and followed Kari out into the hallway. A steady but gentle chatter came from the main room. What if the redhead was out there still? Kari had no idea how the woman would know her, but the way she watched them had been chilling.

Kari managed to keep walking. Adolphys had said no one would bother them here. She had no choice but to believe him.

As they stepped into the main room, her fears dissolved: there were only a handful of people, and none of them had red hair. As relief loosened the tension in her shoulders, Vivianne drew a sharp breath.

"Nic! Tom! Kari, I have some friends over here."

Kari quirked a brow at the two men who stood by the bar. They turned as Viv called their names, and waved. They were disheveled and dirty, their faces barely clear of grime. Their patchy clothes smelled of body odor so much, Kari didn't even connect with the realization that her sense of smell had returned.

"Viv!" called one. He was missing several teeth. "Who knew you'd be at this fine establishment!"

Adolphys stood on the other side of the bar, hands braced on the counter. "I suppose you two'll want some oats."

"Please," Vivianne said. "And I'll pay for these two, as well."

"That's kind of yeh," said the other man.

Vivianne beamed. "Kari, this Nic and Tom." She gestured at them; Tom was the man missing teeth. While Nic had his teeth intact, his hair was thin and ash-colored, as if he were much older than his smooth skin depicted. "I see them now and then when I travel Taris. They're…"

"Nomadic," said Tom. "We live off the grace of the land." He nudged Nic. "Been awhile since we seen a demon up close, eh, Nic? Usually they dead when we do."

Kari's jaw clenched. Adolphys reappeared, followed by a short woman with shoulder-length hair. They dropped off four bowls of steaming oats. Vivianne handed over more coins, which the tavern owner took with a nod before following the woman away.

"Thanks so much, Viv," Nic sighed happily as he took a bowl.

"It's nothing," Vivianne said with a smile. She handed Kari a bowl. There was a smattering of brown dust and a dollop of golden honey atop a bed of grayish white slop.

"Though I do have a favor to ask," Vivianne continued as she turned to Tom and Nic. "I wondered if you two had seen a...demon of sorts around?"

Kari paused in scooping oatmeal.

"Funny you ask," Tom mumbled, his mouth full. "This mornin', we passed some camps we frequent." He looked to Nic. "They was all dead, right Nic?"

Nic nodded. "'E's right, Viv. 'Cept one. Said they was attacked by a big monster in the night."

"Mutant, they called it," Tom added.

"Right. We hurried off right quick, just in case. Came here."

Vivianne's hands tightened around her bowl. "That's horrible."

Nic scraped oatmeal into his mouth. "Tha's the risk of livin' out here, eh?"

Kari's heart clenched at such frankness.

Vivianne bowed her head. "It is dangerous. Which direction did you two come from?"

"West," Tom answered, as Nic's cheeks bulged with oats. "You usually head south, dontcha?"

"Yes. And this time is no different. I must make it to Angel Cross."

Tom's brow drew together. "You sure you gonna keep on, Viv? I tell ya, the way that camp looked…"

"Yes," Vivianne interrupted with a smile. "My destination is south."

Nic shook his head of dirty, ash-colored hair. "Leas'ways, ya gotta demon to keep ya safe, eh?"

He smiled at Kari. She managed a grimace, recalling the way that thing had withstood her electricity as if it were nothing.

"We thank yus for the food and all," Tom said as he returned his empty bowl, practically licked clean, to the counter. "Mighty kind of ya."

"It's nothing, for all you two have done for me."

"Be careful, Viv," Nic said, patting her arm. He and Tom turned to leave. Kari watched as the two men exited the tavern, the door creaking shut behind them.

So the demon, or whatever it was, had gone west. Vivianne laid her bowl on the counter, mostly untouched.

"I won't ask you to come with me—"

"Of course I'm coming," Kari said quickly. "I'm not scared of whatever that thing is."

Vivianne gave her a smile that shrank a little when Adolphys reappeared.

"If it calms any fears, that thing hasn't been seen all morning. Since you two got here, actually."

Kari's brow knitted. Why did it follow them so intently if it was just going to go somewhere else?

"That does ease a little, thank you," Vivianne said graciously. "Perhaps if we make haste, we won't need to fear."

Adolphys gathered the bowls. Kari handed him her empty one.

"I'd offer you a horse, but mine don't take too kindly to demons." He raised his brows at Kari. "Instead, I'll allow you a snip of my ivy."

164

"That would be extremely gracious of you, sir," Vivianne said. "Thank you so much!"

As Adolphys headed outside, Vivianne tossed her large pack over her shoulders.

"Well, Kari...if you're sure you'll stay with me—"

"Of course I am," Kari insisted. She wouldn't leave Vivianne's side just because she was scared of some maybe-demon.

Next time, I'll call the lightning again. That will be strong enough to stop it. I know it.

 Chapter Nineteen

Outside, Kari covered her nose with her shirt. It wasn't quite enough to dispel the scent of the ivy, but she closed her eyes and followed the sound of Vivianne's footsteps.

After Adolphys had bagged a few cuttings of ivy, and Vivianne tied them to her waist, he helped Kari step over the ivy that made an ankle-high wall around his tavern.

"I expect you two know by now to be careful and make haste."

Vivianne nodded. "Thank you so much for taking us in for the night."

Adolphys waved a hand and faced the tavern. "Send people my way, eh? Been short on coin lately."

"I will spread the greatness of your service far and wide," Vivianne said graciously.

Kari shifted her weight. Finally, Vivianne joined her and guided her away. After a few dozen feet, Kari finally dropped her shirt and breathed in deep. Except for the faint smell wafting from the bag at Vivianne's belt, the air was clear.

"I hope I never smell that again," Kari sighed.

Vivianne chuckled. "With luck, you won't."

They walked miles west, nearing the main path again before resuming their journey south. As night fell, they found some shelter under some large, thickly clustered trees. When Vivianne piled some wood together, Kari stepped forward.

"I want to light the fire this time."

Vivianne watched her, a glint of understanding in her eye. "That would be very helpful. I need to skin the rabbits."

As she turned away, lightning danced at Kari's fingertips. How easy it came to her, her power. She'd trained for years with Kiki for this control. She wouldn't let that purple beast best her again. This time, she would protect her friend.

She held her hands over the pile of dry wood. After a tingling moment, tiny bolts flitted free to tease the wood with light touches. Kari gritted her teeth and called for more electricity. It welled inside of her and burst, releasing arcs of lightning that bounded in several directions before she could recall it.

Most of the bright yellow streaks scattered into open air, dissipating into the atmosphere, but one struck a patch of grass and caught flame. With a hiss, Kari leapt to her feet and stomped on it, burning through the soles of her ragged leather shoes. An angry growl escaped. Eventually, the dry dirt and grass were fire-free, if blackened.

When she turned back to Vivianne, she smiled softly as she placed a freshly skinned rabbit on a nearby rock.

Determined to show she could do it, Kari moved back to the pile of wood to try again.

"Where did you learn it?" Vivianne asked. "It isn't magic, is it? Demons cannot—"

"It's not magic," Kari mumbled. "And I could do it since I was born. It's easier…"

The human's bright eyes watched her expectantly. "Easier…?"

A spark flit off Kari's fingers, and she clenched her fists to cut off its power. "I practiced for many years, and I got better, but it's always been easier when I am in my wolf form." Kari hesitated a breath before continuing, "My father did not approve. He and my mother rarely shifted from their wolf forms. My father always said the lightning was rare, dangerous, and something I ought not to have."

Vivianne nodded. "It *can* be dangerous. Lightning is the wildest of the elements, a branch of fire. It's strong-willed and flashy, but powerful." Moving beside Kari, she couldn't contain a grin as she added, "Like you."

The flames Kari produced lit up the darkness creeping around them.

A beat of silence passed. Vivianne asked, "Where are your mother and father?"

Kari looked at her, thinking about the other times she had revealed her past—once, to Kiki, and a second time to Joseph and Anne before she killed them. Who better to hear her story than someone who collected stories for a living?

After spearing some of the rabbits and leaning them over the flickering flames, Kari leaned back. "They died. More than five years ago now."

Something akin to pity flit across Vivianne's face, but she quickly masked it with a smooth, saddened interest.

"What happened?"

As she had told Kiki, Kari told Vivianne. The adult humans had come to find their cave, their numbers, and weapons, only an additional hindrance to the suddenness of their appearance. They took Kari home with them, mistaking her for a human girl. She stayed with them rather than fight and die, as her mother had wished, all the while hoping for a time to avenge her parents. She trailed off as she approached the part where she *did* kill them.

Vivianne looked at her, a different expression in her eyes. "Human or demon, no one deserves to have their parents taken from them. I...I probably would've wanted revenge."

Kari's chest burned with an emotion she couldn't explain. She opened her mouth to reply but froze when her ear flicked, catching an odd sound. The crunching of grass and dirt underfoot.

She swung her head around and bared her teeth at the darkness, a low growl settling in her throat.

"What is it?" Vivianne whispered.

Before Kari could reply, a tall form of bright colors appeared out of the night. Crimson faded into yellow and orange, shimmering around exposed knees and thighs in golden, sheer cloth. Waves of red hair framed eyes that burned like coals.

A human, a woman, who's yellow eyes made Kari's skin crawl.

She jumped to her feet. "You!"

It was the woman from the tavern, the one who had watched them. She entered their camp, appearing to float. Straight-backed, with more confidence than even the most arrogant soldier. She smelled of smoke and ash, as if she'd just left the scene of a bonfire. Kari wrinkled her nose.

Vivianne stood, too. A gentle touch on Kari's wrist made her breathe.

"Hello," Vivianne said, managing to sound cheerful rather than surprised. "You were at the Weary Traveler as well, weren't you?"

"Indeed, I was," the woman said with a slight smile. "I'd stopped in the area, hearing about a creature troubling the people here. I saw none...instead, I found you."

A lilt in her voice made Kari's throat tighten. Those coal-like eyes flicked to her.

"Do you know us?" Vivianne asked. "I have traveled far and wide, and—"

The woman flung out her hands, and flames leapt free. Kari jumped up, heart pounding.

Magic! Fire…fire witch!

"Hey!" Vivianne shouted.

"Why are you with this demon?" the woman's voice hissed from within the crackling blaze.

Kari's legs twitched, trembled. The fire enclosed them in a wide circle before she could think to run, rising well above their heads.

"What are you doing?!" Vivianne demanded.

"I asked a question. This demon—are you waiting to kill it?"

The heat around them made it hard to breathe. Kari's lungs fought to pull in air, her eyes wild.

"No! She's my friend!"

The woman laughed, too cold a sound for someone who controlled magic flames. "How odd, but no matter. I have seen demon wiles befall many men. All the better that I am here to rescue you from this one."

Kari couldn't move or think as the Fire Witch raised her hands. Sweat dripped from her forehead and down her neck. Heat stifled her thoughts. Her gasps came out haggard.

Dimly, sparks flickered at her fingertips.

I can't let her kill me.

Just like that demon…like those men at Briar's Glen.

A rustle of clothes and a swish of hair—Vivianne leapt between them, arms thrown out.

"No!" Even standing so strong and tall, her voice quivered. "If you try to kill her, I will do whatever I can to stop you."

Kari's stomach flipped. "Viv…Vivianne, don't," she gasped.

To her shock, the Fire Witch lowered her arms. "Who are you?"

"Vivianne Coreum. If you are a mage trained in Glimmer View, I went there once."

"Why are you with this demon?"

170

"I told you. She's my friend."

A line in the Fire Witch's jaw ticked. "Do you have any idea? This demon is dangerous. Beyond others. She is—"

"You're wrong," Vivianne said, her voice low. "I've traveled with her for days now. Whatever you think she is, you're wrong."

With a shrug of loose shoulders, the ring of fire died to embers. "Very well. I have made a pact to not hurt fellow humans. If you will stand beside *this* demon, though, your life is forfeit. Remember that I offered this kindness."

Kari's ears twitched. *This* demon?

Vivianne lowered her arms, hands balled into fists. "Just leave."

The Fire Witch looked to Kari. Their eyes met, and Kari's chest ached with fear. Such hatred, and for what? Kari didn't know this woman.

"Remember this face and the heat of my flames. I will be the one to snuff out your life."

With a swish of smoke and fiery cloth, the woman disappeared. Vivianne waved a hand through the air, coughing, then gasped.

"The rabbits!"

She scrambled to remove the burning meat from the fire. Kari watched her dazedly, brow furrowing.

"I don't understand."

Vivianne laid the blackened rabbits on the grass and looked up at her.

"She was a fanatic, Kari. They exist here and there, and especially in Glimmer View. Their goal is to eradicate all demons." She shook her head. "A worthless task. Forget her. Sit with me, and let's eat."

Kari shook herself and obeyed. Though the rabbit was charred black, she barely tasted it.

She didn't know how the Fire Witch knew about her—had she seen her attack the guards at Briar's Glen, perhaps?—but she had seemed too calm to be called *fanatic*. It was as if she had come looking for Kari specifically.

CHAPTER TWENTY

Kari didn't relax until sunlight rose over their heads the next morning. Even Vivianne's attempts at conversation went nowhere; Kari could only think of the Fire Witch, and how Vivianne had said she was likely a hunter of demons. That didn't surprise Kari; she knew the main reason humans learned magic was to fight off demons.

What bothered her was how the Fire Witch seemed to know her.

At midday, they stopped to eat the last of their rabbits. As Vivianne cooked them, she looked up at Kari. Her eyes, so bright and carefree, were filled with excitement. She appeared determined to forget the night before, so Kari would try to do the same.

"We're almost there." Vivianne gestured to the mountain range to the west. "Those mountains are my landmark. We should be less than a week from Angel Cross now!"

The mountains were much clearer now, and Kari could see they curved, blocking off an entire area of land. What would be beyond them?

Vivianne stamped out the fire and handed Kari her share of lunch. "I have something to tell you, though," she said, her voice hesitant.

"What?"

"Angel Cross is an ancient town. They've been around for a long, long time. In fact, the first stories of the demon rising came from the people there." She sighed and continued, "Point is...well...they don't allow demons inside."

Kari's tail twitched. She wasn't bothered, she told herself. Demons weren't allowed in most places.

Vivianne waved her hand. "My business there is short, a week or two at most. If you wait outside town, I can visit between my workdays. And you can come with me on my travels, if you want."

"Yeah, alright."

As they walked, Vivianne excitedly told her about Angel Cross; every detail of every building, the history, and the people that helped her glue her books together. Kari was disappointed she wouldn't be able to see it in person.

The next day, they ventured around a rectangular field of tall, yellow grass with a pointed building in the center. "It's sacred ground, of a sort," Vivianne explained. "I've never felt comfortable walking in there."

Kari didn't disagree. The grass was stiff, and hard, and would have been no joy to walk through.

Their wide path took them closer to the mountains. Kari's nightmares returned, more vivid and mysterious than before. She dreamt less of Kiki and more of the field under a thunderous sky, but now the grass was dark with blood.

Vivianne tried to appease her night-terrors with more stories, but Kari was past the point of help. She cried and whimpered in her sleep as she dreamt of Kiki, the death of her parents, and the field of bloody grass.

During the days, Kari took to studying Vivianne's map. She enjoyed looking at it, noting discrepancies from Snow Shade. There were more villages in the south than she had been told, as well as a long, winding river that separated the eastern edge of the continent from the west. The northeastern corner of the map drew her eye; detailed there was a desert, the sands depicted with yellow, wavy lines. In Snow Shade, that part of the map portrayed lush land.

"What about this?" she asked Vivianne, pointing to the north-eastern corner. "Is it truly yellow land like this?"

Vivianne pursed her lips. "Yes. The woman who told me the story of Nagaris came from this desert, back when it was a jungle. No one knows why the land died, and no one is alive now to remember what it was. Except her, I suppose."

Kari frowned and turned her attention instead to the Demon Sea that separated Kestos from Taris. Might she be crossing that sea at Vivianne's side soon?

As they walked, Kari tried to keep tabs on their location with the map. Except for the field of yellow grass, though, there were no landmarks by which to judge one's position. Instead, a few times a day, she would hold out the map and ask Vivianne their location. She never tired of pointing.

"Around here," she'd say. "We're close now."

The mountains that covered the land to their right also took up a large portion of the map, curving around the depiction of a thick forest and man-made structures. Kari paused in tracing the mountain peaks with a claw. She squinted at them, trying to read the tiny scribbles that labeled what was there.

A forest in the south.

"What is it, Kari?"

She held out the map. "What's in there?"

"Raziac Village. That's where it's said The Fracturing happened. But it's been some time since I've been there."

"What's it like?"

Vivianne tapped her lip with a finger. "Well…the village is secluded, but Lord Izulu—Alton—is very kind. Outsiders are generally welcome. I've even heard of some demons passing through harmlessly. They're surrounded by that massive forest, which has its own air of mystery and danger, if you listen to the tales. Demons hide there, as well."

"Demons?" Kari scowled at the map. Mother had not confirmed that Zina was a demon, but she could not be human to live in a forest like that. Unless…she was in the village?

"Yes. The village has a fair fighting force, and they rather pride themselves on their demon hunting."

Kari grimaced. "When did you last go?"

"A few years. I stop by to meet Lord Alton. We share notes on mysteries." Vivianne smiled. "He is a kind, curious man. And fair."

"What about…a woman. Named Zina?"

Vivianne cocked her head, thoughtful. "The name doesn't sound familiar…of course, it has been years since I've been back. Is Zina a friend of yours?"

Kari bit her lip. "I've never met her. My mother told me to find her in a forest in the south."

"If you'd like to, we can stop by before we hit Snake Bay. Lord Alton was always cordial, even with demons. And it's been too long since I've gone to Raziac Forest. For someone like me, that place is truly something to behold."

The sixth day after the Fire Witch's attack, the sight of spiked, wooden walls was clearly in their sights. When Kari pointed them out, Vivianne squinted, smiled, and quickened her pace.

"It's there!" she said. "If we hurry, we might reach it tomorrow night!"

Kari started to grin, but it faltered as the silhouette of something thick, tall, and bulky appeared on the hill before them. It was humanoid in appearance, bipedal and muscular, but too large and ungainly to be a human.

Vivianne slowed to a walk before stopping. Kari stood beside her. The shape was familiar, but the angle of sunlight obscured any obvious features.

Vivianne was the first to react. She reached for the bag at her waist, the ivy from Adolphys. "Kari—"

She cut off in a gasp of panic as the thing lurched onto all fours and bounded down the hill at them. Kari's mind blurred, but her body reacted automatically: she jumped to intercept the beast, her claws sparking with lightning.

The purple-skinned monster was different, she thought vaguely: its arms longer and threaded with thick, dark red veins. Its eyes popped. The elongated mouth was the only thing the same, yet it offered no comfort: the sight of a hundred black, jagged teeth made Kari's fear spike to mind-numbing levels.

Kari glanced back at Vivianne. She'd gotten the ivy out, and a knife.

Something thick and heavy slammed into Kari's chest, throwing her aside. The breath left her lungs in one smooth motion. As she hit the ground and rolled over the hard earth, she gasped before jumping to her feet again. The beast barreled past her, heading straight for Vivianne.

"Kill you!" the mutation shouted, its voice garbled and deep.

"Kari!" Vivianne shouted, her voice high. She had thrown her bag aside. In one hand, she held a knife; in the other, the ivy. The smell of it seared Kari's nostrils. The creature hesitated, snarling.

Kari roared and ran, tackling the beast from the side. She dug her claws and teeth deep into its broad back, tasting blood. Electricity sparked at her call.

Work. Work this time!

The beast let out an annoyed sound before plucking Kari off and tossing her aside. She flew several feet and landed on the ground again with a huff. Before she could draw breath, the monster was on her, pinning her to the earth with one hand around her throat.

Kari grabbed its wrist. Electricity flared, but the sparks were tepid and few. The monster leaned closer, opening its maw to reveal rows of sharp, black teeth dripping with dark saliva.

"Wolf demon," it grunted. "Take you. Yes."

"Let me go!" Kari screamed. Her body throbbed, demanding she not move. Something was broken, and she willed it to heal. Lightning crackled around her hands, crisping the grass around her.

Footsteps staggered closer, and the familiar, acrid aroma burned her throat.

The beast let out a roar of outrage. It released Kari and spun around to Vivianne; her blade dipped in sticky blood. The ivy was wrapped around the knuckles of her other hand, like a horrible travesty of a glove. She swung her fist at the creature; it shied away, baring its teeth.

Kari froze, slack-jawed, at the sight of Vivianne standing there. The monster lunged at Vivianne. Vivianne swept her blade, catching a scrap of flesh. The beast danced back with a snarl.

Kari moved, jogging, ignoring the burn of her ribs. *I can help. I have to help.*

Her body screamed as she lunged. Her claws struck the creature's face, tearing through flesh and something much slimier than blood. The beast screamed, throwing its head back and revealing the bloody hole where its eye had been.

"Kari, run!" Vivianne grabbed Kari's wrist and tugged her along. The ivy irritated her skin.

"Your bag!"

"Forget it! Make it to town!"

They ran, their feed pounding the ground. Kari's breath burned in her chest, made worse by the ivy so nearby. Her body throbbed with agony. She staggered, her feet slipping.

With a frustrated grunt, Kari ripped free of Vivianne's grip. "Leave me!"

Vivianne faced her. "No! I won't—"

Her eyes widened, and Kari spun as the purple-skinned monster tackled her again. She hit the ground hard, the breath forced from her lungs. Pain blinded her as agony tore through her core.

One of its long-fingered hands pressed against her stomach, earning a pitiful whimper of pain. Blood dribbled from its empty socket and dripped onto Kari's shirt.

"Mistress…wants you…"

"What—"

Vivianne's hoarse scream rang in her ears. She swung her knife at the creature's back. The creature swung out a hand, and Vivianne flew out of sight.

"R-run!" Kari gasped. She grabbed the mutation's arms and squeezed her eyes shut.

Viv had to run. She could make it to Angel Cross. Kari didn't care about anything else, didn't care if this thing was going to kill her after it took her wherever it wanted to. As long as Vivianne…

Come on. Give me another bolt! I have to…

The beast gargled a laugh, slobbering and snarling. Kari's lightning surged through her body and went nowhere. Long, clawed fingers wrapped around her skull and squeezed until she released her grip to beat at the hand.

The beast leapt off her, leaving Kari to pant and wince. Her head pounded; her vision blurred—

An inhuman scream tore through the air; the sound more piercing than thunder could ever be. Kari shot up to see the beast hovering over Vivianne, holding down her arms with its own. Her dagger protruded from its neck, but that hadn't stopped it; its teeth, so sharp and jagged, were buried in her shoulder.

"NO!" Kari roared, her voice thundering. Her legs wobbled as she bounded the distance toward them.

The beast ripped free of Vivianne with a spray of blood, smiling over its shoulder. It stood, teeth dripping crimson.

Fury mashed with Kari's panic. With a cry that shook the earth, a snap of light erupted from the sky. A lurid bolt crashed into the purple beast with a fiery hiss.

The beast was thrown back, its roar guttural. Smoke drifted from the blackened flesh that had been its back, the smell abhorrent. As it pushed itself up to glare, Kari's body vibrated.

I'll…I'll…!

"Be back…get the wolf demon," it grunted before turning and fleeing.

Kari's chest heaved as she watched the mutation disappear into the distance, running on all fours like some hideous travesty of an animal. Her claws clenched, her eyes flashing red. The tingling, burning rage was in her gut, coursing and powerful, but it was too late to do any good.

A gurgling, pitiful whine interrupted her thoughts. She looked down at Vivianne and felt a stab of pain replace the anger. Vivianne's face, usually so carefree and peaceful, was distorted with pain. Blood flowed heavily between her fingers, staining the ground even as they pressed the wound. As Kari watched, she started to shake, her mind painting pictures of Kiki's face contorted with a similar agony.

"No!" Kari cried, dropping to the ground beside her. *Not again, not again.* "Wait, Viv! Wait!" she yelled, reaching for her bag, but they'd left it behind. Shock made her cold and numb.

Vivianne's other hand was cold, but the grip was strong around Kari's wrist.

"K-Kari." Her words came out in a garble, blood pooling out of her lips. "I-it's o-kay."

Kari's grip tightened on the leather back. She felt hot tears invade her eyes and she angrily wiped them away.

"T-take my…b-bag…to…"

"I will," Kari muttered hoarsely.

"Thank you." Vivianne's grip tightened on her wrist, her eyes welling with emotions and words she couldn't express. Kari bit back a sob and leaned over her.

Again, a friend had died. Would everyone she learned to love be taken from her?

She felt Vivianne's grip loosen. With a tiny, wet thud, her arm fell into the pool of blood around her body. Kari finally pulled away to see Vivianne's bright blue eyes, staring at the sky above them.

So like Kiki.

Ignoring her clothes as they ripped and fell away as tattered cloth, Kari shifted forms. She padded a fair distance away from Vivianne and started to dig.

It was well into evening when Kari deemed the hole large enough. She climbed out, shifted back into her now naked self, and carefully dragged Vivianne into it.

"Bye, Viv," she murmured before filling the hole again. Once nothing was left but a pile of dirt, Kari sat back, numb and sick.

What would she do now? All her new plans, so carefully laid out over the last few weeks, melted before her eyes. There would be no magical trip around the world, no companion to take her to see all these amazing sights.

Once Kari felt sufficiently cried out, her eyes puffed and red, she got up and made her way to Vivianne's bag. It lay flopped on its side where Viv had dropped it. Caked dirt and dewy grass fell away as Kari lifted it.

Her chest empty, Kari slowly removed everything that was not part of Vivianne's scribe work from the bag. If she could feel any pleasure at all, she might have been contented to find a few dried fruits, a fist's worth of old cheese, and even a couple sets of baggy clothes. She shoved it all into her own long-since-empty bag. The people of Angel Cross would need none of these things.

Deliberately slow, Kari pulled on a shirt and pants before closing Vivianne's bag and heaved it over her shoulder.

How close they had been. If only they had avoided the beast for a few more hours, then maybe Vivianne would have made it to town.

If only Kari had been strong enough to kill the mutation. Her chest tightened at the thought, restricting her breathing to gasping breaths. If she *had* made it in time to see Kiki, would the same have happened? Would she have been shunted aside as easily as a weakling child while her friend was murdered?

Though she longed to kill it, the beast did not reappear as Kari walked. She mounted the hill it had first appeared on, but only a vague, musty scent was left behind as proof of its presence. Its scent was neither human nor demon, just as Vivianne had said.

As Kari came out on level ground, she made out the wide front gate of Angel Cross beyond miles more of grasslands. She estimated she'd reach the town by morning if she walked all night.

Kari trudged along with Vivianne's pack. It felt much heavier, even with the things she had removed—how had Vivianne carried it for so long?—but she shouldered it. The night was quiet as if it were mourning Vivianne, too. Several hours passed, and pitch-black gave way to a dull dawn.

Kari came within shouting distance of Angel Cross as the sun crawled over the sky behind her. She paused, listening intently for any humans, but all was silent.

Staying low and quiet, Kari jogged closer. Tall grass faded into patches, then gravelly earth. She winced at every *crunch* her feet made. The gate wasn't very tall; it would be easy for someone to see or hear her. Luck, for once, was on Kari's side; she crept close and laid Vivianne's pack on the ground beside the gate.

Her hands trembled at the sight of it, crumpled and blood-stained, without its smiling owner. Lips twisting, she turned and ran from the town of Angel Cross.

Late midday, Kari stumbled to a stop, unable to stay awake any longer. She curled underneath a grouping of bushes and slept. When she awoke, grief clawing at her insides, she continued to walk.

Where would she go now? Thoughts of Snake Bay and Kestos across the sea occurred to her; perhaps she could find Lightglen, Vivianne's home. Though her heart twisted at the idea, someone had to find her family and tell them what happened to their daughter, right?

Kari reached for her bag before realizing Vivianne's map would not be in there; she had forgotten to grab it. Curling her fists, she was distracted from cursing herself by the harsh call of a bird flying overhead.

She looked up to see a massive hawk careening on the wind. It swooped, flapped its too-large wings, and disappeared over the western mountain peaks.

Raziac Forest and Village. She and Vivianne were to go there next, so Kari could see the mysterious forest. And, maybe, her mother's friend.

Lord Alton is fair, even with demons.

What else was left?

Kari turned west and headed toward the mountains.

CHAPTER TWENTY-ONE

Standing at the base of the mountain, the peaks reaching well into the sky, revealed a valley path. A well-worn dirt trail twisted through shadows by thick, crowded trees. Kari followed this to a massive lake. A river snaked away from her, disappearing into more trees. These were taller and denser, obscuring what lay beyond.

She'd grown around trees as a wolf, but these weren't pine like the ones on the northern mountains. The smell was damp rather than tart, and the leaves were numerous and supple, rustling in the slightest breeze. Heart thumping, she followed the path as it curved around the lake.

The clear-blue water glistened, and beneath the surface teemed groups of silver fish. Kari paused to get water but didn't bother to try to catch any food here; she had no desire to get wet.

She paused as she came to the next line of trees. Their branches were tangled, and underbrush crowded around the trunks, shrouding the area beyond the sunlight. Her eyes strained to see within the natural darkness of the forest, but soon she could make out every branch and leaf. She twitched her ears, listening intently, and heard nothing odd. Aside from the stray twitter of birds, the forest was quiet, seemingly empty.

Vivianne had said this place harbored demons, but Kari welcomed a fight.

She dove in, making her way through the maze of trunks. A new path carved a way through. She followed it, her ears tense. The river flowed to her left, peeking between trunks and bushes. Thick roots threatened to trip her, and low-hanging branches snagged at her clothes and hair. Her breaths soon came out hard, and her steps began to drag.

Occasional breaks in the tree branches allowed for a glimpse of sunlight, although it was hardly enough to guide her path. After hours of walking, she tiredly laughed at the idea of traversing this thick forest with Vivianne and her over-large pack.

Within the cover of the trees, bird song and the chatter of squirrels came together in an unlikely harmony. Rather than try to hunt them in such impossible terrain, Kari dug in her pack for what was left of her food and pondered what lay ahead.

What if Raziac Village changed since Vivianne had been there last? What if the people saw her and decided they would not stand for her barging into their home?

Her footsteps, already dragging, slowed even more at the possibility of another Briar's Glen. She didn't want to face more anger, and she didn't want to be provoked to hurt more people.

When Kari broke through a final line of bushes and came again to the full sight of the river ahead. A small bridge arched over it, leading the way to a final line of trees. Beyond them, she could see smoke and the shapes of buildings. The smell of human was pungent, but not altogether revolting.

Tentative steps carried her onward; she came to the trees, her breath held, and crossed through them.

Raziac Village was spacious, if only because things were spread out over flat land. Shops settled in the center; she could see the orange heat of the smith's furnace between buildings and smell the warm bread and raw meat of the baker and butcher. Smaller structures, likely the homes of the villagers, were settled against the eastern edge of town. In the west lay farmland, sprawling farther than she cared to look.

And the humans. There weren't many, but still more than Snow Shade's populace. Even with more space, they crowded, passing from building to building or pausing to chat in the middle of town. Kari stood frozen near the trees, refusing to go any closer.

Her time with Anne and Joseph taught her that humans feared demons. The guards of Briar's Glen had reinforced that thought, while her time with Kiki and Vivianne had countered this notion.

What kind of humans would these be?

She watched the town for a long time, wondering where to go. Where would the lord be? She needed to find him. Vivianne had said he would be cordial to her. Maybe he could help her.

Her first step within the boundaries of Raziac Village was not met with screams or yells. She took another, then one more, and soon she was cutting a path through town. Her feet carried her instinctually toward the smell of bread. She had no money, she realized, having failed to take with her whatever Vivianne had carried. Maybe they would at least start by pointing her in the direction of Lord Alton.

As Kari approached the door of the small bakery, her stomach quivered at the thought of fresh bread—perhaps she would be able to offer them something in exchange for a small bite.

Hot pain pierced her back. She fell against the door, catching herself on her hands, and let out a long, low hiss. Her hand trembled as it reached behind her and froze as she fingered the shaft of an arrow. Turning on the spot revealed half a dozen humans armed with bows, the tips of more arrows pointed at her.

Demon hunters, prideful warriors trained to kill things like her. At least their weapons, thankfully, didn't glow with the white light that would enable them to do more than pierce her flesh.

"You, demon! What are you doing here?!" one of the men yelled. He looked only a little older than her, but fiercer, with dark skin and thick eyebrows.

Instead of answering, Kari tried to grab the arrow; her claws could only tap the shaft, spreading the stinging pain. She ground her teeth, her chest tingling with anger, and wished sorely that it would fall out so she could heal.

She winced. Her head throbbed, and she froze as something clattered to the ground at her feet. She glanced down to see the arrow there, broken in two. Her skull pounded again, and the skin of her back began to itch as it pinched itself together.

A whistle of air signaled another arrow. Kari ducked, and it stabbed the door with a heavy *thuck*.

"Speak, beast!" the man roared again.

Kari shot a scowl at the man who had shot her. "I'm searching for your lord. I heard—"

"Ha! What could you want with our lord, demon? He has no time for hellspawn like you!"

Kari continued to glare at him, even as her insides turned to ice. "I'll leave."

She turned back to the forest and began to walk, wincing only a little as her muscles stretched around the healing arrow wound. Her heart and stomach ached, but there was nothing to it. She'd have to make another plan. Vivianne had been wrong; this place would not accept her.

The hunters were in her way. She curved around them as best as she could; as she passed by, the man who had spoken tackled her. The impact took the breath from her as they tumbled to the ground. The stench of his body odor filled her nose.

She struggled, reaching for his body, then hesitated. She didn't want to hurt him. Even as the thought rose, her insides tingled, and electricity sparked at her claws. Would his armor shred as easily as the men from Briar's Glen?

"Let...let me go," she growled as they grappled. "I don't want to—"

His arm slipped around her throat, cutting off her words in a choked gasp. His weight pressed her body into the ground, trapping one of her arms under her.

Hot, ragged breath brushed her ear. "You're not going anywhere. No demon has left here alive since I've joined the guard, and I plan to keep that record."

Kari writhed. His arm tightened against her throat, and her efforts doubled even as she fought to breathe. He grunted, holding her with everything he had, and pulled her neck back. She strained against him, gasping, and slapped at his arm with one hand. Her fingers curled, her claws scraping against his forearm. He hissed as she drew blood, but still did not release her.

"Let the girl go, Jarus," an older man's voice ordered from somewhere behind them. "The lord has ordered peace, even for demons who do no harm."

The lord!

"Al...Al..." Kari tried to gasp. The man squeezed, cutting her words off in a choke.

"Come on, Roland! We all know what treacherous creatures they are. Only last week one of our children was taken and eaten by them! Why risk it? I'm doing the world a favor by ridding us of this one."

Kari panicked, feeling the man's grip tighten even more in his anger. She felt so weak. Her vision popped with black spots, and finally, she called to the electricity inside of her. She wouldn't die, not like this.

She heard the thunder, and knew they did too; the guards gasped, and the man holding her stiffened. Sparks formed on her fingertips, flaring with the hot, determined anger that burned in her chest—she'd kill him and all the others if she must. She removed her hand from the man's arm and reached instead for his sides, where she knew his leather armor would not protect him.

A new voice, calm and yet loud enough to be heard by everyone, shattered through her anger.

"Release her at once, unless you are prepared to submit a formal hearing for the things she has done to this village. I doubt she has done anything to be judged by."

It was the voice of a young man, but the rumble of thunder quieted. The guard let go of Kari. She fell flat and crawled away, gasping for air, as the man stepped back.

Once the tingling anger was gone again, Kari looked up at the male who had called for her release. He was entirely unimpressive, barely even a man, with cropped dark red hair and lightly-tanned skin. His dark brown breeches and forest green tunic were of a fine make, much nicer than she had seen of the people here so far. Even his boots, though obviously worn, were finer than anything Kari had ever donned. She frowned at him, but he was busy talking to an older male with peppered-gray hair and dressed in fine white robes.

The boy finally turned and made his way over to her. He had a soft, kind face, with barely any youth left in his features. He extended a hand and smiled, ignoring her glare.

"Do you need help getting up? Don't worry. My men won't hurt you."

His men? This cannot be Lord Alton.

Kari scoffed, knocking his hand away before climbing to her feet and rubbing her throat. Who was this boy, and why did he interrupt his fellow humans in killing her?

He didn't so much as raise his eyebrows at her anger. "There's no need to be so jumpy. You can go if you'd like."

The boy stepped back from her. His men did the same, although they looked less happy about it.

"Why?" she rasped. "Why are you helping me?"

"Because I don't find it right that people hurt demons without good reason. I've been trying to spread the sentiment, but it's a hard lesson to learn." He tilted his head as he studied her. "What's your name?"

"Kari." She chewed her lip but finally managed to ask, "Are you Lord Alton?"

His soft expression finally changed; his brow scrunched, and his lips thinned. "No, miss. My name is Ari. Lord Alton was my father. He died a few years ago."

Kari felt her heart sink. Lord Alton was dead. What now?

"That seems to have shocked you. Did you know my father…?"

She shook her head. "No. A…friend told me he might be here and…" Kari trailed off. "Never mind. I'll leave now."

As she moved to step around him, Ari held out an arm to stop her.

"Please, wait. What did you come to see my father for?"

A tiny, longing part of her wished to confide in this boy lord. Her chest felt hollowed; so soon after Vivianne's death, she was not ready for another disappointment.

Two friends, two empty holes in my heart.

Before Kari could insist on leaving, her stomach let out a low rumble. Her face flushed with shame.

Ari glanced at the bakery behind her. "We can speak of my father and your friend later. Will you join me for lunch?"

She stuttered, her mouth refusing to form real words, as Ari gently guided her to the door. He frowned at the arrow protruding there, ripped it free, and tossed it aside before pulling the door open for her.

Inside the bakery, Ari walked to the counter. A tall, sturdy-looking man stood on the other side, his face red and shiny from the heat of the ovens. As she stopped to stand behind Ari, the baker lifted a tray of loaves onto the counter.

When the baker spoke his voice easily filled the room, as towering and strong as his figure.

"The regular order? I'll get it to you in a second." His face split into a huge grin as he added, "New lady friend?"

Kari felt a shock run through her at the grin and the tone. *Lady friend?* As in, what, a lover of sorts? Did this man not notice her ears?

Ari chuckled politely. "No, not at all. She's merely passing through. Thought I'd treat her to a quick meal."

The baker smiled knowingly. "Okay, give me a minute," he said, disappearing into a room somewhere behind the counter, leaving the two of them in complete silence.

Lord Alton isn't here. Viv hadn't said anything about anyone named Ari. Now what? No matter how nice this stupid boy is, I can't possibly stay here. Can I?

Kari felt her face burn. She turned around, ears twitching in agitation. Not a moment later, she felt a tap on her shoulder. She glanced over her shoulder to see Ari, his expression one of worry.

"Is that blood from one of my men?" he asked, his eyebrows knit together. "I saw the arrow on the door and figured they must have missed. Honestly, they're terrible shots."

Kari frowned, reaching for her back again. Her claws touched the dried blood around the hole in her ragged shirt, but she couldn't feel anything on her actual skin. The itching pain had stopped, and she'd forgotten about it.

"Yes."

Ari's lips tightened. "May I look at it?"

Kari's eyebrows shot up of their own accord.

Ari held up his hands. "Please. I'm well trained in medicine and healing."

Kari managed a sneer, thinking of Lord Isaac back in Snow Shade. Such a man would have never even considered touching one of his peasant's wounds. "You're a lord. Why would you dabble with medicine?"

"It is necessary to understand if one wants to remain alive. May I?"

She glared at him a moment longer. With a reluctant jerk of her shoulders, she turned her head back around.

His fingers, much too calloused for a lord's hands, were still gentle as they felt around where the wound had been. He traced the skin of her back with care, not prodding or poking, but feeling. His touch tingled, but not the way the fire in her chest did. It was lighter, sending electricity to her toes.

Kari's face warmed again. She pulled away, turned to him, and crossed her arms over her chest.

"Well?"

There was something amusing about him looking perturbed, his frown troubled and his brows almost touching. Before he could reply, the baker came back through the door holding a loaf of bread so large he had to hold it in his two beefy hands. It was golden brown, delicious smelling, and inlaid with seeds. Smiling, the baker handed it to Kari.

"Thank you, Gorth," Ari replied with a grin, dropping a few silver coins into the baker's hand and leading her to the door again.

"Thank you," she echoed to him, more for the appearance of manners than gratitude.

"It is no problem. If you need a place to stay, I have some bed space available. We could talk of my father, or—"

Kari shook her head, interrupting him. "Thanks for your help, but I hope that we won't ever have to cross paths again." Her voice choked a little as she blurted out, "It doesn't ever seem to end well."

As she turned to run back into the shadow of the forest, he grabbed her wrist. Like his inspection of her back, it was a gentle touch, not demanding or forceful.

"Wait—"

She spun and ripped away from him all the same. His eyes widened with what she assumed was fear.

"Leave me alone!"

She ran back across town. The hunters who guarded the village were gone, leaving an open path straight to the forest. She vanished into the confines of the trees and bushes, swearing to never see that human boy again.

Underneath a layer of exhaustion and grief, Kari was angry. Angry that those guards had attacked her and did not pay for it, angry that Kiki *and* Vivianne were gone forever, and angry that Lord Alton was gone. And most of all, she was furious that her heart itched to turn back around and to see the boy lord.

Ari.

He had been kind without real cause, and she would be lying if she tried to tell herself it hadn't felt pleasant.

She thrust the thoughts down and away. She was lonely, but that did not mean she should cling to every person who was ever nice to her—not that it was a long list.

She recalled the feel of his touch on her wrist and scoffed, forcibly shaking him from her mind. Tucking half the loaf into her slim pack, she lay down, her back against the tree.

Sleep it off. Her jumbled feelings were simply an after-effect of losing Vivianne so recently. It re-opened the not-so-old wound that Kiki's death had left behind. In time, Kari could be back to her old self again.

Just as lonely, just as miserable.

She growled, rubbing the heels of her palms into her eyes. When sleep took her, her mind was blessedly empty.

Kari walked a forest path, though not one made of wide, prickly pine. Instead, these trees were stockier and cramped, their branches tangling together as they grew out and up. The smell of them was different, too. Older, more earthen.

She walked not knowing her destination. Above the treetops, the sky thundered. The electricity was in the air, her energy. A storm was brewing, intense with a power no one could fathom. She could destroy towns, or fields, or even mountains, maybe. She was the master of it all. She was the one...

192

Kari blinked and found herself instead in the field of morthiem lilies. They waved daintily, prettily, uselessly. In the center of them stood Kiki. As Kari reached for her, the girl's head fell back, cut nearly in half. The blood gushed and Kari's throat seized, torn between a scream and a choking desire to vomit.

The dream slipped away as Kari opened her eyes. She rubbed her face, digging her fingers into her eyes.

She didn't want to see Kiki like that anymore. Would nightmares like these continue until she was driven mad?

Unease and sorrow twisted her insides. She forced herself to stand, to prepare for another day, but the quiet around her reminded her of her solitude.

Her eyes burned. She missed Mother, and Father, and her friends. How could her parents have lost to the humans? How could the two friends who smiled so warmly die so horribly? Kari gritted her teeth, trying to swallow around the tears in her throat.

Her mind again recalled Lord Ari. Like Kiki and Vivianne, he hadn't flinched at the sight of her. Despite what she was, he had welcomed her as they had.

She and Kiki had planned to leave Snow Shade and the northern mountains for a "normal" life. They would have gone anywhere and everywhere until they found a place where they could both be accepted. Kari twisted her hands together. She knew Kiki would have insisted they stay the night at least. Besides, she'd wanted to ask if anyone in the village knew who Zina was.

Kari sat and thought long and hard. When she finally climbed to her feet, she was resolved.

No. He was only being nice because I knew his father's name. He would not allow me to stay here. Look at his men, how they attacked me without question!

Kiki is not here now, and I'm better off alone.

The sky visible through the treetops began to darken, casting the forest in a murky, gloomy air. Kari walked nonstop, eyes and ears sharp for the lake and the trail that led out of the mountains. She suspected she had gotten turned around somewhere. She hadn't seen the river since leaving the village yesterday; in her haste, she had run right past it, rather than along it.

And now she was lost in Raziac Forest.

A rustling sound from the bushes behind made her tense. Turning to the source of the noise, Kari allowed electricity to run through her fingers.

After a lifetime of waiting, nothing happened. She called more lightning. Once it formed tiny arcs that bounced between her fingertips, she flicked them at the bushes. Bundles of green leaves caught flame. Nothing leapt free to attack her.

Kari grumbled, stomping the flames out before turning around and starting to walk again.

"Stupid squirrels..." she muttered seconds before she was tackled to the ground from behind. A breathless grunt left her lungs. She squirmed, trying to dislodge whatever was on her. It was heavy, its breath hot and stinking. She gagged as she tried to breathe.

"Finally found you," the creature said, and Kari stiffened, recognizing the voice. "Shadows said this way...but I looked all day..."

"You!" Kari hissed. It was the voice of the bruise-colored mutation, the one who had ripped out Vivianne's throat. Its smell wafted into her nose, the scent of old meat. "Get off of me!"

The creature shifted its weight, freeing her upper half. She roared and charged her body with electricity, but the creature only responded by growling.

"Bring...the wolf demon...Mistress wants you. Come. Or..."

Without warning, Kari felt the sharpness of something dig into her shoulder. She screamed as long, sharp teeth crunched through her flesh and into the bone beneath.

Her blood was hot as it dripped off her shoulder. Kari's scream became a roar as more lightning crackled off her skin. The creature tensed, breathing deeply, and released its hold on her shoulder.

"Wolf demon," it said again in its deep, gravelly voice. "Come to Mistress."

"I don't know your mistress!" Kari roared. "You...you killed Vivianne!"

The creature's claws dug into her back. "Human. Shadows said to remove it. Get wolf demon."

The mutation made a sloppy, wet sound, licking its lips. Kari roared again, thrashing, her lightning flaring out in wild arcs. The creature's claws dug deeper, and she felt her blood dribbling free, pooling underneath her body.

Her vision blurred, but she knew the wound would heal soon. She would be strong enough, and she would avenge Vivianne's death, too.

"I eat humans...Delicious, bloody morsels. But Mistress said to bring you alive. Come."

The beast removed its claws from her side before it shifted off her. Before she could conjure the strength to move, it bit into her shoulder again.

"Come," it gargled around a mouthful of blood and flesh. Kari's mind swam from the pain. Her electricity was sporadic and weakening. The beast began to drag her.

Kari dug her claws into the ground, trying to find ahold to stop the mutation from taking her wherever its mistress waited.

Is this what I deserve? she wondered. *I killed two humans, maybe more at Briar's Glen, and two more had to die because of my failure.*

Her blood was pouring. The wound vibrated, trying to heal. Her vision swam, and the tingling healing stopped. A gargled groan slipped free. Would she even survive a trip to this mistress?

I...I don't want to die.

The burn was dull in her chest, but it was present. It thrummed angrily, like a swarm of bees, but she was too weak to accept it.

The softest rustle caught her ear, distracting her from the dull screen of pain. It was quickly followed by a *swish* and *thuck*. The beast

195

shuddered, hissing angrily. There was a distinct whistling and more *thucks*.

Time froze until the creature finally fell on top of her, limp and heavy, blood flowing from its head. Kari squirmed, her vision darkening, and she stilled.

Someone lifted the body off and pushed it aside. The breath in her lungs left in one great gasp. She reached for her shoulder with the opposite hand, afraid to feel how mangled the flesh was. It was vibrating again, the feeling of needles drawing her skin together, tiny piece by piece. Her head throbbed, and she drew a sharp breath through her teeth.

"Kari? Are you okay?"

She was shocked out of her daze to recognize Ari's voice. Too stunned to speak, she flinched when his fingers touched the slashes on her back.

"Stay still, Kari. Please. I can help you. You only have to trust me for this moment."

Her healing capability seemed to have found a limit. Her head pounded, blinding her. Reluctantly, she did as he bid and trusted him to do what he would. It stung, but she waited patiently as he dabbed the wounds with something cool. He hesitated.

"There it is again."

"What?" Kari rasped, a growl to her voice.

"Your wounds appear to have closed on their own. It was as such with the arrow, too. But these are still raw and pink. Not completely fresh, and not entirely gone, either. I don't understand it." Kari flinched as his gentle fingers ran over one of the slashes. "I will cover the deepest ones, but...I think maybe the others will be fine."

Kari offered an impatient and weak snort. Ari did as he said, fastening soft, cotton bandages onto her shoulder and part of her back. Afterward, he helped her stand.

She winced in pain as she stood straight, stretching the wounds in the process. Her vision was slow to focus, but she looked down at the thing that had attacked her.

Riddled with arrows, one through its skull and a few in its back and side, it was indeed the same huge, purple, veined beast that had taken Vivianne's life. And if its words were true, it had only done so because of Kari. Unwilling tears burned her eyes.

"Kari?" Ari's voice was soft. "Are you alright?"

Her face screwed up. "It…killed my friend."

Ari didn't say anything. He knelt to pack the supplies he had used to help her. When he stood again, he removed the leather vest he wore. He held it out to her.

"Your clothes are ruined."

Kari glared at him and spared a glance down at herself. The shirt she had taken from Vivianne covered her front, if loosely. The back must be in tatters now. She took his jacket and slipped it over her clothes with a small wince.

"Come back with me, Kari. I did what I could with those wounds, but if you don't have a good rest, they won't heal properly."

The look in his eyes was one of stern kindness. Kari wanted to argue that she was fine, that her healing ability would take care of it, but the words died on her lips.

He took her hesitancy as an answer, grabbing her hand and leading her away. As before, his touch was electric. While she pondered the feeling and the bow and quiver slung over his shoulder, he guided her through the forest with ease.

"Do you just walk around the forest?"

Ari's laughter was light. "No. I heard…thunder. It didn't seem a coincidence that thunder boomed the day you came to the village. When I came to investigate, wondering if you were hurt, I heard your scream."

Kari stared at his back. "You…followed the sound of thunder. Knowing it might have been me."

He glanced back at her. "We can discuss that later, if you wish. Watch your step."

She fell silent, following his winding path. He had no problem finding his way; within an hour they came to the river, crossed the bridge, and entered Raziac Village again.

The stars in the night sky sparkled above them as Ari led her past the shops. Kari tried not to stumble, clenching her teeth against the pain and exhaustion threatening to overwhelm her.

"Won't your people be upset that I have returned?" she grumbled as she followed him to the base of a small hill. He led the way up, and she thought her wounds began to bleed again.

"I will deal with them. We're almost there." Ari was sure to stay by her side as they walked. He didn't reach out to help her, but his presence was reassuring.

At last, they came level again, and Kari paused to gape at the large house atop the hill. It was only one story high, sprawling with a tall, peaked roof, far too large for one simple boy. Kari glanced at him, wondering how big of a family he had. He was too young for children, but was he married? And how naïve was he to bring a stranger into his home, especially a demon?

Ari pushed open the door and hurried her inside. After closing it, he nudged her through the sparsely decorated main room toward a hallway and through the first door on the left.

"You can sleep here," he said, leading her to the biggest bed Kari had ever seen. "Please, don't be so tense. I give my word you are safe here."

"Where is your family?" Kari asked, her voice hard from pain.

Ari looked at her. After a moment, he laughed softly.

"I am all alone here." He undid the covers so Kari could climb in, and she hesitantly did so. "Please do not leave tonight, Kari. I'll look at your wounds again in the morning after you've had some rest."

She pursed her lips and didn't say anything. Ari was still smiling softly as he turned and left her alone.

No family? She searched the wide room, noting a wooden cupboard for clothes and another side room, possibly for bathing. His personal sleeping quarters must be much larger, and the hallway through the rest of the house had many more doors aside from this one.

How could that one boy live here all alone?

Kari sat up in the bed, fiddling with the edges of the leather jacket still around her shoulders. She was in a human house again; even so, she did not feel the way she had in Anne and Joseph's home. Ari's home was inherently comfortable and welcoming.

Her fingers stilled on the lower hem of the jacket. She pulled it off and tossed it onto the floor.

I can't do this. I don't need his help.

Thumping onto her side, she fell into an uneasy sleep.

CHAPTER TWENTY-TWO

Kiki was on the ground, tears in her eyes. She stared up at Kari, silently pleading. Between them stood Lian, his eyes sharp, dark, and cold.

If Kari didn't stop him, he'd keep hurting her and Kiki.

She advanced on him, shoving him back and rushing to Kiki's side. He hit the ground behind her with a grunt.

"Let's go. He won't follow us."

She helped Kiki to her feet. Her friend's smile dropped, and her eyes widened, staring over Kari's shoulder. She spun around to glare at Lian, only to stumble back at the sight of the mutated not-demon.

"Kiki," she gasped. "Kiki, run!"

Kari turned to run with her, but Kiki was gone. In her place was another form, another body; a young woman with waves of brown hair and unseeing eyes.

Kari shot up in a cold sweat, her legs tangled in the too-soft sheets. She pushed them off angrily, glancing around the room. It was empty.

Reaching around to touch her back, Kari could feel the wounds that Ari had left exposed. Now it was new, smooth flesh. She stood from the bed and waited for the pain. There was none, not even from the bite on her shoulder.

Who does that boy think he is? Insisting on bringing me to his home. Helping me... Surely, he'll want something in return.

She felt heat rise to her face—whether from shame or anger, she didn't know.

Finally, Kari could stand it no longer. She crossed the room and opened the door noiselessly. Ari was nowhere to be seen in the main room, and his scent was everywhere. Kari made her way to the front door and stepped outside to a light purple sky and an early morning breeze. She wouldn't be caught dead snooping around his house.

Kari's ears flickered, and she shivered slightly. She hadn't paid it much attention yesterday, but this village was oddly cold, chilling enough for her to feel it despite her wolf blood. She pondered if this freezing weather was due to the mountain range that enclosed the forest, the river, and Ari's tiny village.

The village... Kari looked down upon the buildings from atop Ari's hill, watching as the early risers milled about. Between the hill and the center of town was a stone wall curved around a small garden of flowers. A shape, something winged, hovered over them—a decorative piece, perhaps.

Beyond this garden were the shops: she found the bakery Ari had taken her to the day before, smoke already rising from its chimney, and thought of the bread he'd given her. Maybe she could eat that for breakfast.

Beside the bakery was the butcher, and across the path lay another smoking chimney, this one wide and made of stone. The other shops remained boarded up, not due to open for several more hours.

Against the forest on the far right was the tallest structure of the village, rising two stories and lined with wooden spikes. Kari could make out the shape of a thick, burly man outside as he paced before a line of twenty or so men. She frowned; demon hunters were definitely not something she wanted to mix with again anytime soon.

"Do you find yourself well, child?" a soft, familiar voice muttered from somewhere behind her. She spun on the spot to face the old man with peppered gray hair who had spoken for her.

"You need have no fear," the old man said kindly. He crossed his arms beneath the massive sleeves of his white robes. "Are you cold, child? Lord Ari has spare clothes you could borrow, I am sure."

Kari's ears flickered. "You smell...different," she muttered. "Not like other humans. You're...pure."

The man inclined his head. "I am the archbishop of Raziac Village. My soul is as pure as is possible in this world in which we live."

Kari felt fear creep up her spine—the title "archbishop" did not sit well with her. Hadn't she learned in Snow Shade that they had something to do with holy magic?

The old man held up his hands in a placating gesture. "I do not mean to be the cause of your unease, child. Lord Ari asked me to make sure you found comfort until he could return from his morning duties."

Kari relaxed slightly, equally annoyed and pleased for his kindness, even in his absence.

"My name is Roland, child. What should I call you?"

"Kari," she replied after a moment's hesitation.

Roland's smile crinkled his eyes. "It has been quite a long time since we had the company of a friendly demon in Raziac. Not only have the people needed your presence—Lord Ari has, too. It is too easy to forget good will and faith."

"I suppose..."

"Come back inside, child. I will fix you a meal. If you would like, we could find something for you to wear for the time being. By the time you have finished, I believe Lord Ari will have returned."

Roland stepped past Kari and entered Ari's huge home. She stared as he disappeared through the doorway. Vivianne had spoken for the accepting nature of this village, but Kari had never imagined anything to this degree.

The sun had barely broken through the kitchen window when Kari's keen ears caught the sound of footsteps. She tensed in her chair, dropping a chicken bone onto her plate with a clatter. Ari strode in, looking slightly harassed.

"By the gods, Roland! Where did these new men come from? Not even Linus can—Oh! Kari!"

Ari turned to her, irritation melting from his face in an instant. Kari wondered what sort of expressions he could fake, as all lords must. "I'm glad to see you up. I hope Roland has not bored you too much with his stories."

"No," she said, flashing her eyes briefly to meet Ari's before returning her attention to the chicken bone in her hands. Once upon a time, she *would* have been uninterested in stories. Most of Roland's stories, however, had concerned the late Lord of Raziac Village, filling gaps in the stories Vivianne had shared. He'd been a kind, fair man, and Kari wished she could have met him.

Ari smiled at her before turning to Roland again. "I will be by to meditate later, Roland. This morning has unsettled me more than usual."

Roland bowed to Ari. "I will be at the temple. Will you show Kari the village, or…?"

A knowing smile crept onto Roland's face, one of amusement. He found joy in the idea of Lord Ari parading her around the village. Likely she would be of interest to them. Kari dug her claws into the bone, splintering it.

"That's not necessary," she grumbled through gritted teeth. "I only stayed so you could check my wounds. I'm healed now, so I need to leave."

An odd look passed over Ari's face, as if he was hurt by her words. His pleasant mask returned quickly. "Of course you may leave, Kari. But surely you know that we can make a place for you here. My father set the standards years ago. Demons are not strictly unwelcome if they can live in peace with us. It is not uncommon that even demons become lost—"

Her chair squealed as she pushed away from the table and stood.

"I am not *lost*," she growled. "And I am not a pet you can lock up at home while you go tend to your duties. If you will check my wounds, do it now. Then I'll be on my way."

Ari's face became impassive. "As you wish," he said, moving across the kitchen and opening a large cupboard. "I will be by in an hour, Roland."

Roland bowed again and left without another word. Kari watched him leave and felt a pang of guilt as the door closed with a click—she had not even thanked him.

Ari returned to the table with some bandages, balls of fluffy cotton, and a bottle of lemon-colored liquid. Kari turned away from him and hiked up what was left of her shirt, regretting now her refusal of anything new when Roland had offered.

"I hope you will at least take something from my house to wear or allow me to replace these clothes."

Kari huffed.

His touch was soft on her back and shoulder as he removed the old bandages; the liquid stung when he applied it. He did not put new bandages on her back.

"I did not mean to offend you," he muttered while he worked. "The men who attacked you have been reprimanded. We do not hunt demons here, not without cause like that. I thought that maybe we could help you. It is not that you seem lost, but…"

"I will not live off the pity of humans," Kari spat, a little more angrily than she intended.

Ari chuckled, surprising her. He stepped back, pulling her tattered shirt back down. "I do not pity you, Kari. Quite the contrary, you

204

remind me of myself. I had to learn to accept help from those around me, too. You are not so alone, you know."

She snorted and turned to him. "Thank your...bishop. He was rather kind to me."

"Roland will be most pleased to hear your thanks."

Kari frowned. She saw nothing of the falsity Lord Isaac of Snow Shade had shown in this boy's face. If he was being true, that meant he trusted her. But why? Because she had not actively hurt his people?

Kiki and Vivianne had been the same, endlessly kind, and naïve...and look where that had gotten them.

Ari packed his supplies. "Your wounds are almost entirely healed. I've never seen such restorative powers firsthand before. I think it will only leave a little scarring."

Kari glared at his back and crossed the kitchen to the door. Her hand was on the knob when Ari spoke again.

"Goodbye, Kari."

Without returning his farewell, she left.

CHAPTER
TWENTY-THREE

Kari wanted to avoid going back into the forest—the purple mutation's attack still sent phantom burns down her back that made her teeth grind—but she had to leave this accursed village. Once she returned to the forest, she was sure she could find the path Ari had followed.

Thinking of Ari made her stomach clench. She didn't understand his desire to help her. Why couldn't he wince or glare at the sight of her, as many other humans had? Instead, he presented her with kindness she knew she didn't deserve.

Kari forced him from her mind and focused on her task of leaving. After skirting the boundaries of the village, she could find nothing except a wall of trees and bushes.

"How can these infernal humans stand this?" Kari grumbled to herself. She remembered Vivianne's disdain for the village of Raziac and its forest, and now she understood—even her mountain home had not been this densely packed with trees.

She strode around the spiked building that housed the demon hunters, skirting the edge of the tree line without actually entering the dark depths of the forest. Her body was tense, waiting for the shout of a guard. No matter what Ari told her, Kari would not blindly trust a human to leave her be.

She stopped with a huff and looked past the spiked walls of Raziac's garrison. The sun would soon set beyond the mountain range, and she did *not* want to be lost in the forest at night again.

"Can I help you?"

Kari's skin prickled with alarm and she spun to face a towering, burly man. His left eye was concealed behind a black patch, but his right eye was stern as it looked down at her. Kari's ears bent back, and her tail twitched.

The man gazed at her for a moment longer. He rumbled, "If you need help finding something, the lord's home is the other direction."

Her teeth clenched at his words. "I have already been to his house, and I don't need your lord to help me with anything. I was leaving."

The man shrugged and turned toward the wide double doors of the garrison. Kari faced the trees again, her fists clenched. They loomed over her, gloomy and a little menacing, but she'd be damned if she returned to *Lord* Ari and his pampering.

The darkening sky disappeared behind a canopy of dark green leaves and thick branches as Kari delved into the wood. After some huffing and shoving of bushes, she made it to the river and decided to follow it.

Every step was slow and careful. Every sound made her pause and crackle with electricity. Her ears twitched and flickered, and at the snapping of a breaking twig, Kari would crouch, ready to fight. When nothing leapt out at her, she resumed her tense journey.

The trees allowed no sign of the sky, so Kari had no indication of how long she had been walking when she finally stopped to rest. Her skin was covered in goosebumps from the chill, an unnatural thing for her. Growling, she crossed her arms, tucking her hands into her pits. The night wind tickled her back where the shirt had been torn.

Kari glanced around her immediate area. Aside from the river, nothing looked or smelled familiar. Even so, she knew if she followed it, she would eventually find her way out again.

As she grew tired, Kari shifted forms. Her ruined clothes fell to tatters on the ground, forgotten; she had a couple more pairs along with the last fistful of bread Ari had first given her. Light brown fur spread along her body, instantly dispelling the strangely cold air.

She snuffled along the banks of the river before finding a large bush to huddle under for the night. In the forest where she belonged, her dreams were blessedly mundane.

The next day, Kari made breakfast and lunch of any fearless squirrels that braved her path. Her foot slipped in the wet earth along the river when a sharp *snap* reverberated through the trees.

She spun to find the source of the sound; teeth bared in a half-hearted growl. The forest responded with silence.

Kari was thankful that whatever it was, it definitely could not be the purple-skinned beast again. The air was also not poisoned by the sour smell of demon. Nonetheless, something had made the sound, something bigger than another squirrel.

"Who's there?" she asked, fingers tense.

To her stunning surprise, a woman's voice answered. "The word on the wind is true…"

Did she know this voice? Kari froze, cocking her ears. All was still and quiet, even the birdsong was muted. *Where is she?*

"My sisters did not believe me. Wolf demons have long been gone from this part of the world, and yet here you are. *You* are the one they've spoken of."

"Who are you?" Kari demanded in a growl. "Are…are you the mistress? Did you send that purple creature after me?"

The speaker laughed—it was not a happy sound.

"No, but I saw the creature. It took your friend's life."

Kari was numb, staring at the brush around her. Still, the woman did not emerge to face her. "W-what?"

"I told her her life was forfeit. She decided to stand by you, you, the demon who would birth the storm that will destroy the world. And now she is dead."

Her words made no sense. Vivianne was dead...because Kari could control lightning?

"What do you mean?" Kari ventured in a voice that cracked. "What does this mean? Vivianne..."

"You appeared to be nothing remarkable, merely another demon who will perish in time at the hands of another, until I saw your lightning for myself. You are the wolf demon of legend I have searched for all these years. Tell me, demon scum, are you ready for death?"

As the threat registered, electricity sparked from Kari's claws and raced up her arms. Her ear caught a sizzling *fwoom*; she dodged to the side as an arc of fire blasted past her. Wide eyes watched as the flames dissipated mid-air.

Fire magic. The Fire Witch from the plains.

"You!" Kari spun to glare across the river toward its origin. "Why did you attack us?!" Realization scalded her. "Vivianne...you saw that monster—"

A bright, orange glow erupted in the middle of her vision. Kari ducked to the side as another swirl of burning energy sped past her.

"You are certainly quicker than most prey I seek," the voice muttered, still echoing in the dense trees.

Kari thought she could make out the silhouette of a tall form, long and thin, before the ground erupted all around her. Plumes of liquid fire spurt from the earth, bubbling onto her arms and legs with a hiss.

Kari howled and jumped away, patting out the flames on her scorched pants. Her arms were burned, badly; her flesh now dark and raw from the fire she hadn't dodged. The smell and sight of burnt flesh made her stomach twist with disgust.

As she watched, though, the skin lightened until the burns were barely pink. A tug in the back of her skull made her wince.

"Come easily to me, storm-bringer, and it will be swift," the Fire Witch spoke again. "Fire is destructive, decisive. But it can hurt when it wants to."

Kari growled wearily. Her legs throbbed with pain; they hadn't healed like her arms had.

The ground shook again, and she tensed to jump. As her feet left the ground, something wrapped around her ankle and dragged her back to the forest floor. She fell hard with a huff, her hands automatically reaching to free herself. A strangled cry escaped her throat at the sight of a blazing hand wrapped around her ankle. The skin between its fingers blistered, the pain unbearable.

Her vision popped with black dots, her thoughts dancing between panic and agony. It had to stop; she had to destroy this cowardly Fire Witch.

Her eyes flashed red, followed by the forming of heaviness in the air that prickled the fur on her ears. Kari roared, and with it came a dozen lightning bolts that stabbed around her with a crash. The pools of flame rippled and hissed as the lightning forced it back, gouging great divots in the earth all around her. When the lightning settled again, a small, electric barrier stood around Kari's legs, deflecting the splashing lava.

Once the space around her was free of fire, Kari directed her attention forward. The bolts thrust out, into the depth of the leaves and branches—where they touched, they scorched but left behind no free flames.

Kari listened eagerly for a scream or a cry, but nothing came. She stumbled forward, intent to at least see who had attacked her, only to fall back with a cry. When fresh flames didn't leap out of the foliage at her, she knew she was alone again.

Her trembling gaze fell to her legs, and she grimaced—it was no wonder they wouldn't carry her forward. Her thighs were bright red, raw, and blistering, throbbing with every pulse of her heart. And her ankle…

Kari leaned forward to look closer at it, and her stomach twisted into knots.

Though the blisters were fewer, the skin was swollen and striped in charred black where the fiery fingers had touched. Kari didn't know anything about burns, and as exhausted as she felt, she didn't imagine her natural healing would work anytime soon.

While she stared at her ankle, at a loss for what to do, the life of the forest returned in the form of twittering birds. Their songs were soothing, lulling Kari's thoughts away from panic and into exhaustion. She forcefully shook herself; she'd be a fool to stay where the Fire Witch could find her.

She dragged her legs to stand and released a gasp of agony. She was able to stand with the help of nearby shrubs, but as soon as any weight went to her damaged ankle, she faltered again. With a hiss, Kari threw all her weight on her left leg and hobbled into the safety of the trees, away from the river. She followed it by sound, rather than sight, hoping the Fire Witch would not reappear anytime soon.

Kari imagined night was falling again when she collapsed against a thick tree. The gentle trickling of the river was a dull sound on her ears, where her blood pounded. Her skin was clammy, and her body trembled with pain and hunger, but the squirrels that had abided her presence before seemed to think better of it now. Kari slumped to the ground where she stood, gritting her teeth as she stretched her legs out in front of her.

She stared at the burns on her thighs. She thought of them healing, *willed* them to heal, but was met with a pain like a spike being thrust into her eye.

The thought of Ari with his medicine bag full of remedies and bandages flit through her mind. Why did it seem that she always turned to humans when in need? It was exceptionally un-demon of her. She did not need Ari. She had only let him help before because it had been easier than fighting him.

Kari reached forward to touch the skin of her ruined ankle. The skin felt leathery and thick and was numb to the touch.

What would Mother do? Her mother and father never spoke of power for healing like the type that had shown itself in Kari. How did they heal wounds?

A long-forgotten memory sprung up, filling Kari's eyes with fresh tears.

"My toy fell in the fire last night. I couldn't leave it…I had to get it back. Father said the burns will heal in a couple of weeks." Kiki showed Kari the leaves her father had wrapped around her hand.

He chewed leaves into a mush and put them on the burn. What kind of leaves were they?

Kari looked at the shrubbery all around her—all identical. What were the chances any of them was the one that would help her? Little, she figured, since she was on the opposite end of the continent.

After a moment's hesitation, she reached for the closest bush, hissing when she rolled onto her burnt thigh, and ripped a bundle of leaves off. She looked over them carefully, tiny, spear-shaped things, but could recall nothing more about Kiki's burns.

Kari tossed the leaves into her mouth and chewed. Her mouth was dry, and the leaves were sour, but she chewed them into a paste and spat a sticky glob of light green goo. Gingerly, she spread some on each thigh, wincing at the contact. The rest went to her ankle.

Any instant relief that Kari might have expected was dashed immediately as her burns throbbed in rhythm with each other. She leaned back against the tree, thinking angrily that the pain would keep her awake all night.

Kiki sat by a large crackling fire, her back facing Kari. A breeze ruffled her hair, making it whip all around her. Kari approached her friend and sat beside her.

"What should we practice today, Kiki?"

Kiki didn't answer.

"Kiki? Are you okay?" Kari pulled her gaze away from the fire, grin faltering when she caught sight of her friend. The girl was ghostly pale, her eyes gray and unseeing as she stared into the fire. A thin line of red crossed her throat; a steady stream of blood trickled down her collarbone into her tunic.

"Kiki?!" Kari shuddered, turning to grasp her by the shoulders, but her fingers went through them. As she stared, her eyes widening, Kiki's head turned with a nasty crack and squish of bones and blood.

"You did this," Kiki said with a voice full of pure venom. She had never sounded so furious. "You did this, you did this. You did this!"

With each word, her voice became louder until she was screaming. Kari fell back, covering her ears, yet Kiki's voice continued to roar in her mind, never-ending.

Kari awoke with a cry, gasping as her legs jarred. She blinked at the hazy world around her, wondering for a moment where she was. Slowly, her eyes adjusted, noting the thick trees and bushes. Weak sunlight splintered through the leaves above.

Her heart pounded as she tried to calm her breaths. Why would she dream something like that? Why would Kiki…

Kari shook herself. She couldn't do anything about it now. Instead, letting out a hard breath, she forced her attention to her legs.

The green globs had stayed overnight, but the skin around it looked the same. Kari huffed angrily. By the ache in her head, she wasn't ready to heal any of it herself yet.

Digging her claws into the thick bark, Kari used the tree to get up. Dense shrubs served as crutches as she shuffled away from Raziac and the site of the Fire Witch's attack.

By midday, Kari had scrounged up some meager berries to go with the last of her rock-hard bread. Her skin was still clammy, and she was exhausted; so tired any lightning she managed to call fizzled before it left her fingers. Vision popping with black spots, she walked with her head bowed, every movement threatening to take what was left of her consciousness.

Kari ripped and chewed more leaves as she stumbled along, trying to ignore the throbbing in her thighs and the sickening emptiness of her stomach. *This weakness is unbearable*, she thought as she paused to spread more green goo on her burns. How did humans live without restorative powers like hers?

The sun was curving around to hide behind the mountains when Kari broke through the trees and came upon the river again, a thicker part of it than she'd yet seen. She stumbled forward. Without the help of the trees, she fell to her knees. Kari's vision blurred as she dragged her legs over the ground and toward the water.

When she was close enough to dip her fingers in, she collapsed, her head *thunking* against the hard shore. Something slimy and cold brushed against her fingertips. *Fish.* She couldn't summon the energy to reach for one.

Pathetic, she thought to herself with a groan. *Pathetic to let a simple burn do this to me.*

She heard Kiki's laughter and felt blessedly pleased for such a sound.

"You can't even break a rock!" her voice called from somewhere in the distance, echoing and quiet.

"I could," Kari mumbled. The voice spoke again, closer and deeper, the words incoherent. She swirled her fingers in the water and edged a little closer, the water rushing over her burns and providing an intense wave of relief that gave way to blessedly dreamless slumber.

Chapter Twenty-Four

"Are you awake, Kari?"

Her eyes snapped open at the softness of his voice. Her vision swam a little until she could discern the blurry form of Ari's red hair matched against his face. He stood in the doorway of the room she'd slept in before.

A low growl settled in her throat. "You again."

"Please, Kari," he muttered, almost pleading. "You must know by now I only want to help you. Let me work, okay?"

Without waiting for a response, Ari stepped closer to remove the covers. She felt a rush of cool air and flinched.

"This will only take a moment," he muttered and bent over her legs. His too-gentle hands gripped her thighs. Kari tensed, rigid as he moved down to her ankle.

"I think with another day or two of rest, you should be able to walk fine on this ankle. I can keep cleaning and bandaging this, but the burns are severe."

"How did I get here?"

Ari's smile faded. "One of the fishing men caught sight of you at Lacamose River yesterday. He alerted Linus, who told me he had seen you leave a few days ago."

"Linus?"

"The man with the patch." Ari pointed at his left eye. "He described you as—what were his exact words?—ah, 'determined and surly.'"

Kari huffed and Ari chuckled lightly.

"Linus' men went back, found you, and carried you here."

"Are they not the same ones who wanted to have me killed?"

Ari's gaze did not waver. "I told you they had been reprimanded, and many here do not share their sentiments, I promise you. As long as you are here, Kari, you will not be harmed—not by my people." He pursed his lips as he added, "I can't say much for the forest, though. That place is quite out of my domain. Most of my men are too cowardly to even enter it."

Kari had nothing to say. She knew her rudeness toward Ari was unfounded. He did not owe her anything, and she could never repay it. What could a demon offer a human?

He turned to leave the room. "I will bring you something solid to eat now that you're awake."

As he disappeared through the doorway, Kari pushed into a sitting position and looked over herself. She was dressed in a simple white shift that went a little below her knees. She wondered how she'd changed and what happened to her other clothes, then promptly forgot about them when she noticed the lack of burns on her arms. They were gone, and the ones on her legs nearly so. She lightly touched the skin, raw and pink, and felt only a tiny sting of pain.

Rolling her ankle in circles brought no pain; she swung her legs over the bed and planted her bare feet on the cold wood. She leaned forward, testing the weight on her ankle. It throbbed but held. Laying her hand on the headboard of the bed, she stood on shaky legs.

Ari reentered with a plate of sliced meat. Kari sat again, ignoring the stupid smile that settled on his face.

"Eat slowly. I admit I don't know much of demon eating habits, but when humans don't eat enough over the course of a few days, they can get sick if they eat too much too suddenly."

Kari took the plate from him and picked a strip from it. The meat was deliciously seasoned and soft, melting in her mouth—so much better than Anne's cooking had been. She ate with gusto, stopping after a few pieces, and then she asked the question that was bubbling at her lips.

"Why do you insist on this? I'm a demon. You should leave me to my own fate."

Ari's brow furrowed. "It is as much as I would do for anyone. I learned not too long ago that the prejudices between humans and demons are often ill-founded. To live in hatred and distrust…it grows tiring, does it not?"

Kari looked away from him and didn't reply.

"May I?" Ari gestured to the bed. Kari moved so he could sit beside her.

"I, too, was rash and angry once. I hated demon kind. Forgive me," he said with a lopsided smile. "But the circumstances allowed little more than that."

Kari tilted her head—how well she knew.

"When I was on the brink, when I might have doomed the village with my childish anger, someone showed me a better way."

"Your bishop?"

"No, not Roland, though he tried." Ari smiled softly. "I made friendly acquaintance with that of a different sort. He helped me in a way I had never imagined one of his kind could…but he died shortly after we met. His name was Revi."

Kari furrowed her brows. "I'm sorry."

Ari shook his head. "I only mean that things could be different for you. You don't need to run from this place. A lonely, winding road muddled with anger and doubt…you should allow yourself something more, as I did. Demon or human, we are allowed that much."

Kari mulled over his words. With Vivianne gone, all she had left was the mention of this village willing to accept her. Because of her, though, Vivianne had died, and so had Kiki.

"I can't stay here," Kari hissed. "Already, I've caused too much trouble—"

Ari frowned. "You haven't bothered us at all. Please believe me when I say that."

"You don't *know* me. You don't know what I've done or what I'm capable of." Kari laid a hand on her face, wishing she could hide somewhere and never see the world again. "I'm dangerous," she managed in a thick voice. "I'm not meant to be here, or anywhere with humans. I *shouldn't* be here."

Ari grabbed her wrist and gently pulled her hand away from her face. "There is no 'meant to be,' Kari. If there is, and it doesn't suit you, shouldn't you work to change that? I don't believe any of us have our fates etched out in stone. Do you?"

Kari stared at him.

"How can I—" she finally began, only to be interrupted by a chilling scream. Kari flinched and moved to get up, but Ari laid his hand on her shoulder.

"No. Stay here," he said, standing and crossing the room. Kari's heart thudded in her chest.

Kari rose as another yell broke the silence. She turned to the only window in the room, settled in between the bed and a wooden closet. Through the large panes of glass, Kari saw Roland's temple, opalescent and peaked, settled some ways from the rest of town. She craned her head and noted thick, dark smoke billowing from the outer structures.

Fire.

The Fire Witch had chased her from the plains. She could have easily found this village, too. She would kill the people here, as she had presumably let Vivianne die, because of Kari.

No. No more.

She turned and left the room, shoving her way through the front door. At the sight of the hill's descent, she hesitated. She gritted her teeth and walked, each step slow and careful. It was arduous, but she finally came on level ground, her forehead dotted with sweat and her ankle throbbing.

The villagers were scattered. Young children fled the smoke, running toward Roland's temple. Adults rushed past with buckets of water or handfuls of weapons. She followed the biggest group, alert for signs of Ari. What did he intend to do?

With a flapping of robes, Roland ran past Kari, pausing when he caught sight of her.

"What are you doing out here? Ari gave express orders that you must rest!"

She rolled her eyes. "I'm fine. Your homes are on fire! Let me help!"

Roland nodded, but still gave her a stern look before continuing on his way.

The chaos spread quickly as Kari limped along. Tiny flames decorated the buildings, catching and igniting. As she watched, a blaze exploded, destroying half of the bakery. A large woman with short, mousy hair knelt not far from the smoldering structure, her face in her hands. Kari hesitated before laying a hand on her shoulder.

"This isn't the time. They need your help." She gestured to the smith, surrounded by twenty or so people who splashed water on the leaping, dancing flames.

The woman looked up at her, bloodshot eyes widening with alarm. She followed Kari's gaze, then nodded, stood, and ran to help.

The small rush of adrenaline kept Kari going as she looked around, trying to spot Ari amongst the disorder. Where would the lord be if he wanted to defend his people against such a threat?

She sensed a sudden blast of power, pure and bright, further ahead—holy magic. Several more buildings passed before she saw him and froze.

219

Ari stood facing the forest, a bow and arrow in his hands. It wasn't the weapon that gave her pause, but rather the white energy that hugged his form, a luster on his skin. At the sight of it, Kari's mouth dried.

Why hadn't she sensed it or smelled it on him as she had with Roland? The boy lord who had helped her on multiple occasions could wield the blessed magic learned purely for the ability to easily kill demons. Why hone such an ability if his desire was not to kill demon kind?

He pulled back the fearsome-looking white arrow, and as Kari watched, he let loose. It flew, slicing through the heat and smoke, clearing the air as it headed for the center of a pitch-black cloud. The cloud enveloped it, thinning only a little.

He lowered his bow, waited a moment, and then cursed before drawing another arrow from the quiver on his back.

The cloud changed color abruptly as Ari was lining up his arrow. Kari recognized the glow settling deep within it. Her ankle roared with pain as she ran to the boy, tackling him to the ground as a massive beam of fire blasted the air where he had been standing.

Ari rolled over and gripped her with unbelievable strength, intending to shove her off. His grip burned. She hissed, and he hesitated at the sight of her.

"Kari! What are you doing out here?" he demanded, sounding furious. She wiggled away from his hands, the touch still burning her skin. He let her go.

"We have to move!" Kari growled at him. She felt heat rising from the earth in waves and knew what would happen next.

Ari glanced back at the cloud. Then he grabbed her around the upper arm and tugged her to her feet. She felt him tense, and the heat emanating from the ground abated.

"What is this?" The voice reverberated impossibly all around them.

"Kari, go back to the house!" Ari yelled. He picked up his bow and arrow.

"You can't fight it, idiot!"

The black cloud expanded and rushed toward them. Kari coughed as it enveloped them and felt Ari's grip on her arm again. His touch stung, but not as it had before. Her breaths came easier.

"You are human, are you not?" The voice was quieter now, the speaker only a few feet away from them. Kari growled, but the smoke was obscuring the Fire Witch. "What is it with this demon that attracts your kind? And you, beast." Kari felt bubbling heat erupt under her feet. She jumped away, wrenching herself from Ari's grasp. "You should have chosen to succumb to your wounds. Now you will only know suffering."

Spears of flame erupted in the air around her, scorching newly healed skin as they licked her arms and legs. Kari stumbled and fell, her palms landing flat on the burning earth, and screamed. The pain returned tenfold, blinding her, and everything turned red.

"Enough!" Ari's yell hit her ears dully. He let loose a rush of white energy that cooled the ground and cleared the air. As the calming warmth of the light touched her, her skin crawled.

She looked at Ari as he turned to her, his eyes riddled with confusion. The look made her insides burn and tingle with something primal.

"Kari?" he muttered. "Your eyes…they're…"

She crawled to her feet, the pain from her burns numbed, though not yet healed. She thought nothing of them. She wanted to grab him…but why?

He caught her wrist as she approached him. His grip was warm, his scent familiar and mildly comforting; it was of the wood and campfire smoke. The primal feeling sank away and only then did Kari realize how familiar it felt—it was electric, a burning that told her she could do anything, defeat any threat. Ari was not a danger, though. Not to her.

"Kari, what's wrong?"

The red haze slid away. Kari stumbled back, muscles limp. The pain in her ankle was blinding. Ari caught her around the arms.

The voice that reminded her of burns and pain erupted in laughter. Kari's head twisted to finally set eyes, once more, on the Fire Witch.

She was a half-foot taller than Kari, her dress flowing in shades of red, orange, and yellow. The colors blended, giving the impression that she was on fire. In the light of day, her face was drawn and ivory, her eyes glowering orange and framed by long locks of bright red, free-flowing hair.

"Who are you?" Ari demanded. He managed to hold Kari steady with one hand while unsheathing a dagger from his waist. The blade glowed brightly as he held it away from her.

The woman looked him over curiously. "You are Lord of this village, with people to protect. Why do you settle with this filth?"

Ari didn't answer.

"I thought to run her out of town. I had no real intention of killing the good folk here—"

Kari snarled. "You admitted you let Vivianne—"

"You are demon hunters, yes?"

"We defend ourselves to any extent required," Ari retorted.

The woman sneered. "Imagine my surprise when I found her here, coupled with a human boy…helping him…not unlike the time before, with the girl. A disgrace to demons, is it not?"

Kari growled ferociously and made to jump at the woman, but Ari held out his arm, preventing any such movement.

"You will leave," he said to the fire-caster. "She has done nothing to you."

The woman's smoldering eyes glanced between them, a knowing sneer on her painted lips. "You do not yet know. But you will."

Before Ari could demand an explanation, the woman melted into a puddle of liquid fire and dissolved into the ground.

He slowly relaxed, releasing Kari and sheathing his dagger again. He sighed and the glow on his skin vanished.

"Kari, why did you come out here?"

She glared. "Don't ask me stupid questions."

"Is it stupid? Should I expect you, a demon who—if nothing else—despises me, to come to the aid of my people when trouble brews?"

Her scowl wavered. "I don't despise you."

Ari turned fully to her and looked her up and down, brows rising; the new burns that had been inflicted were fading already.

"Does your ankle hurt?"

Kari glanced at her bandaged leg. The bandages were peeling off, and without the threat of the Fire Witch to distract her, the pain was maddening.

"Some," she grumbled.

"Come, then. It's the least you can do for making me worry."

Most of the fires had been put out, leaving a mess of blackened buildings and the smell of smoke thick upon the air. Ari gave assurances as he passed through the village: he would help rebuild everything and ensure that the witch would not return. Kari followed behind him silently, marveling at the certainty and passion he showed for his people.

Finally, they made it to the bottom of Ari's hill. Kari stared up at it apprehensively, but when Ari offered to help her, she stubbornly made her way up alone. He stayed a few paces behind her until they had entered the house again.

Ari led her to the same bedroom and ordered her to stay while he got his supplies. She collapsed onto the edge of the bed and looked at her palms. They had been burned so badly, but now there was nothing to show for it. She squeezed her hands into fists.

The tingling anger had come back. Was it because of the pain? It seemed to only appear when she was hurt badly enough, or in real danger, as in Snow Shade and Briar's Glen.

And that wasn't all. When she'd seen Ari, it was as if he were an enemy too. She knew that to be false. As much as her face burned and her stomach fluttered, she knew that he was a far cry from someone who would hurt her.

Ari returned, breaking her thought. He rubbed a cream that smelled of leaves on her arms, where the burns had not completely faded.

"Do you know what that woman was talking about?" he asked as he did this. "She seemed to know you."

A line in Kari's jaw ticked. "She found…Vivianne and I in the plains. She kept talking about how…I'm dangerous and…" She drew a sharp breath. "I think she let Viv die because she stood beside me."

Like you did.

She winced as Ari removed the old bandage from her ankle and applied a different cream to it.

"Viv said she was probably a…fanatic. Someone who hunts demons."

Finished, Ari sat back. "Many people believe that demons are inherently dangerous and must be destroyed. That goes double for humans who practice magic. None of that matters now, though. Right now, I want you to focus on healing this." He frowned up at her. "Your walk down the hill made the skin crack."

"It will be fine," Kari muttered.

Ari quirked an eyebrow. "I have no doubt you think so. But even a demon like you must fear the thought of losing a limb if these injuries don't heal properly."

"You underestimate me."

Ari chuckled and packed his things. "Probably. I'll bring something for dinner." He approached the door, pausing before stepping out. "And Kari…Vivianne's death was not your fault."

Kari sat back in the bed and rubbed her hands over her face. She knew that. She knew she could not take the blame for Kiki's or Vivianne's deaths.

Still, the Fire Witch had insisted on *her* life. Not some demon, but her, a wolf demon with the ability to control lightning.

CHAPTER TWENTY-FIVE

The next day, Kari woke to the sun peeking through her window. She sat up with a yawn and tugged the covers off to assess the recent damage to her body.

Her arms were back to normal, her ankle nearly so. She breathed in deeply and willed the rest of it to heal. She was surprised by a small burst of pain in the side of her head, and then she felt the skin begin to itch with healing power.

She gritted her teeth uncomfortably as the shiny burns edged away into unblemished skin. Once the healing finished, she swung her legs over the bed to rest her feet on the floor. She turned and tensed her ankle—no more pain.

Pleased, Kari got to her feet and made her way to the door. As she reached out to grab the handle, she paused, noting a pair of leather boots against the wall. A folded note lay on top of them, and a pile of clothes leaned against them.

Kari hesitated before reaching down and opening the note. She pursed her lips as she read.

Kari,

Here are some clothes—I had the best of the village to help me with the sizes. Our local leatherworker made the boots. When Linus' men brought you here from the river, I could hardly stand to see the burns on your feet. I tried my best to make the measurements exact. I hope they all fit.

Yours,

Ari

Kari slowly mouthed the last couple sentences to herself before tossing the note aside and looking down at the boots and clothes. The boots were calf-high, finely crafted with dark leather, and stitched with pale yellow streaks, like little bolts of lightning. Unfolding the pile of clothes revealed a simple off-white short-sleeve tunic and a pair of dark green breeches. She frowned, irritated.

Great, she thought, *now I owe him even more.*

Nonetheless, now that Kari was out of bed, she felt ridiculous standing there. There was nothing to it. With an irritated huff she changed, pulling the new clothes and boots on and tucked the leggings in before lacing them. She loved the way they fit…but she would never tell Ari that.

Kari fiddled with the tunic, first tucking it in, then pulling it out again. Then she pulled the legs of the breeches back out of the boots and settled with them that way. Once satisfied, she left the room, closing the door behind her.

Ari was walking toward her from the left, carrying a tray laden with hotcakes, eggs, and strips of venison. Kari's mouth watered.

"Morning, Kari!" he greeted with a smile. "Does it all fit well?"

She glanced at the boots and her fresh clothes. "Yeah," she mumbled.

"Good. I was bringing you breakfast before I left." He walked past her into the main room and laid the tray on a small table there. "You can eat here. After that…I suppose the day is yours. I won't be back until evening, I think."

Ari turned to leave. Kari glared at his back.

"How can you make me food and provide new garments and not demand that I help you with the damage to the village? That woman followed *me* here. Even if I don't know why, it is my fault this happened." She ground her teeth. "You are the most irritatingly generous human I have ever met."

Ari faced her. "I suppose I'll take that as a compliment," he said drily. "If you wish to help, I will gladly accept any aid you can give me. But I would never force that responsibility upon you. This is my village, and regardless of what attacks us, it is my job to oversee repairs. The blame is not on you for what happened."

Kari stared blankly at him. "How can you say it is not my fault? She came here looking for me. You should be kicking me out, banishing me—"

"I hate to think of the places and things you've seen," he said solemnly. "Raziac is not the same. So long as you remain within the mountain ranges here, I will do everything in my power to keep you safe."

Kari clenched her fists, but she couldn't be mad. He *had* protected her. He had kept that woman well away and helped to heal the wounds left behind by her flames.

So why did she feel so tangled up inside?

When she didn't reply, Ari smiled again. "I'll see you soon, then, I imagine?"

She ground her teeth. As the smell of the meat wafted up to her nose, Kari found herself forgetting her irritation as she dug into her breakfast.

When she finished, Kari jogged down the hill, looking around for Ari as she came level with the village. The place was alive with noise: chattering of passing villagers, the steady *ping, ping, ping* of metal hitting metal, and the happy yelling of children playing. After several minutes of glancing about and pacing the outer rim of town, she couldn't figure out where the boy lord had gone.

"It is a pleasant morning for a stroll, eh, girl?"

Kari's tail twitched at the sound of the gruff voice. She turned to see the tall, eye-patched man approaching her. Linus.

"I'm not *strolling*. I'm trying to find Ari."

Linus looked down at her sternly, and then let out a booming laugh. "Oh, I see why our little lord has taken a liking to you."

Her face reddened. Before she could release a biting reply, Linus gripped her shoulder and turned her around.

"He'll be there, the lord." Linus pointed with a thick finger toward a cluster of buildings to the left of the smith—the bakery, of course. "Tell him not to forget his appointment with me. Now that the winter winds are finally warming, hunting season will be upon us soon."

With that, Linus left. Kari turned away from him, flustered and annoyed thinking of Linus' declaration of Ari's *affection* for her. He was a human—what did he know of Kari enough to *like* her?

The bustle of the village was even more prominent as Kari broke into the boundaries of the town. She was wary, her muscles tense, as she entered the thick of the populace. A group of children ran by her, laughing and screaming. She froze, her ears bent back in anxiety. Being so close to so many humans again felt wrong.

Kari felt a tug on her tail and gasped, spinning to face the offender. A little boy looked up at her, his face pudgy and his eyes shiny with something akin to happiness.

"You're Lord Ari's friend, aren't you?" he gasped, breathless from playing.

She didn't know what to say. She hadn't really considered him a friend.

"Come on, Thomas!" A taller boy ran up to the little one and grabbed him by the hand. "Sorry, miss," the taller one muttered to her with a respectful nod. He tugged Thomas away, who waved ecstatically.

"Tell Lord Ari thank you for protecting us!"

Kari watched the two boys catch up with their friends.

What in the hell?

She stood there, stunned, until the sound of people approaching her caught her ear. She spun to face a crowd of a dozen villagers chattering excitedly as they walked toward her. They poured around her, some smiling as they caught her eye. Before she knew it, they dispersed. Even disguised as a human, the people of Snow Shade had never been so accepting as these of Raziac Village.

The sound of Ari's voice on the wind brought her back to focus. She followed it, rounding the smith to find a cluster of people facing a wooden platform. Ari stood on it with a sheet of paper in his hand and Roland at his side.

"Mary, Louis, Maxwell, and…Daryn, to the homes," he said, scratching marks on his sheet as four people broke away from the crowd to go where he had indicated.

Ari named off a few more groups of villagers until there were only ten people unassigned, along with Kari. Ari rolled up his parchment and handed it to Roland.

"The rest of you can come with me to begin the repairs on the bakery. It was damaged the most in the attack."

The group muttered in agreement, then dispersed to gather supplies and get working. Ari jumped off the stage and made his way to her.

"So, Kari, what do you know of architecture or repairs?"

Kari blinked at him. "Nothing."

Ari nodded in understanding. "I'll mostly be covering the roof, so you can help me with that. It takes a lot of upper body strength, and I don't have a lot of men who fit that quality besides Linus' guards. And I'm strictly forbidden from using them for roofing."

She took a second to look over Ari's form. While his arms were lined and tight with thin muscle, he didn't look especially strong to her.

Ari caught her eye. She flushed, and he smiled.

"No, I'm not very bulky myself. But my power gives me enough strength to get by. Come."

Kari hesitated. She felt the heat in her face still and caught Roland's eye. He smiled kindly, not taunting, or teasing the way Linus did. She spun around to follow Ari.

Ari led her around the front of the smith. It was separated into two open spaces set beyond the low roof, one with a huge furnace and the other with several anvils. Hammers of a dozen sizes hung on a back wall.

A hulking, broad-shouldered man with dark, glistening skin was pulling a strip of red-hot steel from the furnace. As Ari and Kari approached, he walked it over to a barrel of water and dunked the metal in with a *hiss*.

"Lord!" he said, turning to face them. The shadow of a beard lined the lower half of his face, giving him an unpleasant look; his eyes shone with pure, unbridled joy. The smith pulled the steel from the water and laid it on an anvil before removing one of his massive gloves and shaking hands with Ari. "What can I do for you, son?"

"We're going to start the work on the bakery. I need some nails, wood, and metal. In sheets, if you have it," Ari replied.

"Sheets of metal?" the smith questioned, turning to his back wall. He carried back a stack of wood planks and a sack that jingled and laid them on an unused anvil.

"Yes, if you could spare some, Ammiras. I think it will help solidify the roof."

The smith, Ammiras, glanced between the two of them. He shrugged and went back to the wall. He disappeared through a door Kari hadn't noticed.

Ari grabbed the sack and tied it to his belt before hefting the planks. "If you could take the steel, Kari?"

Ammiras returned a moment later with a stack of thin silver sheets tied together with twine. He held them out for Kari.

"Good luck, Lord Ari!" Ammiras said. Ari waved goodbye to the smith and led Kari toward the blackened, crumbling building that was the bakery.

"What can you use these bits of metal for?" she asked as they walked. In Snow Shade, the roofs were made of wood and thatch—never anything remotely relating to iron or steel.

"I'll tell you as soon as we're up there," Ari replied. Soon the two of them joined the other ten workers assigned to the bakery. They had put up new walls for half of the structure and were working with the next half.

"Almost done, Lord!" a tall, reedy male replied as Ari approached them.

"Good work, Avery," Ari said, clapping him on the back. He stepped into the bakery and laid his supplies on the charred wooden counter. Kari watched as he dragged a ten-step ladder over to the closest wall and propped it up.

"I want to start in here," Ari said, gesturing above them. "We can use the sheets of metal with the planks of wood to layer the roof. If we align them right, we can nail the metal into the wood…"

Kari looked at the metal in her hands. After a moment, she laid the stack down and pulled two sheets from it. After lining them side by side, she knelt.

"What are you—"

Ari drew a sharp breath as Kari called electricity to her fingers. It zapped between her digits. Letting out a breath, she willed the lightning to the metal sheets.

It arced from her fingertips, wanting to go everywhere at once, but she managed to control it. Soon she was drawing her fingers back and forth between the two sheets of metal, the lightning melting what it touched until the sheets melded together into a bigger piece.

Kari stood once she was done. She looked at Ari and frowned at his expression of shock.

"This would be easier, yes?"

Ari collected himself and nodded. "Much easier. I never asked, how can you do that?"

Kari shrugged off his question. She separated the stack of metal into twos and melted them together as she did the first set.

Ari cleared his throat. "That will be a great help."

The two of them started to work. Kari didn't know anything about building, so she followed Ari's instruction. She used electricity to meld metal, and her superior strength to lift beams or hold planks in place. Ari impressed everyone with a spectacular strength unbefitting his size, though the white glow made Kari flinch away from him. By the time the sun was beginning to set, her head was pounding from the physical exertion.

"I think that will work." Ari ran his arm across his brow to wipe away the sweat pooling there. Kari slumped to the ground. The outer walls were finished, as well as most of the roof. "Are you feeling well, Kari?"

"I'm fine."

He gave her a knowing look and turned to his rag-tag team of builders. "That will be enough for today. We will commence tomorrow, before midday."

One by one, the villagers finished what they were doing. They left, thanking, or clapping Ari on the shoulder. Some of them spared Kari a small smile.

Once everyone had left, Ari turned to her again. "To home, then?"

She shuffled along behind him, her head pounding so much she didn't have the strength to remind him it was *his* home.

The two of them climbed the hill and entered Ari's house as darkness fell over the village. He made a quick dinner of meat and potatoes while Kari relaxed at the kitchen table, idly watching him.

It perplexed her why Ari would prepare his own meals if he was indeed the lord of this tiny village; he should have maids and helpers, as Lord Isaac had. He should not be building homes and fighting battles with strange women, and certainly not cooking his own meals.

He set a large ham before her, sliced and glistening, then added potatoes and bread before taking a chair opposite her.

"Thank you for your help, Kari. Things went so smoothly today, and it's all thanks to you."

Kari, her mouth already full of potatoes, and her plate stacked with a dozen of slices of ham, rolled her eyes. With some difficulty, she swallowed.

"I'm sure you and your people would have gotten along just fine without me, as you have before."

"Possibly, but there would have been complications. I don't have many men to spare for work like this. When it comes down to it, my builders are farmers, midwives, smiths, and gatherers. On occasion, I must borrow seamstresses as well. A little extra muscle never hurts."

She didn't reply. She shoveled more ham and potatoes into her mouth and swallowed again before taking a big gulp of water from a mug Ari pushed toward her.

"Was the strain much for you?" he asked. "I saw you grasping your temple a few times, as if it hurt."

Kari spared him a glance. "Nothing is too much for me. I was fine."

Ari stabbed a piece of ham with his fork and brought it to his mouth. He chewed slowly and swallowed. "I would not shame you for it, Kari. We all have times when we weaken, even a little, and—"

"Why didn't you tell me you had holy magic?" Kari demanded suddenly, cutting across his words. Ari blinked at her. She felt foolish at the outburst but went on. "Don't play dumb, Ari. You had it with the Fire Witch, and you used it today. You claim to not want to hurt demons, so why? Why have such an ability?"

Ari relaxed, a smile settling on his face that irritated her further. "I didn't mean it as a secret from you. It's something I have always had. It was bred in me, not learned like most magics."

Born with it? That was impossible—everything she'd ever learned about magic said so. It could only be learned from years of hard training. How could this be?

It's like me and my lightning.

Kari's frown deepened. When Ari's smile didn't fade, she looked away with a huff.

233

Ari chewed more ham and swallowed before speaking again. "I know what holy magic does for your kind. I have trained for years to be able to control it. Even now, it only presents itself when I call it. I would never use it to hurt you." He took a drink from his goblet. "I don't know what you've gone through, and I may never know. Yet I see the pain in your eyes. I know you have guarded yourself off from the world, probably for a very long time."

She didn't reply except to clench her jaw, so he continued. "But now you've seen for yourself how well you could fit in here. I have spare rooms you could use, or we could have a small house built outside the village if you wish. Roland and Linus appreciate your company. I…" He cleared his throat. "That is, we would love if you chose to make Raziac your ho—"

Kari pushed away from the table. "I will finish this business with the bakery, and then I will leave." She stood, gathered her dishes, and laid them on the counter.

Ari's smile finally faded. At first, Kari felt like smiling herself. As his eyes averted from hers, though, she felt some odd emptiness in her stomach. As if she had lost something dear to her.

Didn't he understand yet? She couldn't care for someone else and lose them again.

"You may do as you wish, of course," Ari said finally. "I will clean up."

Kari hesitated, but left the kitchen and returned to the bedroom she had been using.

Closing the door behind her, Kari moved to the bed and sat on it. Her stomach tangled with fluttering anger, but it was a different sort than she had known. It was something hungrier, something that clawed at her heart. She thought she recognized it from the time before she had met Vivianne. Grief, loneliness; a desire to be wanted someplace.

Kari bent to unlace her boots. She laid them beside the bed, once more noting the handsome craftsmanship before lying back on the feather pillows. She tugged the thick quilt over herself.

I could not live here, she reminded herself, and realized how ridiculous that sounded. Had she not planned to, after Viv's death? She realized something about Ari had changed that in her. The thought of him being in danger was painful.

With a huff, Kari rolled onto her side and closed her eyes.

CHAPTER TWENTY-SIX

The darkness was thick and smoky, so deep that Kari's eyes couldn't penetrate it. She couldn't see, couldn't smell, and couldn't hear.

"Where am I?!" she cried. Even her voice was swallowed, reverberating in her ears.

The darkness bubbled around her. She backed away, and froze as the silhouette of a thin, frail figure emerged, outlined in an ashen glow.

"Hello?" Kari called to the figure. The bubbling shadows popped and hissed around her.

The figure glowed with gray light. Kari forced her way through the darkness, feeling the bubbling mass attach to her like oozy tendrils. She ripped away from the shadows angrily, making her way to the steely light.

"Who are you? Wait!" Kari stepped forward into a puddle of something thick and viscous; her foot stuck.

"Kari…" the ghostly voice came off the figure as wisps of dark gray smoke.

"Help me!" Kari pleaded as the darkness swallowed her other foot with a wet, sucking noise.

"Why did you come here, Kari?" The smoke-made words drifted around her, filling the dark space with haze. "Was it not enough to send me here?"

Kari's heart thudded against her ribs. This old dream was familiar, and so was the voice. "Kiki?! Where are we? Where are you?!"

"I am here." Kiki's voice was more prominent now, louder. Her ashy silhouette glowed brightly, diminishing the shadows significantly. Kari could still not move her feet. "I have been here, Kari. Where have you been? Why did you send me here?"

Kari reached down, gripping her ankles to free one of her feet. As she bent, her arm slid against something slimy. She recoiled too slowly. A thick string of black ooze wrapped around her elbow and pulled her into a solid wall of black. She struggled, her cry choking.

Kiki solidified before her. Or Kari thought it must be Kiki—she had the same long, blonde hair and pale face—but her features were drawn, her face gaunt. Her eyes, once full of love and childish joy, were now sunken and empty of everything except contempt.

"Kiki, what is going on?!" Kari demanded, still trying to wrench her arm free.

"This is where you damned me, Kari. When I died, I came here. I have long tried to call you to me, so that we may share eternity here. It is the least you could do for ending my life so harshly."

"Kiki! I did not kill you!"

Kiki's eyes flared to life. Suddenly, she was a breath away from Kari, their noses almost touching. Kari drew breath and realized there was no scent on Kiki, not even one of death.

"You did not...? But who, I wonder, could have cut my throat with such speed and skill that I did not even sense a presence near? Who could have known I would be there? Tell me, Kari," Kiki hissed, leaning in even closer, "of all demons of the world, which has powers even equivalent to yours? No regular demon could have sent me to this hell!"

Kiki reached up and grabbed her shoulders. The darkness converged around them, cocooning them in. Kari yelled and struggled.

"This is no regular afterlife. What scriptures would have told of this place? I have lived an eternity here, Kari. I see time above me, moving placidly

237

without me. I saw my father, alone and sad. I saw you, leaving behind our mountain home." Waves of red-hot anger like flames rolled off her. "If I must be trapped here, I thought, I must have my old friend Kari."

Kari roared, finding she couldn't pull away. Gooey drops of ooze dripped down her head. "I DID NOT KILL YOU! Kiki, please listen to me!"

"Enough!" Kiki screamed, a ghastly, high-pitched noise that made Kari whimper. "You will join me here." Her breath frosted against Kari's ear. "I will share eternity with you."

Kari's breath came in short gasps as the shadows closed around them. Still, the lack of scent met her senses, and she paled. Even in death, a body would have a scent. Yet Kiki...

"This isn't your true body. That's why I can't smell you."

Kiki's grip tightened. "The shadows have told me my connection between body and soul was destroyed at death. But you would know that."

"No! Kiki, I do not have the power to remove souls!"

"There will be plenty of time for your lies, Kari," Kiki hissed.

She felt the shadow pooling around her waist in a sticky mess.

"Kari!"

A new voice. It was quiet, indistinct. Kiki pulled away from her to turn to the sound.

"Wake up!"

The dark tendrils wrapped around her squeezed. Kari hissed in pain.

"NO!" Kiki cried, her form shimmering. A flash of blinding light exploded in the darkness. Kari gasped and clenched her eyes shut, struggling endlessly. Finally, she felt Kiki's grip loosen and release her.

Kari sat up with a gasp. Cold sweat ran down her forehead. Her elbow stung, and her feet were unnaturally cold. The darkness was still present around her, though not nearly as thick. For a heart-wrenching moment, she thought of Vivianne—Vivianne and her bright fires that kept the darkness at bay.

In the gloom of her bedchambers, Kari could make out the shape of someone kneeling beside her.

"Gods above," Ari whispered. A faint white glow encircled his hands, fading every second. "I have never seen anything like that."

She looked up at him blearily, and blinked, feeling the hardwood floor below her. "How did I get down here?" The covers were strewn all around her, tangled in her legs.

"I heard you scream," Ari muttered. "I came in here, thinking the Fire Witch had come back. You were…" He was pale with worry, which shocked her. "You were entangled in some kind of smoke. I couldn't get near you and you didn't seem to hear me."

Kari felt a chill run up her spine. She pulled her legs to her chest and wrapped her arms around them.

He grabbed the blanket from the ground and wrapped it around her. He hesitated, then scooped her up in his arms and lifted her back onto the bed. Kari stiffened as his arms wrapped around her and did not relax even when he let go.

"What was that, Kari?" Ari asked in a whisper. "Where were you?"

She remembered Kiki. She had thought it was a dream, a nightmare. She knew better, though: Kiki was alive, somehow, in that blackness. Someone had put her there and made Kiki believe it was Kari who murdered her.

Tears, hot and stinging, pricked the corners of her eyes. She squeezed them shut, but the tears only leaked free.

"I don't know what that was."

Ari didn't say anything. She half-expected him to expel her from his home. This, she thought, must be a breaking point—if she did not bring Fire Witches to his village, she brought mysterious dark energies to his home.

"If it is okay with you, I will sleep right outside, in the main room, tonight," Ari said instead, standing straight. Kari finally opened her eyes to look at him. "I barely heard you from my room…it was almost like a dream. I can't imagine what would have happened if I hadn't woken up." He looked distraught by the idea.

"If you must," she muttered in the toughest voice she could manage.

Ari nodded. "Good night, Kari."

She lay awake for a time, afraid to fall asleep and into that dark world again. Never had she imagined shadows could be so threatening. A quiet, dry sob crept from her throat. She was all alone, hated by the world. Her parents were dead. Her best friend murdered and blamed Kari for it.

The tears were warm as they left her eyes and down her face, dripping into the nape of her neck. What was left to her now, besides the darkness that Kiki had shown her? Should she be there? Was that what Kari deserved, for not being able to save her friend, her family, or even Vivianne?

CHAPTER
TWENTY-SEVEN

Kari awoke to the smell of frying meat. She stumbled out of bed, hastily dressed, and scrambled toward the smell. She entered the kitchen to see Roland sitting at the table, along with Linus. Ari laid a platter of meats and eggs in the middle of the table.

"Please, sit," he said with a tired smile.

"Mornin', girl," Linus grunted at her as she sat. She grunted in return.

Roland looked up from a thick, dusty tome. He smiled at Kari and returned to his readings.

Ari served them all, starting with her. "I was about to wake you." His eyes were shadowed with dark circles.

"Did you not sleep?"

"Not much, I'm afraid," he answered. Once he had gone around the table, he sat between Linus and Kari.

"So, Lord Ari," Linus said in between bites of egg and fried fish, "when will you gather the groups for the hunting parties?"

"I will assign some men later today," Ari replied. "We will need many. Raziac Forest is dangerous at the best of times, but with that Fire Witch running about…" He pinched the bridge of his nose.

"I'll go with a hunting group if your men can stomach me," Kari grumbled. "I can sense prey better anyway."

Ari smiled weakly at her. "I can't—"

"Oh, shut up and let her," Linus growled. "Juris of the Hunt knows my men can't stalk prey to save their lives. They're too damn noisy."

Kari grinned. Ari glanced at Linus with playful annoyance. "As you wish," he said. "If you will scrounge up a small group today, then possibly we can find time tomorrow. Before noon." He glanced at Roland, who gave a quick nod and returned to his tome.

"What is that book?" Kari asked as she started to eat.

"Oh, I'm researching something for Lord Ari," Roland said, delicately turning a page. "Not much luck yet, though…"

Kari tried to get a look at one of the pages, but the writing was so tiny and faded she couldn't get a good idea of what it said. She shrugged and returned to her breakfast.

The same group of ten met Kari and Ari at the bakery a little before high noon. Ari gave them all a quick summary of what else needed to be done and sent everyone to their tasks. Kari felt glad to focus on something besides Kiki; she poured every ounce of her attention into rebuilding the rest of the roof. Within two hours, it was done, and she was fitting a new window next to the repaired door.

The sun graced the top of the sky as everyone stepped back to look at the bakery. Ari shaded his face from the sun with his hand and smiled.

"That will do it. Thank you, everyone."

As the group dispersed, Ari grabbed a young man by the shoulder. "Could you get me a status report for the other groups?"

Kari stared at the bakery. It was polished and new, the smell of wood strong in her nose. She felt a rush of pride having been involved in its creation.

"We would not have dreamed of getting it done so quickly without you," Ari said, drawing her attention. "Thank you."

She shrugged. "You saved my life. This is a weak repayment."

Ari gazed at her before turning away. "Well, let's see if we can't get Linus to round up some men for a hunt."

Kari followed him through the village toward the barracks. "As lord, can't you command them to go? It's as if you're asking permission."

Ari tittered. "I *am* asking permission. Even without the set rules of our town, Linus is hardly a pushover. He only lets some of his men go at a time, and I do not have precise control over them, even with my title. The rest must stay to guard the borders, especially if I'm not present."

Kari noticed the little boy who had grabbed her tail across the way—Thomas, she recalled. He met her eye and waved wildly. She felt a flush in her cheeks and looked away.

"Hi, Lord Ari!"

Ari looked in his direction and waved back. "Hello, Thomas. What're you up to today?"

"Sammy is going to take me fishing! He helped me make my own pole yesterday!"

Ari laughed. "That's great. Catch a big one for me!"

Thomas nodded enthusiastically. He waved at Kari again before turning away.

Her tail twitched in agitation while her stomach buzzed with something pleasant.

Within minutes, the two of them entered the barracks. Kari felt anxious as he led her through the wide double doors and into a large sparring area. Ten or fifteen men were scattered around, clashing weapons or fists against dummies while another dozen or so practiced

243

archery above them. Kari winced at the sound of every drawn bow-string.

"You're safe. They have no reason to harm you," Ari said as they mounted a set of wooden steps. Kari didn't reply.

Linus stood on a balcony at the top of the stairs. He faced away from them, yelling at some young lad who looked utterly terrified.

"I'm not here to train little boys, son! You came here to be a better fighter, yes? To defend the village?"

The male nodded furiously, his eyes wide and his lips a shaky line.

"Use your tongue, boy! The gods know you have it for a reason."

"Y-yes, Master Linus!"

"Then I want no more talk of this nonsense. You will toughen up, or you can go back to your mother's tailor shop. Would you like to make pretty dresses for the rest of your life, boy?"

The male shook his head of ginger hair.

Linus grunted. "Go back to training. I'm sick of your pitiful face today."

The ginger male gave a half bow and took off without another word or glance back. Linus turned to Ari and Kari.

"That was mighty unkind of you, Linus," Ari teased.

Linus scoffed and rolled his one eye. "You should hear the grumbling I put up with here. It's worse than my lordship."

Ari quirked an eyebrow and Kari chortled.

"Anyway, Linus," Ari continued with an amused glance at her, "I'm here to see how many men could accompany a hunt tomorrow."

Linus scratched under his massive chin. "How many will you be needing?"

"Maybe ten? We could do with a few good elk, and we'd need many men to carry back what we find."

"Half," Kari muttered.

244

Ari raised his eyebrows at her. "Elk are heavy. It'd take three or four men to carry one——"

"Five or six men, plus you and me. The rest are too much. We won't find anything with so many humans."

Ari regarded her a moment longer before nodding at Linus. "The lady has spoken."

Linus watched their exchange with a glint in his black eye. "Aye, I can get you five good men. You can take the red head, as well. A good trip into the forest will decide whether he's worth my time."

Ari laughed. "Have them ready for my command tomorrow morning."

Linus nodded. "Any word from Roland?"

"Not yet. I hope to see him on our way back."

The two of them discussed more details about the hunting trip while Kari wondered if this talk of Roland had to do with the old tome he was reading. As she opened her mouth to ask, her stomach interrupted with a mighty rumble.

"Dinner time it is," Ari said with a laugh. "See you, Linus."

The barrack's master waved the two of them off as they descended the steps and made their way back through town.

Ari led the way to the butcher as the sun sank below the mountains. The darkness spreading across the sky made Kari pause, reminding her vividly of the night before. She had rarely known fear like this; usually, enemies came in a more solid form. How could she fight actual shadows?

As Ari opened the door to the meat shop and the smell assailed her nostrils, she forgot about everything else. The counter was topped with a dozen types of meat and cuts: legs and ribs of venison, slabs of meat that could've been a cow or some other beast. She wandered to a whole duck, her mouth watering at the sight of it glazed and golden brown.

A door behind the counter opened with a clunk, and a pretty, brown-haired girl entered with a tub of something heavy in her arms.

"Hullo, Milord," she muttered.

Ari raced around the counter to help her lay the tub atop the counter. Kari watched as the girl's face flushed red and she batted her eyelashes at him.

"Thank you!" she exclaimed, wiping her hands off on her apron as Ari returned to Kari's side. "What can I get you?"

"This duck and some of that stew, if you please, Julia."

Julia pulled the bird off the counter. She wrapped it, slapped it back onto the counter, and turned to the tub of steaming stew.

"This is quite a feast, Lord," she said as she ladled some into a large clay bowl.

"My house has been teeming with guests lately."

Julia glanced over the counter at Kari. They met gazes, and Kari noted her eyes were a surprisingly vivid shade of light blue. The color reminded Kari of Vivianne, though not as bright.

Julia came around the counter and handed Ari the bowl. She spared him a flirty look and flashed him a bright smile.

"Will I see you again soon, Milord?"

Kari grabbed the duck off the counter and followed Ari out of the shop. "I'm sure," he said vaguely. "Have a good night, Julia. Tell your father thanks for the meat, as usual!"

Kari caught a glimpse of a sullen Julia as the door closed behind them.

"That girl desires you," she said as they trudged through the village.

"What makes you say that?"

Kari huffed. "She stares at you and flutters her eyes. She is like a little wolf pup yearning for attention."

He laughed. They came upon his front door and he opened it for her. "Julia is young, that's all. Any handsome young man who enters her shop gets the same treatment, I'm sure."

Kari walked through the hall toward the kitchen. "I don't think so," she said, laying the duck on the table.

"It is a moot point, anyway," Ari replied as he set the clay bowl beside the bird and set the table for dinner. "I wouldn't have time for a woman like that."

She took a bowl from him and poured some of the stew for herself. She quirked an eyebrow at him as he cut into the duck. "What time is there to have, besides for mating? You want children, don't you?"

Ari choked another laugh. "Someday, yes. I mean that Julia is not the girl for me. I have known her her entire life. She is sweet, yes, but also impatient and innocent. She knows nothing outside her father's shop."

"So, she wouldn't help out with your duties, is that it?" Kari asked with a sneer. "The lord needs a woman's help?"

The idea was laughable, having grown up in Snow Shade, where the women were nothing more than pretty faces who did housework. As long as Kari lived with them, Anne never helped Joseph with hunting. Even Lord Isaac's two women were utterly useless ornaments.

Ari met her gaze without a hint of bashfulness. "Well, yes. If I were to choose my woman, those are the qualities that I would look for."

Kari watched him as he served the sliced duck, but he didn't say anything more. He wanted a woman, not for her looks or as a servant of the house, but as an equal. It was a strange thought, coming from a human. It reminded Kari of her parents.

There had been undeniable love between her parents, one Kari had never seen between Anne and Joseph. Her parents had loved her with equal intensity, and she was stronger for it. Where else would she have found a pair more inseparable, one that worked and lived as a unit rather than a pair of individuals?

If only they had told me the things I needed to know before...

Her brow furrowed; she cut the thought off there. In the blank space of her thoughts, Kiki emerged, and Kari frowned, her eyes burning.

She sighed heavily. So, so many questions; she felt that was all she had. Endless questions and no answers.

CHAPTER TWENTY-EIGHT

As Kari made her way to the kitchen the next morning, she heard the distinct, slow voice of Roland. She was hardly surprised to see he and Linus had joined them again, and pondered briefly on the ease of that acceptance, before taking the chair next to Linus. Ari looked up at her from beside Roland and smiled. Dark circles were under his eyes again.

"Morning, Kari. Did you sleep well?"

She shrugged. Ari's eyebrows drew together. Kari was about to snap at him for worrying about her when Roland cleared his throat.

"Lord Ari, if we may go somewhere to talk…?"

"No, tell me here, Roland."

Roland cleared his throat again and leaned over the table. "I have found the passage that describes the things that you told me."

Ari put down his fork. "Excellent. What did it say?"

"It is an ancient form of power, my lord," Roland said. "The scripture is rather unclear about *what* it is or where it came from. It only tells that pure light extinguishes it." He frowned. "Your own ability is quite pure, it is true. I think, *maybe*, you could do this. But…" Roland glanced at Kari.

"What are you two gawking at me for?" she demanded.

Ari's brow furrowed. "My apologies, Kari. I asked Roland to help me find out about the darkness that enveloped you the other night. I was up most of that night myself, but could find nothing in my small collection of books."

"And while I did find this passage," Roland said, gesturing to the dusty old tome, "it does not make the situation any easier. Kari's being—that is, the demon soul she possesses—would make this a deadly act against her life."

"And what exactly would you be doing to me?"

Roland looked down at his book. "It sounds as if a spectral being has latched itself onto you. In time, they would drag you into the 'Other World,' as it is called here. Once your soul leaves this world, it is unlikely that it can come back."

Kari frowned. Kiki…was that where she was? She was stuck in some other world, a type of Yutemi?

"What can we do?" Ari asked.

"There is a ritual of sorts. Lord Ari would channel his blessed magic into the 'inflicted one,' it says," Roland looked up at Kari with the smallest smile on his face. "It doesn't explain much else. Much of this relies on you, Lord Ari. So much pure energy…it would be beyond dangerous."

Kari thought of the burn from Ari's glowing hands when he gripped her arms days ago. That was a fraction of his power. What would it feel like, an onslaught of white magic on her body and soul?

"I will do nothing without your word, Kari," Ari said.

She looked at him.

"I will do what I can to help you. I will manage my powers as much as I can to lessen the pain. But I will not do anything unless you say so."

She longed to ask him why, why did he bother, why did he care? Instead, she turned to Roland. "She—the shadow—it's infecting me? Like I'm sick?"

"In a way," Roland replied.

"So, I'm in danger regardless?"

Roland furrowed his brow, then nodded.

"Fine." Kari shoveled food into her mouth. "I will help Ari with his hunt, and then we can do this." She pushed away from the table and left the room. As she closed the door behind her, she heard Linus' gruff voice.

"Ah, I have waited years to see a woman who could match your lordly insolence."

Kari was gazing uneasily into the forest when she heard the creak of the door behind her. Ari exited the house, a bow and quiver over one shoulder and a sword at his waist.

"Are you nervous?" she asked, gesturing to his weaponry.

Ari led her down the hill. "This is standard for the forest. Before, demons would spawn daily from its depths. Things have changed, but there's still the fire woman to consider."

Kari followed him as he headed toward the line of trees closest to the barracks. From this far, Kari's keen eyes could see a small group of men waiting for them.

"I don't think your arrows and steel will hurt her."

"As it is, this is the only power I have against her. She is human, so my holy magic had no effect except to smother her heat."

Kari frowned. "Your power doesn't hurt humans? Why not?"

"It is a caveat that comes with this type of power," Ari replied. "Humans cannot be harmed, because they are not inherently…evil."

He shrugged at the look on her face. "Gods know that isn't true, but it isn't as if humans are my main worry. For them, steel usually works well enough."

They came upon the hunting group as the sun broke the mountain tops. Ari shielded his face to get a look at his men.

They stood at attention as Ari approached, their backs straight and their eyes forward. Each was armed with a short sword, and some had weapons of their own. Kari stood back nervously.

"Five of you," Ari said, looking them over. "Are we missing one? Present!"

The men called out their names from the left, pounding their fists against their chests as they did so:

"Wilcoth!"

"Bakri!"

"Milak!"

"Mikael!"

"Ryael!"

Ari pondered them a moment longer. Kari wondered what he was looking for when the thought clicked.

"I'm sorry, Master Ari!" a whining, wheezing voice called from behind them.

Kari and Ari turned to see the ginger-haired boy Linus was scolding the day before. He stopped as he came upon Ari and bent over, breathing heavily. He looked pathetically tiny compared to the rest of Ari's men, with scrawny arms and chicken-like legs.

"What is your name?" Ari asked him.

"Greglin Mattis," he gasped.

"You will address me as 'lord,' and you will not be late again."

Greglin stood straight, his face paler than usual. The dash of freckles across his nose brightened. "Yes, Lord!"

Ari nodded and gestured to the others. Greglin raced past him to stand with them.

"We will enter the forest now…" Ari trailed off, a look of exasperation forming on his face. "Greglin, have you no weapons?"

Greglin's face reddened. The other men were beginning to grin.

"I f-forgot, Lord."

Ari stared at him a moment longer. Finally, he said with an amused smile, "Will someone please lend Greglin a weapon for to-day?"

Ryael unhooked his sword and handed it to the sweating red-head.

"Right. Let's head out."

Ari led his troop of six men and Kari into the forest. As soon as they entered the barrier of trees, the dense leaves obscured the morning sun. Kari walked quickly to catch up with Ari, her ears flickering frantically.

The boy lord didn't say anything as she came to his side. He was a different person; completely relaxed, yet deadly serious, with his bow in his hand.

The walk was a boring one. Kari could hear Ari's men whispering amongst themselves about women, weapons, and what they might do after the hunt. She listened to them for a time, thinking it silly how easily pleased human boys were, when a sudden crashing from behind made her spin. She faced the source of the sound, her teeth bared and electricity crackling along her claws.

Greglin looked up at her from the ground with a nervous stare. Ari's men stood around him, shaking their heads and smirking at the ginger boy.

"Time for a break, is it?" Ari called a few feet behind Kari.

"Greglin is a clumsy fool, Lord!" Mikael called back.

"S-sorry!" Greglin cried as he stood again.

Ari appeared at Kari's side again. "In front, if you please," he told Greglin before moving on again.

After another quarter-hour, Ari slowed his pace and stopped at a small clearing. He turned and waited for his men to circle him. Kari stopped beside them and sniffed around, trying to catch a solid scent. The forest all around them smelled of a thousand things, including elk. The smells were so numerous it was impossible to decide which way to turn.

Gods, why didn't Mother and Father teach me more?

Kari was surprised when Ari spoke. "We're coming upon the beginning of their territory. We're downwind right now, so if we're quiet, we could get a couple here without having to go much farther."

His men nodded in response and unsheathed and unslung various weapons. Mikael and Ryael each had an identical spear. Milak wielded a heavy axe. Bakri swung a longbow over his shoulder. Wilcoth bore a long sword that shone a little in the dim lighting. Greglin shakily unsheathed Ryael's extra blade.

Once they were ready, Ari nodded and turned away. He weaved through the bushes, keeping low, his steps barely making a sound. Kari followed him silently, her eyes cutting through the darkness. Behind her followed Greglin and the rest, who still clomped along, though much quieter.

Ari held up his fist. Kari froze on instinct at the swiftness of his movement, and relaxed when the rest of his men did the same.

So humans have silent cues, too.

Ari nodded his head to the right and the rest of them followed his gaze. In between two thick rowan trees, Kari could see the movement of something thick, furry, and brown. It glided through the bushes gracefully, chewing as it walked. A pair of massive antlers easily knocked aside low-hanging branches.

Behind Kari, Greglin whimpered. Milak crept past him and next to Kari. He tapped Ari on the shoulder and pointed to himself. Ari nodded.

With a grin, Milak carefully slunk around them and into the greenery.

Kari waited, her breath held. She longed to kill the elk herself. It was alone, such easy prey for her, but she sensed this trip into the woods was more for training than it was need for food.

Her head snapped up at the sound of the elk letting out a low, groaning sound. It cocked its head in their direction.

Milak jumped out of the trees. His dark brown eyes gleamed with delight as he let out a raucous cry and came down on the elk's back. His axe lodged deep into the beast's throat and sliced down, easily severing the head. It fell to the ground with a *thump*, and shortly after, the body followed.

Ari and his men joined Milak. Kari followed along behind, the tangy smell of blood filling her nose.

Milak lifted the elk's head by the antlers and held it up. Bakri gave a whoop and raced to his side to clasp him on the shoulder. Ari stopped to study the kill.

"A clean cut."

Milak pounded his free fist against his chest. "Thank you, Lord."

"It is messy, though," Ari continued, ignoring Milak. "And rather…crude. This sort of absent-minded killing might suit a war, Milak, but the creatures of Raziac deserve a little more grace."

Milak's face reddened slightly. He looked half abashed, half annoyed.

"Yes, Lord."

"Gut it and clean it. You and Bakri will carry this one. Wilcoth, if you will aid them?"

Ari's men did as he bid. Kari watched them cut open the elk with deft hands, removing the innards and cutting the skin away from the bone. She glanced at Ari, who faced away from them again.

Kari had believed only wolves spoke of honor and a graceful death for their prey. As long as the job was done, why would a human care?

Soon Bakri, Milak, and Wilcoth hefted the meat, and they were off. Ari moved slower this time, curving around the forest along a serpentine path. Every several yards he would stop, search the ground, and head in a different direction until Kari was sure they were lost.

It must have been around noon when he stopped again, crouching low.

Ari held up a hand. With two fingers he pointed forward; again, no one moved. Kari wondered what this signal meant.

Slowly, Ari slipped an arrow from the quiver at his back. He nocked it to his bow and drew the string to his cheek. Kari watched him align the arrowhead. She glimpsed a large, dark shape as he let go.

The arrow whistled and struck into the hind of the beast with a *thuck*. Ari had another arrow ready and let loose as the creature turned to them. The point stabbed in between two brown eyes; the elk stumbled, dead before it hit the ground.

The hunting party climbed over bramble and around trees to Ari's kill. He removed his arrows and cleaned them before sticking them back in his quiver.

"Prepare this one, then we will round our way back," Ari said. "It grows late. Mikael, will you and Ryael help Greglin—"

"We can take this one ourselves, Lord," Ryael said with a grunt as he cut away the flesh. Greglin's gaze lowered.

"As you wish. But hurry. We will go on, see if we can't get one more," Ari said, leading Kari, Greglin, Bakri, Milak, and Wilcoth onward. She noted Greglin, looking downcast. He fingered the hilt of the blade at his side, staring off into space as they walked. Frowning, she moved faster to catch up with Ari.

"Do you tire, Kari?"

"No," she murmured. "I could carry these things."

Ari led her around a thick tree and sidestepped a thorny bush. "That is what my men are for. They learn the art of a swift kill and bear the weight of it."

"Then why am I here?" Kari growled. "I don't like this forest. The only reason I agreed to come was to help you."

Ari's eyebrows drew together, but he didn't reply. She rolled her eyes with a huff.

After a long time, he muttered, "I did not want to leave you alone."

Kari's heart thudded uncomfortably. She glanced at Ari, but he was gazing ahead, carefully leading them around another tree.

"I was sure that the shadowy force from the other night would only affect you as darkness fell… But I had a fear in my heart. I couldn't leave you there. Forgive me. You may take the next kill if you wish."

She was taken aback by his words and found herself blushing as anger welled in her chest. How *dare* he? She was not a weak pup that needed watching!

At the same time, though, she felt a tiny prickle of something akin to pleasure; it felt *good* to be looked after for the first time in so long.

Ari extended his arm, stopping Kari in her tracks. His eyes were wide, alert. Her pulse quickened, her pleasure dispelled. She flicked her ears and tried to catch a strange scent or sound.

There was the steady *crunch* and *snap* of broken branches not far off, somewhere straight ahead. More than a deer was approaching.

Then there was another sound, something melodic. Off-tune and quiet, it hardly reached Kari's ears beneath the cracking of trees.

What was music doing out here, in the forest? Where was it coming from? Kari's legs tensed, as if to walk toward it.

"What is it, Lord…?" Greglin asked, but Ari held up a hand for silence. She wondered if Ari heard the music, too.

The crunching grew closer and louder, drowning out the musical notes. When Kari could not easily find them again, she felt her jaw tighten. She did not even care that some hulking thing was meandering through the trees toward them. Behind her, Milak grunted.

"My lord—"

Ari whipped an arrow free and nocked it, letting it fly toward the sound. Gleaming white, the arrow disappeared between the branches ahead of them, hissing as it flew.

A loud, angry roar echoed through the trees. Ari pulled another arrow from his quiver.

"Drop the meat and ready yourselves. It's a demon."

At the word *demon*, Kari's mind cleared; she tensed, ready to fight. The men drew their weapons as Ryael and Mikael joined them.

"Is it break time now? Gods, I'm starving."

"A demon is coming," Bakri hissed at them.

Kari listened intently as it lumbered to them, roaring all the time. The branches ahead of them creaked and broke, revealing the large snout and fuzzy black head of a bearish creature five feet above them. It snuffled through the trees and bellowed once more.

"Juris, help us!" someone gasped behind her.

"MEN, ARMS!" Ari cried, loosing another arrow. The meat-bearers dropped everything except their weapons and raced to his side. Bakri let loose an arrow from his own bow, but his aim was off; the arrow whistled to the side and lodged in a bush.

The bear demon broke through the final barrier of thick bushes and paused to glower at the pitiful group of hunters. Kari stared back at it.

She had seen glimpses of bears on her mountain home, but never a demon-blooded one. This one was more than ten feet tall, towering over them with beady black eyes and yellow fangs. Black fur covered its body, except for the belly and the top of its head; those were protected by thousands of tiny little plates, like armor. Ari's two arrows looked measly sticking out of its thick arm and shoulder.

"MEAT!" the demon roared so tremendously the trees shook. It thrashed toward them.

Ari's men scrambled, running in all different directions. Kari jumped onto a low-hanging branch out of the way. She turned to the demon, ready to jump onto its back, when she saw Greglin. His red

257

head was a shock of color in the greens and browns of the forest. He stumbled away from the bear, clumsily trying to free his sword as he ran.

"Greglin, DUCK!" Ari yelled.

With a cry, Greglin fell to the ground as the bear swiped a mighty paw over his head. He crawled a few feet away and spun around, finally unsheathing his sword and holding it out.

The bear bellowed angrily, the sound shaking the branch on which Kari was perched. It raised a huge foot to stomp the boy, only to let out a harsh, gargling whine. It stumbled forward, narrowly missing Greglin. A steady trickle of blood seeped around the glimmering blade in its ankle. Kari caught sight of Ari rolling away as the bear spun, swinging its paw around to catch him.

Ari's men, thrilled by his attack, rushed the demon. They jabbed with spears and swords, though the demon easily whacked away most of their attacks.

Greglin rejoined the fray, sword firmly in hand. He stabbed the blade deep into the bear's inner knee, eliciting another outraged cry. The demon stomped and thrashed, scattering the men once more. As they dispersed, Kari did not see Ari go in any direction. She scanned for him, thinking he must have joined Greglin. Yet the pale redhead skirted around the bear, alone.

She saw the bear stoop low to poke at something on the ground. She craned her neck around its hulking mass; there lay Ari, splayed out on the forest floor, his eyes closed. As Kari watched, the demon, chuckling loudly, raised a claw high above his limp body.

"Weakling humans!" it rumbled. "Kill you all!"

"No!" Kari roared. With a growl and a rumble of thunder, she leapt from the tree branch and landed on the demon's mighty back. It jerked and twisted, trying to reach her. She dug her claws in between his thick scales. Using them as handholds, she crawled up its back.

"Get off!" the demon roared, thrashing.

The air grew heavy with energy and Kari knew that it would come if she called it now. She hoped the humans below were out of the way because she couldn't shout a warning; her teeth clattered with every wild swing of the demon's body.

Her eyes flashed; with another crash of thunder, a blinding, jagged bolt of lightning shot through the air to strike the demon's head.

The smell of burnt flesh assailed the air. The demon stumbled, its roar fading to a grunting growl, and then it fell. Kari barely clung on as it crashed onto the hard forest floor. She gagged at the smell and crawled up the demon's shoulder.

It was covered in a wide, black, smoking burn. Piercing dark eyes rolled, showing the whites. With one final shudder, it lay still.

Kari nimbly jumped off the bear and walked around it until she spotted the humans. Ari's men were huddled in a circle around his body. Her breath drew short. Why hadn't he risen yet?

Milak saw her approach and nodded his head. The rest of them turned to face her. After a moment's hesitation, they pounded their fists against their chests in respect, as they did for Ari. Her face reddened.

"Is he...?" She couldn't produce the words. She could only see Kiki and Vivianne, both killed by something much stronger than either of them.

"He lives," Wilcoth said from his kneeling position at Ari's side. Kari's insides melted with relief. "I think he may have bumped his head, is all."

"Will we carry him back with the meat?" Bakri asked.

"Do we have enough manpower for that?" Ryael replied with a snort.

"Does anyone even know the way?" Milak asked quietly.

The men fell silent. Kari glanced between them. They did not fear her, even now. Even though she had made the sky crash down, they accepted her. She let out a breath and stepped forward.

Ryael and Mikael parted so she could stand before Ari and Wilcoth.

"I can carry him. And…" She raised her head to sniff at the air. Her senses were weaker in this form, but she thought she recognized a scent on the wind. As a wolf, it might be easier. "I may be able to lead us back to the river."

The men looked skeptical, eyeing her tiny body. Kari frowned. She removed the leather boots Ari had given her, unwilling to have them destroyed, and shifted forms. Her clothes tore and fell away, replaced by golden brown fur as she bent forward on four legs.

Greglin's eyes widened considerably, and his face paled. The others showed similar signs of shock but said nothing. Kari bent forward and nudged Ari's face with her nose. She looked up at his men.

"Oh!" Ryael said. He bent to sit Ari up so she could bend her head under him. With help, Ryael dragged Ari up and draped him over her back. She shifted her shoulders so he wouldn't easily fall off, and one of the guards grabbed her boots. Satisfied, she turned on the spot with a flick of her tail.

Kari lifted her nose as she walked, following the familiar scent of the river. If she could get them that far, they could lead the way back home.

How ironic, she thought with thin annoyance, *that I will find my way back to the place I don't want to be.*

Even as the thought crossed her mind, she wondered how true that was.

As Kari walked, she vaguely registered the warmth of Ari's body on hers. It was comforting, in a way, the way his heart beat in rhythm with her own.

She thought about the lightning she had called. It had come so easy to her, as if it were always meant to be so simple. She recalled trying, and failing, to start a simple fire because her electricity was too uncontrollable. What made that different now? Was it this place, this forest? Was it the adrenaline of the moment? Was it…

She glanced over her shoulder, caught a glimpse of Ari's red hair, and forced her mind away from it.

Kari led Ari's men through the forest for the better part of an hour. The trees finally thinned, revealing the bright rays of an afternoon sun. Kari snuffled through a large bush, and broke the barrier of the forest. The sound and gleam of steadily running water met her eyes and ears.

Ari's men broke through after her and let out cheers at the sight of the river. Kari allowed them to take the lead, instead following Greglin as they headed southeast.

Greglin was fidgety, shuffling his feet as he walked. Kari watched him, wondering why he would ever join the barracks. Hunting and training seemed far out of his comfort zone.

He glanced at her over his shoulder and gave her a weak smile. He slowed his pace so he could walk beside her.

"So...have you always been able to change form?"

Kari gave him a blank look. He looked uncomfortable.

"Do you understand our language still?" he asked.

Kari's ears twitched and she nodded.

"But you can't speak?"

Kari shook her head. With her parents, she had been able to speak telepathically, but she didn't know if that would be possible with humans. For all she knew, it would throw them over the edge. Wouldn't a different consciousness entering your own be overwhelming?

Greglin fell quiet. Kari relished the silence, enjoying the sound of the river running beside them as they walked. Her thoughts wandered, recalling suddenly the bizarre music she had heard. It vanished with the bear's appearance and did not return, yet she wondered who had been making it.

The ginger boy muttered, "I could never be brave like Mast-Lord Ari. But my father admires him. The way he looked at me sometimes...I had to get out of there. I really thought I could do this." His grip on the hilt of his sword shook.

Kari glanced up to see a minuscule tear leak out of Greglin's eye. She huffed and nudged him with her shoulder. When he looked down at her, she rolled her eyes and tapped the scabbard hanging at his waist with her snout.

Greglin stared at her blankly, his eyes a little bloodshot. He looked down at his sword. "I...I hurt the demon."

Kari nodded and tilted her head back, gesturing at Ari.

"Lord Ari...is it my fault he's hurt?"

Kari shook her head and let out a low growl, trying to communicate her thoughts. Before she could make another gesture, Ari's hand shifted up her side and gripped a tuft of her fur. He twitched and groaned.

"What...?"

She stopped.

Greglin gasped, "Lord Ari!"

The other men stopped and turned to them. They repeated Greglin's call as Ari sat up on Kari's back. His hands ran over her, stopping below her ears. Kari's body shivered with pleasure at his touch; she silently reprimanded herself.

"K-Kari...?"

She hunched her shoulders so he could climb off her back. He stared at her, his mouth open and his eyes wide.

"Lord Ari! Are you well?" Wilcoth asked.

Ari tore his gaze away from Kari to look at his men. "Yes. My head only hurts a little. What happened?"

Mikael handed him his bow and quiver. "Kari killed the demon."

"She called down the sky, is what she did," Bakri said loudly, mimicking the sound of thunder with his mouth, blowing out his cheeks.

Ari chuckled softly. "Your lightning? You are astounding, Kari. Thank you."

She spared him the most unconcerned gaze she could muster.

"And all of you are safe as well." Ari laid his hand on his head. "As shamed as I am to have fallen, I'm glad our hunt was a success." He looked up at his men. "Let us continue to the village and take this meat to the butcher."

The men agreed and continued through the trees. Greglin scrambled to catch up with them, apparently unwilling to share his insecurities in front of the lord. Ari and Kari followed the procession.

"You carried me all the way here?" he asked as they came to the bridge that enabled them to cross the river. When she did not reply, he said, "That is a great honor, Kari. You could have easily left us all behind. I owe you much."

He fell silent. She walked beside him, enjoying the feeling of the hard ground beneath her paws and the deep scent of the forest. With a surge of unease, she realized she was *happy* to be returning home with Ari. To have the chance to return here whenever she wanted.

Kari nudged Ari's hand with her nose. He looked down at her, smiled, and ran his hand along her back, eliciting another small tingle of pleasure. Side by side, they followed Ari's men back home.

CHAPTER
TWENTY-NINE

Before they broke the boundaries of the forest, Kari paused to shift back into her humanoid form. She shook out her shoulders and stretched her fingers, but as Ari turned back to wait for her, she realized the coolness of the breeze touched her everywhere. She instinctively wrapped her arms around herself.

She was *naked*, and about to walk in front of a bunch of humans!

Kari leapt behind a tree, her face on fire. How could she have forgotten? Of all the times she had shifted…she was becoming too comfortable and careless.

If Ari saw anything, he acted otherwise. His voice, even and kind, came from the other side of the tree.

"Kari, what's wrong?"

"My…my clothes," she muttered, cursing herself. *How could she forget?*

Silence answered her. He uttered a short, slightly choked "Ah." After a rustle of clothes, his long jacket appeared at her side. She snatched it and slipped it on, her face still unpleasantly warm. The jacket just reached down to her mid-thigh, and buttoned up to cover her front. She stepped out from behind the tree, refusing to look up from the ground.

"I did not know you had that ability," Ari said, facing away from her. "I have never seen a demon who was able to shift shape."

"My parents could, too," she muttered, as resolute as he was to pretend her slip-up had not happened. They returned to town.

"It is extraordinary," he commented, finally smiling at her. His cheeks were tinged with pink. "Your fur is beautiful."

Kari's face reddened even more. She didn't reply.

"Let's see," he continued, holding up his hand and counting off on his fingers, "you killed the demon. Protected my men. Honored me with a ride out of the forest. I am incredibly humbled by you, Kari."

She scoffed. "You can thank me with the ritual tonight, and by not killing me." She paused and muttered, "And maybe some more clothes."

Ari chuckled. "Of course. We can pick up some things for the ritual on our way to Roland's temple. He gave me a list of supplies this morning."

At last Kari, Ari, and his men entered the village. His men let out sighs of relief and turned to Ari, who nodded. Then they gave Kari a respectful nod and left for the butcher. Greglin alone was left, looking worn and shamed.

"You may return, Greglin," Ari said. "Send Linus a report on my behalf."

Greglin looked positively frightened; even so, he pounded his fist against his chest and left them.

"He is afraid."

"I know. Linus is tough on him, but that's the only way Greglin will find his own strength."

She watched the ginger boy disappear in the distance. "I understand that," she murmured.

Ari led her around the shops. First, he took her to a small, simple building with a tidy sign hanging over the door. *Finely made clothes for all occasions!* it said.

The inside was brightly lit and full of tall racks heavy with coats, dresses, pants, and shirts. Kari ran a finger down the sleeve of a silky shirt, but there were also leather, cotton, and fleece things.

"Mornin', Lord!" called a lanky, red-headed woman with a freckled face. Stepping into the middle of the room, her eyes darted to Kari, a politely curious glance. "How's my son doin'?"

"Morning, Melony. He will give his first report to Linus today."

Melony clasped her hands against her chest. "Thank the gods." She closed her eyes a moment, as if praying. Then she smiled wide, looked at Ari, and propped her fists on her hips. "So, what can I get ya'?"

Ari gestured at Kari. Without him saying a word, Melony hopped to a nearby rack and removed a dress. Kari took an involuntary step back, her ears flicking.

"Something more…practical, if you please?" Ari said quickly. Melony looked over her shoulder at him. He smiled. "The things we'll be doing are unsuitable for a dress."

She stuck out her bottom lip and instead reached for a long shirt and simple pants. "These're the best I've got on short notice, my lord."

"They'll do perfectly. Later I will request formal replacements."

Melony nodded. She charged him ten silvers and allowed Kari to change in her backroom. Amongst piles of ribbon, string, and cloth, Kari slipped off Ari's jacket and pulled on the shirt and pants. Returning to the main room, she handed the jacket back without meeting his eye.

"Thank you," she muttered.

"It's nothing," he said under his breath. Louder, he called, "Thank you, Melony!"

"Tell that Greglin he'd better be home for supper!"

Kari plucked at the shirt while Ari led the way to another shop, this one for herbs and potion-making, where he purchased bundles of sweet-smelling leaves and candles. Then he stopped at the butcher and purchased a freshly cooked, fist-sized quail for each of them.

She twirled the browned quail in her hands. Its roasted smell wafted, mouthwatering. "Are you sure you're well enough to do this? Roland said it would be strenuous, and you—"

"I will manage," Ari said as he sorted through various herbs and different types of candles. He looked up at her with tired eyes set against a wide smile. "Trust me."

They had enough time to finish their lunch, then they rounded a corner and headed toward Roland's temple.

Kari's stomach squirmed as they approached; as if the quail sought revenge for having been feathered and roasted. She swallowed hard, resolved to do this. She wanted to see Kiki again and explain that she had not been the one to kill her.

And if Roland was right, Kiki would kill her if they didn't do something.

Life after death was never something Kari had discussed with her parents. When the subject had been breached by the humans in Snow Shade, she had scoffed at the idea. What did death matter to her when she might die any day? This, though, was something she would have never fathomed; Kiki was the nicest person Kari had ever known. Why did she not find peace in an afterlife?

Ari opened the large double doors and ushered her inside. The temple's pointed ceiling appeared endless with panes of glass that highlighted the darkening sky. Kari found herself staring for some time before Ari called her attention from across the room.

She crossed the broad, whitewashed, wooden floor. A stack of wooden benches lay against either end of the massive single room.

"Do people not visit often?" she asked, thinking of Snow Shade. The church there was much smaller and filled to the brim with people every seven days.

"We have a day of blessing once a month." Ari led her to a broad-backed chair at the end of the room and stepped behind it. He pulled on a string Kari wouldn't have noticed, revealing a wooden door that opened to a set of descending steps. "Close it behind you. Roland doesn't like people down here," he told her before climbing in and disappearing into the darkness of the basement.

She followed him, reaching up and tugging the wooden hatch shut behind her. She caught Ari's scent and followed him through a small doorway until she came to another, smaller room.

Flickering torches provided light, revealing a storage chamber of sorts. One wall was lined with shelves stacked with books, vials, bottles, and jars. Another held the beautiful painting of a handsome, bearded man with dark red hair and even darker emerald eyes, reminding her of pine trees. His face was lined with age, though the corners of his mouth were curved, as if he couldn't help but smile.

"Who is this?" Kari asked as Ari placed the candles around the room.

"My father. Lord Alton."

She studied the painting a little longer. *The one I came here to meet.*

"Why is it down here?"

Ari began lighting the candles. His voice was tight as he said, "On the night of his passing, I had the painting moved down here. I could not handle seeing it for some time."

Kari turned to him. He had arranged the candles in a large circle. "You should move it to your house. He should be honored, not hidden away in a dusty tomb."

He laughed softly. "You're right, Kari. I fully intend to move it to my home. The main room, maybe. Perhaps that is when you will tell me of your friend who sent you here looking for him." Ari gave her a wry smile. "Stand here, please." He indicated to the middle of the circle. She stood where he gestured. "If I may ask, where is your family, Kari?"

Kari pursed her lips, taken aback by the sudden question. "Another time."

Ari nodded. He stepped outside the circle and sat. "Please sit opposite me."

She did as he said. The heat from so many lit candles made her skin warm and tingly. The smell of the melting wax wafted all around her, mingling with another scent. She scrunched her nose.

"What is that smell?"

"The candles. They are made of a special wax that helps clear the mind and settle the soul. Forgive me, but I will need all the help I can get for this."

Ari took a deep breath and closed his eyes. A white glow spread from his fingertips, up his arms, and across his shoulders. Within minutes, the light outlined his form. Kari winced and leaned away from him.

"Are you ready, Kari?" his voice was a whisper, barely audible.

Her ears flickered. "Yes," she replied just as quietly.

Ari let out his breath. As he exhaled, a warm gust of shimmering wind blew forth. It passed over the candles without the barest flicker of a flame; Kari hissed through her teeth as it washed over her. First it tingled, then it stung, a thousand white-hot needles prickling every bit of exposed flesh. It was gone before it became unbearable; she forced herself to relax, trying to calm her breathing.

He placed his hands on the ground between them. He grunted, his muscles tensed, and suddenly the entire floor was aglow. Kari gasped in pain.

"Don't move," Ari muttered. She barely managed to obey him as the white heat threatened to scorch her skin. "Give...me...your hand."

Kari flinched as she reached across the candle flames to grab his hand. He entwined his fingers with hers and threw his head back. His eyes, once vibrantly green, were two flames of pure white.

His grip burned. The air was stifling, drawing the breath right out of her lungs. He squeezed her hand, and she breathed a little easier.

Ari waved his free hand through the air, and all at once, the candles were extinguished. Kari squinted against his glow, now the only light in the room. The burning sensation intensified.

His grip tightened and he gritted his teeth. She watched him through narrowed eyes. Shock flashed over his face, and he grunted again.

The light blinked out for the briefest second. Kari gasped as the burning suddenly disappeared before it returned full force, searing even through her new pants. The darkness, lingering beyond Ari's glow, felt heavy and alive; it loomed all around them, only kept at bay by his power.

At the edge of her vision, Kari saw something. She twisted around, still holding tightly to his hand. At the edge of the light was a flicker in the darkness, a shift of gray. Her eyes widened as fingers reached from the deep, hulking blackness. Soon a hand was revealed, then an arm. Soon there was a shoulder attached to the neck, and head, of Kiki. She dragged elongated, inhuman claws along the stone, hissing when she got too close to the light.

Ari loosened his grip on her hand. She turned back to him. His eyes were wide, taking in the sight of the darkness with recognition she couldn't fathom. Then the expression was replaced with a calm fierceness as he looked at Kiki. The white fireballs had disappeared from his eyes, but the glow around him remained.

Kiki dragged her body from the shadows and crawled around the circle, her eyes on Kari.

"What is this?" she whispered. "I cannot reach you…"

"I summoned you," Ari said, loud and clear, his voice ringing.

Her head snapped to him.

"And who are you?" She crouched low, like an angry cat. "I do not know you, have never seen…"

"What is your purpose here? What is your name?"

Kiki's face twisted into a malignant sneer, an expression she would have never made while alive. "Did Kari not tell you? She killed me, banished me to some shadowy afterlife. I'm here for revenge."

Kari grimaced, opened her mouth to argue; the scorching heat in the air seared her throat.

"Revenge will not settle your spirit," Ari said softly.

"What do you know of revenge or spirits?!" Kiki yelled, unleashing a wave of darkness that crashed against Ari's unwavering brightness.

"I admit I know little," he replied, still speaking gently. "I know this: your hatred is unfounded. Kari has never hurt any of my people. I read the pain in her eyes the last time I witnessed your interaction with her. She misses you, and she mourns you. She could not possibly have done this deed."

Kiki screamed. Kari winced. The girl's face transformed with rage; she clawed at her own face, tortured by the agony and anger she felt.

"SHE IS THE MOST EVIL, THE MOST FOUL! SHE KILLED THE PEOPLE WHO TOOK HER IN! SHE KILLED ME! SHE IS THE REASON EVERYONE AROUND HER DIES! SHE IS A MURDERER!"

"Please," Ari whispered, "calm."

His words floated through the room as a warm, soft, breeze. Kari felt her breathing slow. Likewise, Kiki seemed to relax, slumping against the ground. The shadows around her pulsed, buzzing like angry bees. Ari spared them a glance.

"Your murder was a shameful thing. And yet, Kari is not without honor. She could never have done this to you." Ari's gaze flickered to the impeding shadows and clenched his fists. His white glow pulsed, fighting back the darkness. "I believe your true murderer revels over the trickery in the shadows. Even now, they are angry—"

The shadows. Kari's thoughts whirred, recalling the purple beast and its mistress. She flinched as a dozen somethings all spoke at once, hissing over each other.

Kill Kari…

She betrayed you.

Your blood is on her hands…

Ari glanced around the room as the voices, raspy and thin, emerged from all around them. Kiki shook every time one spoke.

"Enough," he growled. His glow pulsed again, and the darkness frothed. Inky bubbles erupted from the ground around Kiki's hands. They began to pop, each time dribbling smoking plumes of more shadow.

"Ari," Kari whimpered.

He pushed himself up to one foot, hand drifting to the dagger strapped to his thigh, yet he didn't draw it. "I don't know what you are, or why you're here, but you won't remain."

Kiki's body quaked with silent sobs. The monstrous obscurity around her wiggled with hissing laughter.

Flee, young lord.

You are nothing.

To the great night, your light will fail.

Ears pinned back, Kari looked to Ari. The color drained from his face, and that scared her more than the monstrous darkness did.

He clenched his hand, then slammed his fist onto the ground. Blazing, ivory light erupted, forcing Kari to turn her head. The dazzling, bright burn washed over her, feathering her skin with licks of uncomfortable warmth.

Yet her own whimper was engulfed by the hissing of the shadows as they dissipated.

Only when the silence was long and thick did Kari turn back around. Ari's shoulders were slack, his head bowed. She thought of reaching for him until Kiki raised her head again, ash-colored eyes filled with shimmering tears.

"Please help me. I don't know where I am or why. It's so dark."

Kari's eyes burned with her own tears. How she longed to grab Kiki and hold her, to make all of this go away.

"Someone has wronged you greatly," Ari said, weakness cracking each word. "But it was not Kari who did this to you. You know that, don't you?"

Kiki let out a choking sob that shook her whole body.

"I will make this right, Kiki!" Kari cried, despite the burning air. "I will do anything, everything, it takes to release you!"

"Kari," Kiki sobbed. "It's so dark. She said…she said you couldn't come. Not unless I brought you. But I…you can't! It would destroy you. It would…"

Her words faded into choking gasps. Kari reached for her with trembling fingers, only to flinch back as a glow flared into Kiki.

It came from Ari. Once it swathed Kiki in its light, he slumped, his face tightened with effort.

"It is time, Kiki," he rasped. "You must release her."

"Wait," Kari gasped. "Who did this? Kiki?"

Kiki's head was already dipping. The whiteness of the room pulsed, and Kari's friend sunk into the ground. Once her darkness had dispersed completely, swallowed by Ari's light, the room flashed before fading to normal. Ari fell to his hands with a grunt, his arms trembling.

Kari stared at the place Kiki had been before realizing the burn from the ground and air was gone. She turned to Ari as he began to shake.

"Ari?"

He heaved, releasing the contents of their light lunch. He wiped his mouth and met her eye. His face was tinged green and shiny with sweat.

"Sorry, Kari…" He sat up shakily. "Your skin…you're burned."

Kari glanced down at her arms to see raw, red skin that throbbed and stung. The edges of her shirt had been burned away.

"I will survive," she grumbled. "Are you…?"

"Just weak," Ari replied. He dug into his pocket and pulled out some bright green leaves. "Chew these and apply them. They will ease the pain," he whispered hoarsely, handing them to her. She shoved them in her mouth and did as he bid. Slowly, Ari stood on shaky legs. "I will have to ask Roland to clean up in here," he muttered and walked around the candles to the door.

Kari had finished applying some of the green mush to her last burn when he stumbled against the wall with a groan. She got up and made her way over to him, using her arm to help him balance.

"Thank you," Ari said. He looked down at her legs again and winced. "I am so sorry, Kari."

"It's nothing," she replied, trying to ignore the throbbing as she pulled his arm over her shoulders. "Can I ask something?"

"Of course."

"When you saw Kiki, and the darkness surrounding her, you seemed shocked. Not surprised or scared, though. More like you'd seen them before."

She felt Ari tense, his hand balling into a fist next to her arm.

"It's…I can't talk about it now," he said shortly.

Kari glanced at his face. The boy lord wore an expression of agonizing fury, a tangle of emotions she wouldn't have believed him capable of.

"Alright. Let's get back. Your home is quite a walk away."

Ari snorted. "You're right. The more I think about it, the hill was not an ideal place to put a house."

The two of them stumbled uneasily up the stairs. Kari glanced back at the room before the natural darkness swallowed it up. How would she save Kiki when she didn't know where she was or how to get there?

"I did what I could to protect her spirit," Ari whispered softly. "I gave her some *Mikeo*, a fragment of my light. It will help keep the darkness at bay until we can find a way to release her."

Kari frowned at him. "What do you mean, 'we'? And is that why you're so weak?"

He pushed open the hidden doorway and climbed out. He reached down to help Kari, who gritted her teeth in pain as the burns on her legs throbbed.

"I would never dream of leaving you to traverse a plane of darkness so powerful, not by yourself," Ari said plainly. "In any case, it will take some time and research. Until then, I hope that Kiki will have some peace knowing that you will come for her."

Kari's insides burned with gratefulness as well as embarrassment. She closed the door and helped Ari out of the temple.

"Tell me about your friend who led you here," Ari rasped as they walked. "It will keep my mind off the discomfort."

She hesitated, but it was a small thing to ask for after what he'd just done for her.

Kari swallowed. "Her name was Vivianne. I met her while walking from the northern mountains," she said as the two of them started up the sloping hill. "I had abandoned my home and was looking for a place to go...she was kind to me. She offered to take me with her as she traveled the world. She was a scribe."

Ari chuckled weakly. "Ah. Yes, I remember a vivacious young woman coming by years ago, when I was only a boy. She practically hounded my father for all the history we held here."

Kari grinned. "As we came further south," she grunted, shouldering much of Ari's weight, "she mentioned your father. Said the people here were relatively fair for demons like me. She said we could stop by on our way to the ships."

Ari was silent for a time. "But that purple beast..."

Kari felt a clench in her gut. "Yes. It killed her outside the town of Angel Cross."

Neither of them said anything. They walked laboriously until finally, the hill leveled.

"Her death was not your fault. Neither was Kiki's. You know that, right?"

Kari stiffened and didn't reply. When they reached his door, she allowed Ari to pull away and open it.

"I have often thought things happen for a reason. They must. It is a terrible thing that your friend Vivianne died, after so short a time of getting to know her." He looked back at Kari. "But I'm grateful that it allowed me to meet you. I'm sure Vivianne would be proud that you have found a home here."

When Kari didn't say anything, Ari smiled at her. He limped into his home, leaving the door wide open behind him.

Home. The word had meant so little for the last several years of her life.

"Home" was where everything was taken from her. "Home" was where she reluctantly returned every night because she was too fearful and weak to make her own life in the woods.

Home was not a place for her. But now...

Pushing her fears and pain aside, Kari followed him, closing the door with a resolute *click*.

CHAPTER THIRTY

That night, Kari's dreams were blessedly free of darkness, and returned to the norm of thunderstorms over the plains of Taris. These were their own type of mystery, although one she could happily ignore.

The following day, she joined Ari as he discussed the hunt with Linus, specifically mentioning Kari's aid in defeating the bear demon. She pretended to ignore him, and tried not to notice the surly barracks master's grin.

Afterward, Ari led her through town, where he was stopped often by villagers. A few had respectful complaints about supplies. While he appeased them with promises to help, she looked to the forest. It seemed less ominous now, after her fight with the bear demon. She recalled her desires to leave Raziac Village. She'd done what she needed to here; what other reason was there for her to remain?

Her brow furrowed, recalling another goal tied to this place, this forest. She'd forgotten her mother's order.

"Ari, is there anyone here named Zina?"

He thought for a moment, pursing his lips. "No…no, I don't believe I know that name, and I *should* know everyone here."

That is so much to memorize, Kari thought. She sighed.

"Who is she?" he asked.

"I don't know. My mother told me to find her in the south, but no one seems to know her."

If Zina was not here, she had to be elsewhere. Should Kari leave Raziac and go look for her? There must be some reason her mother had wanted her to find Zina.

She felt Ari's eyes. She looked to see him watching her and felt her stomach flip.

"Let's go see Telda," he said. "She's…well, you'll like her."

Frowning, Kari followed him to the bakery. When they entered, it was not to see the large man Kari had met her first time in the village. Instead, there was a woman, her hair short, curly, and brown, her face round. Kari had seen her once, crying in front of this shop when the Fire Witch attacked.

"Well, if it ain't the young lord," the woman said in a jovial voice as she straightened from behind the counter. "Come to take my monthly fees?"

Ari snorted. "Telda, this is Kari. Kari, Telda. She's Gorth's wife. The baker," he added.

"I wondered when you'd come by," Telda said, her eyes glittering. "Quite the girl, from what I hear, eh? Helped ya rebuild our shop an' everything."

Kari started to shake her head as Telda's smile grew wider.

"Thinkin' of stayin' here?"

"I…no," Kari muttered. She felt Ari shift beside her and worried he'd be offended that she had no desire to stay.

Telda nodded. "Of course, it's strange, ain't it? Bein' around people like us?"

"What do you mean?"

278

Telda gestured at Ari, who quirked a brow. "Well, our young lord…he ain't very cultured, is he? I heard ya came from the north, so I figure he must seem a regular bumpkin."

Kari laughed.

Ari grumbled with mirth. "Maybe I will accept your annual fees early."

The door creaked open behind them, and a woman walked in.

Telda waved a hand at Kari and Ari. "Be gone with ya. We have a business, aye? Go on!"

The woman tilted her head to Ari as they passed. When they left the bakery, Ari headed away from town, towards the trees.

"Does everyone here treat you with such indifference?" Kari asked, lips twitching.

Ari's shoulders slumped a little, but he managed a laugh.

"Some of them. They were close to my father, so I suppose it's natural for them. Telda…she's something of a mother to me. When my mother left, Telda was always kind. Stern, too." He chuckled, quieter this time.

"What happened with your mother?"

Ari stopped walking. They were near the edge of the forest now.

"She left when I was very young," he said without looking at her. "She journeyed for an herbal remedy and didn't come back. After months passed with no word, my father assumed she was dead. It's been years now."

Kari could have cut the silence with her claws. She was sorry she asked.

She took a few tentative steps until she stood at his side.

"I used to live in the northern mountains. My parents and I were the only wolf demons in the land. At least, that's what my mother told me." Her fingers curled into fists as her eyes burned.

Ari's hand reached for hers. She stiffened but allowed his fingers to unclench her fist. His touch was warm, a gentle contrast to the cool air of the coming evening. "What happened?"

Kari glanced at him. She wanted to tell him, she realized. It was an itchy need inside of her, a desire for Ari to know everything.

How would he react when she told him?

"Humans came," she said, her voice low. "They'd seen me at the base of the mountain and followed me. They attacked my parents. Even though Mother and Father were the strongest demons I'd ever known, they were felled. The humans took me home, mistaking me for one of them."

Ari said nothing. Kari steeled herself to continue.

"I…I vowed that I would end their lives. I trained for years until I was strong enough. Kiki helped me, even though she didn't want me to take a human life." Kari turned to him, her eyes burning with angry tears. "And then I killed them. They deserved it, so I did it."

Still, Ari didn't reply. Her stomach twisted into knots. She had confessed to the murders Kiki had accused her of committing. Would he still want her to stay?

He slowly turned to her, his face calm. "We do things we regret, Kari. I understand your need for revenge. If I knew what kept my mother from home, I…" He trailed off and let out a heavy breath. "Can I show you something?"

Kari frowned. "What?"

"It's in the forest, a little ways in."

She nodded, and he led her a little more west along the tree line. When they came upon a spot that appeared wholly random to her, they entered the forest.

"What if we find another demon?"

Ari cut a path through the trees and bushes; there was no trail to follow. "They don't come this way. They stay more to the north."

The trees and bushes enveloped them, caressing them with the smells and sounds of the natural forest. It was as calming as the village outside, despite the dangers it also represented. Ari continued at a left angle. Kari wondered what he could possibly want to show her out here.

The sound of gently running water was on the air, and yet they did not come to the river that snaked through the forest. Instead, Ari continued at a westward angle, cutting through underbrush and around huddled trees. They came to a row of large bushes. He paused to glance at her.

"Just through here," he said before pushing through.

She followed, stepping onto the bank of the roaring river that sparkled with a moonlight hue. The water was faster here, rushing as it cascaded from a waterfall. Rocks jutted out from the bottom, spraying the tops of their boots with water.

The sound and sight of it was mesmerizing. Kari walked to the falls and held out a hand to catch a trickle as it fell. Icy water splashed over her hand.

Ari stood at her side, smiling.

"My mother showed me this place. I come here sometimes to think."

Kari watched him, waiting. He dropped his gaze to the water splashing near their feet.

"I don't blame you for your past, Kari. No one here would. I've done foolish things I regret for the sake of retribution, too." He rubbed the back of his head. "But the importance is in the present. I know you wouldn't hurt us. My people would never give you cause to do so. They will treat you like family if you let them. You saw Telda."

Kari snorted. "How can you say you know I won't hurt you? You've barely known me. Demons are evil. They lie and kill, anything to get their way."

"I don't know you as well as Kiki, or even your friend Vivianne, might have known you," he admitted. "But I have the faith to know that you are better than the lesser of your species. There are evil humans too, Kari. Would you lump me with them as well?"

She bit her lip, twisting her fingers in the icy water.

He reached a hesitant hand out and laid it on hers. She stiffened and looked up at him.

"I…I know we just met, but…I want you to stay with me, Kari."

Kari blinked. The icy water was still falling on their entangled hands. Without realizing it, she had wrapped her fingers around his. She disentangled herself and pulled away.

"I don't belong here."

Ari laughed, a sound that made her heart quiver. "Kari, no one has ever belonged somewhere more. I have cherished your company, truly. You believe me, don't you?"

Kari's brow furrowed. Her stomach fluttered as if she had eaten a still-living bird. "I…"

What argument did she have? She was a demon, yes, but his people did not mind her presence. Most of them gladly accepted it.

But I need to find Zina. Mother wished it.

A hopeless quest, her traitorous mind argued. *I only wanted acceptance, and I have felt that here.*

"You have had a hard life," Ari continued in a whisper. "It's obvious people—humans—have done nothing but hurt you. If you let me, I…"

He trailed off. Kari waited, holding her breath.

"I would like to be a good piece in your life," he continued, his voice hoarse. "I…I would be so happy if you chose to stay here. With me."

Kari slowly shook her head. Her feet moved without permission, taking her a step away from the waterfall. From him.

"With you? What does that mean?"

Ari turned to her. Even in the dim light of the forest, he seemed to glow. A silhouette of sunshine, all on his own. "I…Kari, I'm falling in love with you."

Kari stiffened. Her stomach and head exploded with differing feelings: one grew hot, making her sick, while the other buzzed, filling her with useless mush.

"I'm sorry to be so forward," he murmured. "I haven't felt like this before. I…"

"You're the lord of a human village," Kari managed, her voice cracking. "How can you possibly say—"

"I don't care about that," Ari said with a frown. "You're you, no matter who or what you are."

He hadn't moved toward her, for which she was grateful; her body was fighting between running for the trees and falling to the ground in a heap. She didn't want to be provoked to do either.

"You can't say you love me. There's…there's plenty of worthier girls." Kari's words came without her conscious thought. "What… what about Julia, the meat shop girl?"

As soon as the words left her mouth, Kari's heart felt as if it were being squeezed by hands as icy as the waterfall.

Ari cocked his head at her, the corners of his lips lifting.

"Is that truly what you think? The best woman for me is the one who knows nothing outside this village, or even her father's shop?"

"No. But…"

"I'm not a fool, Kari," he said, stepping closer.

Her legs trembled. Part of her told her to run, but the other screamed louder. *Stay.*

"I know there would be boundaries for us to overcome, but believe me when I say we could do it together. You deserve a happier life than you've known. Let me help make that happen."

"We're destined to fight each other," Kari ground out, desperate to find something that might make him leave her and this conversation. Her heart squeezed again. "That's the nature between humans and demons, isn't it? We have been enemies since the beginning of time. You can't have me, and you can't put me in a place above your people. I'm a demon. I'm evil. I'm…"

Ari didn't speak again. His movements were careful, smooth and slow. His arms gently encircled her, pulling her against his chest. She was stunned; being in his arms made her thoughts quiet and her stomach less fluttery.

Since her parents' deaths, Kari had felt she had to set herself against the world. Yet here, with him, she could believe that there might be another way to do things.

Before her mind could register more than a heady buzz, he leaned closer. Their lips were almost touching. Kari held her breath and didn't move.

When he pressed his lips to hers, everything else melted away. She pressed her hands against his back, relishing the warmth of him. Her heart erupted with glorious static and flames.

I could do anything, she thought suddenly. *As long as I have Ari, I could do anything at all.*

CHAPTER THIRTY-ONE

Before Kari knew it, autumn was upon them. It chilled the air with sharp winds and colored the leaves of the trees, although the larger part of the forest remained quite green and lively.

"The forest never withers, not even in the dead of winter," Ari explained when she pointed this out. "It's strange, but it's always been this way."

It was odd, but not unlike Kiki's morthiem lilies. In a way, it felt as if Kiki was blessing her choice to stay in Raziac Village. Though Kari was gladdened by the thought, it also made her shameful; while she was finding comfort and even love, Kiki's soul was trapped.

I will find you and free you, somehow, Kari promised in the dark of night, when she thought Kiki might hear her. Determination made her warm. She *would* save Kiki from whatever had her trapped.

Kari learned things she never expected living with Ari, such as how to broker trade deals and ensure the village would not go hungry in the winter. With Roland, she learned that Taris once had two great wars between humans and demons, with neither side really "winning"—demons still plagued the land, if with less violence than their ancestors.

"Fortunately, men learned a way to fight the demons back. The demons would need a strong rallying point to fully conquer the world. If they could organize…"

"Or find a leader," Kari suggested, thinking of Ari.

Roland smiled. "Yes. If they could find a particularly smart, or strong, demon to lead them, we might be in trouble."

When she might be attempting to study history books but found them too boring, Linus taught her the psychology of warfare, specifically how the chaos of battle affects the minds of men.

"You must make sure they are strong of body and will, or they will crack under the strain."

"Not that we deal with that much in Raziac," Ari broke in wryly.

In their free time, she and Ari walked the streets of town, soothed by the peace of his people even as they prepared for the coming chill of winter. It was nothing like Snow Shade, where even as she masqueraded as a human, everyone looked down on her. Here, despite her ears and tail, she was an equal. This was the life she and Kiki had dreamed of living, and she was determined to live it to the fullest in her friend's honor.

As winter came, Kari thought often of Snow Shade. Those blizzards were harsh and biting; in Raziac Village, the snow came gently, blanketing the ground and lining the buildings with frost. The cold of it was bitter, though, chilling to the bone, even for her.

The year ended. Rather than avoid celebrating it as Kari might have done in Snow Shade, she gladly joined Ari and his entire village around a large, crackling bonfire. He spoke of good fortune and happiness, and love for him showed in the face of every man, woman, and child. Kari watched him from a place beside Roland, her heart in her throat, as he thanked everyone for all that they did for him.

The weeks and months continued to pass. As they traded the bitter cold for soft grass and gentle breezes, Kari was glad. Wilcoth was chosen as Lieutenant under Linus, and after months of training, Greglin was finally settling in at the barracks.

At her insistence that she do more than get his provisions every few days, Ari taught her how to read through reports and respond to letters from other towns. It was monotonous, tedious work, but she found she didn't mind it all that much, especially when Ari sat at her side.

"How it's going?" Ari asked, laying a hand on her shoulder.

Her eyebrows relaxed, and her shoulders straightened at his touch.

"Telda needs more of those spices…cinnamon, I think?"

Ari nodded. "She was happy to remind me a little while ago."

"And Briar's Glen still writes rude letters," Kari said, holding up a page scrawled from top to bottom with messy writing.

Briar's Glen. She hadn't liked the place since she'd been attacked there. After doing Ari's paperwork, she hated it more. It was a booming town full of good trade, and easily supplied much of the things used in Raziac Village, yet their responses and offers were crudely written and full of deceit. Ari told her that Briar's Glen overvalued much of their product and charged them far above asking price. Yet, there wasn't another option for things such as spices and silks.

There were two other villages to trade with in the south: Snake Bay to the northwest, which provided salmon and salts; and Angel Cross, southward and east of the mountains.

Ari had never been to Angel Cross, but he corresponded often with their lord, Lucas, and said they were the holders of many of the old legends of Taris. The name, for instance, was given to it because a literal angel had blessed the town after conquering a great demon. Kari rolled her eyes at him—even Vivianne wouldn't have believed a story like that. In any case, the town of Angel Cross did not make for good trade, unless one wanted parchment and ink.

Ari took the Briar's Glen letter from her. He skimmed it, shrugging.

"We'll figure it out later."

"How was this morning?" she asked with a smile.

"Good. It appears Greglin will move up to a training position soon. Other than that, it's smooth sailing until the hunt in a few weeks. Linus is preparing some new men for it now, but he wants to have the ceremony for Wilcoth's promotion first. I have to help him plan that tomorrow—"

A series of loud, sharp knocks interrupted him. Kari's head shot to the hall.

"I'll see who it is," Ari said with a frown.

She stood from the table as he left, her ears flickering when the front door opened.

"Lord Ari," a breathless voice said.

"Whoa," Ari replied. "What is it?"

Kari left the kitchen and entered the hall. Ari stood in the doorway facing Wilcoth. He was bent over, hair matted to his head with sweat. He smelled of salt and blood.

"What happened?" she asked sharply.

Ari glanced at her. Wilcoth lifted his head to look at them.

"Something in the forest," he gasped. "Men are hurt—scouts—there was so much blood. You have to come."

Without a word, Ari rushed back down the hall to get his herb kit. Kari fetched Wilcoth a cup of water.

"Thank you," he breathed after he had gulped it down. "I have to go tell Linus what I saw. Can you tell Ari? It was at the river, near the bridge. I couldn't..." He flinched as if struck by the memory. "I couldn't carry them back with me."

"I will," Kari promised. "Go."

He nodded and ran back down the hill. Ari appeared again, bow and quiver slung over his shoulder, and medicine pouch around his waist.

"Let's go."

They rushed toward the trees. Some villagers milled about this time of day; they paused as the two of them ran.

"What is it, Lord Ari?"

"Lord?"

"It's alright!" he called as he passed them. "Return to your homes!"

Before long, they were in the forest and running to the river. They broke through a final line of bushes to a scene that made Kari freeze, her gut twisting with disgust and fear. Ari stopped a step ahead of her with a sharp intake of breath. His hands curled at his sides.

Upon the banks of the river lay the scattered remains of three men. By the smell of them, some had died only recently. Their blood dribbled slowly onto the grass around them.

Leaning against the bridge was a young male, barely alive. His breath came in shattered gasps. Ari rushed to his side and fell to his knees, hands going to the pouches at his waist.

"What happened?" he asked while Kari inspected the bodies.

The boy gurgled an answer too quiet for her to make out. She knelt beside the body of another young male. His chest was slashed with four long claw marks, but instead of torn flesh, the edges of the wounds were blackened.

She frowned and knelt closer, gingerly plucking apart his leather vest. The wounds were made by something inhuman, yes. What could do this? She hesitated before drawing her head over his body and breathing in deeply.

Blood, sweat, fear. And beneath it all was the tiniest, almost insignificant smell of burnt flesh.

Ari cursed behind her. She jerked around as he closed the eyes of the boy leaning against the bridge. He slowly got to his feet and turned to her.

"A demon. That was all he could tell me."

"Ari, these wounds…"

Before she could continue, a loud rustle sounded behind them, followed by a man's grunt. Branches cracked, and something hard hit the ground.

"Who's there?" Ari called sharply.

"Sorry, Lord, it's me," Wilcoth's voice sounded from beneath the bushes. Soon he emerged, looking frazzled. "I fell, tripped over a damned root."

"Wilcoth." A layer of tension released from Ari's shoulders. "What is it?"

He pounded a fist on his chest. "Linus, Lord. He told me he needed you right away."

Kari frowned. "Ari, these wounds are strange. Could that boy really tell you nothing else?"

"No. He...his life gave out before..." He shook his head. "What does Linus want, Wilcoth? This...this is the work of some type of demon, and I need to..."

"He wouldn't say, Lord."

"I can investigate further," Kari murmured, glancing over the bodies again. "And come back if I find anything."

Ari frowned. "We don't know what did this, Kari."

She recalled the scent of charred flesh on the body that lay a few feet away from her. She was sure she knew, even if Ari didn't realize it yet.

"I can handle whatever it is. If not, I won't pursue it. I promise. Linus needs you."

Ari searched her face, his lips tight.

"I can go with her, Lord," Wilcoth suggested.

They both turned to him.

"I'm not much, but I guarantee her safety." He unstrapped the spear from his back—a reward for making Lieutenant—and looked at Ari with fierce determination.

Still, Ari seemed hesitant. He let out a breath. "I will go see Linus and come to find you as soon as I can. Don't go far."

Wilcoth and Kari nodded. Ari glanced between them, the troubled look marring his face. Finally, he turned and rushed back to the village.

Kari watched him disappear into the foliage before turning back to the body. The wounds on his chest were unusual, hardly even bleeding. The skin around them was reddened; the edges of the wounds themselves dark, as if made with flaming claws.

"What do you think it is?"

She chewed her lip. "Nothing good. Come on."

They ran until they were both breathless. Kari had caught a faint scent of smoke and followed it to a tiny clearing, but found nothing. The smell ended in the bushes; there was no sign of a fire.

She leaned against a tree to catch her breath. Wilcoth's hard gasps filled the space beside her. She felt bad that he had come with her. He'd done quite enough running around today.

"We're pretty far in," he said between breaths.

"Yeah," Kari agreed reluctantly. "We should return soon. Ari would have a hard time finding us."

Wilcoth took a moment to catch his breath. Then he said, "It was brave of you. To come out here like this."

She looked to him with a cocked brow. "What would you have me do? Let whoever did that get away?"

He laughed humorlessly. "Well, I might have expected you to follow the lord back into town. I didn't expect it'd be this easy."

Kari frowned, turning fully to face him. "What do you mean?"

"I mean that it was kind of you, for me that is, to leave behind the safety of your human hovel. Very noble."

She stared at him, not understanding, and stumbled back with a hiss when his face began to bubble and shift.

"Wilcoth—"

Her companion wasn't Wilcoth anymore; maybe it never had been. His entire being was hazy, as if he was standing behind a foggy slab of glass. His hair grew, his face curving and shrinking. Even his weapons and leather armor were a falsity, melting into the shape of flowing robes in the hued colors of a fire.

It took only seconds and Wilcoth was gone, replaced by the Fire Witch.

"You!" Kari roared.

The last of Wilcoth faded off her, leaving the figure of a slim woman. "Oh yes."

"What did you do with Wilcoth?!"

"Oh, he is laying about somewhere, I suspect. Not dead. *You* are the scum I am after."

Kari growled. "You killed those men at the river!"

The witch's shoulders rose and fell with carelessness. "Every war has casualties. When the great demon of our time is defeated, their deaths will be noted as grand sacrifices."

"Enough!" Lightning crackled at Kari's fingertips. "Enough of this! How could you do that, but claim I am a monster? You don't even know who I am!"

"Quite the contrary," the witch said smoothly. "I have known about you for many years."

"How? Who are you?!"

"The same old question," the witch sighed. "I'm your death, Kari Kasente. Does that satisfy you? I have trained for years to have the honor of destroying you myself."

"Why?" Kari roared. Thunder boomed over them. "I have never hurt you, never even seen you before you attacked me!"

Streams of glowing fire laced down the woman's arms. Kari tensed, but the Fire Witch did not make a move.

"Not yet, perhaps. But who wants to take chances?" She looked idly at her fingers, where the fire was coalescing into minuscule orbs. "A creature like you, you're tainted. You don't deserve life, and I will gladly snuff it out. Of course, there is the matter of your home and those who so blindly accept you." She sneered, raising her glowering orange eyes to Kari again. "You see those mountain peaks to the east? There is a path that leads to an opening in the crag. Meet me there before nightfall. If you do, I will leave the pitiful village alone. If you don't, I will be forced to melt the skin from their bones. Anyone who ever dared to allow a *demon* into their home will die, and the blame will be yours."

Kari snarled and a bolt of lightning burst through the air. It struck the ground the Fire Witch had been, but she extended a pair of flaming skeletal wings that lifted her to safety.

"East, Kari," she said with a sneer and spun, her wings carrying her away.

Kari clenched her fists. She ought to return to Ari, to tell him what had happened. The Fire Witch had transformed into Wilcoth and tricked them. The image of her bubbling face made Kari gag.

No, she couldn't risk the witch returning to the village. She would kill them all if Kari did not find her and stop her.

Kari forced herself to move, and soon she was jogging through the forest.

After an hour of following the river, Kari approached the wide lake that marked the mountain valley that would lead to the rest of Taris. She stopped briefly to peer into the water, noting its ghostly blue tinge, before looking up again. The mountain range that she passed through so long ago was ahead of her. With her keen eyes, she could see a barely-concealed path between two thick trees.

With a flick of her ears, Kari ran to the path and picked her way through the trees and bushes that had grown from misuse. She stopped several times to smell the air. The woman's scent was weak here, but Kari knew she'd never forget that smokey smell.

She ducked under a thick branch, and the path opened onto a rocky mountain trail. The woman's smell was stronger. As Kari ascended the slope, she caught glimpses of charred rock and branches. She quickened her pace, eager to rid herself and Raziac of this woman once and for all.

And maybe she would discover the Fire Witch's ultimate reason for hunting her.

Kari began to huff as the slope steepened and angled around sharp rocks. She jogged when she could, but the higher she climbed, the more perilous the path became. She picked her way over loose rock, clinging to thick bushes that grew from the walls.

Finally, mercifully, the path opened into a rocky clearing. Kari climbed down one last ledge and dropped onto level ground. The rocky summit was vast, and empty, save for the strewn-about bones of small animals.

"Where are you, Witch?!" she roared. The mountain walls echoed the noise back to her.

Kari waited, electricity sparking at her fingertips, but only her echoes answered. Grinding her teeth, she started to cross the clearing.

Something bright and hot flared at her side, too large and fast for her to dodge. Kari slammed into the rock wall and hit the ground, throwing her arms up to cover her face with a cry. The burns were light, and healed quickly.

Wincing, she lowered her arms to glare at the Fire Witch. The woman smiled down at her, smoke drifting from her hands.

"I'm more excited than I have been in years. I didn't think you would actually sacrifice yourself for them."

"I'm not here to die," Kari growled, and lunged. Her claws swiped at the sneering face, sparks leaving a streak of static energy in the air. The woman moved with supernatural speed. She fell back, easily dodging Kari's attack, and swept to the side to land a fire-charged punch in Kari's ribcage.

With a gasp, Kari rolled to the side, the smell of her burning flesh filling her nose. She willed her side to heal, and winced as a sharp pain reverberated through her mind. Healing wouldn't be an option much longer.

"You are young and slow. Weak. It's almost boring to kill you this way."

Kari's eyes flashed and thunder boomed with her cry. The sky darkened and the heavy feeling of static filled the air.

She barely registered the sound of the Fire Witch laughing when the ground began to shake. She stumbled, losing her concentration. A spare bolt of electric energy shot from her fingers. It struck the Fire Witch, only for her to knock it aside with the back of her hand. The lightning crackled and boomed as it struck rock instead, blasting aside pebbles and dirt.

The woman gritted her teeth, massaging her hand with the other. "It isn't magic, what you do. We knew that. Still, my sister's lightning hurts a bit more than yours."

Kari stared, frozen. The Fire Witch's lips pulled back into a nasty smile, and she leapt forward. Kari stumbled back, slicing with her claws. Fingers made of flame caught her around the wrist, eliciting a high-pitched scream.

The Witch jerked Kari closer. Her mind, blank with pain and shock, couldn't stop her body from staggering forward. She had her other hand. She could kill the woman now; she was close enough—

Something hard hit her at the base of her skull. As she fell, a voice spoke.

"I've thought of the most wonderful plan."

And everything was gone.

CHAPTER THIRTY-TWO

Kari felt as though her head would split in two. She groaned, dragging her hand to touch her forehead, and winced as her wrist flared with pain.

The mountain valley was colored in the violet hues of the coming night, and it was empty. She was alone.

Kari scrambled to her feet, tensing her wrist with a wince.

"Where are you?" she called, her voice little more than a rasp. "Come out and finish me! It's what you wanted!"

She turned a slow circle, waiting for the Fire Witch to appear with blazes of fiery light, but there was no one around.

Kari's brow furrowed. Where could she have gone? She had wanted to fight Kari to the death, and she'd had no better chance. Her face burning with shame, Kari realized she'd lost the fight.

So why wasn't she dead?

She recalled words, a whisper just before she'd lost consciousness. She hadn't understood them, but now each icy syllable dripped into her gut.

I've thought of the most wonderful plan.

Kari shambled, turning her back to the entrance of the valley.

What else could the woman have meant? What other games could she play with Kari's life that did not involve Raziac Village and the people there?

Heart pounding, Kari climbed the ledge out of the valley. She slipped and scrambled back down the mountain slope.

She ran as fast as her legs would carry her, wishing she'd thought to bring extra clothes for an emergency shifting—her wolf form would've been much faster.

Her chest burned with the effort, but thankfully, the route was mostly downhill. Soon she was rounding the lake and vaulting the river. Her feet pounded the earth as she made for the last strip of forest.

A bulky body emerged from the foliage, impeding her path. She skidded to a stop, her legs trembling, and her breaths hard.

Wilcoth stood before her, his face strained. Dried blood trickled from his temple, and leaves were tangled in his hair.

"Wilcoth," she gasped. She'd let herself forget about him, but now wasn't the time to worry. He was okay. "We have to—"

"What are you doing, Kari?"

She stared at him. "I'm…I have to get back! The witch—"

"You…I heard screams, woke me up," he said. His face screwed up in concentration, as if he was having a hard time piecing together his thoughts. "I…went to see what happened, and…"

"We don't have *time*! The village is—"

"You…you attacked them," he muttered. His hand slowly went to the sword at his waist. "I…I saw you walking back earlier…"

He trailed off uncertainly, his eyes squinted in pain. She stared at him, her mouth slack. She remembered the way the witch's face had bubbled, shifting from Wilcoth's image to her own. Understanding slowly clicked into place.

"Wilcoth…no. No, what you saw wasn't me. Please, you have to listen!"

"I…don't understand," he admitted wearily.

"Let me find Ari. Please, Wilcoth. If you ever trusted me at all, let me by."

He stared at her with bleary eyes. He stumbled back a step. "Don't…don't hurt them."

Kari bit back a whine. "Hide here, Wilcoth. Rest. I'll come back with Ari."

He looked torn, but his hand finally fell away from his sword. He slumped onto the ground, holding his head.

Heart blistering, Kari raced through the last strip of forest. There was barely any light in the sky left when she finally made it to the village. She stopped in her tracks.

Chaos. Any building not reduced to smoldering wood was broken or in a stage of collapse. Every villager seemed to have fled. The silence was deafening. Ears flickering uneasily, Kari entered town, trying to find evidence of life. Her heart was in her stomach as she glanced around corners and inside every ruined building. How could the Fire Witch have gone to this level of destruction? This was Kari's *home*; her home was destroyed, and she had been unable to prevent it.

She could find no one alive. She walked past a few bodies charred beyond recognition, the flesh still smoking. Every step brought her closer to the center of town. Unease prickled her insides, making her sick. The bakery stood, though barely. Julia's precious meat shop was in shambles, the apothecary too. There were no bodies to be found near them, but that did nothing to quell her fear.

Where was Ari? Roland? Linus? Had they been felled as well?

Was she to be left nothing but death and loneliness again?

"You!"

The shout was sudden, hoarse, and angry, and made Kari flinch. It was a male's voice, one she recognized. As she turned around to meet him, her heart trembled.

It was Ari, bow in hand, the nocked arrow glowing white and pointed at her heart. Breathtaking worry melted into relief.

"Oh, Ari," she groaned. "Thank the gods. Where is everyone?"

He said nothing. There was a long burn across his cheek. All things considered, she was grateful that was his only wound.

Sighing, she stepped closer. "Is anyone hurt? Did—"

"Don't move, Kari!" he snapped. "Don't come any closer."

Kari froze, tried to puzzle together what he meant, and failed. "What are you talking about, Ari?"

"Enough!" he yelled, unleashing a wave of white energy that made Kari flinch away. "I won't hesitate this time!" Even as he said the harsh words, tears came to his eyes. "For what you did, the people you killed…this time, I won't let you run away!"

The blood drained from Kari's face. *She* killed?

I've thought of the most wonderful plan.

"Ari, no!" Kari shouted. "You have to listen to me! Wilcoth, he—"

Her words cut off in a strangled gasp as the arrow whizzed past her head, clipping her ear. It was a mere flicker of pain, but Kari retreated from him all the same.

"Wilcoth never returned! What did you do with him, Kari?!"

"I didn't hurt him, Ari, I swear! We went together, but it wasn't him! The witch, she—"

He laughed, but it was harsh and mean. "Why the games now? I saw you do this with your own hands! I saw your eyes, glowing red as they did before. I had thought it strange, but didn't speak of it. Now…" He gritted his teeth. "Tell me why! Why did you do this?! I gave everything to you. I trusted you!"

Kari felt hot tears burn the corners of her eyes. *What is this? Why is this happening again?*

"I could never do this!" she roared back at him.

His face was set, the anger in his gaze unwavering. She had never seen him look so furious.

Ari flung aside his bow and unsheathed the sword at his waist. The long, silver blade glowed bright white in the dying light of the sun. Kari longed to step back, but her body was stiff and unmoving. Every instinct screamed to run, yet she continued to stare at him, angrily disbelieving.

How could I have trusted him…? The thought sprang unbidden, clenching her heart in an icy grasp.

"You *did* do this. And I was too afraid to stop you. Not now, Kari. I will protect what is left."

Ari rushed her, sword raised. Kari jumped back, fingertips glowing with yellow sparks. The power was there, and part of her cried to use it. Her fingers curled. She could not strike against the boy she had loved.

He was strengthened by his rage, swiping and stabbing until she was out of breath again. She swept aside and ducked, all the while feeling the sparks of energy on her claws.

As the glowing sword swept by one more time, Kari stepped back, only for her foot to slip on a bit of charred wood. She stumbled, landing hard on her backside with a grunt. Ari hesitated only a moment before approaching her and raising his sword.

Kari's eyes flashed, and a bolt of lightning struck the ground beside him. Ari jumped to the side. She got to her feet and ran after him—she would make him see reason.

Ari was stunned as she advanced but quickly brought his sword up again. She knocked it away with a hiss of pain and gripped the collar of his smoldered vest.

"Stop this!" she cried. "Listen to me!"

Ari's eyes were stony, unforgiving. She couldn't imagine what he'd seen; he was a man possessed, a man she no longer knew.

"I can't stop. Not now," he whispered, his voice cracking slightly and betraying his resolve. "I loved you. Now...now I can't stop until you are dead."

Kari's heart plummeted. Icy hands gripped her throat. She let out a choke of despair. Her grip on Ari loosened.

Raw, unbridled hopelessness threatened to engulf her. Her legs trembled and her heart felt shredded into infinitesimal pieces. What could she say? What could she do to make him see that it had been the Fire Witch, not her? She didn't even know what the witch had done, who was hurt, who was still alive.

Kari opened her mouth to speak, to try and find reason between them.

A sharp pain invaded her gut. With a gasp, she looked down to see the blade of Ari's sword embedded there. His trembling hand gripped the hilt.

She stared, unbelieving. She felt a hot rush of blood well in her throat, and coughed, spewing it onto Ari's chest.

His grip tightened. The sword flashed brilliantly. Kari screamed, falling to her knees. He pulled his blade free, releasing a torrent of crimson.

"Now everyone will be safe," he whispered hoarsely, his voice trembling and strained. "And you...can be at peace."

His eyes glistened. He clenched them shut, though not before a tear slipped free. As he cried, lifeblood seeped from the wound in Kari's stomach. Her power to heal failed her, her demonic energy too weak to combat his blessed power. She coughed more blood and collapsed onto her side.

"I...I love..."

EPILOGUE

Not for the first time, Zina cursed that hot-headed fire mage. Even now, she could hear Riniko's gloating.

I did it, Zina! I did what no one else could do. The Catalyst of lore is dead, and the world is safe!

How could she be so damn foolish? If the divinations were true, and Kari was the one, simple bodily death would not stop her.

Zina slipped in between the trees that guarded Raziac Village from the depths of the forest, her crimson robes silently swishing with her movement. It was growing late, but still, the place was appalling to see. No building had been spared, leaving charred, crumbled walls. Wafts of dark black smoke drifted into the air, the smell of scorched wood and bones abhorrent.

Zina knew that Riniko hated demons, but why did she have to do this? The humans here should not have been casualties. She committed the very sin she feared Kari would one day exceed. Perhaps Riniko preferred the world to burn under her fiery justice, rather than the hand of a demon.

Zina skirted around the outer edges of the village, careful to remain out of sight. She'd long since learned to hide away from this place and its people, and desired to keep her secrecy.

She just had to find Kari and leave, preferably without anyone knowing.

Zina drifted around two more crumbling, smoking buildings until she caught sight of the survivors. Despite the utter destruction, most of the villagers were alive. They huddled together around a massive funeral pyre topped with bodies. In front was the redheaded boy Zina knew had recently come into lordship. In his right hand was a flickering torch.

She was certain Kari would not be salvageable if her body was burned. She'd have to get personally involved now.

The Lord of Raziac was speaking, his voice barely loud enough for Zina to pick out snippets of what he said. He was blessing the dead, praying for them to go safely on in their afterlives. Would he wish the same for Kari, who he thought had done this to his home? Who he had killed for it?

Raising her arms to shoulder height, Zina stepped closer to the cluster of villagers. White smoke drifted into the air from her fingertips and quickly coated Raziac Village in a thick fog. Ari's words cut off as he sensed the magic. He whipped around, but the smoke obscured her. There was only the fog, heavy and opaque.

The villagers whispered and cowered as Zina and the fog descended upon them. Ari shouted for them to be calm, he would handle this. She could see the light of the torch as he passed it to someone else, and then she felt a light burning sensation in the middle of her mist.

Eyes narrowing, Zina pushed back against Ari's energy. The villagers shuffled away from him and the pyre, trying to find safety outside of the fog. Soon their noisy movements and whimpers halted. One by one, with heavy thumps, the villagers fell to the ground. Zina made her way to the pyre, where the redheaded lord had fallen to his knees. His head nodded as he tried to remain awake, to fight the white smoke he didn't understand.

With a wave of Zina's hand, the Lord of Raziac fell aside with the rest of them, into a dreamless slumber.

The haze thinned as she stepped up to the pile of wood and bodies. She knew none of the faces there, young, or old, and with a twinge of annoyance, she wondered where Kari might be. Ari would not dig a grave for her, would he? It was their tradition, as she understood it, that all dead be burned regardless of their life tribulations.

A patch of yellow amidst the sea of browns and grays caught Zina's eye. She reached out, her eyes narrowed, and made a grasping motion with her fingers. As if by an invisible hand, Kari was slowly lifted from the back of the pyre, the movement causing an older man's corpse to topple into her place. Kari limply drifted free, her face pale with death. Dried blood coated her front, and she smelled of smoke. Zina wrinkled her nose as Kari floated off the pyre and into her arms.

"At last, we meet," she murmured as she stepped away from the other bodies. Kari was practically weightless in her arms. "Though I wish it were under different circumstances."

Years ago, when Zina had set her eyes on the wolf demon child, she wondered what would come of their relationship. Would Kari flourish under her parents' guidance, or become a lackluster demon with an ordinary, perhaps violent, life?

When Zina saw the electricity sparking from the young demon's teeth, she knew. One day, they would meet again. Everything would be different then.

Careful not to step on the sleeping villagers, Zina left them and their funeral pyre. With a jerk of her head, the pyre lit, becoming a roaring flame that would soon wake them with its heat.

Zina hefted Kari more comfortably and made her way back into the forest.

She hoped the little lord would not miss Kari within the flames. The price she would have to pay to call Kari back from the brink would be costly, and she would hate for him to come along and ruin it with some petty idea of revenge.

She would do it, though. She'd promised, after all, to keep the little wolf demon safe. Zina did not believe in the divinations anyway. Prophecies were useless, rarely reliable, unless one believed them and fulfilled it by their belief.

It did not matter that Kari's existence was detailed finely. The extremes to which Riniko had gone to kill Kari did not give true basis to the prophecy's validity. It only proved that Kari would be in danger, probably from many enemies. It was up to Zina to ensure she remain safe. If that meant preventing Kari's supposed descent into storm and destruction, Zina would do what was necessary.

Destined or not, Kari required this from her.

Acknowledgments

I would like to acknowledge those fabulous writers on Twitter's #writingcommunity who helped lift me up and accepted me and my writing. Some of you are very special and dear to me, and I will be thankful every day that we met!

I would be remiss to leave out my lovely husband, who doesn't really get it, but tries very hard all the same.

From the bottom of my heart, thank you to everyone at Shadow Spark Publishing for accepting me as part of their very real family. It is like home here within the light and darkness.

And absolutely, my every ounce of gratitude and love goes to my brother, who has been with me from the beginning. Without him, I wouldn't have written half of the things I have, nor nearly as well. Thank you, Guine, for always being by my side. I love you so much, and I (and Kari) would be lost without you.

Valerie Storm

Valerie Storm was raised in Tucson, Arizona. Growing up, she fell in love with everything fantasy. When she wasn't playing video games, she was writing. By age ten, she began to write her own stories as a way to escape reality. When these stories became a full-length series, she considered the path to sharing with other children & children-at-heart looking for a place to call home.

She can be found on twitter @Valerie_Storm

What was Ari thinking? Find out!

Subscribe to my newsletter for updates on the series as it's written and receive Ari's perspective for the lead up of this book's climactic finale!

Made in the USA
Las Vegas, NV
16 June 2022

50332644R00177